## Defiance and Surrender

"Why, you pompous peacock!" Alexandra shrieked. "I have no intention of changing my behavior to suit your standards!"

Smothering a smile at Alexandra's indignation, Nicholas replied, "Nevertheless, your behavior is not befitting that of a duchess nor of my prospective wife. In the future, I shall expect better of you."

Nicholas strode purposefully toward her. The spicy scent of his shaving soap reached up to assault her senses as he neared. She could feel a warm glow starting in the tips of her toes and running all the way up to her flushed cheeks.

Placing his hand under her chin, Nicholas tipped up her face to stare into the bright blue of her eyes. "I think you are in need of taming, my dear, sweet Alexandra. I fear I will have to undertake the task myself."

Alexandra's senses reeled at the feel of Nicholas's lips on hers. Her hands came around his waist, under the satin of his robe, to draw him nearer to her.

"My sweet," he murmured. "We may not view the world through the same eyes, but I think we shall suit, nevertheless."

# HEARTFIRE ROMANCES

## SWEET TEXAS NIGHTS
(2610, $3.75)

by Vivian Vaughan

Meg Britton grew up on the railroads, working proudly at her father's side. Nothing was going to stop them from setting the rails clear to Silver Creek, Texas—certainly not some crazy prospector. As Meg set out to confront the old coot, she planned her strategy with cool precision. But soon she was speechless with shock. For instead of a harmless geezer, she found a boldly handsome stranger whose determination matched her own.

## CAPTIVE DESIRE
(2612, $3.75)

by Jane Archer

Victoria Malone fancied herself a great adventuress, but being kidnapped was too much excitement for even Victoria! Especially when her arrogant kidnapper thought she was part of Red Duke's outlaw gang. Trying to convince the overbearing, handsome stranger that she had been an innocent bystander when the stagecoach was robbed, proved futile. But when he thought he could maker her confess by crushing her to his warm, broad chest, by caressing her with his strong, capable hands, Victoria was willing to admit to anything. . . .

## LAWLESS ECSTASY
(2613, $3.75)

by Susan Sackett

Abra Beaumont could spot a thief a mile away. After all, her father was once one of the best. But he'd been on the right side of the law for years now, and she wasn't about to let a man like Dash Thorne lead him astray with some wild plan for stealing the Tear of Allah, the world's most fabulous ruby. Dash was just the sort of man she most distrusted—sophisticated, handsome, and altogether too sure of his considerable charm. Abra shivered at the devilish gleam in his blue eyes and swore he would need more than smooth kisses and skilled caresses to rob her of her virtue . . . and much more than sweet promises to steal her heart!

# BRAZEN VIRGINIA BRIDE

## MILLIE CRISWELL

**ZEBRA BOOKS**
**KENSINGTON PUBLISHING CORP.**

ZEBRA BOOKS

are published by

Kensington Publishing Corp.
475 Park Avenue South
New York, NY 10016

First printing: December, 1990

Printed in the United States of America

TO
LARRY
MY HERO, MY HUSBAND, MY BEST FRIEND

# PART ONE

# BOUND BY FATE

*The nobly born must nobly meet his fate.*

—Euripides

# Prologue

*Blackstone Manor, England, June, 1744*

She would never be the Duke of Blackstone's mistress, Catherine Williston vowed, tramping through the dew-dampened grass to meet her lover one last time.

The morning air was crisp. The sun had not yet made its appearance this first day of June. She drew her cloak tight about her, warding off the chill that seeped through the warm wool and thin satin of her slippers.

The sight of the gazebo, so pristine and white, conjured up memories of her time spent there with Charles. Times of loving and passion. Times of betrayal.

A single tear flowed down her cheek as the guilt of her perfidy tore through her soul. She had betrayed her best friend, her childhood companion—Charles's wife, Sarah. Sarah, who had been kindness itself, opening up her home and heart to an orphaned friend, betrayed by the one person she trusted—herself.

She had tried the past two years to keep her feelings for Charles hidden. Charles was the husband of her dearest friend, she had told herself. She had no right to love him. But still her feelings burned hot, like a flame raging out of control, threatening to destroy her.

When she came to recognize the same fires burning within Charles, it was too late. They had acted on impulse rather than reason, and now she knew it was time to depart.

As she approached the latticed building, Catherine observed Charles standing tall and erect, hands clenched behind his back, staring out toward the river. His brown hair blew gently in the breeze. Today she would bid farewell to the only man she would ever love. Her heart constricted painfully.

Charles turned, his face brightening with pleasure as he caught sight of Catherine coming toward him. "My love," he called, opening his arms to receive the red-haired beauty.

Catherine stopped, unwilling to become ensnared in Charles's welcoming embrace. She had to remain true to her convictions or all would be lost. It would do neither of them any good to prolong the inevitable. She saw the look of hurt and confusion in his eyes before he dropped his arms to his sides.

"I have come to a decision," she said, rubbing her arms against the early morning chill.

"I can see by your set expression, you have not looked favorably upon my offer. You do not love me, then?"

Taking a deep breath, Catherine swallowed the tears that threatened to choke off her response. "It is because I love you that I cannot consent to become your mistress. What we have done in a moment of passion and weakness was wrong. I will not hurt Sarah or you by remaining a part of your life."

Stepping forward, Charles placed his hands on Catherine's shoulders. "I love you. This is no mere dalliance on my part. I want to marry you."

"That is not possible," Catherine said softly, shaking her head. "Don't you see the futility of it all? You are a duke—a lord of the realm. Even if divorce were possible, which it is not, I am only a vicar's daughter—

a commoner. Our love can never be.'' She turned away, unable to face the disappointment on Charles's face.

"But I love you. Does that mean nothing?''

Turning to face him, she blinked back her tears. "Your love will remain a brilliant memory in my heart, but I must look to my future as well as to yours. You have a son. Have you forgotten, Nicholas? Do you wish to jeopardize his inheritance, his birthright, by bringing shame and dishonor upon the name of Fortune?''

"But I can't bear the thought of seeing you day after day, pretending you don't exist. I love you too much.'' Charles wept openly, unashamedly before the woman he adored.

Reaching up, Catherine tenderly caressed his cheek. In all the years she had known him, she had never seen Charles cry. His tears were like bullets ripping into her heart. Taking a deep breath, she finally replied, "That is why I am leaving.''

"Leaving!'' Charles's face contorted in pain at her admission. "You can't leave. Where would you go? You have no money—no family.''

"I have decided to accept Samuel Courtland's proposal of marriage.''

The silence that fell at this statement was relieved by the shrill cry of a robin calling to its mate from the branches overhead. Charles's brown eyes narrowed into thin slits; his face reddened in anger. "Courtland is only a merchant. You would prefer to marry that boorish colonial rather than remain here as my mistress?''

"He has made me an honorable offer,'' she insisted.

"You do not love him.'' It was a statement of fact, not a question.

Catherine shook her head. "No. I do not love him, but he professes to love me, and in time I may be able to return his affection.'' She knew it was a lie, and she could see by the expression on his face that he knew it too.

Grabbing her, he pulled her roughly to him. "Catherine, I will never see you again. Please don't leave me."

"It is for the best. Our love was not meant to be. Perhaps in another place, another time, but not now."

Turning away, his shoulders slumped in defeat, Charles faced the water, looking out at the murky depths below. He couldn't bear to lose Catherine. If only there was a way to bind her to him. After several minutes of silence, he turned back to gaze at her pale features.

"If you must leave, then I ask that you leave a part of yourself with me."

A soft smile touched her lips. "Charles, you know you will always have my heart."

Taking the small, cold hand within his grasp, he placed a kiss upon it. "As you shall have mine, but there is one more thing that I desire."

Her brow wrinkling in puzzlement, Catherine replied, "I do not understand."

"I wish to betroth my son, Nicholas, to your first-born daughter."

Catherine gasped. "He is to be the duke. It cannot be," she protested, shaking her head in denial.

"You must promise to do this. It is the only way we shall ever be united. Don't you understand? Through our children we shall become one."

She didn't understand, but why should she make their parting more difficult than it already was? What harm could it do? She might never have children, and if she did, they might all be boys.

At the look of pleading on Charles's face, a smile found its way through her mask of uncertainty. "If it means that much to you, I will agree."

"You will sign papers to that effect?"

12

She nodded her acquiescence. "If it is your wish."

Charles's smile emerged as brilliant as the summer sun that now appeared overhead. "It is my wish—my very fervent wish."

# Chapter One

*Blackstone Manor, England, March, 1774*

The acrid stench of death filled the darkened room. Charles Edward Fortune, Third Duke of Blackstone, lay dying.

The heavy blue velvet drapes were drawn against the late afternoon sun. A single candle burned on the nightstand, illuminating the faces of the brothers who waited anxiously by the bedside of their father.

"Nicholas," the frail voice called out, the effort to speak causing a spasm of coughing to overtake him.

The tall, dark-haired man bent down, leaning over the emaciated form on the bed. "Yes, Father. I am here." He pressed his ear close to the dying man's face, which was white but surprisingly serene in the last stages of his life.

A gnarled hand reached out, grasping the stronger one. "I fear I will leave you this night."

Nicholas glanced over at the ashen face of his younger brother, Basil, who stood quietly on the other side of the bed. Funny, he thought, it was the first time he could recall a show of concern on Basil's face for someone other than himself. Perhaps he did have some feelings, after all. He looked back down at his father.

"You mustn't speak so, Father," Nicholas finally

replied. "You must fight to battle the ravages of this disease."

"This battle is over, my son. You will carry on as duke when I am gone."

Nicholas squeezed the feeble hand. "I will miss you."

"And I you, but there is something I must tell you before I depart this world." Charles's voice grew weaker, the rattle in his chest becoming more pronounced with every breath he took. "There is a stipulation in my will."

Nicholas and Basil exchanged startled glances before Nicholas replied, "A stipulation? I do not understand."

"I pray you will forgive me. I never meant to hurt you. I. . . ." The gurgling sound within Charles's chest grew louder, finally drowning out the words he had wanted to speak. A deafening silence filled the room.

Nicholas stared down at the still form before him. Reaching over, he closed the eyes that stared out so hideously in death.

"What do you suppose he meant?" Basil asked. He hadn't missed the fact his father had no last-minute words for him. There was no recognition for the son whose presence always went unnoticed. Only for Nicholas—always for Nicholas. Was he always to live in the shadow of his older brother? It was Nicholas who was smarter, stronger, more handsome. Even at his father's deathbed Nicholas came first. A feeling of bitterness welled up inside him.

Nicholas shook his head. "I suppose we will know soon enough. I will advise the solicitor, Mr. Abernathy, that the reading of the will shall commence two days hence. That will give us time to prepare a proper burial."

"But . . . are you not curious as to the mystery behind father's deathbed pronouncement?"

16

Nicholas stared in contempt at his brother and his morbid curiosity. The animosity reflected in the brown of Basil's eyes could not be hidden within the folds of his pale, flaccid face. "Curiosity is a dangerous affliction. It has been known to create trouble where none exists and bring down those who dare to delve too deeply. It would be wise to attend only to those matters which concern you," he advised.

The brown eyes narrowed. Basil crossed to the door and paused. "As you wish. But do not be surprised if the father you so revered has done you a great injustice. It is only fitting that you should be hurt by his death, as I have been while he lived." He threw Nicholas one last derisive look before exiting the room.

Nicholas stared at the door and then at the lifeless form on the bed. *I never meant to hurt you.* The words so recently uttered hung ominous and portent, like the knell of death so recently come to claim the Duke of Blackstone.

Pacing back and forth across the highly polished parquet floor of the library, Nicholas glanced out the Palladian window that looked out over the rear garden, observing the rain that gently beat against the panes of glass. The formal reading of the will had ended an hour ago. Only he and the solicitor remained to go over the final details.

"Are you quite certain that this will and agreement are valid—binding in a court of law?" Nicholas asked, turning to face the lawyer.

Phinneas Abernathy swallowed. His protruding Adam's apple bobbed nervously up and down like a cork upon the water as he stared into the set features of the new Duke of Blackstone. "Quite sure, my lord. Dispatches have already been sent to Virginia, notifying the Courtlands of your father's demise. The agreement appears to be in order."

The agreement. How neatly he had been backed into a corner with no means of escape, Nicholas thought. He was trapped by a title and a fortune, and his father's misplaced motivations. He remembered how Basil had laughed when the will had been read. He could laugh. Basil had no title to boast of, but he also had no yoke of matrimony hanging about his neck to weigh him down.

"What will happen if I refuse to comply with the agreement?" Nicholas asked finally, staring at the red-faced lawyer.

"Your title, of course, would remain intact, but your fortune and estates would revert to your brother."

Nicholas snorted contemptuously. Basil as the owner of Blackstone! That notion was too absurd to consider. Basil would squander the monies and decimate the estate until the magnificent old stone manor was nothing more than a pile of rubble. Nicholas couldn't let that happen, whatever the cost.

"What if the Courtland woman is unwilling to marry?"

The lawyer shook his head. "She is bound by the agreement as tightly as you are. Apparently she is eager to wed. I have a document with her signature affixed."

Nicholas banged his fist on the massive walnut desk, causing Phinneas Abernathy to leap from his chair. "By God, what a wretched state of affairs. Suppose she is as ugly as rotted horseflesh."

Stuffing the legal documents into his leather pouch as quickly as he could, Phinneas replied, "My lord, you have only to marry the woman. Once the marriage is consummated, you will be free to take your ease with whomever strikes your fancy."

The image of Sabrina Montgomery rose quickly to Nicholas's mind. Sabrina. The thought of her ripe, ample breasts brought a familiar tightening to his loins.

18

"If you will excuse me, Mister Abernathy, I have a pressing engagement in London that cannot wait."

Phinneas hid his smile, not wishing to offend the duke. He knew with a certainty the direction of Lord Blackstone's thoughts at the moment. "Of course, my lord," he answered, watching the duke exit the room.

It was common knowledge that Nicholas Fortune was quite taken with his mistress, Sabrina Montgomery. Her pair of distinguishing attributes could take any man's mind off his problems. Why should the duke not avail himself of a little succor to ease his troubled mind? Phinneas thought enviously, wondering if Nicholas Fortune knew just how lucky he really was.

The morning shower had ended, leaving in its wake a glorious springlike day. The sunlight filtered in through the partially opened shutters, landing unnoticed on the two naked lovers entwined so rapturously upon the bed.

Sabrina Montgomery's silver strands of hair were decorously arranged upon the white satin pillow. She watched in satisfaction as Nicholas took first one rigid nipple then the other into his mouth, sucking furiously upon her breasts.

It was her inordinately large breasts that had first attracted Nicholas to her. Of course, that had been her intention all along. She had Nicholas right where she wanted him, and she intended to keep him there until she became the next Duchess of Blackstone.

"Take me, Nicholas," she cried, clasping him in her arms. "You are driving me mad with desire."

Only too happy to accommodate his willing mistress, Nicholas embraced her with a desperation that drove all conscious thought from his mind.

A short time later, his lust spent, Nicholas leaned back against the mahogany headboard, drawing Sabrina into his embrace. He would miss the voracious

19

widow, he thought, squeezing the milky globes tenderly. She had been an adequate mistress these past two years, but that was over now. It was time to put his affairs in order and prepare for his journey to Virginia.

He couldn't hide the look of disgust crossing his face as he thought of his upcoming marriage to the colonial commoner who was probably as stimulating as dried toast. Small wonder she was eager to wed. There was probably not a man in the entire colony of Virginia who would have her.

"Nicholas, what is it? What has put such a dreadful expression on your face?" Sabrina asked, rubbing his cheek with her fingertips. He was such a handsome man. Not effeminate or timid like some of the others she had bedded. She could see why everyone called him "The Black Duke." With his thick ebony hair and compelling black eyes, he had set many a heart aflutter. Of course, that was before they had met.

She had managed to keep Nicholas contented these many months and had been amply rewarded for her services. She deemed herself fortunate to have attracted the attention of such a wealthy protector after her husband, Cecil, had died. Not to mention the fact that Nicholas's virility was a perfect match for her insatiable appetite where matters of the flesh were concerned. She could feel the familiar throb building once again and was disconcerted to see Nicholas preparing to rise.

Giving Sabrina one last kiss upon the cheek, Nicholas proceeded to dress. "I have had some disturbing news today," he said, stepping into his black broadcloth breeches.

A shadow of alarm crossed Sabrina's perfectly sculpted features. "What has happened?" she asked, fearful of the disturbing look she read upon his face. She wanted nothing to stand in her way of becoming Nicholas's wife, unless, of course, the Blackstone fortune had dwindled.

"My father left implicit instructions in his will. I am to travel to the colonies to claim a bride."

Sabrina gasped, clutching her chest. "That cannot be! I thought after all we had been to each other that I would become your wife."

Nicholas's eyebrows shot up at her astonishing disclosure. "You have presumed too much, madam. I never made any promise to you in that regard."

Scrambling off the bed, Sabrina wrapped her arms about his waist. "But I love you. I want to marry you."

Extricating himself from her embrace, Nicholas looked with distaste upon the scene his mistress was creating. He detested vulgar displays of emotion calculated to strip a man of his masculinity. "Get hold of yourself, madam. Have you no pride? I would never marry you. You have been a pleasant diversion, nothing more."

Nicholas's cold statement cut Sabrina to the quick. For two years she had contrived her seduction of Nicholas Fortune. She was so certain she had been successful in winning his heart. But she could see now that the gossip mongers had been right—the Black Duke had no heart.

Her eyes hardened into bits of green glass. "How dare you speak to me as if I were nothing more than a whore. I am a respectable widow. Many men have vied for my favors, but I chose to give them only to you."

Nicholas snorted, shrugging into his coat. "And you have been amply paid for your efforts . . . just like a whore," he said.

"I will make you sorry you were every born. Just you wait and see," Sabrina cried out.

Pausing at the door, Nicholas turned. "I'm afraid my father has already robbed you of that privilege, my dear."

* * *

Holding the brandy up to the light, Nicholas studied the amber clarity of the liquid before gulping it down. Placing his glass upon the desk, he poured himself another.

He had escaped into the dark-paneled sanctuary of the library shortly after his unpleasant visit to Sabrina's rooms earlier today. That had been a bloody mess, he thought, shaking his head. He downed another glass of brandy. The fiery liquid warmed his innards as effectively as the fire blazing so brightly in the massive stone fireplace.

Leaning back in the red leather chair, Nicholas surveyed the room, taking great pleasure in his surroundings. The library had always been his favorite room in the large mansion. Culture and refinement enfolded him within their bosom. Here he was surrounded by his books, his brandy, and the tasteful artwork that adorned the walls.

It was a beautifully appointed room, just like all the others at Blackstone. The manor had been built over two hundred years ago, and still it stood proud and strong like the country it had sprung from.

How in bloody hell was he going to survive in the unsophisticated, backward colony of Virginia? he asked himself, holding the sides of his head. No matter if it was only until he could fulfill his distasteful obligation. It was common knowledge that the colonials were socially inferior to the British. He would still have to rusticate there like some backwoods bumpkin, and to make matters worse, he would have to bring that provincial Courtland wench into his home—introduce her into society, set her up as the Duchess of Blackstone. By God, it was too much to be borne. He took another swallow of the liquor.

"My lord." The stentorious tone of his butler intruded into his misery.

Looking up, Nicholas focused his attention on the implacable features of Bellows, who stood rigidly in the

22

doorway. He was garbed in the familiar black velvet livery of Blackstone Manor.

"My lord, I have just received word that the prime minister is on his way here to see you."

Nicholas's head jerked up; he straightened his slouching posture. "Lord North is coming to see me?"

Bellows nodded his assent. "Yes, my lord. He should be here shortly."

"Show him right in when he arrives."

"Very good, sir," Bellows replied, bowing before making his exit.

What the devil was the prime minister doing calling on him at this hour of the night? he wondered. Nicholas straightened his stock, smoothing down the black velvet of his frock coat. He brushed back the unruly strands of hair that had escaped from his queue. Perhaps it had something to with his father's death. Charles Fortune was well respected in the House of Lords. He looked up as the library door opened once again.

"The Prime Minister, Lord North," Bellows announced.

Nicholas stood up as the heavy man with the drooping, jowly cheeks came forward to greet him. "My lord, I am honored by your visit," Nicholas said, bowing.

"Good evening, Lord Blackstone. I hope I have not come at an inconvenient time." The bulging myopic eyes seem to take in everything at once before landing on Nicholas's face.

"Not at all, my lord. I was just having a bit of brandy. Would you care to join me?"

Taking a seat by the fire, Lord North replied, "Don't mind if I do. It's a might nasty out this evening. A spot of brandy might be just the thing to warm a body up."

Nicholas fetched the liquor and took a seat opposite the prime minister in one of the blue velvet wing

23

chairs. "To what do I owe the honor of this visit, my lord? I presume you are not here for purely social reasons."

A calculating look entered Lord North's eyes. "Quite right, Lord Blackstone, quite right. Although I do wish to convey my deepest sympathy on the loss of your father. He was a just and honorable man."

Nicholas inclined his head.

Taking a sip of the brandy and dabbing at his lips with the lace ruffled handkerchief he pulled out of his sleeve, the prime minister cleared his throat. "I have come on a matter of the utmost urgency," he said, leaning forward in his seat. "The Boston Mobility's seditious act of disposing hundreds of cases of tea last December has precipitated the Crown to call for some rather harsh measures."

"I do not wish to offer offense, but I fail to see what the rebellious lot of Boston has to do with me," Nicholas interjected.

Lord North pushed his massive bulk out of the chair and stood, his back to the fire. "We are aware of the fact that you will be sailing to the colonies to claim a wife."

"That is true. But I sail for Virginia, not Massachusetts Bay."

"Quite. But your presence in Virginia could prove to be very valuable to the Crown."

Standing up, Nicholas leaned his arm against the mantel. "Please, go on."

"We are not pleased with Lord Dunmore's performance in handling the upstart colonials in the Virginia colony. They have been far too outspoken . . . especially that young lawyer Patrick Henry."

"But what does all this have to do with me?"

"I assume you will be taking your father's seat in the House of Lords." At the inclination of Nicholas's head, Lord North continued, "The seat carries with it a large measure of responsibility toward the king and to En-

24

3/12/16 to B.M —

Brogan Virginia Brûlé — 1 wt

M. Cruiwell

gland. We wish for you to exercise this responsibility by becoming an aide to Lord Dunmore.''

Nicholas tried to hide the astonishment he felt at this news. "You wish for me to spy on Lord Dunmore? John Murray is my friend. I find the entire prospect highly distasteful.''

Lord North's eyebrows rose in an affronted expression. "I think the term 'spy' is rather a harsh one. We prefer to think of it as observation and guidance. The tea dumped in Boston Harbor has brewed an ill will here at home. We are going to take measures to close the Port of Boston.'' Lord North paused at Nicholas's sharp intake of breath. "We do not expect the colonies to react favorably. We need you there to apprise us of the local sentiments—to report on any other activities you encounter.''

Damn, but the old bastard had put him in one hell of a spot, Nicholas fumed. To refuse would be a dereliction of his duty; to comply, a deception against his friend. He had little choice in the matter. The dogmatic prime minister had seen to that.

"What say you, Lord Blackstone? Do you serve king and country, or merely yourself?''

The black eyes smoldered in resentment like two clumps of coal ready to ignite a growing indignation. "You have no need to remind me of my duty to the King. The Blackstones have stood behind the Crown for centuries. I shall go to Virginia and do your bidding. It is but another distasteful agreement I find myself obliged to fulfill.''

# Chapter Two

*Williamsburg, Virginia, May, 1774*

The charming brick Georgian house facing Duke of Gloucester Street stood serenely beneath two white flowering dogwood trees, belying the furor that was taking place within its walls.

Alexandra Courtland faced her mother across her parents' sunlit bedchamber. Her expression was clouded in anger as she held the letter up they had just received informing them of Charles Fortune's death.

"How could you do this to me, Mother? You have ruined my life forever," she accused.

Catherine's face colored with guilt. If only that missive hadn't arrived today, she thought. Well, it was bound to have happened sooner or later. "Please calm down, Alexandra. I know you have cause to be upset, but shouting will change nothing," she said, staring at the defiant set of her daughter's chin. She had seen that expression often enough in the past nineteen years to know she was going to have a difficult time convincing Alexandra of her duty.

"Calm down? How can I calm down? My life is over." Walking to the window, Alexandra pulled the red brocade fabric back to peer out at the street below. She had always thought to marry Tom Farley one day.

The strapping blond cooper had been her childhood friend and confidant. It was understood that they would cement their mutual affection within the bonds of matrimony. How, then, could her mother expect her to entertain the idea of marriage to someone else?

Catherine watched as Alexandra pressed her forehead against the glass, her face a study in abject misery. It was such a beautiful face. Alexandra had grown into a lovely young lady—a headstrong one, but lovely nonetheless. Remorse overwhelmed her at what she was putting her daughter through. Taking a deep breath, she said, "I would not ask you to do it if my life did not depend on it."

The wild mane of black hair swung back and forth in denial as Alexandra spun about to face her mother. "I won't do it. How can you ask me? He's an Englishman—a nobleman," she spat. To think her own mother had betrothed her to a duke! It was the ultimate humiliation. For months she had done nothing but rant and rave about the oppressive English aristocracy, and here she was practically engaged to one of them.

"I could be prosecuted for what I have done if you do not go through with the marriage to Nicholas Fortune. Forgery is a serious offense."

Alexandra's blue eyes widened in alarm. "Mother, what have you done?"

Dropping down on the featherbed, Catherine covered her face in mortification. "I am so ashamed," she said, sobbing.

Rushing over to the four-poster bed, Alexandra took a seat next to her mother, drawing her into her embrace. "Don't cry. There must be a way we can repair the damage. Tell me what it is you have done."

Catherine hesitantly recounted all the details of her former alliance with Charles Fortune. Alexandra listened, mouth agape, at her mother's revelations. She was stunned to find out that her mother had a past. She could see the moments of happiness and sadness

28

reflected in her mother's eyes as she relived her memories from long ago.

"So you see, Alex, I had no alternative but to forge your name on the document," Catherine confessed, shortening her daughter's name to the frequently used nickname that Alexandra abhorred.

"But why? The duke was three thousand miles away. Surely he never would have known."

Taking Alexandra's hand in hers, Catherine replied, "I don't expect you to understand. Maybe someday when you have fallen in love you will. I made Charles a promise. It was the only thing I could leave him with. We corresponded over the years, mostly through Sarah at first, but then directly, after she died giving birth to their second son. Charles never let me forget the promise I had made him."

"Did father know?" Alexandra asked, her eyes wide in anticipation of the answer.

Catherine's smile was thoughtful. "Yes. Your father has been most understanding throughout our marriage, but I fear his level of compassion will be sorely taxed if he finds out that I have committed an illegal act."

"But why did you? I still don't understand."

Catherine's eyes filled with tears once again. "I received a letter from Charles about a year ago. He wrote to tell me he was dying. He begged to have me formalize our agreement by having you sign the document. I couldn't bring myself to ask that of you. I signed your name."

A glitter of hope entered Alexandra's eyes. "But it's not legal. I cannot be held responsible."

"That is true, Alex, but I can."

Rising from the bed, Alexandra paced nervously back and forth across the red and green Turkish rug; the blue taffeta of her skirt swished softly over the floor. There must be something they could do, she thought desperately. Glancing over at the tearstained face of her mother, she felt a dull ache form in her chest.

"Will you try and have the duke break the contract?" she asked. "If he decides to void the agreement, no one will get hurt."

Catherine nodded. "I will try. But I can't promise he will agree. What if he desires this union? Will you capitulate?" She watched a multitude of emotions filter across her daughter's face. So much rested on her decision.

A long silence drew out between mother and daughter. The tall-case clock in the hall chimed two, signaling to Alexandra that her father would soon be home for dinner. How much did he know of all this? she wondered, finally asking, "Does father know of the agreement?"

"Yes, but he thinks you are eager for the match. He was surprised at first, because of your sentiments toward the Crown, but I reassured him that you were doing this to please me. I'm sorry," Catherine said, dabbing at her eyes with the linen handkerchief.

Alexandra sighed deeply. "I will marry your duke if I have to, Mother," she said, her voice edged in anger, "but I will never conform to his aristocratic ways. He and the King of England may view us colonials as illegitimate children of the Crown, but I view myself as an American. Nicholas Fortune will rue the day he ever laid eyes on me if he thinks to change that fact."

Duke of Gloucester Street was teeming with activity as Alexandra made her way down the broad, dusty, tree-lined thoroughfare. Dozens of draft and saddle horses were tied up in front of the well-furnished shops and business establishments she passed on her way to the printing office. It was her intention to purchase the latest edition of the *Virginia Gazette*. The newspaper was widely read throughout the colonies, its prose highly acclaimed. She was proud that such a distinguished paper was published right here in her town.

Williamsburg was a flurry of excitement during this hectic week of Publick Times. Burgesses from the various counties throughout the colony met here twice a year when the General Assembly held sessions in the Capital. The population of the quiet country town increased three times its normal size; every tavern and inn was filled to capacity.

Alexandra paused, waving at Mr. Anderson, the proprietor of the Wetherburn Tavern. He was attempting to placate a group of irate men who apparently had been denied lodging in his establishment. The tavern accommodated up to five persons in a bed, but evidently there were no beds to be had this day. Although the Wetherburn was not considered as fine a hostelry as the Raleigh Tavern across the street, it was still a handsome structure famous for its liquors and lively dances.

Hurrying on, Alexandra wrinkled her nose in disgust at the pungent smell of animal manure that wafted through the air. It was really getting to be quite a nuisance having pigs and sheep roaming the streets at will, she thought, lifting her gown, careful of where she stepped.

Walking in the direction of the printer's, Alexandra frowned, thinking of the confrontation she had had with her mother this morning. She had used the excuse of purchasing the newspaper as a means of escaping the guilt-ridden looks her mother had flashed her throughout the afternoon meal. She shook her head in consternation as she thought of the horrible predicament she now found herself in.

Spotting the familiar wooden sign with the red painted image of a printing press, Alexandra turned and made her way up the steps to the door.

"Good afternoon, Mister Dixon," Alexandra said, smiling at the gray-haired man as she entered. He was wearing a brown leather apron; his fingers bore the telltale stains of the black printer's ink he used regularly. The shop smelled of newsprint and leather and the sweet odor of tobacco Mister Dixon always smoked.

John Dixon looked up, pleased to see one of his best customers entering the shop. It was no secret to anyone who knew Alexandra Courtland that she had a penchant for reading. "Good day, mistress. How may I serve you this fine afternoon?"

"I am here to purchase a newspaper. But first, I would like to browse through your books."

The printer smiled knowingly. "Certainly. There are several new editions just come off the press in the back room. Take all the time you want."

The leatherbound editions drew Alexandra's immediate attention. She was drawn like a magnet to the shelves of calfskin-covered books whose gilt-embossed lettering made them valuable treasures indeed.

Spying a copy of *Two Treatises of Civil Government* by John Locke, Alexandra picked it up, gazing reverently at the book that had made such an impact on her thinking. Locke had set down in writing everything that she so fervently believed in: freedom from taxation without the people's consent; freedom to rebel if the government failed to respect the law. It was the last doctrine she secretly held to her heart. It was her fondest wish that one day the American colonies would break free from the tyrannical hold of their mother country.

Engrossed in her perusal, she failed to notice that she was no longer alone.

"It would seem that your reading material is inappropriate for a girl of such tender years. Wouldn't you find a lighthearted romance more to your liking?"

Alexandra spun around at the precise, clipped words that could have been uttered only by a pompous, overbearing Englishman. No American would dare comment on another person's reading preference. Tender years indeed, she thought angrily.

32

The hot retort she was about to utter died on her lips as she stared into the fathomless black eyes of the man before her. He was looking down at her and standing very close. She felt a moment of unease. Everything about the man was black save his skin: his eyes, his hair, his suit of clothes. Even the cane he carried was deep ebony, topped by a knob of gold. He was very handsome, for an Englishman, she admitted grudgingly, though a mite pale for her taste. At the questioning expression on the gentleman's face, Alexandra realized she was staring.

Choosing to hide her embarrassment behind a scathing retort, she said, "I fail to see how the choice of my reading material is any of your business, sir. It might do you Englishmen some good to study the words of Locke. Perhaps you'd learn a thing or two."

The stranger's right eyebrow shot up at her insolent suggestion, but the staid expression on his face remained unaltered. "I shall take your recommendation under advisement," he replied dryly.

Alexandra nodded curtly before turning to exit the room. Why did she suddenly feel as if she had just been put in her place? These Englishmen were a cool lot, she thought. They probably had ice water running through their veins.

Handing Mister Dixon her coin, Alexandra hurried out the door, eager to put some distance between herself and the disturbing dark-haired stranger.

The dining room was aglow with candlelight as the Courtland family gathered for their evening meal. The green Chinese wallpaper was a stunning backdrop for the lovely gilded looking glass hanging over the Hepplewhite serpentine mahogany sideboard.

The mirror reflected the look of boredom that the eldest daughter of the Courtland family wore on her face. Alexandra grimaced as she looked around at the somber faces of her family. Supper was certainly proving to be a tedious affair this evening, she thought, taking another bite of her ham. Everyone seemed so quiet, not at all like the boisterous group that usually gathered about the long mahogany table.

Glancing over at her father, whose peppered head of hair was bent in concentration over his dinner, Alexandra found herself wondering what he would think if he knew about her mother's dishonesty. How did he feel knowing his wife had loved another man before him?

Her mother's face was unusually pale, as if she could read the disquieting thoughts Alexandra was having about her. The red of her hair, tempered by strands of white, shone brilliantly in the light of the twelve candles which gleamed from the brass chandelier overhead. Catherine Courtland was still an attractive woman, despite the fact that she was fifty years of age. It was understandable why Charles Fortune had fallen in love with her. Her beauty went beneath the surface of her skin. She was kind, generous, and caring. It would have been impossible for her not to help her mother out of her predicament, Alexandra realized.

Alicia, her younger sister by three years, was staring dreamily into her plate of ham and sweet potatoes. Alexandra didn't think Alicia knew what was on the fork that she put reflexively into her mouth. She must be in love. Only that affliction could produce such a look of total indigestion. Alexandra smiled inwardly. Poor Alicia. She was so shy and reserved. It was no wonder she was having a difficult time attracting boys her own age. She was certainly pretty enough. She had Mother's flaming hair and alabaster complexion; her large blue eyes glowed with the innocence of youth. Whoever the boy was who had captured her heart was very lucky.

The only family member at the table who seemed to be enjoying his meal was her older brother, Benjamin.

He looked as if he didn't have a care in the world, but Alexandra knew differently.

The colonial cause had affected all of them in one way or another. The rising hostility between England and her colonies made the future uncertain for a man of Benjamin's age. He was presently studying law with Mister Wythe, who lived only a short distance away. He had only one more year of studies to complete before he would be eligible to practice the profession. At twenty-three, Benjamin was anxious to conclude his schooling so he could marry. He had had his eye on the daughter of the local cabinetmaker for quite a while.

Prudence Adams was a sweet, unassuming girl. She was passably pretty, terribly serious, and madly in love with Ben. She would be a welcome addition to their family.

Deciding that the somber atmosphere at the table had gone on long enough, Alexandra prepared to enlighten her family about the stranger she had encountered at the printer's office earlier that afternoon. "You will never guess what happened to me today," she said, breaking the silence.

Four pairs of eyes looked up simultaneously.

Benjamin smiled widely. "What's that, Alex? Don't tell me old Tom has finally popped the question!" he teased.

Alexandra could feel a warm blush stealing over her cheeks. She chanced a peek at her mother, who was also blushing. "Don't be silly," she replied offhandedly. She thought she heard Alicia breathe a sign of relief. "I met the oddest man today at Mister Dixon's printing office. He had the audacity to take me to task over my reading of John Locke's book *Two Treatises of Civil Government*. There I was, minding my own business, when an arrogant, ill-mannered—"

"Excuse me, miss," Betsy Tibbs, the housekeeper, interrupted, smiling apologetically at Alexandra as she came into the room, closing the door behind her.

"There's a very proper gentleman out in the hall asking to see you, Missus Courtland. Says it's of the utmost urgency, or some such. Should I tell him to come back?"

Catherine smiled at the pretty, plump servant. "Bring him in, Betsy. We are finished with our meal." She watched as Betsy hurried out into the entry hall to retrieve the uninvited guest. "I have no idea who could be calling at this hour. Does anyone else?" Catherine asked.

"Well, it's obviously someone sadly lacking in manners. Imagine showing up at someone's house during their suppertime! I personally have had enough of rude, obnoxious people for one. . . ." Alexandra's words froze in her mouth as she spied the man coming through the dining room door. "It's him!" she shouted, pointing an accusing finger at the dark-haired stranger in the doorway.

Catherine stood to greet the guest, puzzled by Alexandra's rudeness.

"Alexandra, where are your manners?" Samuel Courtland scolded, giving his daughter a reproving look. Rising from his chair, he threw his napkin down upon the table. "Please excuse my daughter, sir. She is rather high-strung."

Alexandra shot her father a penetrating look of annoyance before turning back to stare at the stranger. He came forward, bowing courteously, his black tricorn hat held firmly in the crook of his left arm.

"Forgive my intrusion. I am unaccustomed to the dining habits of the colonies. I have only just arrived."

"Think nothing of it. Please come in. I am Samuel Courtland and this is my wife, Catherine. How may we help you?"

"I am Nicholas Fortune, Duke of Blackstone."

Catherine and Alexandra exchanged quick, nervous glances. An uncomfortable silence filled the room at the stranger's revelation.

Catherine reeled, her face paling. "We did not expect you so soon, your grace. We have only just received word of your father's death," she said, recovering her aplomb.

" 'Twas a shame about the duke," Samuel offered. "I met him many years ago in England. Please accept our condolences."

Nicholas inclined his head. "I have come regarding the agreement between my father and your wife," he said, staring accusingly at Catherine, whose cheeks reddened under his scrutiny. She was probably feeling guilty about coercing his father into such a ridiculous agreement, he thought.

Taking a deep breath, Catherine said, "If you will follow Samuel and me into the parlor, my lord, we can discuss the situation in private." Turning to her daughter, who sat transfixed in her seat, her face as white as the glass of milk in front of her, she added, "Please come into the parlor, Alexandra." She then addressed the others. "Ben, I would like you and Alicia to retire now. We have business to discuss."

Nicholas witnessed the whole scene unfold before him as if he were watching a melodrama. The red-haired child smiled sweetly at her parents, bidding them good night like a dutiful daughter. The son stared at him with obvious dislike before pushing back his chair, grumbling his farewells, and departing the room.

The only one who remained was the black-haired wench he had encountered earlier at the printer's office. Just his luck to be saddled with a sharp-tongued seditionist, he thought disgustedly. He preferred his women a bit more biddable and definitely more well rounded. Why, compared to Sabrina's lush figure, this girl's body was that of a boy. He scowled, not realizing he had been staring at her chest until he heard her say, "Have I spilled something on my gown, my lord? I thought I must have, the way you have been scrutinizing my person."

Looking up, Nicholas caught the look of accusation in her eyes. He bit back the smile that rose to his lips and replied smoothly, "Beg pardon. I meant no disrespect."

Samuel cleared his throat. "Shall we adjourn to the parlor," he suggested. "We will be much more comfortable there."

Rising from her seat, Alexandra gathered up the folds of her gown and glided to the door, refusing to look at the duke. It would have to be him, she thought. Of all the Englishmen in the world, he had to be her duke. She couldn't go through with this marriage. He was every bit as arrogant and haughty as she had feared he would be.

"Please be seated, Lord Blackstone," Catherine said.

Taking a seat on the rose brocade settee, Nicholas glanced about the elegantly furnished room, noting the matching rose brocade festoons that hung at the windows and the exquisite rose and green Aubusson carpet that hugged the floor. There were several Chippendale mahogany chairs scattered about, and a lovely, ornately carved Queen Anne highboy that stood in the corner. Apparently, Samuel Courtland did quite well for a merchant, Nicholas thought, impressed despite himself. He hadn't expected to find so many fine possessions in the home of a colonial.

"May I offer you some refreshment, my lord?" Catherine inquired graciously.

"A cup of tea would be nice," Nicholas replied.

"We don't drink tea in this house, your grace," Alexandra interjected. " 'Tis a bit too expensive for our taste." She sat upon the Chippendale side chair, smiling innocently at him.

At least she wasn't ugly, Nicholas thought, but that tongue of hers would have to be stilled. "A brandy will do nicely," he said, continuing his observation of his future bride.

She wasn't very tall, and she was as slender as a willow tree. Perhaps she would plump out a bit after her first child, he thought hopefully. Women's breasts were known to enlarge considerably during pregnancy. Her hair was as black as his. She had most of it hidden beneath a demure white linen mobcap. The blue of her eyes reminded him of brilliant sapphires. They sparkled like jewels whenever she was angry, which apparently was most of the time.

Alexandra moved restlessly in her seat, aware of the duke's assessing gaze. From the displeased expression on his face, she could tell he found her lacking. Unconsciously she sat up a little straighter, thrusting her chest out. She was not overly endowed, but she certainly had enough to keep most men interested. She reddened as her eyes met his across the room. She thought she saw the corner of his mouth twitch. Her eyes narrowed. By God, he was laughing at her! How she would love to wipe that look of superiority off his face with the palm of her hand.

"Here you are, my lord," Samuel said, placing the snifter of brandy in Nicholas's hands. "Since the original agreement was between your father and my wife, I am going to let Catherine handle this affair."

Nicholas's eyebrow rose. "That is highly irregular, is it not?"

"Not in the colonies, my lord," Catherine assured him. "Women have a few more rights and privileges here than they do in England."

Nicholas glanced over to see the smug smile plastered on Alexandra's face. "Very well," he conceded, taking a sip of his brandy. These damn colonials know nothing of proper decorum, he thought.

Catherine took a deep breath, relieved that Samuel was seated next to her on the loveseat. "As you know, the original agreement between your father and me was drawn up many years ago. Your mother and father and I were very close friends. When I decided to

39

travel to the colonies to marry Samuel, Charles insisted on uniting the families by the marital agreement.

"I have discussed this situation with Alexandra only this morning. She has agreed to release you from any obligation the agreement stipulates."

A look of surprise registered on Nicholas's face. So the little rebel desired her own independence as well as the colonies', he thought. Pity he would have to disappoint her.

"That is most generous of your daughter, madam." He saw the look of hope that entered Alexandra's eyes. "But I am afraid my father has left me no recourse but to marry. If I fail to comply with the agreement as written, I shall have to forfeit my lands and fortune. That is something I am unwilling to do." There was a bitter edge of cynicism in his voice.

Alexandra's face fell. Blinking back the tears that suddenly surfaced, she bit the inside of her lip to keep from crying out. The tiny hope she'd held within her breast was gone—crushed by the words Nicholas Fortune spoke. She would have to marry the aristocratic nobleman. The thought of binding herself to this man filled her with despair.

Catherine stared with sadness at the two young people before her. Nicholas's face was hard, remote; Alexandra's drawn and pale. She shook her head. Charles, my love, she thought, what have we done?

# Chapter Three

The morning air was comfortably warm as Nicholas walked the mile from the Governor's Palace, where he temporarily resided, to the Capitol to keep his appointment with Lord Dunmore.

The white flowering dogwoods and blooming pink azaleas made a splendid sight as he turned from the Palace Green onto Duke of Gloucester Street. The air was scented with the fragrant perfume of lilac mingled with the offensive odor of backyard privies and animal droppings.

A brisk walk was just what he needed to clear his thoughts after his illuminating encounter with Alexandra Courtland last evening. He could tell she would not make an obedient wife. Her dislike of him was evident in every look she gave him—in every word she spoke. He heaved a sigh. What a bother this whole, tedious affair was going to be. There would have to be some semblance of a courtship before their engagement could be announced. It wouldn't do to flout the proprieties.

How the devil was he going to find the time to court his lovely betrothed and still involve himself in the government of the colony? he wondered. Dunmore had been very insistent about seeing him promptly at ten o'clock this morning.

Doffing his hat at two overweight matrons who stuck their noses in the air as he passed, Nicholas realized that life in Virginia and life with a Virginian was not going to be a pleasant experience—not by any stretch of the imagination.

Approaching the handsome brick Capitol building, the Union Jack flying proudly overhead from the hexagonal cupola, he was impressed by the imposing structure. It was surrounded by a wall of brick, putting forth the image of strength, solidity, and sovereignty.

Nearing the grassy area to the east of the building known as the Exchange, Nicholas observed merchants and men of affairs who gathered to transact cash business and settle debts. He spotted two well-dressed gentlemen on the steps leading up to the building. Probably burgesses, he surmised, judging from the heated discussion they were having. Walking forward to make their acquaintance, he prepared to introduce himself.

"Excuse me, gentlemen. I am newly arrived and wondered if you might inform me as to the whereabouts of Governor Dunmore."

Both men paused in their conversation and turned to stare at the intruder. The red-haired man smiled, proffering his hand. "Thomas Jefferson at your service, and this is my good friend Patrick Henry. Are you by any chance the new aide to Governor Dunmore we have been told to expect?"

Nicholas bowed. "Nicholas Fortune, Duke of Blackstone. It is a pleasure to make your acquaintance. My business here is both personal and political," he replied.

"We've heard you've come to fetch a wife," Patrick Henry said, a smile breaking out on his thin, angular face. "Word travels fast in the colonies, my lord."

"So I've heard, Mister Henry. And not all the information you receive is favorable to the Crown . . . or so I'm told."

"The winds of dissent blow hard, Lord Blackstone.

42

Let us hope they can be stifled with reason and prudent measures," Jefferson interjected.

"Yes. Small winds often gather into gales of fury," Henry warned. "Perhaps when you have seen which way the wind blows here in Virginia, you will be able to counsel our illustrious governor."

Dipping his head slightly, Nicholas replied, "Thank you for your direction, gentlemen. Now if you will excuse me, I have an appointment with Lord Dunmore."

"You'll find him in the council chamber on the second floor," Jefferson said.

Offering his thanks, Nicholas hurried inside and up the stairs to his meeting. He entered the walnut paneled room to discover that the governor, seated at the long oval table, was alone. Apparently, the meeting of the council had already taken place.

"Come in, Nicholas. Have a seat," Dunmore said. "You've arrived too late for the meeting, I'm afraid." There was a hint of censure in his voice.

"My apologies, my lord. I was engaged in a discussion with a Mister Jefferson and a Mister Henry; I fear I lost track of the time."

"I must say your choice of company is most curious, Nicholas," he said with a significant lifting of his brows. "Jefferson and Henry are both troublemakers. They are indicative of the general populace of these colonies. I have never found a group of more insolent malcontents in all the years I have served the Crown."

"You expect trouble, then?"

"The colonial pot simmers ominously. When it will boil over is anybody's guess."

"I thought most of the trouble brewing was in Massachusetts, not here in Virginia."

"True, true. But these traitors to the Crown have banded together. They have express riders spreading their seeds of sedition and discontent up and down the Atlantic seaboard. I fear we will see things coming to a head in Boston now that Hutchinson has been replaced by Gage."

Nicholas shook his head. "I don't understand how the colonies can expect protection from England yet refuse to pay the taxes that support that very protection."

"They're a prickly, stiff-necked breed of people. For years the colonies have existed solely for the benefit of the mother country. Now, because of rabble rousers like Samuel Adams and our own Patrick Henry, they cry out that taxation is unjust."

Pausing to light a clay pipe, Lord Dunmore continued, "Enough of this political talk. What of your plans to wed? Have you set a date for the wedding?"

Nicholas frowned. "Does everyone in Virginia know of my plans?"

"I'm afraid the arrival of a duke, and the fact that he is planning to marry a commoner, have provided fodder for the gossip mill. Every woman between the ages of eight and eighty will view your engagement as the personification of romance."

"If they only knew," Nicholas said, snorting.

Lord Dunmore viewed Nicholas with shrewd consideration. He steepled his fingers in front of his chest, a satisfied expression on his face. "Your engagement is going to prove very useful to the Crown, Lord Blackstone."

"How so?" Nicholas questioned, leery of the look on John Murray's face.

"We are going to have a grandiose ball in honor of the occasion. The local citizenry will be invited to observe how nobility and the common man, or in this case woman, can unite peaceably . . . lovingly."

Rising to his feet, Nicholas placed his hands upon the brightly colored tapestry that covered the table. "I don't think that would be wise, my lord."

"Why ever not? I think it's a splendid idea."

"My betrothed is not predisposed to our marriage.

44

She will not be easily persuaded to attend such a function. I fear her sympathies lie with the colonial cause."

Lord Dunmore's laughter filled the room, echoing off the walls of the chamber. "I've heard the Courtland wench is a feisty little thing. Beautiful, though, quite beautiful. Surely you can bring her to heel, Nicholas. You're an Englishman, by God. She's just a woman— and a colonial at that. Show her who's in charge. As the King shall rule absolute over his colonies, so shall you over Alexandra Courtland."

The cooper's shop was located at the western end of the main street. Alexandra approached the white clapboard building with trepidation. She was going to tell Tom of her decision to marry Nicholas Fortune.

Pushing the gate open, she entered the yard. Barrels and kegs of various shapes and sizes were stacked in neat rows waiting to be delivered. These were the common containers used for storing and shipping all kinds of goods from nails to delicate china cups. The most important container, vital to Virginia's economy, was the tobacco hogshead. It was in these four-foot-high barrels that the planters shipped their tobacco to England in exchange for imported goods.

As Alexandra opened the door to the shop, her nose was immediately assaulted by the pungent odor of freshly cut pine. Tom looked up as she entered, his face somber. The sunlight reflecting off his curly blond hair made it look very much like the light-colored wood shavings at her feet.

"I wondered when you would finally get around to telling me your joyous news," Tom said.

Alexandra reeled as if stricken at the hostile expression on Tom's face and the animosity in his voice. "Who told you?"

"Ben was here first thing this morning. It seems not

every member of your family is pleased with your decision."

"There are extenuating circumstances I am not at liberty to divulge."

Tom sneered. "Like money and position?"

"No! How can you think that?" Alexandra shouted.

Tom stood up, kicking the barrel he was working on out of his way. "What do you expect me to think? I thought you and I were going to get married."

The look of hurt and confusion on Tom's face pierced her heart. "As did I. But things have changed. All I can tell you is that the marriage to Nicholas Fortune was arranged before I was born."

"You don't have to agree. Your father would never force you."

"I already have. The marriage will take place as planned," she said, turning away, unable to face the look of disgust on Tom's face. She felt the tears roll down her face and then a firm hand on her shoulder.

"Don't do this, Alex. I love you. We belong together. Marrying a member of the nobility goes against everything you believe in. Surely you cannot mean to turn your back on the fight for freedom."

Alexandra spun about, wiping her eyes with the back of her hand. "My marriage will not change how I feel about America. I am as true to the cause as I ever was."

"What about your feelings toward me?" he asked, pulling her into his embrace.

"I will always care for you, Tom. Nothing will ever change that. But I must marry the duke. I hope you can understand." She looked at him beseechingly.

"I understand nothing," he ground out, shoving her away. You have always been stubborn and headstrong. You should try to be more tractable, like your sister."

Alexandra's eyes widened. "Alicia . . . what does she have to do with all this?" Her eyes narrowed in suspicion as she recalled her sister's odd behavior at dinner the other night. "You haven't encouraged her, have you?"

Tom smiled maliciously. "Don't tell me you're jealous. No, I haven't encouraged Alicia, but maybe I will. She stops by here often enough. Perhaps next time I shall be more hospitable."

Alexandra's eyes flashed in anger. "Well, let's just hope she won't become an old maid waiting for you to propose. If you had made your declaration six months ago, none of this would have happened." She pushed open the door; the cool air was a balm to her heated cheeks.

"Alexandra, wait," Tom called out.

Pausing in her tracks, she turned. "I have waited too long as it is. Now time has run out. Good-bye, Tom. I wish you well." Hurrying out the gate, her tears slid slowly down her cheeks as she walked the short distance home.

A tall, thin, distinguished-looking gentleman dressed in black broadcloth breeches and frock coat waited patiently on the front porch of the Courtland house. Banging the S-curved knocker once again, a bit more impatiently this time, he was relieved to hear footsteps approaching the door.

The door opened slowly to reveal a short, plump woman dressed in a plain gray gown with a white starched apron and white ruffled mobcap. She was rather pretty in a common sort of way, William Habersham thought. Indentured servant, no doubt. If he were a betting man, he would wager his last shilling on it.

"May I help you?" Betsy asked, observing the stiff-looking gentleman with the droll expression.

"I have come from the Duke of Blackstone with a message for Mistress Courtland."

"Which Mistress Courtland might you be referring

to, sir? We have three residing in this house.'' Betsy
smiled inwardly at the look of annoyance that passed
over the Englishman's face.

"I believe his lordship was referring to his betrothed,
Mistress Alexandra Courtland.''

"Well, why didn't you say so? Come in and wait in
the hall. I won't be a minute. By the way, what did
you say your name was?''

Straightening his posture and tilting up his chin, the
messenger replied, "I am Habersham, the duke's
valet.'' He was proud of his exalted position and
wanted to make sure this colonial house servant knew
it.

Betsy curtsied, not surprised to find the staid gentleman's eyes glued to her generous bosom. Smiling, she
winked, causing the man to blush. "I'll fetch Miss Alex
for you.''

Watching the housekeeper hurry up the stairs, Habersham was afforded the most delightful view of her
fetching posterior. He stuck his finger inside the collar
of his shirt, trying to loosen the tightness he was feeling
at the moment.

Betsy knocked softly on Alexandra's door, uncertain
if she had fallen asleep. The poor girl had come home
a short while ago with tears in her eyes and an expression of anguish on her face. Betsy knew it had something to do with the cooper, Tom Farley, but she dared
not question Alexandra in the state she was in.

"Yes," a small voice replied from the other side of
the door.

"It's me, miss," Betsy said, sticking her head in the
door, relieved to find Alexandra up and sitting at her
dressing table. "Are you feeling up to company?''

"Is Tom here?" Alexandra asked, her face brightening. He had come to apologize for his ill treatment
of her, she thought happily.

Shaking her head, Betsy replied, "No, Miss Alex.

48

'Tis the duke's valet. Says he has a message for you from his lordship.''

"Very well. Tell him I shan't be a moment," she said, sighing deeply. She should have known Tom wouldn't come. He was much too proud to admit it when he was wrong.

"Wait till you see this one, Miss Alex." Betsy's face was bright with mischief. "He's so serious; he could scare the crows if we set him out in the garden."

A small smile touched Alexandra's lips. "Betsy, shame on you. What would mother say? You know she doesn't like us to speak ill of others."

"Go on with you, Miss Alex. I happened to hear all those unkind things you said about the duke the other night when you were getting ready for bed." She folded her arms, waiting for Alexandra to deny it.

A faint blush stole over Alexandra's cheeks. "Eavesdropper!" she said, smiling. "You had best get downstairs and keep our scarecrow busy while I make myself presentable."

"Right you are, miss."

Alexandra smiled thoughtfully as she watched the housekeeper depart. Betsy had worked for the Courtland family for almost fifteen years. She had indentured herself when her husband died and left her penniless at the age of twenty. After her seven years of servitude was up, Betsy found she was unable to leave and had stayed on with the only family she had ever known. Every one of the Courtlands agreed that they would be lost without the helpful, cheerful countenance of Betsy Tibbs.

A short time later, Alexandra descended the stairs to find Betsy and a gawky-looking gentleman, who reminded her of a crane rather than a scarecrow, engaged in what appeared to be a minor flirtation. Clearing her throat, she almost laughed aloud at the guilty expressions they each wore as they quickly separated.

"I understand you wish to see me," she said, facing the red-faced valet.

Squaring his shoulders, Habersham reached into his pocket, extracting a sheet of cream-colored parchment. Handing it to Alexandra, he said, "Lord Blackstone wishes a reply, your ladyship."

Being addressed as nobility set Alexandra's teeth on edge. She tore open the red wax seal, which bore the Blackstone crest. In neat script was a very properly worded message indicating the duke's desire to call on her this evening on a matter of the utmost importance. "Tell Lord Blackstone I shall expect him at nine o'clock."

Bowing, Habersham replied, "Very good, madam."

Alexandra waited for him to take his leave, and when he didn't she cocked her eyebrow at him and asked, "Was there something else?"

Turning as red as a Virginia cardinal, Habersham swallowed. "Might I bid good day to your charming housekeeper?"

Alex bit back a smile. "You'll find Betsy in the kitchen helping Chloe with dinner. Just follow the path to the rear of the house."

Deciding to cheer herself up, Alexandra ventured into the parlor, seating herself at the lovely walnut spinet. She hadn't played for awhile and flexed her fingers over the keyboard. Jumping into a rousing rendition of *"Lovely Nancy,"* and singing merrily at the top of her voice, she found her spirits improving immensely. She was never quite as adept as Alicia when it came to exhibiting her musical talent. She distinctly remembered Mister Peabody, the music master, telling her that her singing could be likened to that of a tree frog. She giggled at the memory.

Perhaps she should sing for his lordship this evening . . . it could very well prompt him to change his mind about their marriage. Laughing gaily, she continued to stroke the keys.

* * *

As the carriage pulled up in front of the two-story house, Nicholas adjusted his cravat and smoothed the velvet of his frock coat. Tonight he would formally propose to the ebony-haired beauty who was destined to become his wife. He checked his coat pocket one more time to make certain he had the ring. He felt as nervous as a schoolboy; his palms were actually sweating. He shook his head. Thirty-three years old and his bloody palms were sweating.

Alighting from the carriage, Nicholas made his way to the door. He was ushered into the parlor by the little blonde maid he had met the other night. "Miss Alex will be right down, your lordship," she informed him. Alex—short for Alexandra. How quaint, he thought.

"Mister and Missus Courtland said I was to give you their humblest apologies for not being present tonight. They have gone to the theater to see Mister Shakespeare's play."

At least they displayed a modicum of culture, Nicholas reflected, flecking an imaginary spec of dust off his coat sleeve. "That is quite all right. My business is with Mistress Alexandra."

Betsy smiled. "I'm to chaperon you tonight, but seeing as how you're a duke and all, I expect I can leave you two to your privacy."

Nicholas's brow shot up. "Your faith in my character gladdens my heart," he said, his words laced with sarcasm.

Giggling, Betsy replied, "Go on with you, your lordship." She waved her hand at him. "I'll be in the study working on my cross-stitch if Miss Alex needs me."

"I'll be sure to convey your message." He watched the maid bustle out of the room and smiled despite himself. These Americans were a strange lot, he decided, taking a seat on the settee.

51

A moment later, his eyes were drawn to the opening of the door. Alexandra floated into the room in a gown of blue satin over a white ruffled lace petticoat. The square-necked bodice revealed a good deal more flesh than he had previously observed. The modesty piece, or fichu, was nowhere to be seen, and the gentle curve of her breasts swelled provocatively over the edge of the gown. It appeared he had grossly underestimated Alexandra's charms, he thought, standing as she entered.

"Good evening, my lord," Alexandra said, dipping into a curtsy. She was pleased by the look of admiration reflected in Nicholas Fortune's eyes. After the disparaging looks he had given her the other day, she had been determined to prove she was every inch a woman. She wasn't about to let this English nobleman mock her.

"You look lovely this evening," Nicholas said.

"Thank you, my lord. Won't you have a seat?"

"I think under the circumstances it might be more appropriate if you were to call me Nicholas."

Fanning her cheeks with her long, dark lashes, she replied, "As you wish. Would you care for a brandy, or perhaps some Madeira?"

"I'll have whatever you are having."

Unaccustomed to spirits, but not wishing to seem unsophisticated, Alexandra poured two glasses of the rich Madeira. Handing Nicholas a glass, she took a seat next to him on the settee. He looked very handsome this evening. His shoulders were much wider than she had first thought; his skin didn't look nearly so pale in the glow of the candlelight. She sipped thoughtfully at her wine.

"Were you aware that Madeira is purported to be an aphrodisiac of sorts?"

Alexandra choked on the wine, and her cheeks reddened. "I hadn't heard that. How interesting," she sputtered.

Nicholas's lips twitched in amusement. She really was quite an innocent, he thought. Quite a cry from worldly Sabrina. "Your maid wished for me to convey that she will be in the study if you should happen to need her."

Alexandra smiled. "I'm surprised she is not in here, sitting right across from us. Betsy is usually very protective."

"I believe she said she was going to trust me because I am a duke." Alexandra's tinkling laughter was very pleasant to Nicholas's ears. She was beautiful when she smiled; her teeth were as straight and white as the finest set of matched pearls.

"Betsy is very taken with nobility."

"But you are not?"

"I believe all men should be treated as equals. I do not believe in the divine right of kings. If God wanted kings to be divine, he would have had them rule in heaven."

"But your own father is a member of the aristocracy here in Virginia. How can you look down your nose at British nobility when this is so?"

"My father worked hard to achieve what he has. It wasn't handed to him on a silver platter. He didn't wait around for someone to die so he could inherit their wealth." She had been speaking in generalities, but she could see by the angry glint in Nicholas's eyes that he thought she was referring to him.

"I am proud to carry on my father's tradition. My family has been a part of English history for generations," he said.

"I'm sure it has. But don't you see? With your title and your fortune, you are as much a slave to your way of life as the slaves that toil here in Virginia."

"Everyone is bound to something."

"Not I," Alexandra stated emphatically. "I am free . . . independent."

"Are you forgetting that you are bound to me?"

The question hung in the air, sending a shiver of apprehension into the pit of her stomach. "Only by a piece of paper," she finally replied.

"My dear, sweet, innocent child. When you become my wife, you will be bound to me by bonds forged tighter than any you have ever imagined." He reached out to pick up the curl that lay against her breast. "What is mine, I keep."

Alexandra swallowed, not liking the direction the conversation was taking. "I believe your message said you had something important to discuss." Nicholas's smile warmed her as thoroughly as the Madeira. She couldn't control the arrhythmic beating of her heart.

Reaching into his pocket, Nicholas extracted the ring, his expression suddenly serious. Getting down on one knee, he took Alexandra's hand in his. "Would you do me the very great honor of becoming my wife?"

A million denials rose to her throat, but she didn't voice them. She was like a mouse caught in a trap with no means of escape. "Yes," she whispered, "I will marry you." He placed a magnificent diamond solitaire on the finger of her left hand. It seemed to mock her as it sparkled in the light of the candles.

Resuming his seat, Nicholas placed his arm around Alexandra's shoulders, pulling her into his embrace. "I believe it is customary to seal the engagement with a kiss." His look was expectant.

Blushing to the very tips of her satin slippers, Alexandra nodded. Nicholas's lips were soft as velvet as they covered hers. She was expecting only a perfunctory buss on the lips and was therefore surprised when he tightened his hold, deepening the kiss. He moved his mouth over hers, devouring its softness. The blood began to pound in her brain; her insides felt quavery, like a jar of quince jelly. She had been wrong about the ice water; Nicholas's blood definitely ran hot.

Raising his mouth from hers, Nicholas gazed deeply into Alexandra's eyes. The wild sapphires had mellowed with passion. "I believe our vows are sealed," he said.

"Yes," she choked out, unable to catch her breath.

" 'Tis but the first bond we forge this night, Alexandra," he said, running his finger gently over the swell of her bosom. " 'Tis merely the first."

# Chapter Four

*London, England, May, 1774*

Sabrina Montgomery sat back against the red velvet cushions of her sofa, observing the short, rather rotund individual before her. Her new protector. What a joke! If Nicholas could see her now, he would laugh in her face.

Nicholas. How she missed him. His looks—his lithe body—the magical way his hands moved over her flesh. She sighed, looking with distaste upon her new lover, Basil Fortune.

How alike Nicholas and Basil were in many ways: their condescending attitudes, their belief in the superiority of men over women. But how different they were in others. In looks especially. Basil was a good head shorter than his brother. Where Nicholas's stomach had been hard and flat, Basil's was soft—flabby. Years of drinking, gambling, and self-indulgence had turned Basil dissolute. It was hard to believe that he was five years younger than his brother.

Of course, there was no comparison when it came to judging the brothers in bed. Basil was an ineffectual, fumbling fool who thought he was God's gift to women. It was getting increasingly difficult to feign satisfaction in his arms.

She almost hated Nicholas for leaving her desperate enough to accept Basil's protection. If it wasn't for the fact that Basil had promised to make her a wealthy woman, she would have booted him out on his rear. She was the kind of woman who liked to hedge her bets.

"Will you quit staring at me," Basil yelled, looking up from the copy of the will he was reading. "I can feel your eyes on me clear over here."

Sabrina smiled seductively. "Can I help it if I can't keep my eyes off you? Why don't you come and sit over here on the sofa." She patted the space next to her.

Basil preened under her flattery. "This is terribly important to us, my dear. Your base instincts will have to wait. I have just gone over the will my father left. I intend to get what was rightfully mine in the first place."

Sabrina stared at her long, red-lacquered nails, a bored expression on her face. "I really don't know why you are wasting your time. Your father named Nicholas as heir, not you. There is nothing you can do to change that. Nicholas is out of reach, and so is his fortune."

Basil's eyes narrowed, his lips thinning to a sneer. "That is where you are wrong, my dear. He doesn't inherit the money unless he marries the colonial. If we can prevent him from doing so, the estates and the money will be mine."

"I really don't understand how you could possibly do that, darling. Nicholas is in Virginia, and we are here." Noting the exasperation on Basil's face, she smiled inwardly. He thought she was such a fool, but she had plans of her own.

Basil stood, throwing the document down on the desk. "What I'm getting at is that you and I are going to prevent Nicholas's engagement. We sail to Virginia immediately. I have booked passage on the schooner *Sally Ann*. She leaves for Virginia on Monday.''

Sabrina masked the excitement his words instilled in her. She would be able to see Nicholas again. Surely he had missed her. That colonial peasant would offer no competition to her grace and beauty. She smiled confidently. Once she had Nicholas back in her bed, she was certain she could convince him to reconsider his position where she was concerned. It wouldn't be that difficult to dispose of his new wife once he had inherited his fortune. Then he would be free to marry her, and she would become the Duchess. She gazed at Basil, wide-eyed and innocent. ''But how do you propose to prevent it?''

Walking around behind her, Basil reached over to cup Sabrina's large breasts in his hands. He rubbed them provocatively, squeezing the nipples until they hardened, pleased when he heard her soft moan of pleasure. ''You are going to prevent it, my beauty. You and your lush body and lovely breasts. Even my brother has his weaknesses.''

Coming around the front of the sofa, he dropped down beside her. Drawing her gown down off her shoulders, he revealed the massive globes to his view. God, she was magnificent, he thought, feeling himself harden. Her nipples jutted out proudly. He kissed them, nipping and biting, until she cried out for release.

''Do not torture me so, Basil. You know I will do whatever you ask. Just touch me.''

Basil's smile was full of satisfaction. How fortunate to have inherited such an insatiable slut as Sabrina! One had only to fondle her pendulous breasts and she would spread her legs for more. Reaching up under the skirt of her gown, he let his fingers trail up her thigh, pleased by the fact that Sabrina never wore anything beneath her clothes. It made things so much easier.

He knew how to get whatever he wanted from her. Cupping her woman's mound, he squeezed until he saw her eyes glaze over. "We are going to prevent big brother from inheriting the Blackstone fortune. When he fails to fulfill the agreement my father set forth, everything he is supposed to inherit will come to me." He laughed harshly, squeezing the wet mound harder. "I shall become the Lord of Blackstone Manor, and you, my delectable tart, shall be my lady."

"Oh, Basil," Sabrina cried, arching her body up, "you are everything that your brother is not."

A smug expression crossed his face. Finally he had found something he could do better than Nicholas. And who would know better than Nicholas's former mistress, he thought.

"I will have my revenge on Nicholas and my father, and so shall you, my sweet. When Nicholas finds himself stripped of his estates and fortune, he will know what it is like to be second best—to take the leavings. I shall look forward to that day."

# Chapter Five

The storming of the palace on this warm May day had nothing to do with the May 12th edict by the Boston Committee of Correspondence that the colonies should suspend their trade with Britain.

Rather, it had to do with one very overwrought Alexandra Courtland, who had just read Nicholas Fortune's edict in the most current issue of the *Virginia Gazette*, announcing their engagement ball at the Governor's Palace on the 20th of May.

"How could he do it?" she muttered, marching through the wrought-iron gates like an army of one. The lion and the unicorn sitting atop the brick wall on either side of the gate looked down on the invasion of the angry woman.

With newspaper in hand, Alexandra boldly knocked on the wide double doors, waiting but a few moments for them to be thrown open. The doorman, dressed in blue and gold livery, made a leg, bowing from the waist. "May I help you, madam?" He quirked an eyebrow at Alexandra's less than courtly attire. She was dressed in a plain pink sprigged muslin day gown; her white mobcap was slightly askew from the hurried trek to the palace.

Throwing her shoulders back and pulling herself up to her full five-foot, three-inch height, she replied, "I wish to see the Duke of Blackstone."

Alexandra was ushered into the entry hall, a lovely black walnut paneled room with a beautiful black and white marble floor and fireplace. The royal arms were displayed proudly above the mantel, and there was an impressive collection of muskets, swords, and sabers mounted on the walls.

It was obvious that these symbols of power were there to remind whoever entered these walls that the authority of the Crown was vested in the governor residing here. As if one needed to be reminded, Alexandra fumed, thinking of the red-coated soldiers who'd made their presence known, dotting the landscape like an epidemic of the pox. She took a seat on one of the red-and-white gingham covered chairs and waited. A few moments later, the duke's valet arrived.

"Mistress Courtland, whatever are you doing here at this hour of the morning?" Habersham demanded, looking about to see who had accompanied the young woman. He had to admit when informed of her presence that he had hoped the lovely housekeeper, Betsy, might be with her.

Alexandra jumped up. "I am quite alone, and I am here to see the duke."

Crossing his arms over his chest, Habersham braced his feet apart in a stance that implied intimidation. "That is quite impossible, madam. His lordship is still dressing."

Alexandra's eyes narrowed a fraction at the overbearing valet. She was going to confront Nicholas and no one, including this lanky whooping crane of a man, was going to stop her. Nodding in compliance, she made to leave, hoping that Habersham would relax his posture. She didn't have long to wait. As quickly as it took him to unfold his arms, Alexandra darted past him, running down the hallway and up the stairway to her left.

"Come back, miss," the valet shouted. "You are not allowed above stairs."

With determination in every step Alexandra hurried up the wide walnut stairway; Habersham's heavy footsteps sounded right behind her. Reaching the landing, she paused briefly, quickly surveying the various rooms to decide which one Nicholas occupied. She chose the northeast bedroom, remembering how elegant it had been when she'd used it to freshen up the night of the Christmas ball.

Placing her hand on the latch, she was just about to open the door when she spied Habersham, red faced and breathing deeply, coming around the corner. "No, miss, you mustn't," she heard him shout. Throwing caution to the wind, she pushed open the door.

As the door banged open, Nicholas spun around from the shaving mirror, razor in hand, one side of his face full of soap. He stared in stunned silence at the sight of his betrothed rushing forward, Habersham on her heels.

Alexandra skidded to a halt, almost losing her balance when Habersham plowed into her from behind. The air left her lungs from the impact. Her mouth fell open; her eyes widened in shock at the sight of Nicholas, bare-chested, his face covered with shaving soap.

"I am sorry, your grace. I tried to stop her," Habersham apologized, throwing Alexandra a hostile look.

Impervious to the valet's anger, Alexandra stood transfixed, the sight of Nicholas's partially naked body too interesting to let go of. At the sound of Nicholas's voice, she raised her eyes from the muscular chest to stare into the black velvet of his eyes, unable to halt the blush that rose to her cheeks.

"You may leave us, Habersham," Nicholas said.

"But, your lordship . . ."

63

Nicholas's face hardened; his voice dripped cold with authority. "I said, you may leave."

Alexandra couldn't help the spiteful smirk she bestowed upon the disgruntled servant. She basked in her moment of triumph, but her victory was short lived when she saw that Nicholas's angry glare was now directed at her. She swallowed her nervousness.

Wiping the soap from his face with a towel, Nicholas said in a voice that was quiet yet chilling, "Would you care to explain yourself, madam? While I am flattered that you have gone to such lengths to seek me out, I feel it is most unseemly, considering my position here on the governor's staff."

Placing her hands on her hips, Alexandra glared at the insolent man before her, watching as he stepped over to the bed to retrieve a red satin robe. "You needn't be flattered, you conceited, arrogant . . ." She groped for just the right word, and when none came forth she spat out, ". . . Englishman." Taking the newspaper concealed behind her skirts, she threw it at him, watching it land at his feet. "How dare you print such lies in the *Gazette?* I have not agreed to participate in any such farce."

Bending over to pick up the offending paper, Nicholas refolded it, slapping it across his left hand. "Do not give me cause to punish you like a recalcitrant child, Alexandra. I assure you, as your betrothed, I have that authority."

She gasped, taking a step backward. "You would dare to strike me?"

"I am used to having people follow my orders. I will not stand for your impertinence, nor your rudeness to my servants."

"My rudeness! Why, that awful man practically ran me down! 'Tis a wonder I wasn't injured having to run as quickly as I did."

Smothering a smile at Alexandra's indignation, Nicholas replied, "Nevertheless, your behavior is not

64

befitting that of a duchess, nor of my prospective wife. In the future, I shall expect better of you.''

''Why, you pompous peacock!'' she shrieked. ''I have no intention of changing my behavior to suit your standards. Neither have I any desire to be a duchess. The whole concept of nobility is ludicrous and . . . and disgusting!'' She folded her arms across her chest, lifting her chin.

Nicholas's mouth tightened. ''More's the pity. I think you would make a lovely duchess.'' He spoke the words smoothly, belying the annoyance he felt as he closed the distance between them.

Alexandra knew a moment of fear as she watched Nicholas coming toward her with a purposeful stride. She did not like the glint of anger she saw in his eyes, nor the stubborn set of his chin. Her mother had warned her that her rash tongue and quick temper would get her into trouble someday. It appeared she'd been right.

The spicy scent of Nicholas's shaving soap reached up to assault her senses as he neared. His robe was open, revealing a lightly furred patch of dark hair on his chest which disappeared into the waistband of his breeches. She could feel a warm glow starting in the tips of her toes and running all the way up to her flushed cheeks.

Placing his hand under Alexandra's chin, Nicholas tipped up her face to stare into the bright blue of her eyes. They shone as clear as the brilliant summer sky. She was incredibly lovely, he thought. Her skin was milky white, her lips full and sensual, holding the promise of paradise.

''I think you are in need of taming, my dear, sweet Alexandra. I fear I will have to undertake the task myself.'' He felt her stiffen at his words, but she did not speak. Lowering his head, he placed his lips lightly over hers, drinking in the sweet taste of her honeyed lips.

Alexandra's senses reeled at the feel of Nicholas's lips on her own. She had thought of little else since the night they had sealed their engagement. Her hands came around his waist, under the satin of his robe, to draw him nearer to her. His skin burned hot. She felt the corded muscles of his back ripple beneath her hands.

Nicholas's arms engulfed her. His kiss deepened, drawing a response from deep within her soul. His hands came up to cup her breasts lightly, the thumbs moving lightly over her stiffened nipples. The touch of his hands on her breasts set every nerve ending in her body on fire. She tingled in all the forbidden, unexplored areas of her body.

As their bodies pressed closer together, forged like molten metal, Alexandra could feel a hard bulge pressing into her knotted abdomen. Snapping back to her senses, she pushed herself out of his embrace. "Do not think to tame me like a cat, with kisses and caresses, my lord. I am no simpering tabby. It will not work." Her breathing was labored. The words she uttered sounded hoarse, strange to her ears.

Nicholas's smile was self-assured. "You think like such a child, Alexandra. Pity you don't act more like the woman your body tells me you are." He saw her cheeks redden in anger. "I could have my way with your right now, if I so desired. Your body responds to my touch, even if your mind fights against it."

"You lie!" she shouted, shaking her head, her mobcap falling off to loose the magnificent black curtain of hair. "I feel nothing for you."

Nicholas reached out, wrapping his hand around the long, silky curls. "Shall I prove my mastery once again?" Pulling her forward by the hair before she could protest, he ground his lips over hers more forcibly this time. At the sound of her moan, he lessened the pressure, thrusting his tongue into her mouth.

Alexandra's hands pushed against the hard muscled

planes of Nicholas's chest. But as his tongue darted into her mouth, instead of resisting, her fingers began to knead his flesh of their own volition. God, he was right. She had no protection against this onslaught of her body. She could feel her defenses weakening with every thrust of his tongue.

An odd, hot, tingling feeling was starting to build low in her stomach, spreading down to touch her most intimate of places. She arched her body into his, pressing the painful throb against the hardened bulge in his breeches. She knew not what she wanted, only that this man had the power to assuage the fever in her blood.

Lifting his head, Nicholas smiled tenderly into the passion-filled face of his betrothed. She was innocent of her body's needs and urges. Suddenly he knew that he wanted to teach her everything about the mysteries that existed between a man and a woman. He wanted to plunge into the depths of her desire and take her to that place where no man had ever gone before. "By God, you tempt me, my sweet," he whispered into her ear. "I am hard with the need of you." He held her at arm's length, trying to restore his composure.

Alexandra blushed, mesmerized by the burning desire that glowed in Nicholas's eyes. "I would be lying if I said that my body did not also crave your touch," she admitted, lowering her lashes.

Her honesty touched him. Caressing her cheek, which felt like the down of a baby chick, Nicholas replied, "We may not view the world through the same eyes, but I think we shall suit nonetheless."

The spell was broken. Alexandra stepped back, putting distance between them. "How can you think it? We are two different people from two different worlds. It is not in my nature to be meek and subservient. I cannot sit idly by letting others rule my life—make my plans for me."

Nicholas's lips puckered in annoyance. "If you had had the common courtesy to ask me about the newspaper article instead of drawing that saber-sharp tongue of yours, I'd have explained that I did not place that announcement."

Alexandra's eyebrows shot up. "But if not you, then who?"

Walking over to the brass stand that held his shirt and coat, Nicholas removed his robe. Shrugging into his shirt, he turned back to face Alexandra, fastening it while he talked. "Governor Dunmore would be my guess. He took it into his head that our engagement ball would be the perfect opportunity for the colonials and the King's men to unite peaceably. We are to set an example."

Alexandra shook her head. "It is because of the governor's highhandedness that things are as they are between Virginia and the Crown. He cannot impose his will on others and not expect retaliation."

"I did try to dissuade Lord Dunmore, but he was adamant. Would you be willing to concede to the ball for my sake?"

Walking over to the window, Alexandra peered down at the sunlit formal garden below. The green holly maze offered few avenues of escape, reminding her of her present predicament. "I guess I should be grateful that you are asking instead of ordering, my lord," she said, turning to face him, the corners of her mouth tipping up into a smile.

Nicholas grinned, displaying even white teeth. "It sometimes becomes necessary to alter one's tactics when faced with insurmountable odds. Orders do not appear to work well with you."

"You're learning, my Lord Blackstone, you're learning. Now if only the governor was as astute, we could save ourselves a lot of trouble."

Nicholas's forehead creased in a frown. "Do you anticipate trouble?"

Cautious not to reveal anything that could be used against the colony, Alexandra replied, "I have no knowledge to base my predictions on. But in my opinion, the colonies will release their fury like a teakettle blowing off steam to release the pressure that builds within."

Interesting that Alexandra should use the same word, "fury," as Mister Henry, Nicholas thought. If the common people felt as strongly as the burgesses about the so-called injustices being heaped upon them by the Crown, perhaps it was time for England to pay more heed to their outcries for equity. He would send a dispatch to Lord North immediately, informing him of the need for more conciliatory measures.

"Are you listening to me, Nicholas? I said, I will attend the ball as you have requested."

Snapping back from his thoughts, Nicholas smiled. Taking Alexandra's hand in his, he brought it to his lips, kissing it tenderly. "I shall look forward to holding you in my arms once again."

"You mean to dance, of course?" she asked, offering a smile.

"Of course," he replied innocently, squeezing the hand that he held. "Now, you had best be on your way before you endanger your reputation."

"If one were brave, one could do without a reputation," Alexandra said, shocked by her own boldness.

"And are you that brave?" There was no mistaking the hidden meaning in his question as he looked first at her and then at the bed.

Smiling coquettishly, a faint pink tinge to her cheeks, Alexandra pretended to consider the question. "Alas, no. I find I am bound by convention as strictly as you are."

"You will find, my sweet, that you are bound by desire even more." He tickled the palm of her hand with his tongue.

Tremors of yearning rocketed through her like fireworks ready to erupt, giving truth to his bold statement. She took a deep breath, fighting for composure.

Looking into the depths of Alexandra's eyes, Nicholas whispered, "There is no way to loose the hold that I have upon you now."


The afternoon sun beat down unmercifully on the women of the Courtland household, who had gathered in the rear yard by the kitchen to perform the burdensome chore of making soap.

Wiping the beads of perspiration off her brow as she leaned over the leach barrel, Alexandra added more ashes to the water. She was setting the leach, or making the lye, that would trickle down from the barrel into the large wooden tub below.

"Do you think the lye is strong enough, Alex?" Alicia asked, wrinkling her nose at the caustic odor.

"If it will bear up an egg or potato, then it is," Betsy declared, wiping her hands on her apron.

"Well, it smells strong enough to float a ship upon," Alexandra said. "Let's get it into the grease so we can get this over with." Making soap had to be the worst task of any that had to be performed all year, Alexandra thought, helping Betsy cart the tub over to the great copper pot that Chloe had suspended over the outdoor fire. Chloe's face was drenched in sweat as she leaned over the pot, stirring in the lye.

"I hate this chore. I think it's worse than making candles," Alicia groaned.

Alexandra smiled, her sister's thoughts mirroring her own exactly.

"I knows you do, honey. But iff'n we don't make de soap, you ain't going to have nothin' to wash your pretty face wid," Chloe remarked.

How Chloe could always keep her sense of humor was beyond Alexandra's understanding. She stared at the kind, ebony face of their cook. Chloe always performed the most arduous of tasks with a smile on her face. She had cooked for the Courtland family for over ten years, during nine and one-half of which she had been a free woman of color—one of the few free blacks in Williamsburg.

Samuel Courtland did not hold with slavery. He had signed Chloe's manumission papers shortly after receiving her from a client who owed him money. Alexandra remembered the snide remarks her father had received at his action from some of his friends and neighbors. He had shrugged them off, saying, ". . . if a man can't live by his principles, then he has no business living at all."

Smiling ruefully, Alexandra thought about her conversation and behavior with Nicholas this morning. She blushed, thinking of how ardently she had responded to his kisses. She couldn't let his persuasive lips sway her from the principles of independence and equality that she believed in. She needed to remain firm in her convictions if she was going to survive marriage to such a virile opponent.

"What be puttin' that secret smile on your face, Miss Alex?" Chloe asked, her black eyes twinkling. "It couldn't be dat handsome duke I hear you is fixin' to marry, could it?" She chuckled.

Cheeks glowing, Alexandra smiled at the ageless black woman. No one really knew how old Chloe was. Her face was free of wrinkles; her head of hair was still as black as her face. When Alex would ask Chloe her age, she would just smile and reply, "Old enough to swat your bottom, missy."

"Chloe Brown, you hush. Mother is going to skin us alive if we don't get this soap finished," Alexandra chided, hoping the heat from the fire would disguise her burning complexion.

"You is right about dat, chile. At the rate we's goin', we ain't never goin' to get done."

Alexandra sighed, seeing the truth of her words. It took about six bushels of ashes and twenty-four pounds of grease to make one barrel of soap. With her mother insisting on a full barrel, they had several more hours' worth of work ahead of them before they reached their goal.

Now that she had decided on attending the engagement ball at the Governor's Palace, she wanted to get finished so she could make her plans for the dress she was going to wear. It had to be something absolutely dazzling that Nicholas would approve of.

Frowning, Alexandra shook her head at the direction her thoughts were taking. What was happening to her? One little kiss and caress, and she was becoming as pliant as worn shoe leather. Her eyes lit with mischief as a wonderfully outrageous idea came to mind. Nicholas just might be in for a few surprises the night of the ball, she decided. Shouting to Alicia and Betsy to bring more lye, Alexandra resumed her work with enthusiasm.

It was three days until the engagement ball. Pacing nervously across the pine floors of her bedroom, Alexandra cast anxious glances at Betsy, who sat in the old, wooden rocker, sewing furiously upon Alexandra's gown.

Each evening after supper, the two women sequestered themselves in Alexandra's blue-and-white floral-papered bedroom to work on the dress.

"Do you think you will have it done in time, Betsy?" Alexandra asked for the third time in just as many minutes.

Betsy sighed, shaking her head at the younger woman. "If I have to stop each time you ask me that, Miss Alex, then I'm not too sure."

Alexandra smiled sheepishly. "I know I'm being terribly impatient, but I just can't wait to see Nicholas's face when I arrive in that gown. It has to be perfect."

"Why do you want to embarrass him, miss? Don't

you like the duke? I found him to be quite a nice gentleman.''

"Of course I like him,'' Alexandra protested, suddenly realizing the truth of her words. She hadn't seen Nicholas in over a week since their confrontation at the palace, but she found herself thinking about him more than she cared to admit. "It's just that, he's so stuffy—so serious. And he's too damn self-assured. He needs to be shown that we Americans don't need to conform to old-fashioned British ideals. I don't want to present the image of a simpering, demure miss. I want to embody the very essence of the independent American spirit. Besides, he wants me to behave more like a duchess, and that is exactly what I am going to do.''

Holding up the shimmering blue satin dress shot with threads of silver, Betsy shook her head. "You're sure to do that in this, Miss Alex. But your mother and father are not going to approve of your showing so much bosom in public.''

Unable to hide the smug expression that crossed her lips, Alexandra held up a white lace fichu, waving it as if it were a flag of victory. "They won't know until it's too late. And besides, it's mother's fault that I'm getting married in the first place. She can't expect me to go docilely to the altar without some small sign of protest, now, can she?''

"And your father?''

"Once father arrives, he will remove himself to the card room and won't even know that I exist.''

"I hope you are right, miss,'' Betsy said, looking skeptically at the headstrong woman. "I wouldn't want them blaming me for your scandalous behavior.''

"Oh, Betsy, don't. . . .''

A knock on the door interrupted Alexandra's train of thought. "Quick, Betsy, hide the dress. I don't want anyone to see it before the ball.''

"Alex, can I come in?'' Alicia shouted through the door.

Hurrying to open it, Alexandra smiled innocently at her sister's annoyed expression.

"What took you so long?" Alicia questioned, noticing Betsy for the first time. "Oh, hello, Betsy. I didn't know you were in here."

Betsy curtsied. "I was just helping turn down the covers, miss."

Alicia glanced over at the blue satin coverlet which hadn't been touched and then back at the pair of women, suspicion bright in her blue eyes.

"What do you want, Alicia?" Alexandra chimed in, hoping to distract her nosy sister. Alicia was a notorious snoop, always eavesdropping and spying on other people's activities. It was going to get her into trouble one of these days.

Plopping down on the bed, Alicia tugged nervously on the folds of her skirt. "I wished to ask you something."

"I'll be going now, miss," Betsy said, her hand on the door knob.

"Will you be bringing me my cup of hot milk later?" Alexandra asked.

"Yes, miss. You can count on it," she said, giving Alexandra a sly glance before departing.

"What was that all about?" Alicia asked.

"I'm sure I don't know what you're talking about," Alexandra replied, taking a seat next to her sister. "Now, what is it you wish to ask me?"

A warm glow covered Alicia's cheeks. "I'm not sure how to go about this."

"For heaven's sake, Alicia, just get on with it," Alexandra said, her words ringing with impatience. She was not in the mood to put up with Alicia's vacillation when she had a dress that she needed to finish.

"Are you aware that Tom is planning to attend your engagement ball?"

"Why, no! How do you know that?"

Staring at the hands in her lap, Alicia blushed. "I

passed by his shop on my way home from the milliner's."

"Alicia! That was most unseemly of you. Tom is much too busy to put up with visits from you."

"He didn't seem to mind," Alicia said, jutting her chin out stubbornly. "He told me to come by whenever I wanted."

Alexandra didn't want to hurt her younger sister. She knew Tom was trying to get back at her for marrying Nicholas. "Tom is just being polite. You're not to bother him again."

Jumping up, Alicia faced her sister, her expression mutinous. "You can't dictate to me. You're just jealous because Tom doesn't like you anymore. You have your silly old duke. Why can't I have Tom?"

Alicia's spiteful words stung. Alexandra had cared for Tom so long it was difficult to accept that he might be interested in someone else. "Alicia, I'm just trying to keep you from getting hurt. Tom is upset with me for marrying Nicholas. I don't want him using you to get back at me."

"You're just being hateful," Alicia screamed, wiping at the tears streaming down her face. "Tom loves me. I know he does, and I love him. I intend to marry him, and there is nothing you can do about it." She ran for the door.

"Alicia, wait!" Alexandra shouted, but it was too late. Her younger sister had already slammed the door, shutting off any explanation she might have offered.

Staring at the door, Alexandra felt a strange numbness overtake her. She had never had words with her sister before. Shaking her head, her eyes filling with tears, she hugged herself tightly, trying to stop the sudden tremors that shook her body. What a horrible mess. Now she not only had Nicholas to contend with, she had her sister as well.

What had she ever done to deserve all this misery? she wondered. It was all Nicholas Fortune's fault, she reasoned. If he had never come to Virginia, none of this would have happened. She would have married Tom and everything would have gone on as before. Yes, she decided, it was the Duke of Blackstone's fault. And come Saturday night, he was going to be sorry he had ever journeyed to the colonies.

# PART TWO

# BOUND BY DESIRE

*Ah Love! Could you and I with Him conspire*
*To grasp this sorry scheme of things entire*
*Would not we shatter it to bits—and then*
*Remold it nearer to the Heart's Desire!*

—Edward Fitzgerald

# Chapter Six

—

"Are you sure you want to go through with this, Miss Alex?" Betsy asked, surveying the outrageously low-cut dress and ridiculous coiffure that Alexandra had fashioned.

Admiring her reflection in the Chippendale looking glass, Alexandra smiled. "It's just perfect, Betsy. Thank you so much for helping me." The blue satin gown had a square-cut bodice, cut so low the tops of her aureolas could be seen peeking above the neckline. She colored slightly, careful not to take too deep a breath lest she pop completely out of her gown. "Hand me the fichu. It wouldn't do for mother or father to see me before it is time."

"Miss Alex, I think you are making a big mistake. Why, half the population of Williamsburg is going to see your bosoms tonight!" Betsy exclaimed, shaking her thick mop of blonde curls.

Adjusting the empty tea tins she had fashioned into her powdered hair, Alexandra shrugged. "It can't be helped. The Duke of Blackstone wishes for me to conform to my role as his duchess; this is how I view myself." She twirled about; the full skirts of her gown swished softly across the floor. Reaching up, she steadied the small ship's model that rested on top of her head. She smiled, thinking of Benjamin's expression when he recognized it as his own. "Well, what do you think?"

Betsy shook her head, her face a mask of disapproval. "I think your duke is going to contemplate murder when he gets a look at your costume."

"Wonderful!" Alexandra squealed, clapping her hands together. "That is just the reaction I'm hoping for. When Nicholas sees me in this garb, he will realize what a horrible mistake he is making marrying me and probably call off the engagement."

"I wouldn't be too sure of that, miss. He be a proud man. I don't see him as the type to turn tail and run from a challenge."

"Oh, balderdash! When the Duke of Blackstone sees his future duchess, he will probably book passage on the first ship back to England."

The royal carriage Nicholas sent over to pick up his betrothed arrived promptly at eight o'clock. Alexandra was seated across from the elder Courtlands, her head bent slightly forward to keep her coiffure from touching the roof of the coach. Her sister, Alicia, did not join them. She had decided to accompany Benjamin, who had left sometime earlier to pick up Prudence Adams, preferring the boring company of Benjamin's sweetheart to that of her interfering sister.

"I must say, Alex dear, your hair is most unusual," Catherine said, eyeing the monstrosity with aversion. "I didn't think you favored powdering it."

Patting the sides of her hair, Alexandra replied, "Nicholas prefers it this way, Mother. It is what all the nobility do." She watched her mother sink back, a resigned expression covering her face.

Glancing at her father out of the corner of her eye, Alexandra caught his amused expression and smiled. She knew she didn't fool him for a moment. Father was quite aware of her feelings toward the nobility. If he thought it odd that she was marrying one of them, he kept it to himself. He had always deferred to her sensible judgment, as he put it, and apparently was doing so once again. Bless him for his faith in me, Alexandra thought gratefully. She just hoped he would feel some charity toward her after the scene she was sure to create tonight.

As the carriage pulled to a halt in front of the wrought-iron gate, Alexandra's stomach fluttered wildly. Peering out the window, she noted that the stately cupola atop the massive brick Georgian building had been lit, the brilliant illumination signifying the importance of the occasion.

The footman opened the door, helping Catherine and Alexandra to alight. The tile walk was lit by lanterns, guiding the guests to the double doors.

When the Courtlands reached the entry hall, Alexandra grabbed onto her mother's arm. "You and father go ahead. I need to deposit my mantle in the cloakroom." She eyed the room to the right that had been designated for that purpose. "I'll be right along," she assured them, breathing a sigh of relief as she watched her parents move toward the ballroom.

Removing the satin mantle from around her shoulders, she inconspicuously removed the white lace fichu, stuffing it into her reticule. Moving into the entry hall, she caught the lustful gaze of the servant assigned to escort her into the reception.

"Madam," he said, extending his arm, his eyes riveted on her bosom.

Giving him a reproachful glare, Alexandra placed her left hand on his arm and marched into meet her fate.

The palace ballroom was resplendent. From the beautiful turquoise-papered walls to the exquisite trio of crystal chandeliers that hung from sixteen-foot ceilings, the room reflected grace and beauty. Chairs lined the wall in front of the six double-hung windows. The black iron coal stove used to heat the room in winter stood to the right. The large oil portraits of King George and Queen Charlotte seemed to look disapprovingly at her from their resting place on the wall at the far end of the room.

Waiting her turn to be presented to the assemblage, Alexandra surveyed the crowd. She spotted Nicholas at once, talking with her parents on the far side of the room. His back was to her, but she could see that he looked quite handsome in a suit of black velvet. His hair was unpowdered, tied back in a queue with a black velvet ribbon.

Her mother also looked stunning in a gown of green silk, looped up in the polonaise style over a silk petticoat of the same color. Alexandra noted that her father looked quite ill at ease in his finery, constantly reaching into the collar of his shirt to pull the constricting material away from his thick neck. Poor father. He probably wished he were still at home, sitting in his blue battered dressing gown with his feet propped up before him in the comfort of his study.

She quickly recaptured her thoughts as the majordomo announced her name. "Miss Alexandra Courtland." The sound seemed to echo off the walls.

Taking as deep a breath as her dress would allow, Alexandra glided forward, observing the look of mortification on her mother's ashen face. Her father's frown belied the spark of admiration she saw reflected in his eyes.

At the look of horror on Catherine Courtland's face, Nicholas spun around, his mouth dropping open momentarily at the sight of his betrothed coming toward him. He clamped it shut. His eyes narrowed before traveling from the top of Alexandra's outlandish hairstyle, down her painted face, until they came to rest on her wide expanse of bosom. The top of her nipples were plainly visible for all to see. He bit the inside of his cheek. Bloody hell! he thought, clenching his fists as he marched across the room.

Alexandra was tempted to turn tail and run at the look of outrage on Nicholas's red face. The muscle in his cheek was throbbing violently; he looked as if he might burst a blood vessel.

Assuming a smile as he approached, Nicholas bowed before his betrothed. "You will pay dearly for this, my sweet," he promised, bending over to kiss her hand.

Alexandra's eyes widened. "Why, Nicholas, don't you like my gown? I did so want to accommodate your desire that I behave in a manner befitting a duchess." She smiled innocently.

Guiding her to a secluded corner behind the harpsichord, Nicholas made sure his voice was deceptively calm. "If it was your intention to embarrass me, you have succeeded. But you should also be embarrassed. These are your fellow townsmen, come to pay their respects to someone who looks no better than a low-class whore."

Blue flames seared a burning reproach. "Perhaps that is what I view the nobility as . . . whores who prostitute themselves for the King of England."

Nicholas's face purpled with rage. "By God, I'll. . . ." He paused at the sight of the governor and his entourage.

"The honorable governor of the colony of Virginia, Lord Dunmore." The stentorious tones of the major-domo echoed throughout the room.

There was a modest amount of applause as the governor strode forward, smiling and shaking hands with the local populace. His frock coat of red brocade sported shiny brass buttons that matched the buckles on his shoes. On his head he wore a white powdered wig.

"We must go over and present ourselves, Nicholas said, grabbing Alexandra's elbow. "You had better keep that sharp tongue stilled, or I swear, I will rip it out."

"But then, how would I be able to kiss you?" Alexandra taunted, caressing his cheek in an affectionate display.

"Madam, I am warning you," he whispered.

"Oh, Nicholas, you say the sweetest things," Alexandra said loudly enough for the benefit of a pair of middle-aged matrons who were straining their ears to listen.

"Martha did you hear that? The duke really must be in love with Mistress Courtland," the obese lady said, her two chins bobbing excitedly.

"I think it's just beautiful," the wrinkled, white-haired matron replied, dabbing at her eyes with her handkerchief. "Isn't love wonderful?"

Alexandra almost gagged as she listened to the exchange between the two old ladies about her and Nicholas. Love, ha! She looked over at Nicholas's stern visage. His head was held high, his body rigid as he guided her over to the governor. His expression was far from loving at the moment.

"My dear Mistress Courtland," the governor exclaimed, placing a kiss on her hand. "How wonderful of you to attend our gathering."

Dropping into a curtsy, Alexandra flashed him a brilliant smile. "Thank you for hosting such a grand ball in our honor, your grace. It was too, too kind of you."

Nicholas released the breath he was holding. Thank God Alexandra had observed the proprieties. It seemed he had quite a bit to learn about his impetuous betrothed, and it also seemed, she had quite a bit to learn about crossing him.

"That is quite an interesting headpiece you are wearing, my dear. Does it have any special significance?" the governor asked, his eyes straying to the swelled breasts that spilled over the edge of her gown.

Alexandra almost laughed at the lecherous old fool. Smiling sweetly into the governor's flabby face, she replied, "Actually it does, your grace. It is supposed to represent the Boston Tea Party." She heard Lord Dunmore's gasp and Nicholas's choked cough. "I see," he replied. The look he gave Nicholas was edged in ice. "If you will both excuse me, I have other guests to greet."

Nicholas inclined his head at the governor then turned to face his intended. "You go too far, Alexandra. I think we need to go somewhere and talk in private."

"That is impossible, my lord. There is my brother, Benjamin, signaling to me at this very moment. I must attend him."

Glancing over to where Alexandra was pointing, Nicholas spied Benjamin Courtland. "Very well. But do not think we are done with this, my sweet seditionist. No one makes a fool of Nicholas Fortune."

Watching Nicholas stalk away, Alexandra tried to repress the fear that his words instilled. Thank goodness she was surrounded by her family. He wouldn't dare try anything while they were here.

"Alex, you constantly surprise me," Benjamin said, smiling widely as he approached. "I thought you had sold out to the other side, but I see by your bold statement, you're still one of us."

"Thank God you arrived when you did. I came very close to getting my hide pinned against the wall by both the governor and Nicholas," Alexandra confessed.

"If that bastard dares to lay a hand on you. . . ."

"You will do nothing," Alexandra interrupted. "Do you understand? I can handle his lordship." She smiled with more bravado than she felt. "We do not want your position to become jeopardized by a senseless argument with someone on the governor's staff. You must be prudent."

"You are right, as always," Ben said, tweaking her nose. "That ship you wear looks very familiar."

Smiling impishly, Alexandra grabbed his hand. "Come and dance with me. I feel the need for some diversion . . . if you don't think Prudence will mind."

Leading her onto the dance floor, Ben shook his head. "Prudence is upstairs, doing whatever it is you women do when they go up there. Alicia is with her. What's with you and Alicia, anyway? I noticed a slight chill in the air whenever I mentioned your name this evening."

"I'm afraid I made rather a mess of things with her. It seems she fancies herself in love with Tom. I tried to warn her off. I don't want her to get hurt."

The minuet did not allow for intimate conversation, but when brother and sister came together again, Benjamin replied, "Are you sure it is Alicia getting hurt that you are worried about? I know you care deeply for Tom."

Pulling Benjamin off the dance floor, Alexandra paused by the refreshment table. "I did care for Tom very much. He will always have a special place in my heart. But I have come to realize that the love I bore him was of a brotherly nature, not the all-consuming love a woman feels for a man. Anyway, that is all in the past. My only concern now is for Alicia's welfare. I do not want Tom to take out his anger at me by using her."

"Well, if you would care to look over at the far corner of the room, you can see that Tom looks quite taken with our little sister."

Alexandra's eyes followed Benjamin's direction. Alicia was gazing lovingly into Tom's eyes and it appeared Tom was actually enjoying it. "It seems I was mistaken. I will have to rectify matters with Alicia."

Benjamin's expression grew serious; his brow wrinkled in confusion. "Why are you going through with this wedding, Alex? I know you don't love the Duke of Blackstone."

Alexandra could feel her cheeks redden. She longed to tell Ben the truth. They had always been close, but she had promised her mother that she would not reveal the motive behind her marriage. She sighed. "I am marrying him because of someone I love very much. That is all I am going to say."

"Well, it appears your reprieve is at an end. Here comes your betrothed, and by the black expression on his face, I wouldn't want to be in your slippers right now."

Glancing over at Nicholas, who was marching in her direction, Alexandra swallowed. She feared by his angry appearance, it was time to pay the piper. "Perhaps you had best leave us alone. I don't think our meeting is going to be all that pleasant."

"Are you sure? I can stay if you like."

The concern on Ben's face was touching. "Quite sure. Now go and find Prudence. I fear it won't be too difficult; her hair is even higher than mine. I shall see you at home." She kissed him on the cheek, watching him walk away. Gathering her courage, she braced herself for the wrath of Nicholas Fortune.

"I see your watchdog has left," Nicholas said as he approached, smiling vindictively. "I think it is time for our little talk."

Alexandra nodded, the action causing one of the small tins of tea to drop down at Nicholas's feet.

Bending over he retrieved it, looking at it with distaste before handing it back to her. "You should never have humiliated the governor tonight, my sweet. I fear he is even more vengeful than I." He grabbed her hand, pulling her along.

"Where are you taking me?"

"I told you once that you were in need of taming. I think it is time you realize who you are dealing with. I am not some colonial bumpkin you can twist around your little finger. You will soon learn who holds the upper hand in this relationship.''

Alexandra looked about frantically for some sign of her family. Spying Benjamin at the refreshment table, she was just about to call out to him when Nicholas's words stilled her voice.

"I wouldn't do that if I were you. I have knowledge of your brother's activities that I am certain the governor would be very interested in learning.''

A lump of fear rose in her throat; she clutched the tea tin tightly. Nodding in compliance, she followed Nicholas out of the ballroom and up the servants' stairway to the second floor.

Pausing outside the door to Nicholas's bedroom, a wave of apprehension sailed through Alexandra's body like a ship in the throes of a hurricane. Why would he risk ruining her reputation by bringing her to his room? she wondered. Perhaps Betsy was right. Maybe he was going to murder her. She chanced a look at his face, which was hard and unreadable. She swallowed her fear.

"After you,'' Nicholas said, indicating with a wave of his hand that she should enter. The chill in his voice sent a shiver of alarm down her spine as she stepped forward.

The bedroom was much as she remembered. The green paneled walls, trimmed with white molding, were relieved by the bright green-and-purple scenic print on the bed hangings and swags at the windows. There was a mahogany tea table in the center of the room atop a multicolored Turkish rug. The table was flanked by two Queen Anne side chairs upholstered in a lively green-and-white bold gingham check. The candles had been lit, bathing the room in a golden glow, giving off the sweet scent of bayberry.

Alexandra's eyes widened as she heard the sound of the key turning in the lock. She spun around, frightened by the satanical smile Nicholas wore.

"Now we shan't be disturbed," he said, walking over to where she stood. "Take off your dress."

Alexandra gasped, clutching her throat. "Are you crazy? I'll do no such thing." Her heart was pounding so loudly, she was certain he could hear it.

Nicholas's eyes were hard with determination. "If you value your brother's life, you will do exactly as you are told."

Tears filled her eyes, but she blinked them back, vowing not to be intimidated. "I will need help with my hooks," she said, presenting her back to him.

As Nicholas's fingers came in contact with the bare flesh of her back, Alexandra tried to block out the tingling sensations that she felt. As the last hook was undone, the dress fell loosely off her shoulders. She held it up in front of her, trying to shield herself from his gaze.

"It's a bit late for a show of modesty, don't you think? Most of the men in the ballroom know exactly what your breasts look like, even down to the pink blush of your nipples." He couldn't keep the anger out of his voice as he spoke. "Throw the gown on the bed and come here."

Alexandra's cheeks burned in humiliation. She hadn't felt half as embarrassed displaying her charms before the large assemblage as she did right now before Nicholas. The black of his eyes burned with desire as she tossed the gown aside. She stood proudly before him, unwilling to cower or humble herself.

Nicholas fought for control as he stared at the pert breasts so provocatively displayed before him. They were supported by some type of wire stays, with no material to cover their beauty. He took a step forward.

Alexandra braced herself as Nicholas came toward her. She had seen the lust on his face as he stared upon her nakedness. When his hand reached out, her nipples hardened in anticipation of his touch. Closing her eyes, she waited. A moment later those same eyes flew open in surprise when Nicholas grabbed her hair, yanking the various decorations from it.

"Why did you powder your hair?" he asked, throwing the offending items to the floor. "In the future, you are to leave it in its natural state. The powder is hazardous to your health." He pulled the pins out; her hair fell in soft cascades down her back. "Bend over," he said, reaching for the brush that rested on the dresser.

Too astonished to speak, Alexandra did as she was instructed. Bending over from the waist, she watched the powder float to the floor like a flurry of snow. The fine white cosmetic caused her to gag; Nicholas handed her a handkerchief. "Put this over your mouth," he instructed.

The cloth offered little protection from the billows of powder threatening to suffocate her as Nicholas continued his undertaking. A few moments later, a spasm of coughing overtook her; she choked, gasping for air.

Grabbing her about the waist, Nicholas hauled Alexandra over to the partially opened window. His fingers burned as they came in contact with the velvet softness of her breasts. He fought the urge to take the enticing mounds into his hands; he breathed deeply of the cooling air, hoping it would halt his rising ardor.

"Thank you," she choked out, looking up into Nicholas's flushed face; his forehead was damp with drops of perspiration.

Fighting for control, Nicholas sought to take his mind off Alexandra's tempting body. Grabbing the towel from the washstand, he dipped it into the basin of warm water. "You're a mess," he said, wringing out the towel. Cupping the back of her head with his left hand, he proceeded to wash the pasty makeup off her face.

"Ouch! You're hurting me," she said, twisting her head from side to side.

"Stand still. I'll not have a painted harlot for a wife.

You'll not hide your natural beauty behind such artifice.''

She stopped struggling. A warm glow crept through her at Nicholas's statement. He had said she was beautiful.

"There . . . that's much better,'' he pronounced, observing his handiwork. "You look almost respectable.'' His gaze dropped down to her breasts once again.

Blushing, Alexandra covered herself with her hands, producing a hearty chuckle from Nicholas. It was the first time she had heard him laugh; it was a glorious sound, even if it was directed at her.

"Why do you cover yourself? I have already seen everything.''

"And do you like what you see?'' she asked boldly, dropping her arms.

"Very much,'' he choked out, pulling her to him, crushing her naked breasts to the velvet of his coat.

The sensation felt deliciously wanton. Putting her arms about his neck, Alexandra pressed herself into him, giving into her desire. "Kiss me, Nicholas,'' she said.

Lowering his head, Nicholas ravaged her lips with an intensity that frightened and stimulated at the same time. He plunged his tongue into her mouth, exploring the sweetness within. Her skin burned where his hands moved sensually over the naked flesh of her back, finally coming to rest on the soft roundness of her breasts.

Nicholas kissed her face and the side of her mouth, making a path down her neck that sent chills up her spine. Finally he drew the puckered peaks of her breasts between his lips. He plucked and pulled at the rigid nipples until Alexandra thought she would explode with the tautness that was building within the apex of her thighs.

91

"Nicholas," she moaned, her impassioned plea sounding odd to her ears.

Nicholas looked up at the sound of his name on Alexandra's lips. He fought to regain the control that had almost escaped him. Taking a deep breath, he gazed deeply into Alexandra's passion-lit eyes. Bloody hell! he thought. The little minx had almost succeeded in making him forget his objectives. "Do not think you can divert me from my goal, temptress," he said, pushing her away.

Nicholas's words doused the fire in Alexandra's blood as effectively as a thundershower. Glaring at him with burning, reproachful eyes, she replied, "You should be ashamed, luring me up to your room, trying to take advantage of me."

His laugh was scornful. "I was the one in fear of being raped, madam."

The look she shot at him was meant to kill. Crossing to the bed, she retrieved her gown and proceeded to dress. "Would you mind fastening my gown?" She presented him with her back.

After the last hook was done, Nicholas spun Alexandra about. "You may use my brush to fix your hair in a more becoming style."

Offering no thanks, she stared at her reflection in the mirror. Her lips were red and swollen; her hair, still bearing the traces of the white powder, hung about her shoulders in disarray. The low-cut gown, which had made her feel so daring, now only made her feel cheap and common. She closely resembled the whore Nicholas had earlier accused her of being. Turning around, she noticed Nicholas rummaging through the tall chest-on-chest which held his clothes. When he stood, he was holding a white ruffled shirt.

He came forward, ripping the expensive white silk shirt to shreds. Removing the ruffles, he held them up to her view. "I believe you have more use for these than I do."

Her brow wrinkling in puzzlement, Alexandra replied, "I am sure I do not know what you mean."

"Then allow me," Nicholas said, taking the ruffles and inserting them into the bodice of Alexandra's dress.

"What do you think you are doing?" she cried, grabbing onto his hand. "If I had wanted to wear a fichu, I certainly would have."

"Your wants do not concern me at the moment, my sweet, only your proper behavior as befitting your new station in life. Now we are going to go back down to the party, and you are going to offer an apology to Lord Dunmore."

As Alexandra shook her head in denial, her expression became mutinous. "I won't do it . . . you can't make me."

Tipping up her chin, Nicholas smiled self-assuredly. "Would you care to place a wager on that? Say . . . your brother's life?"

The blue eyes glittered dangerously. "How do I know you are not bluffing about Benjamin?"

"Let's just say, his horsemanship has been noticed on several occasions."

Alexandra's face paled. He knew, she thought. If he told the governor about Benjamin riding for the Committee, Ben would go to prison, or worse, hang for treason. She couldn't let that happen. She had to protect Benjamin even if it meant humbling herself before the whole British empire.

"Very well. I'll do it your way," Alexandra said, her bitter words reflected by the animosity on her face, "but remember this, I will repay you someday for your threats of extortion. You will not get away with this."

# Chapter Seven

Surrounded by her silent friends who spoke only when their spines were laid flat, their parchment pages open, Alexandra sat staring at the leatherbound volumes that lined the walls of her father's study. The sweet singing sounds of the blue jay who perched outside the window on the branch of the catalpa tree was the only intrusion into her quiet.

Her thoughts were far away, buried in the events that had occurred six days before at the Governor's Palace. Anger surged through her when she thought of Nicholas. But anger was not the only emotion she felt when the image of his face came to mind. She hungered for him, burned like the flame of a candle—constant and hot.

"Oh, God," she cried, throwing down the book she held. The memory of Nicholas's touch was too vivid in her mind. She couldn't control the throb in her breast or the ache in her loins. "Why can't I stop thinking about him? What spell has he cast over me to make me feel this way?"

At the sound of the door opening, Alexandra jumped up from the worn leather chair, surprised by the sight of her father coming through the door. "Father, we did not expect you home until tomorrow. Did your trip to Richmond go as planned?"

Samuel Courtland dropped the black leather portmanteau on the floor, taking a seat in the tufted red chair behind the walnut desk. The old leather creaked as he seated himself. "Aye, all went well. I contracted for several shipments of tobacco, which I will pick up and ship in the fall."

He smiled. His face creased about his eyes and mouth, revealing his good-natured character. Alexandra could recall few times when her father did not have a smile on his face.

"And how have you fared this past week since your outrageous behavior at the ball? I did not have time to discuss your conduct due to the necessity of my trip, but I do think we need to have a talk, Alex."

A hot blush rose to Alexandra's cheeks as she stood in front of her father's desk. Lowering her eyes, she stared down at the toes of her blue moroccan slippers. "Please don't think ill of me, Father. I can handle anybody's criticism but yours."

"I don't wish to criticize you, my dear. I want only to point out the risk you took by flouting convention as you did. I admire your convictions and your bravery in expressing them, but you must understand the consequences of your actions."

Alexandra's eyes flew up. "I did not cause trouble for you, did I?"

Leaning back in his chair, Samuel lit the clay pipe, puffing repeatedly until clouds of smoke circled over his head like a halo. "My sentiments against the injustices of the Crown are well known. Any trouble I may incur in the future will doubtless be caused by my own rash behavior, not yours. But you must realize that although you disagree with the way Lord Dunmore is governing the colony, he still demands a certain amount of respect for the position that he holds. It does our cause little good to humiliate and anger the man."

"But, Father. . . ."

"Let me finish," Samuel said, holding up his hand to forestall any argument. "Not only did you embarrass the governor, you also caused your mother a great deal of anguish. She found it necessary to apologize repeatedly to the duke."

Blue eyes flashing like summer lightening, Alexandra lifted her chin defiantly. "Nicholas deserved worse than he got." She would never forgive him for forcing her to enter that ballroom looking like a bedraggled witch and making her apologize to that arrogant, self-righteous despot.

"He is your betrothed, Alex. I do not understand why you wished to embarrass a man you intend to marry. Unless of course, you really have no desire to marry him. Is that it?"

Alexandra turned away, unable to face her father's probing stare. She had never been able to lie to him. What could she say? That she was marrying Nicholas only to protect her mother from prosecution? That she was being forced to do something completely against her will? She had to protect her mother at all costs. Turning about, she pasted as bright a smile on her face as she could muster.

"Don't be silly. Of course I want to marry Nicholas. He just makes me mad sometimes. You know how insensitive and autocratic the nobility can be."

Samuel nodded in compliance. "Aye, I know, and I'm relieved that your actions were perpetrated by nothing more than a lover's spat. But that doesn't excuse your behavior. In the future, I shall expect better from you, Alexandra. Do you understand?"

"Yes, Father. I'm very sorry. I wasn't thinking clearly. I shall try to. . . ."

Before Alexandra could finish her statement, Benjamin burst into the room, his face flushed with excitement. "You'll never guess what has happened," he shouted, his breathing labored. "I have just come from the Capitol. The burgesses have been dissolved by the governor. Their protests against the Boston Port Act have resulted in their immediate dismissal.''

Alexandra and her father exchanged startled glances. ''What will happen now, Father?'' Alexandra cried. ''Surely the burgesses will not accept the governor's contemptible action. I know Mister Henry will not accept this lying down.''

Samuel Courtland's expression was grave. Shaking his head, he replied, ''Only harm can come of this deed, I'm afraid. The governor has underestimated Virginia's support for her sister colony of Massachusetts. We must pray that tempers will remain cool and men of integrity and influence will find the means to avert what surely could become a crisis of monstrous proportions.''


The loud voices raised in anger inside the many-dormered Raleigh Tavern this sunny May morning could be heard spilling onto Duke of Gloucester Street. The beautifully appointed Apollo Room, site of many a fancy dress ball, was filled to bursting with the various members of the House of Burgesses, who sat discussing the latest edict by the governor of the colony.

The tallest member of the group, a distinguished-looking gentleman in a suit of dove gray, sat in front of the elegant rose marble fireplace, facing his fellow legislators. ''I fear our overzealous governor has left us no choice but to take the matter of the closing of Boston Harbor into our own hands,'' General George Washington stated. ''We must continue to support our brethren in Massachusetts Bay. A united front is our only hope in winning the repeal of these unsavory taxes.''

John Randolph stood, his face pinched in anger. ''I disagree, General Washington. We cannot go against the dictates of our mother country. To do so would be tantamount to treason.''

A tall, dark-haired gentleman in the rear of the room jumped up. ''Is it treason to desire that the colonies be treated fairly and justly? Must we stand idly by while the King robs us of our livelihood—stealing money out of our very own pockets? I think not, gentlemen. The general is right: we must band together as one voice, loud and strong. Singly, we shall be drowned out," Patrick Henry shouted, his strong resonant voice booming out over the heads of the gathering. There were murmurs of approval at his words.

Benjamin and Alexandra waited furtively outside the door of the Apollo room, listening to the exchanges going on within.

"I told you Mister Henry would speak out against the governor," Alexandra whispered, trying to peek through the crack in the door.

"Move away from there, Alex," Benjamin said, pulling on her arm. "I was foolish to let you talk me into bringing you here."

Following Ben outside, Alexandra paused on the walk in front of the large white clapboard building. She could see the gentlemen through the window, gesturing wildly; the expressions they wore reflected the intensity of their purpose.

"I don't see why I must miss everything simply because I happen to be a woman," Alexandra protested. "I am as well versed in the politics of our time as many of the local gentry closeted inside this building."

Ben smiled, tweaking his sister's nose. "That may be true, Alex, but I don't think your English duke is going to agree. I get the impression that he doesn't think you have many brains."

They walked down the rut-filled street, muddied from yesterday's shower. Alexandra hurried her pace, trying to keep up with her brother's longer stride. "Hmph! Well, you'd just better be grateful that I had enough brains the other night to placate Nicholas about your overt activities, or you would be occupying a cell at the gaol right now."

"I appreciate what you did for me, Alex, though I

think it took more courage than brains to humble yourself before the governor.''

"Never fear. Nicholas Fortune has not heard the last of me where that matter is concerned. I expect to exact my pound of flesh.''

"You had best curb your vengeful tendencies for the time being. I understand mother has invited your duke to supper this evening.''

Alexandra stopped, grabbing onto Ben's arm. "What? How could she do this to me?''

Ben's look was commiserating. "Mother feels responsible for your unkind treatment of the duke and seeks to recompense him for his embarrassment.''

"His embarrassment! I don't believe you. You're teasing, are you not?''

" 'Fraid not, little sister. It seems you'd better get used to eating humble pie around your betrothed,'' Ben said, laughing at Alexandra's look of outrage.

"Humble pie, indeed! We'll just see who chokes on the seeds of disgrace this time.''


Alexandra approached the parlor with a mixture of anticipation and dread. Some small part of her looked forward to seeing Nicholas again, but there was also the part that feared facing him for the first time after their amorous encounter.

Pausing before the brass looking glass in the hallway, she surveyed her appearance one last time. She had worn one of her most conservative gowns—a light blue dimity with eyelet ruffles about the neck and wrists. It was demure in the extreme. With her hair pulled up and fashioned in a knot on the back of her head, she thought she resembled a sedate spinster.

Surely neither her mother nor Nicholas could fault her appearance this evening. It was her intention to present an entirely different Alexandra this evening, one completely opposite from the impetuous, brazen woman of last Saturday night. If Nicholas thought he had her figured out, he would soon find out how wrong he was. Pasting a smile on her face, she smoothed down the folds of her skirt and made her way into the parlor.

Nicholas stood as she entered, looking utterly masculine. His black hair, gleaming in the candlelight, reminded her of shiny black satin. Why hadn't she noticed before how thickly muscled his thighs were? Coming forward, he took her hand, pressing it to his lips. She felt a shudder of awareness dart through her at his action.

"Good evening, Alexandra." His eyes took in her costume. The quirk of his eyebrow told her that he found the contradiction quite amusing.

Alexandra fumed silently at his smugness, choosing to ignore it. Dropping into a curtsy, she replied, "My lord."

Her mother watched the whole exchange in nervous anticipation. Alexandra could almost feel the sigh of relief she emitted. Turning to face her, she smiled. "You look lovely tonight, Mother." Catherine was wearing a gown of rose-colored silk which complimented, rather than detracted from, the red hue of her hair.

A warm blush the exact shade of her gown rose to Catherine's cheeks. "Why . . . why, thank you, dear. How kind of you to notice."

"I can certainly understand where Alexandra gets her beauty, Missus Courtland," Nicholas interjected, smiling at the older woman.

"Thank you, my lord," Catherine replied.

"Please . . . call me Nicholas."

"And you must call me Catherine. We are, after all, going to be family soon."

Alexandra thought she was going to be sick. Why her mother felt she had to welcome the enemy into their camp was beyond her understanding. Her thoughts must have been reflected on her face, for when she glanced over at her father, his eyes were twinkling merrily. Why did she get the feeling he knew more than he let on?

Samuel watched the entire exchange with amusement from his position by the mantel. "What could the governor have been thinking by dissolving the burgesses, Nicholas?" he asked. "I think it was a foolish move on his part."

Eyeing Nicholas from her position on the settee, Alexandra noted the tautness about his mouth, a telltale sign of his annoyance at her father's question. She smiled inwardly.

"I believe the governor has the best interests of the colony at heart, Samuel. He doesn't want a repeat of the trouble in Boston to surface here in Virginia," Nicholas replied, taking a seat next to Alexandra on the settee.

"I think it is the best interest of the King, not Virginia, that Lord Dunmore takes to heart," Alexandra stated, staring into the deep black pools so dangerously close. Her gaze dropped down to Nicholas's lips. She blushed, remembering where they had so recently traveled; her nipples tightened at the memory.

Nicholas smiled knowingly. Picking up her hand, he brushed his lips over her palm. "I do not expect you to understand the intricacies of government, my sweet. Do not bother your pretty head about such matters."

Alexandra straightened, pulling her hand out of his grasp. How dare he treat her like some empty-headed chit! She was about to tell him what she thought of his condescending remark when her mother stood up.

"Supper is served," Catherine blurted, hoping to avert the argument Alexandra's expression told her was imminent. "I do hope you like fried chicken, Nicholas. Chloe, our cook, prides herself on that Virginia specialty."

"Indeed, madam. I am acquiring a taste for many Virginia delicacies." He looked over at Alexandra and smiled, pleased by the blush that covered her cheeks.

Rising to stand, Alexandra waited until her mother and father were out of earshot. "Why doesn't it surprise me that an Englishman would be particularly fond of chicken? After all, it would appear that you both have much in common." She stalked from the room, Nicholas's hearty chuckle following in her wake.

Mercifully, dinner was completed with a modicum of disquietude. Benjamin and Alicia, who were already seated at the table when Nicholas and Alexandra entered, were able to sustain most of the conversation. Alexandra was able to sit back and observe, listening quietly to the exchanges going on around her.

She was grateful for the opportunity to regain her composure and calm herself. She had almost lost her head at Nicholas's prejudiced comments earlier; she vowed not to let that happen again.

Engrossed in her private battle, she did not notice that Nicholas had risen from his chair and was now standing behind hers. When she felt his warm hands on the bare flesh of her arms, gooseflesh broke out instantaneously.

"It is a lovely evening, Alexandra. I thought, perhaps, you might walk with me awhile." The soft velvet of his voice poured over her like Chloe's thick, warm gravy. The challenge in his eyes was unmistakable.

Flashing him a brilliant smile, she excused herself, noting the surprised looks on her parents' faces and the amused look on Ben's. "I would be delighted," she replied.

Nicholas was faintly puzzled by Alexandra's quixotic behavior. One minute she was throwing insults at him, and the next, dazzling him with the radiance of her smile. She definitely presented a challenge, and he was a man who thrived on challenges.

The light of the street lanterns cast a warm glow over the couple, who walked in silence side by side. The grating cry of the crickets' strange mating sounds and the whirring of the locusts in the tree branches overhead were their only company.

Breathing deeply of the jasmine-scented air, Alexandra tried not to notice how Nicholas's hand about her waist made her skin warm, her pulse race. She concentrated on her anger, trying to remember how humiliated he had made her feel such a short time ago; but try as she might, those images receded, while the others, his mouth, his lips, his hands, loomed forth to torment her.

"Are you warm?" Nicholas asked, looking down on Alexandra's flushed face, visible in the light of the street lantern. "Is something wrong?"

Taking another gulp of fresh air, Alexandra smiled. "No," she choked. "Why do you ask?"

"Your skin is warm," he said, placing his fingers on her cheek, running them over her lips. He looked into her eyes; his breath was soft upon her face. "I thought perhaps you had a fever." Gently he placed his lips on her forehead, then added, "Fevers are a dangerous thing. They burn hot, making your blood boil and your skin sizzle."

Pulling out of Nicholas's embrace, Alexandra felt steamy with desire, ill with her need for him. God! How could he always make her feel this way? She hugged herself, trying to control the unfamiliar yearning that filled her body. "I'm fine. Let us continue our walk."

Nicholas nodded, smiling inwardly. Alexandra was weakening. He would tame the stubborn, willful minx. It was his objective—the goal he had set for himself. Once he had her in his bed, she would submit. He would demand total surrender of her mind, her spirit, her heart. He would conquer her as thoroughly as any Englishman vanquishes his adversary. He would show no mercy when she writhed beneath him, begging for release. She would learn who the master was. She would learn as valuable a lesson as these American colonies.

# Chapter Eight

The residents of Williamsburg gathered en masse this first day of June, marching down Duke of Gloucester Street to Bruton Parish Church. The handsome salmon-colored brick building stood as a reminder to the people of the community of the important part religion played in their daily lives. All classes, from slave to planter, assembled each Sunday to receive the sacraments of the Anglican Church.

The service this Sunday was to be different from the others that had been held inside the church. It had been decided, by those who had met at the Raleigh Tavern earlier in the week, that no objections could be raised by the governor to an outpouring of prayer for peace and guidance.

The brightness of the day was in direct contrast to the dark feelings many of the colonists held as they joined together in protest to show their support for their sister colony of Massachusetts.

Alexandra sat in the Courtland pew, her body wedged between the broad shoulders of her brother and those of her betrothed. She had been mortified when Nicholas had shown up at the house shortly after breakfast to escort her and her family to church. She was forced to suffer the disdainful looks and snide remarks of her fellow parishioners as she marched into the church with a member of the hated British aristocracy on her arm.

Looking about the church, Alexandra spotted many familiar faces. Mister Henry and Mister Jefferson were in their respective pews to her right. She saw Henry nod in her direction and was just about to return his greeting when she realized he was acknowledging Nicholas, not her. Her face flamed. How humiliating to be thought of as a Tory sympathizer by someone as important as Patrick Henry!

The governor occupied the large, square pew toward the front of the church. Seated in the red brocade canopied chair provided for his use, he was unable to hide a look of marked indignation as he observed the large assembly that had gathered to protest the King's actions. Maybe now the pompous old coot will realize we mean business, Alexandra thought.

Glancing off to her left, Alexandra looked straight into the penetrating glare of Tom Farley. She offered a small smile, only to have it thrown back in her face when he looked the other way, cutting her dead. She could feel the heat rise to her cheeks and looked down into her lap. She couldn't remember what had ever attracted her to that rude boy in the first place. Her hands shook in anger; she pressed them into her knees, trying to contain her ire at Tom's rebuff.

A warm hand reached out to cover hers. She looked up to find Nicholas's searching gaze upon hers. He squeezed her hand and smiled. The anger she felt melted as quickly as butter on a warm biscuit. She smiled back, realizing, not for the first time, how right his presence felt pressed up against her.

"You could be struck down by having such lascivious thoughts while seated in God's house," Nicholas whispered, his eyes twinkling mischievously.

"Nicholas!" she scolded, louder than she had intended. A number of heads turned her way, causing a slow burn to creep up her neck and land squarely on her cheeks.

At the horrified look her mother directed at her, Alexandra bowed her head, praying for deliverance from the infuriating man at her side.

After the service, the assemblage moved into the churchyard, huddling about in small groups to discuss the recent sermon by the Reverend Price.

Standing beneath the shade of an ancient oak, Alexandra waited for Nicholas, who had paused to discuss the sermon with Lord Dunmore and his entourage. The afternoon was warm, and she was grateful for the protection her straw bonnet afforded. It was tied under her chin by a green velvet ribbon which matched the green chintz dress she wore.

Running her gloved hand over the roughened bark of the tree trunk, she picked off the decaying pieces and tossed them carelessly to the ground while observing her friends, Martha Reynolds and Sally Manning, who stood on the other side of the yard. They appeared to be avoiding her. Usually, the three of them met each Sunday after church to talk of the latest fashions and town gossip. But that was before her alliance to the Duke of Blackstone had been made public. Now, it seemed, she was as much an outcast as Nicholas. She had no desire to align herself with those friends of his who favored the Crown's position. She would rather remain alone than compromise her beliefs any more than she already had.

"What's the matter, Alexandra? Have you suddenly become a pariah within your own community?"

Turning about, she faced the hostile gaze of Tom Farley. The anger she had thought dissolved suddenly resurfaced. Her eyes flashed as blue as the azure sky overhead. "If you fear contamination, don't feel you need to associate with me. I much prefer my company to yours."

"It is too bad your mind is not as sharp as your tongue. Have your senses been dulled by the drugging kisses of

107

your duke?'' He spat the words contemptuously, seeking to wound as he had been wounded.

"That is no concern of yours. Now, if you will excuse me, I shall rejoin my betrothed." Alexandra gathered her skirts, intending to leave, but Tom's hand upon her wrist stayed her departure.

"I saw you the night of the ball. First you arrive looking like the town harlot, then you disappear with your duke only to reappear an hour later looking like a woman who has just come from the bed of her lover. Tell me, Alex, does your duke satisfy your carnal needs? Does he make you cry out in ecstasy when he plunges into your whore's womb?"

"Release Alexandra at once." Nicholas's words were cold and rapier sharp.

Looking up, Tom found Nicholas Fortune's black eyes tearing into him; that gaze was as lethal as a sharpened sword. He dropped Alexandra's wrist.

"Leave us, Alexandra," Nicholas ordered.

Through a veil of tears, Alexandra gazed at Nicholas's menacing visage. Relief flooded through her that he had come. She was unable to control the violent spasms that shook her body when she thought of the horrible things Tom had said to her. They hurt deeply. She had known Tom all her life, yet right now, he was a stranger to her.

At the deadly look on Nicholas's face, fear overshadowed her anguish. Grabbing onto Nicholas's arm, she pleaded, "Let it go, Nicholas. He did not hurt me."

"No one speaks to a lady as this ill-mannered ruffian did and lives to talk about it," Nicholas said, pushing Alexandra aside. He stood scant inches from Tom's face. "You have impugned the honor of my betrothed. I, therefore, challenge you to a duel."

"No!" Alexandra screamed.

Ignoring her outburst, Nicholas continued, "I shall have my second call upon yours this evening to discuss the details. Shall we say, dawn tomorrow?"

"Please, Nicholas," Alexandra begged, looking frantically between his implacable features and those of Tom's fierce countenance.

Tom nodded. "Very well. I shall meet you on the field of honor, but you should know before you waste your life, Alex isn't worth it. I should know. I've sampled her charms myself."

The sound of Alexandra's strangled cry mingled with the crack of Nicholas's fist on Tom's jaw. "You bastard . . . you bloody colonial bastard," Nicholas shouted, oblivious to the stares of the curious onlookers who had gathered to observe the altercation.

Nicholas continued to pummel Tom's face, his anger supplying the additional strength that was no match for the burly cooper.

"Please," Alexandra screamed, "someone stop them!"

A moment later, her brother burst forth from the crowd, pulling Nicholas off of Tom. She blanched at the sight of Tom's bloody face, but it was Nicholas's wounds that commanded her attention. His lip was bleeding, and his knuckles were bloodied and swollen.

Benjamin dispersed the crowd, then turned to face Nicholas and Alexandra. "Take Nicholas home, Alex. I will see to Tom." He looked down at the semiconscious man on the ground and shook his head. "I don't know what this is all about, but I have a pretty good idea. I shall be home shortly to get some answers from both of you."

Alexandra normally would have laughed at Ben's officious manner. It seemed ludicrous that someone of Ben's years would be ordering a man like Nicholas around.

She looked up at Nicholas; his mouth was bleeding freely. Taking her handkerchief from beneath her sleeve, she dabbed at the cut on his lip. He winced but said nothing. "Let's go home, Nicholas," she said, grabbing him about the waist.

Nicholas gave her a crooked grin, moaning at the

pain it caused. "Are all you Courtlands so bossy?" he inquired.

"Only when faced with stubborn fools."

"Ouch! Your words cut deeply, madam."

"No deeper than you deserve. I can't imagine what you must have been thinking to launch yourself at Tom that way."

"You're defending him?" His tone was clearly indignant.

"No. I'm not defending him, and I do appreciate your protecting my honor. But Tom's words, although bitter and false, were bred of jealousy, not hatred. We were to be married before you came."

Trying to mask the surprise her words produced, Nicholas asked, "Do you love him?"

Pushing open the white picket gate in front of her house, Alexandra paused, choosing her words carefully. "I thought I did, but I have since realized that I cared for Tom more like a brother." She did not see the look of relief that crossed over Nicholas's face. "Come into the kitchen. Chloe is still at church, but I think I can find something to put on your lip."

Nicholas followed her down the oyster-shell path to the small brick building at the rear of the house. The smell of freshly baked bread rose up to greet him as he entered.

"Have a seat at the table. I shall fetch a basin of water."

Glancing about the kitchen, Nicholas noted several banked fires in the hearth, burning in preparation of the afternoon meal. Large black pots of cast iron hung from the lug pole that extended across the chimney several feet above the hearth. There were several colorful earthenware crocks lining the shelves of the cupboards, and various utensils of copper and pewter hung from pegs on the whitewashed walls.

A moment later, Alexandra returned, carrying a basin of water and a clean white towel. Setting the items on the scarred trestle table, she walked behind Nicholas, placing her hands on his shoulders. "Let me help you off with your coat, though from the looks of it, we will have to get Betsy to sew it up for you," she said, tugging on the broadcloth material. She loosened his cravat, removed it, and placed the items on a nearby chair. Leaning over him, she dipped the towel in the warm water and proceeded to cleanse his face. His nearness was unsettling. She tried to keep her hand steady and her mind on the matter at hand.

Nicholas observed the tender ministrations with admiration. Alexandra didn't flinch at the sight of blood; she performed her task with quick efficiency. The rose scent of her perfume wafted down to tease his nose each time she bent close to touch his face; his heart pounded at her nearness.

He hadn't realized how fond he had become of the little minx until that blond ox had chosen to attack her with his insults. Feelings of protectiveness swept through him when he thought of how shattered she had been by Farley's unkind words.

The sight of her tears had moved him more than he cared to admit. He'd best be careful. A woman's tears could drown a man—reduce him to nothing. He usually felt disdain when confronted with the obvious ploy of crying that most women used to achieve their wants, but Alexandra's tears were different. Hers sparkled like raindrops, clear and pure—a reflection into her soul.

"There, that should do it," she said, standing back to observe her handiwork. Now that the blood was gone, there was only a slight cut on his lower lip and a darkening bruise on his jaw. Reaching out, she tenderly ran her fingers over the bruise, pulling back quickly when Nicholas winced in pain. "I'm sorry. I wish there was something I could do to make this up to you."

Pulling her onto his lap, Nicholas smiled. "I know of one way you could." He kissed the warm flesh above the neckline of her gown.

111

Alexandra squirmed, feeling the hardened bulge beneath her skirts. Her face warmed; her heart raced. "I must go into the house now, Nicholas. Chloe will be home any moment."

Ignoring her protests, he kissed her neck, her ears, and finally her mouth. She sampled the salty taste of blood as her lips came in contact with his. Her arms came about his neck as his tongue entered to explore the recesses of her mouth. They kissed for several minutes until the gong of the clock on the shelf reminded Alexandra of the lateness of the hour. Lifting her head, she smiled. "I am so relieved you have decided to forget about that stupid duel tomorrow."

Nicholas's eyebrow shot up. "Forget? I haven't forgotten. The duel will take place as planned."

Jumping up, she stared down at him. "You can't mean to fight Tom. He's just a boy compared to you. You'll kill him."

Nicholas couldn't control the smirk that crossed his face. A boy! My God! The *boy* was as tall as he, with arms the size of tree trunks. He eyed Alexandra suspiciously. Perhaps she lied. Maybe she did care about the cooper. Maybe . . . just maybe . . . Farley had been telling the truth when he cast aspersions upon Alexandra's character. He clenched his fists, trying to control the sudden spark of jealousy that threatened to ignite. He would kill the bloody bastard for certain.

"As much as I would like to accommodate you, my sweet, I'm afraid honor demands satisfaction. I must meet Mister Farley."

"But you needn't kill him. Couldn't you just scare him?" Her eyes widened in fear and uncertainty. She couldn't let them fight over her. As flattering and romantic as that notion might be, a man's life was at stake. She would never forgive herself if anything happened to either of them.

"Perhaps he will kill me, Alexandra. You haven't

thought about that possibility. If I am killed, you will be free of our arranged marriage—free of me."

Caressing his cheek, Alexandra replied barely above a whisper. "I do not want my freedom at the cost of your life."

Staring into the guileless blue pools, wet with unshed tears, Nicholas felt a peculiar tug in the region of his heart. "And if I spare your friend, what will you give me in return?"

Brightened by his words, Alexandra smiled. "Anything. Anything you ask."

Grabbing her wrist, Nicholas pulled her into his chest. "Anything, Alexandra? Are you sure? There is much I would ask of you."

The black eyes smoldered like the banked fires in the hearth. Alexandra knew she would sacrifice herself to save Tom. What Nicholas would ask of her was a small price to pay for the life of her childhood friend. What difference would it make if she submitted to Nicholas before they were married? They were engaged and would be married within the year. Many couples in similar circumstances consummated their vows before the ceremony.

The warmth she suddenly felt had nothing to do with the temperature outside. If she were honest with herself, she would have to admit that the thought of bedding Nicholas was as intoxicating as peach brandy.

Standing on tiptoe, she reached up, draping her arms about his neck. "I will yield to anything you desire," she whispered, pressing her lithe body into his.

His arms encircling her, Nicholas pulled her in to feel the hardness of his passion. "You are mine. Never forget it. When I ask, you will give. When I take, I will take all. You will be possessed, consumed, absorbed into my being. We will be one. You will be enslaved by your own passion, and I will be your master."

# Chapter Nine

It was the hour before dawn. The sky was as black as printer's ink. Alexandra looked out the window, judging the distance from her second-story bedroom to the ground.

Her father had expressly forbidden her to attend the duel, but there was no one on earth who could prevent her from watching this morning's confrontation.

Dressed in a pair of Ben's old buckskin breeches and a too-large white linen shirt, Alexandra pushed on the sash until the wooden window moved steadily upward. The cool morning air sent a chill down her arms as it combined with her own nervous tension.

She hadn't had occasion to use the sturdy old holly tree that stood near her bedroom window in years. She smiled thoughtfully as she stepped out onto the thick branch nearest the window, remembering back to the night she had decided to accompany Ben and Tom to the creek to fish for eels.

Of course, the boys hadn't known she was following them that night. If they had, Ben would never have let her come along, especially when she found out what they were really up to.

The night had been unbearably hot; she hadn't been able to sleep. At the sound of voices below her window, Alexandra had looked out to find Ben and Tom, fishing poles in hand, sneaking away from the house. She couldn't resist the temptation to tag along, and so had climbed down the holly tree and followed.

She had gotten much more than she had bargained for that night when she came upon them down by the creek. Her twelve-year-old eyes had widened in astonishment at the sight of her brother and Tom rolling on the ground with the two MacKenzie twins, Adriane and Adelaid. The two buxom sisters were dressed in only their chemises. She had hidden behind the trunk of a huge oak tree, watching as the four participants engaged in all sorts of forbidden delights. Her education had increased a hundredfold that night.

She still giggled to herself each time she spotted the two pious spinsters attending church services on Sunday. She had never revealed to Ben or Tom that she knew just how big a catch they had made that night.

Dropping down to the ground, Alexandra waited, glancing around to make sure no one was about. The piercing cry of a whippoorwill made her start, until she realized he was her only companion this morning.

The duel was to be fought in the open field adjacent to the creek that ran by the cabinetmaker's shop. She would have to hurry if she was going to reach her destination in time. The sun was just beginning to lighten the sky, peeking over the horizon to turn the black morning into a grayish hue.

The city was awake. The glow of candles could be seen in upstairs bedroom windows. The cock-a-doodle-doo of the roosters' crow, announcing the beginning of another day, could be heard in backyard henhouses up and down the main street. Alexandra walked quickly, hoping to be in time for the match.

Nearing the field, she spotted several horses and carriages. Careful to remain hidden behind the trees, she crept steadily forward until she glimpsed Nicholas talking with his valet. She dropped down behind a thick bush of honeysuckle. The sweet, fragrant flowers made her nose itch; her eyes began to water. Damn! Just her luck to pick a honeysuckle bush to hide behind. She had an aversion to them. Pinching her nose, she took a deep breath to keep from sneezing.

Looking toward the opposite end of the clearing, Alexandra spotted Tom with her brother Ben. Ben had agreed to act as Tom's second despite the pleas she had made last night. Covering her mouth to stifle the sneeze that threatened to give her position away, she watched as Nicholas and Tom faced each other on the field of honor.

She held her breath as the two opponents turned their backs to each other; her heart began to thud in her chest. Their pistols looked ominous as they held them high against the gray light of morning. Remembering Nicholas's promise that he would spare Tom's life, she breathed a little easier.

The counting began. On the count of ten the two men would turn and fire. Her heart pounded with every step they took as they marched off their paces. Eight . . . nine . . . ten. They turned. Nicholas's arm went up; he purposely aimed high, missing Tom by shooting over his head. But Tom, seeing his chance for revenge, took careful aim and fired.

Alexandra watched in horror as Nicholas fell to the ground, grabbing his left arm. She burst from the bushes, running forward. "Nicholas," she screamed, dropping down by the injured man's side. She noted how pale his face had become; his arm was bleeding profusely. Ripping the bottom of her shirt, she made a pad to staunch the flow.

"It seems our friend was not as noble as I," Nicholas whispered, his voice laced with pain.

"I'm so sorry. I never thought he would shoot you. Please forgive me," she said, bending over his prostrate form, her tears falling unchecked upon his face.

"My sweet, your tears will surely drown me if this bullet wound does not kill me first," Nicholas said, smiling wanly at her terrified expression. "It is only a nick. Habersham will have me fixed up in no time."

"Right you are, sir," Habersham replied, coming forward with a small leather satchel. He efficiently cleansed and bound the wound, announcing after a few minutes that Nicholas was fit for travel. He helped him to his feet.

"Thank you, old friend. Please get the carriage and bring it 'round. I will wait here for you," Nicholas said.

After Habersham departed, Nicholas turned his attention back to his errant betrothed. "You should not have come here, Alexandra. It is not proper for a woman to attend a man's shooting match."

Bristling with indignation at his ungratefulness, Alexandra crossed her arms firmly over her chest. "How can you think of proprieties at a time like this? You're bleeding, for heaven's sake!"

Cupping her chin with his good hand, Nicholas smiled as if talking to a child. "Your concern is most touching, but that does not excuse your dress or your behavior." His eyes lingered insultingly over her attire. "You must learn to curb these impulsive instincts of yours, Alexandra. A duchess does not behave in this manner."

Alexandra's face reddened. Placing her hands on her hips, she flipped her head back defiantly, the mass of black curls coming loose from beneath the old tricorn hat that she wore. "Your blood may be blue, your grace, but when you bleed, it flows red, just like a commoner's. If you are done upbraiding me, I believe I will go home and change before my parents realize I am gone." She turned to leave, but Nicholas latched onto her arm.

"How did you manage to leave your house unnoticed?"

Swallowing hard, she lifted her chin, boldly meeting his eyes. "I climbed out the window."

"Bloody Christ! You could have been killed. Have you no sense?" The pressure on her arm increased.

"I am not some porcelain doll, Nicholas. I don't break that easily . . . although if you don't release my arm soon, you could prove me wrong."

He stared down at his hand. Suddenly comprehending her words, he pulled it away. At that moment, the carriage arrived and Habersham alighted. "My lord, your carriage awaits."

"Get in," Nicholas ordered, motioning to Alexandra.

Alexandra stood firm. "I have to find Ben. I intend to confront Tom about this cowardly act." She looked back to where her brother and Tom had stood a short time ago, but there was only an empty field of grass.

"As you can see, there is no one left but us. I shall escort you home."

"But your arm."

"Is fine. Now get in. I feel the need to sit down."

Doing as instructed, Alexandra scrambled into the coach, Nicholas following right behind. She took the seat across from him, observing the beads of perspiration dotting his forehead and upper lip. He held onto his injured arm, wincing in pain as the carriage lurched forward.

"Are you all right?" she asked, alarmed by his sudden pallor. "Oh, Nicholas, I never meant for you to be hurt. You must believe that." She moved to take the seat next to his. Removing the handkerchief from his pocket, she gently wiped the sweat from his brow.

"It isn't your fault that your friend Tom is without honor. If I had known he was going to shoot me after I purposely avoided hitting him, I would have aimed to kill." Nicholas's voice was cold, his face filled with contempt.

"Well, I'm relieved that both of you are still alive."

He smiled suggestively. "I hope you will still feel that way when I come to collect my due."

119

Blushing at the implication of his words, Alexandra felt her hand tending his brow suddenly freeze. "I . . . I will not renege. I still have my honor, even if others do not."

As the carriage pulled to a halt in front of Alexandra's house, Nicholas leaned over, placing a kiss as tender as the gentle flutter of angel's wings against her lips. "I am happy to hear it, my sweet," he replied. "I shall return later today to plant my proposition and reap the rewards of our fertile agreement."


Nicholas stared pensively at the document in his hand. It was a copy of the Quartering Act, which was to go into effect today. "Damn," he shouted, banging his fist on the walnut secretary. The brass candlestick toppled over, falling unnoticed to the pine floor.

No wonder the governor had requested an audience with him as soon as possible. Bloody hell, but John was blind about these colonials, he thought, crumpling the parchment and throwing it to the floor. Was the Crown purposely trying to antagonize the situation here in the colonies? It didn't take a political analyst to figure out, after yesterday's show of unity at the church, that these Virginians were joining together in a common cause. He wasn't completely sure of what they hoped to gain, but he knew they had enough determination to succeed in whatever it was they were doing.

They were an independent, unpredictable sort of people. Rubbing his left arm, he thought of Tom Farley's dishonorable behavior. By God! An Englishman would never have thought to pull such a cowardly act.

Standing, he walked to the window. The late afternoon sun shone a brilliant orange ball against the blue expanse of sky—blue as Alexandra's eyes. Alexandra. What was he going to do with her? She was so young, so full of life. Would she ever conform to her role as the Duchess of Blackstone? He smiled, thinking of how outraged Bellows or Habersham would be if they caught her climbing out one of the upstairs bedroom windows at the manor.

A loud rap on the door brought Nicholas out of his reverie. He spun around as the door opened to see Habersham's worried face peering into the room. "Sorry to disturb you, my lord, but Lord Dunmore is most insistent about seeing you," the valet stated.

Nicholas sighed, smoothing back the sides of his hair. "Tell his lordship I shall attend him at once."

Nicholas made his way down the darkened hallway to the suite of rooms the governor occupied. He was ushered into the middle room, so called because it stood between two bedchambers.

The room was impressive, as it was meant to be. Tooled leather from Spain covered the walls. The two double-hung windows which faced the Palace Green were draped in red brocade.

Standing in front of one of a pair of gilt-framed rectangular mirrors that flanked the windows, Nicholas checked his appearance one last time, adjusting his white silk stock.

The door to his immediate right opened; John Murray entered the room from his bedchamber. He smiled as his gaze fell upon Nicholas. "Thank you for being so prompt, Nicholas. I have need to talk to you," he said, indicating one of the red-and-white gingham-covered chairs.

"I presume this has something to do with the Quartering Act," Nicholas replied, seating himself next to the governor.

Assuming a grave expression, the governor nodded. "These upstarts leave us little choice. They must be taught who is in control here. The presence of our soldiers in their homes will soon remind them of England's dominance."

"With all due respect, Governor, I can't help but think that the Crown is making a grave error by instituting this measure. Yesterday's show of Virginia's unity for their sister colony of Massachusetts was a clear example that they do not intend to back down. I don't believe they will meekly step aside while we place our soldiers inside their homes."

Lord Dunmore snickered. "I hope that little radical you've gone and hitched yourself to has not let her political views rub off on you."

Nicholas felt the heat of anger rise up his neck. His left arm twinged; he rubbed at it absently. "Alexandra Courtland has nothing to do with my views . . . and I am very much insulted that you would imply otherwise."

The governor stood, leaning his arm against the mantel of the white marble corner fireplace. "I meant no disrespect. But a woman can have a great deal of influence on a man." Nicholas opened his mouth to protest, but the governor raised his hand to forestall his argument. "The Courtlands have been very outspoken against the Crown. Your intended's blatant act of defiance at the ball leaves me no choice but to set them up as an example."

A feeling of dread surged through Nicholas's veins. He knew it would only be a matter of time before the governor exacted his revenge against Alexandra. Nicholas stood, facing Lord Dunmore. "I take full responsibility for my betrothed's actions. Let me handle her."

"I intend to quarter troops in her home. I have a feeling more goes on there than we are aware of."

"I have dined with the Courtlands. They are a fine class of people. Not ill-bred or coarse like so many of these Virginians."

"True. But that does not exempt them from experiencing the King's justice. There will be soldiers quartered there."

"What if I were to move into the house myself? Would that satisfy the Crown?"

Lord Dunmore crossed to the mahogany card table,

extracting a pinch of snuff from the small brass container which rested on top. Wiping his nose with a fine lace handkerchief, he waved it in the air before stuffing it back inside his coat sleeve.

Nicholas watched the entire display with distaste. If this arrogant pomposity was what the governor of the colony exhibited to his subjects, small wonder they were disgusted with the present state of affairs. Lord Dunmore was a dangerous man to have in a position of authority, Nicholas concluded. Lord North had not yet responded to his last dispatch concerning the political climate here. Perhaps it was time for a stronger statement about the governor's abilities in keeping the peace. Nicholas looked up as Lord Dunmore finally spoke.

"That is a brilliant idea, Nicholas. I would like you to move in today. I will send word to Samuel Courtland immediately."

"I would prefer to tell him myself, your grace. Under the present circumstances, I'm sure you can understand."

"Quite . . . quite. I leave the details in your capable hands. I will expect a full report on any overt activities you may encounter. After all, your first allegiance is to the King."

Nicholas's eyes burned black as the coal in the scuttle. "That is the second time I have been reminded of my allegiance to the Crown," he said, his tone cold and curt. "I do not need to be told by you or anyone else where my loyalties lie. I am first and foremost an Englishman. I will not have my honor questioned or impugned."

"Calm down, Lord Blackstone. I meant no offense. Your loyalty is not in question here, but Mistress Courtland's is. You must realize my position in this matter."

Nicholas moved toward the door. His hand shook; the brass beneath it felt as cold as his heart at the moment. "Your position has never been more clear, Lord Dunmore. I bid you good day." With those words, Nicholas slammed out the door. Reaching his room, he threw open the door, shouting for his valet.

The tall, lanky man loped into the room, a look of alarm on his bony face. "Yes, my lord. I'm here."

"Get the trunks, Habersham. We are leaving this place."

Habersham's face brightened. He couldn't contain the note of hope in his voice when he asked, "Do we travel back to England, my lord?"

"No!" Nicholas shouted, pulling open the wardrobe doors and flinging an armload of clothes onto the bed. "We are to be quartered in the enemy camp."

His brow wrinkled in confusion. "I don't understand, sir. The enemy camp?"

Nicholas reached for the crystal decanter by the bed. Pouring himself a generous portion of brandy, he gulped it down. The fiery brew began to thaw the chill around his heart. The image of Alexandra's flashing blue eyes rose to his mind. He smiled at the stunned servant. "Wear your stoutest armor, my good man. Guard your manhood and your feelings. We enter the Courtland household this day."

A small hexagonal window emitted a bright shaft of light into the cramped, musty attic. As her mother lifted the lid on the battered old leather trunk that she and her sister were hunched over, Alexandra wrinkled her nose at the puffs of dust flying everywhere.

The trunk contained her mother's wedding gown, and it was obvious from the expression on Catherine's face that she cherished the memories it held.

The frown Alexandra wore was indicative of her feelings at the moment. She had no desire to plan her wedding to Nicholas Fortune. Her protests had fallen on deaf ears, however. Her mother had insisted on showing her the wedding dress, which she hoped Alexandra would want to wear.

The trunk creaked and moaned as Catherine pushed up on it, not wanting to allow entry into its musty interior.

"Can't we do this another time, Mother?" Alexandra questioned. "It's so hot up here, and the dust is going to suffocate us."

"Don't be such a grouch, Alex," Alicia chided, "just because you don't want to marry the duke."

Alexandra and her mother exchanged worried glances before Alexandra looked over at her sister and replied, "Oh, hush. You don't know what you're talking about. Of course I want to marry Nicholas. Why else would I be getting married?"

Alicia's smile was spiteful. "Tom told me it was arranged before you were born."

"Tom is a fool . . . and a coward, I might add. You'd be doing yourself a favor to stay away from him," Alexandra warned.

"He is not. You're just angry because he shot your stupid duke. Well, Nicholas deserved it. He should never have. . . ."

"That's enough, Alicia," Catherine snapped, slamming down the lid of the trunk. "Thomas Farley is too old for you. I forbid you to see him again."

Alicia jumped up, a defiant expression on her face. "Tom loves me. I know he does. Alex is just trying to start trouble because she's jealous."

Catherine pushed herself to her feet, taking hold of Alicia's arm. "You had best mind your manners and your tongue, young lady, or else I'll be forced to wash your mouth out with lye soap."

"I'm not a child, Mother. You can't wash my feelings for Tom away with soap."

Alexandra sighed, noting her mother's beseeching look. She stood up and faced her sister. "Alicia, I've told you before, Tom is using you to get back at me.

125

I am not jealous of you. What I felt for Tom is over. I want you to be happy, but Tom is filled with bitterness and hate right now. He tried to kill Nicholas after Nicholas purposely avoided shooting him.''

''You lie! Tom would never do that. He's honorable and good.''

Grabbing onto her sister's shoulders, Alexandra gently shook her. ''Tom behaved like a coward. Don't let your feelings cloud your judgment. See things as they really are, not as you would like them to be.''

Sobbing, Alicia covered her face. ''But I love him,'' she wailed.

Taking her sister into her arms, Alexandra spoke gently. ''Tom needs a friend right now, Alicia. If you care for him, be his friend. Don't pressure him. Give him time to lick his wounds and heal. In time, if you are patient, he may regard you as more than a friend.''

''Do you really think so?'' The youthful look of hopeful innocence shone on her face.

''Yes, I do,'' Alexandra replied, turning to face her mother, who was wringing her hands nervously. ''Isn't that right, Mother?''

''Well . . . I . . . I suppose Alex could be right, dear,'' Catherine admitted, smiling at her youngest child. ''Now, if we all don't want to roast to death up here, I suggest we leave this for now and go down to Margaret Hunter's millinery shop. I hear she has a new shipment of hats just arrived from England.''

''Mother, you know how I feel about buying imported goods,'' Alexandra said.

''I know, dear,'' Catherine replied, patting Alexandra's cheek, ''but it can't hurt to look, now can it?''

Nicholas arrived at the Courtland house a little after three. He had been ushered into the study and was awaiting the arrival of Samuel Courtland.

Sitting in the comfortable, well-worn leather chair, he sipped on the lemonade Betsy had thoughtfully provided. The tart liquid soothed his dry throat. It was bloody hot out. He would never get used to these awful Virginia summers, where your clothes stuck to every inch of your body and your thirst never seemed to get quenched. Damn, but he wished he could go back home to England. At least there the weather was civilized. A person needn't feel like a wrung-out sponge. Wiping his brow, he looked up at the sound of the door opening.

Samuel strode into the room, a welcoming smile on his face at the sight of his future son-in-law. "Nice to see you again, Nicholas," he said, proffering his hand to the immaculately dressed Englishman who had risen at his entrance. Despite the fact that Nicholas Fortune was an Englishman, and the son of his onetime rival, he found he liked the man. Nicholas was courteous, not at all effeminate, like so many of the priggish nobility, and he appeared to have enough strength to keep his headstrong daughter in line. Yes, Alexandra could do far worse than the duke.

"I'm afraid you've just missed Alex. She's gone to the milliner's with her mother and sister."

Nicholas's relief was almost audible. He was not looking forward to Alexandra's reaction when she heard why he had come. "Actually, it is you that I have come to see, Samuel."

Gesturing that Nicholas be seated, Samuel took a chair opposite him. "Tell me how I may help you."

"I'm afraid the news that I bear is not good."

Samuel's eyebrow arched up. Reaching over, he took the clay pipe from the pie-crust table. "Well, let's have it."

"There's been a new edict sent down by the King. Troops are to be quartered."

Jumping up, Samuel threw the pipe down on the table, causing the fragile clay to shatter into several pieces. "By God! King George goes too far. The local populace will never agree to this," he said, pacing the room.

"I'm afraid the governor means to place troops in your home."

Samuel stopped dead in his tracks. "Never! He will have to come and arrest me first!"

Nicholas stood, facing the older, irate gentleman. Samuel's face was red in anger; the vein at his temple throbbed violently. "I assumed that was how you would feel. That is why I have volunteered to take their place. I'm to be quartered here instead."

Before another word could be uttered, the study door burst open and Alexandra stormed into the room, holding a copy of the *Virginia Gazette*. So intent was she on giving her father the news, she did not see Nicholas standing near the window. "Father, have you seen the paper?" she shouted, coming forward to thrust it into his hands. "The governor has declared that troops are to be quartered in our homes. Those damned viperous Englishmen! How *dare* they presume to enter our homes? Why, if I were a man, I would shoot each and every one of them."

Samuel's face reddened. He turned to look at Nicholas, whose face had become a mask of stone. Alexandra, noting her father's discomfort, followed his gaze. Her mouth dropped open at the sight that greeted her eyes.

"Nicholas!" she cried. Oh, God. Would she never learn to curb her tongue? If Nicholas reported to the governor what she had said, they all could be hanged for treason.

"Good afternoon, Alexandra," Nicholas said, coming forward to take her hand, placing a kiss upon it.

Alexandra's hand burned where Nicholas's lips touched. She pulled it back, hiding it behind her skirt. In her agitated state, she had forgotten he had promised to come back to collect his due. She felt the heat rise to her cheeks. "I was not expecting you so soon."

128

"Apparently not. I do not see your loaded pistol anywhere."

Alexandra's cheeks burned crimson. "I was not referring to you. Please excuse my speech."

Looking over at Samuel, who wore what Nicholas would call a humorous expression, he turned back to face his betrothed. "I hate to contradict you, my sweet, but you were, in fact, referring to me." At her look of confusion, he added, "You see, Alexandra, I am to be quartered in your home."

# Chapter Ten

"You're what?" Alexandra screeched. Nicholas Fortune actually had the audacity to stand there looking poised and unperturbed and tell her that he was to be quartered in her house! She could not believe it.

Ignoring her outburst, Nicholas continued, "I was explaining to your father that the governor desires to place troops within your home."

"That pompous, arrogant . . ."

"You have only yourself to blame, Alexandra," Nicholas reminded her. "If you hadn't humiliated the man before a room full of people, I doubt you would have been singled out."

Her blue eyes flashed dangerously. "How *dare* you insinuate that this was my fault?" she said, turning to face her father, who was seated in the chair behind his desk. "Are you going to let this . . . this *Englishman* speak to me in this fashion?"

Placing the flat of his hands on the smooth surface of the desk, Samuel pushed himself out of the chair. "I'm afraid Nicholas may be right. He is your betrothed, Alex. He has the right to speak to you in any way he chooses."

Crossing her arms over her chest, Alexandra spun around, unwilling to let Nicholas or her father see how humiliated she was.

Samuel shook his head at his daughter's show of stubbornness. "If you will excuse me, Nicholas, I will take my leave. Betsy will show you to your room when you are ready."

Extending his hand, Nicholas replied, "My valet will be joining me. I hope that will not inconvenience anyone."

"Not at all," Samuel assured him, turning his attention back to his daughter. "Alexandra, I trust you will be a gracious hostess." The words held an implied warning.

The temperature in the room dropped ten degrees as Alexandra turned back to level an icy stare at her father. She said nothing until Samuel left the room, then spun about, unleashing her fury upon Nicholas. "You planned all of this, didn't you?"

A dark eyebrow rose at her question. "I'm flattered you think me capable of second-guessing the King. But even *I* am not that astute."

"It won't work, you know. Just because you have won my parents over, don't think you will do the same with me. I detest all Englishmen, and you are no different."

Nicholas smiled, closing the distance between them. "Aren't you forgetting that your mother is English? That your heritage is English?"

"Leave my mother out of this. If it wasn't for an Englishman—your father, to be exact—we wouldn't find ourselves in this horrible predicament."

"My father! It was your mother who tricked him into signing that ridiculous marital agreement. Why else would he betroth me to a commoner?"

Alexandra gasped. "My mother never tricked anyone. How dare you say such a thing? You know nothing of their relationship. Why, he . . ." She clamped her hand over her mouth, afraid she had said too much already. What could she have been thinking? she had almost betrayed her mother's confidence.

132

Grabbing her shoulders, Nicholas looked intently into her face. What did the little minx know that she wasn't telling? "Why he *what?*" he probed.

She thought quickly, a mischievous twinkle suddenly lighting her eyes. "Why . . . he probably sought to improve that blue blood of yours with a little color," she replied, relieved when she saw the corners of his mouth turn up. "If you will excuse me," she said, twisting out of his embrace, "I shall see you to your room. Habersham will have to be content with the room over the kitchen. It's the only one that is not occupied at the moment."

A devilish smile crossed Nicholas's face. "I'll be happy to share your bed, my sweet, if all the others are taken."

The words sent a delicious shudder of awareness down Alexandra's spine as visual images of their naked bodies pressed close together in her bed came to mind. Her face grew warm; she wiped her sweating palms on the pink cotton of her skirt. Taking a deep breath, she replied, "I believe we shall be able to provide you with a bed of your own, my lord."

"Pity. I was hoping we would be able to get much better acquainted while I am here." He laughed inwardly at her affronted expression. What fun it was to make her squirm. Living here might prove to be more beneficial than he had originally anticipated.

Eyes like blue lightning flashed in annoyance at the amused expression on Nicholas's face. "Your room will be at the opposite end of the hall from mine. I doubt we will see each other all that often. We probably won't even know that we are living in the same house."

"What a joke," Alexandra muttered, pulling back the covers on her bed. She punched down the soft feather pillow until she had fashioned a comfortable spot in which to lay her head. Climbing beneath the sheet, she wished, not for the first time, that she had never laid eyes on Nicholas Fortune. To think she had actually been foolish enough to believe that she and Nicholas would never see each other!

"Ha! Wishful thinking on my part," she said to herself, lowering her voice when she realized the object of her displeasure might be listening to her through the wall adjoining their rooms.

It was a cruel twist of fate that had placed Nicholas in the room next to hers nearly a week ago. The guest room at the far end of the hall had been stripped for painting, leaving the room next to hers as the obvious choice. The sewing room had been hastily rearranged to accommodate their unwelcome guest.

Try as she might to avoid him, she seemed to run into Nicholas everywhere she went. If she retreated to the study to read, he was there, lounging in her favorite chair with her favorite book. If she chanced to mention that she was going to Mister Dixon's printing office, Nicholas was beside her, offering his escort. It got so she was afraid to pull the chamberpot out from beneath her bed!

"Good night, Habersham." The deep-voiced farewell floated through the plaster wall. Alexandra sat up, her heartbeat quickening at the realization that Nicholas was on the other side of the wall, probably undressing at this very moment.

Unable to restrain herself, she jumped down from the high tester bed, tiptoeing over to the partition. Pressing her ear against the cold surface, she heard the sounds of water splashing. Nicholas was bathing. Closing her eyes, she imagined the water sloshing over his thickly muscled chest, droplets of water clinging to the softly matted hairs. Her nipples hardened in response to the image. Hugging herself, she willed the sudden tightness between her legs to stop.

"Oh, God," she whispered, pressing her head against the wall, "What is the matter with me?"

"Good night, my sweet," came the words loud and distinct. She jumped back, uncertain if she had been hearing things. The unmistakable ring of Nicholas's laughter mocked her. Scrambling onto the bed, she pulled the covers up over her head to block out the infuriating sound.

With the commencement of the humiliating episode of the night before, the battle lines had been drawn. For every icy stare and rude comment that Alexandra shot at Nicholas, a carefully orchestrated bombardment of her senses was made in retaliation.

Alexandra stared miserably at the bowl of strawberry shortcake set before her. It was her very favorite dessert, yet she couldn't enjoy it in the company of the overbearing Englishman. Dinner this afternoon had become an experience in torture. Forced to exhibit her best behavior in front of her parents, she had been unable to defend herself from the sensuous smiles and knowing looks Nicholas slyly directed at her.

Oooh! she fumed silently, smashing the berries and fresh cream together, if only this were Nicholas's head!

"Is everything all right with your dessert, Alex? You are usually able to devour several helpings of short-cake," her mother said, a teasing quality to her voice.

Turning as red as the berries in her dish, Alexandra sat bolt upright. "Really, Mother! I hardly think the amount of food I consume is anyone's business but mine."

Seeing the stricken look on her mother's face, Alexandra immediately felt contrite. What was the matter with her? Perhaps if she had been able to get to sleep last night, she wouldn't be so edgy today. Opening her mouth to apologize, she snapped it shut when Nicholas butted into the conversation.

"I don't think you should speak to your mother in

such a fashion, Alexandra. It shows a complete lack of respect."

Seething with mounting rage at Nicholas's unmitigated gall, Alexandra shot him a venomous look. "How dare you interfere in a family matter! Your presence and your opinion are unwelcome here."

Oblivious to the shocked gasps of Alexandra's family, Nicholas glared reproachfully at his intended. "May I remind you that I am here because of your shrewish behavior in front of the governor."

Her nostrils flaring, Alexandra stood. Picking up the bowl of strawberry shortcake, she dumped it unceremoniously on top of Nicholas's head. "That is what I think of my shrewish behavior," she said, storming out of the room.

Hurrying to reach the safety of her bedroom, she was unaware that Nicholas followed right behind until she heard her name upon his lips. "Alexandra!" The fierceness in his voice stopped her dead in her tracks. She turned, unable to keep the corners of her mouth from twitching at the sight of such a proper nobleman with cake and cream dripping over his head.

Nicholas's eyes narrowed. "You won't be laughing when I am done with you, madam." The vein in his neck throbbed ominously.

Taking her firmly by the arm, Nicholas hauled Alexandra up the stairs. When her kicking and clawing became too much for him to handle, he picked her up, throwing her over his shoulder.

"Put me down, Nicholas. How dare you treat me in such a fashion?" She plummeted his back with her fists.

Kicking open the door to his bedroom, Nicholas strode over to the bed, dumping Alexandra in the middle of it. "Now we shall see who has the last laugh."

The scene the other members of the Courtland household had just witnessed left them momentarily stunned. Recovering from the shock of what her daughter had just done to a member of the nobility, Catherine shook her head sadly. This was all her fault, she thought, staring at the open doorway. Alexandra was never going to reconcile herself to this marriage. Turning her worried expression on her husband, she asked, "Do you think we should go up and see if everything is all right?"

"No, I do not," Samuel replied. "Alexandra will have to learn to curb her impulsive outbursts. I, for one, am happy to turn the job of teaching her restraint over to someone else."

"But what if he strikes her?" Alicia asked, her eyes widening in fear.

Ben motioned to rise, outraged at the possibility.

"Sit down, Benjamin," his father ordered. "The time to play big brother has come to an end. Nicholas is in charge of Alex now."

"But, Samuel," Catherine interrupted, wringing her hands, "you don't really think the duke will harm Alex, do you?"

Rising from the table, Samuel stared at the trio of concerned expressions. Shaking his graying head, he replied, "I have learned it is wise never to try and second-guess the actions of another . . . especially when that other is a man who has been made to look like a fool. I'm afraid Alex has made her bed; now she must learn to lie in it."

Which was exactly what Alexandra was doing at the moment, only it wasn't her bed she was lying in but Nicholas's.

Looking up at the harsh features of her betrothed, Alexandra shrunk back into the mattress. She had never seen Nicholas so angry. She had gone too far this time; she had underestimated the enemy's strength. If Nicholas's look of anger was any indication, she was going to pay most dearly for her mistake.

Staring wide eyed, she gulped as Nicholas stripped off his coat and shirt throwing them onto the floor.

Stepping over to the washstand, he poured a small amount of water into the basin and proceeded to wash the sticky mess from his face. Bending down, he poured the remaining water from the pitcher over his hair to remove the crusted cake and cream.

As she stared in rapt fascination at the play of muscles across Nicholas's back, the thought of escape never entered Alexandra's mind. A nervous quiver started in the pit of her stomach; she hugged herself, trying to squelch the feeling.

Groping blindly for a towel, Nicholas spun around, causing droplets of water to fly every which way. Wiping the moisture off his face, he stared at Alexandra thoughtfully, pondering the punishment he was going to inflict upon her.

Nicholas almost laughed at the uncharacteristic look of fear that covered her face. The time had come to teach her another lesson. Marching to the bed, he grabbed her wrist, hauling her up against him. "I should pull up your gown and give you the spanking you deserve. You know that, don't you?" His voice was silken steel.

Alexandra said nothing. She wasn't going to give Nicholas the excuse to carry out his threat.

"What's the matter, my sweet? Are you finally at a loss for words?" He stared intently into the blue of her eyes, noting the alarm she tried so desperately to conceal. It would be so easy to throw her back on the bed and have his way with her. The thought had preoccupied his mind each night as he lay in his bed listening to her movements through the wall that separated their rooms.

He ran his fingers over the soft fullness of her lower lip. It quivered in response. God, how he wanted her. "What shall your punishment be, my sweet?" His arms encircled her, pulling her into the hardness of his manhood. Her eyes widened in alarm; he felt a mea-

138

sure of satisfaction. He would tame the minx one way or another.

"Shall I strip you naked, Alexandra? Remove your clothing, piece by piece, until you are nude and vulnerable before me?" As he spoke, he could feel her nipples harden against his chest. Rubbing his thumbs over the stiffened peaks, he watched her eyes deepen to blue velvet.

Alexandra could not fight back against the torture Nicholas's erotic words played upon her body. Desire flowed through every pore of her being. She ached for the promise of fulfillment his words portrayed.

"Do you know what I would do to you, my sweet, once I had you naked?" He ran his tongue up and down her neck, causing a fluttering in her stomach like a thousand butterfly wings beating uncontrollably.

"Nicholas," she breathed, "please, I can take no more of your taunts."

Ignoring her pleas, Nicholas ran his tongue into the recesses of her ears, licking and nibbling the sensitive orifices. "This is what I would do to all those hidden places that ache for my touch."

Mindless with wanting, Alexandra's hands played over the naked muscles of Nicholas's chest and back. The soft hairs beneath her fingers sent a jolt of desire down to the apex of her thighs. "Kiss me, Nicholas," she begged, waiting breathlessly, expectantly.

Black eyes locked with blue; the tension between them stretched out as taut as the string on a violin.

"I think not," came the curt reply.

Blinking in confusion, Alexandra was unable to believe what she had just heard. At the sight of Nicholas's satisfied smirk, her cheeks flooded with color. "You bastard!" she screeched, tearing out of his embrace. She walked to the window, hugging herself to quell the torment ready to explode inside of her.

"Your conduct has been most unbecoming, Alexandra. I do not wish to make love to a shrew. When you learn to outgrow your childish antics, then perhaps we can satisfy each other's needs.''

Spinning around, her face contorted in rage, she screamed, ''I have no need for you, Englishman.''

Nicholas laughed. ''You are ill with desire, my sweet. Your body cries out for fulfillment.''

''No!''

''You ache in the center of your being. You are wet with your need of me. Deny it.''

''No! No! No!'' she screamed, bolting for the door.

''Alexandra.''

With tears streaming down her face, she turned at the harshness of the command.

''You can run from me, but you can't run from yourself. We have an agreement. Have you forgotten?''

Wiping her eyes with the sleeve of her dress, she shook her head. ''I have not forgotten,'' she replied, barely above a whisper.

''It is time for me to collect my reward. I believe, you promised me anything I desired if I spared your friend's life.''

The moment she had dreaded and desired was upon her. She took a calming breath before answering. ''I did.''

''Are you prepared to meet your obligation?''

Her mind reeled in confusion; she was puzzled by Nicholas's abrupt change of mind. ''I don't understand. If you wanted my virginity, why didn't you take it earlier when you had the opportunity?''

Nicholas grinned. ''My dear, as much as I would love to partake of that sweet, little body of yours, that is not what I desire from you.''

Cheeks burning in humiliation, Alexandra felt a shudder of apprehension run through her. If Nicholas did not want her body, what did he want? What price had she foolishly agreed to pay?

"What I desire from you is complete obedience and utter capitulation in our relationship."

The words dropped about her like bombshells. Obedience. Capitulation. Her worst nightmare was coming true.

"Please come back and sit down so that I may tell you exactly what it is that I shall require of you."

Too stunned to object, Alexandra walked forward, seating herself on the occasional chair by the fire. Taking a deep breath, she looked up into Nicholas's face. The glow of victory was clearly written there. She swallowed her feeling of foreboding. "What is it you want?"

"Your sentiments against the Crown and our marriage are well known. It has been a cause for embarrassment, not only to me, but to your family as well. I refer to your mother, in particular."

"That's not fair. I was coerced into this engagement."

"Let me finish, if you please. Because of my position on the governor's staff, as well as my rank of nobility, it is imperative that I have a wife who will support me. One who will bring honor to the Fortune name. I have indulged you in our relationship, thus far. Now it is time for you to appease me."

Alexandra could feel her tears threatening to spill. She fought for control. She would not cringe like a battered puppy. She was, after all, made of sterner stuff than that.

"Am I to understand, you wish for me to keep my political opinions to myself? To look the other way at the inequities going on around me here in the colonies? I cannot do that. It goes against everything I believe in."

Standing before her, Nicholas looked down at her brave facade. He admired the fact that she held her convictions so dear, but he was determined to hold her to her word. "You told me that you possessed honor. Did you lie?"

"No, but . . ."

"But, nothing. You either honor your word or I will be compelled to challenge your Mister Farley to another duel. And this time, I will shoot him dead. It would give me the greatest measure of satisfaction, I assure you."

Alexandra couldn't control the look of horror that crossed her face. She was trapped. She had given her word and now she must compromise her principles to keep it. "I will do as you desire," she said, staring at the hands which rested in her lap, her voice filled with defeat and resignation.

Taking hold of her hand, Nicholas gently guided her to her feet. "From now on, for all public purposes, you will behave in a manner befitting your role as my duchess. There will be no more defiant acts of embarrassment nor any seditious speeches in front of my friends. You will conduct yourself with all humility, and you will defer to me in all things. Do I make myself clear?"

Her eyes were as cold as the depths of the Atlantic when she spoke. "If I must play a role to service your needs, then I shall. But never think when I bestow a sweet smile upon you that I mean it. Never think when you take me in your arms and I do not resist, it is because that is where I want to be. My feelings toward you and your country will never change. I shall despise you with every ounce of my being, and I will count the days until my country is free of the tyrannical hold of yours, and I am free of you."

# Chapter Eleven

"You look lovely, Miss Alex," Betsy declared, smoothing out the folds of the rose brocade gown. "Where you be going tonight? It seems you and the duke have been out to one function or another every night this week."

Alexandra frowned at the truth of Betsy's words as she checked her appearance in the looking glass, putting the finishing touches to her hair. Since that horrible afternoon over a week ago, she had been playing her role as the besotted, simple-minded sweetheart to perfection. Nicholas even had the audacity to compliment her on her performance by suggesting that she join a theatrical troupe. He was horribly infuriating, she thought, slamming down the silver filigree hairbrush.

Observing Betsy's questioning glance in the mirror, she smiled. "We are going to the Governor's Palace tonight, Betsy. It seems Lord Dunmore is having a reception to introduce his wife, who is newly arrived from England."

Betsy's eyes lit up at the news. "Oh, do pay attention to what she is wearing, Miss Alex. I'm sure her clothes will be the very latest fashion."

Nodding absently, Alexandra picked up her mantle and gloves from the bed. She sighed, wishing desperately that she could forgo this evening's fete. She didn't know if she could carry off her role in front of a room full of Tories, especially the governor.

Up until now, she had only to contend with two or three of Nicholas's acquaintances. They had dined at the Raleigh with Mister and Missus Winters, an ingratiating couple who fawned all over Nicholas; attended a lively dance at Wetherburn's, where Thaddeus Pembroke, another Tory friend, proceeded to spill wine punch over her brand new gown; and spent an entire evening at the theater with Mister and Missus Arnold, who were both deaf as dirt and talked so loudly throughout the entire performance, she still wasn't certain what play they had actually seen.

She had taken all of them in stride, proud that she had maintained her composure. But tonight would be different. Tonight, she would be a dove in a nest of vipers. She trembled at the thought.

Nicholas awaited her at the bottom of the stairs. He looked splendid in his black satin evening attire. Black like his heart, Alexandra thought uncharitably as she descended the steps to greet him.

"Good evening, Alexandra. I must say you look quite beautiful tonight."

Her smile was perfunctory. "Thank you, my lord," she replied, knowing quite well that the avoidance of his given name would ire him. She was not disappointed when she noticed the slight thinning of his lips.

"I trust you will be on your best behavior this evening. The governor would not take kindly to any insult that might be directed at his wife."

"You needn't worry, my lord. I know my role as your adoring duchess-to-be." She reached up to touch his cheek tenderly, noting how his eyes darkened. "Too bad you will never have the real woman," she taunted. "All you will ever have is a façade."

Placing the satin mantle over her shoulders, Nicholas leaned down and kissed the side of her neck. "Don't

144

be too sure, my sweet. I am a master at pursuit, and you are definitely worth pursuing."

As she stepped out into the warm, dark evening, Alexandra was uncertain if the chills that suddenly tingled her spine were caused by the night air or by Nicholas's intriguing words.

The guests were already assembled in the large ballroom when Nicholas and Alexandra arrived. Coming back to the site of her recent humiliation brought a tightening to her stomach. Nicholas's arm rested possessively around her waist; she was thankful for his presence and support.

There were only ten couples present, but there might as well have been a thousand, she felt so nervous. Fortunately, the governor hadn't arrived yet. At least she would not have to contend with him at the moment.

"There are the Wellingtons," Nicholas advised, pointing to a middle-aged couple across the room. "I knew them back in London. Shall we go over and greet them, my sweet? I know they are looking forward to meeting you."

"Why is that? Surely they have heard that the Duke of Blackstone's affianced is a treason-spouting seditionist."

"Your reputation precedes you," he answered smoothly.

"It would be a pity to disappoint them," Alexandra replied, smiling wickedly, her eyes sparkling with mischief. She almost laughed at the look of horror on Nicholas's face. She couldn't help teasing him; he was terribly stuffy at times.

The piercing black eyes held an unmistakable warning. "Do not think to embarrass me, Alexandra. I assure you, your punishment would be severe."

Smiling seductively, she licked her lips. "Do you mean to strip me naked and have your way with me? Oh, Nicholas, do not tempt me so. I fear I shall become terribly naughty."

145

Nicholas tightened his hold on Alexandra's waist. His smile was wildly erotic. "If I thought you would not object, I would take you upstairs at this very moment and make passionate love to you."

Hiding the turmoil that his words elicited, Alexandra tried to make light of his statement. "But I thought you said you didn't want to make love to a shrew."

Breathing his words into her ear, he replied, "I think perhaps it might be just the cure for your tumultuous emotions. They could be channeled into a much more productive means. I'm sure you have read Mister Shakespeare's work on the subject."

Alexandra's smile turned into a thin-lipped sneer. Choking on her anger, she was unable to voice her retort. How dare he compare her to Kate in *The Taming of the Shrew* she fumed silently, about to voice that very sentiment when she caught sight of the Wellingtons coming toward them. She took a deep breath.

"Lord Blackstone, how wonderful to see you again," Lady Wellington gushed. "This must be your charming betrothed we've heard so much about."

Alexandra pasted a simpering smile on her face as she looked up at the unusually tall woman before her. Lady Wellington had to be close to Nicholas's height, and he was well over six feet. She wasn't terribly attractive but had an arresting face. Alexandra guessed her to be about her mother's age, but her skin was much more wrinkled. She wore a beauty patch in the shape of a heart next to her mouth, and her hair was powdered in a style that only added more inches to her height.

Standing next to her was Lord Wellington. He was not nearly as tall as his wife, but what he lacked in height he made up for in heft. They were the most incongruous-looking couple she had ever laid eyes upon. She waited for Nicholas to complete the introductions.

"It is a pleasure to meet you, my dear. Nicholas is certainly a lucky man," Lady Wellington said.

"Indeed I am, Johanna. It is not every man that is as fortunate as I to have a bride-to-be as lovely as Alexandra." He looked down at her with adoring eyes.

"I say, Nicholas," Frederick Wellington interjected, "what do you know about this non-importation business that we have just been advised about? Do you think these malcontents are serious about refusing to buy goods from England?"

Nicholas could feel Alexandra's body stiffen at Lord Wellington's words. Why did Frederick always have the knack of talking about the wrong thing at the wrong time? "It is my opinion that the colonials believe that the means justify the end. So far, it is only the tea that has been affected. We will just have to wait and see which way the wind blows . . . to use the words of Mister Henry."

"Mister Henry! That loud-mouthed, rabble-rousing troublemaker. I'm surprised he hasn't been tried for treason," Frederick stated.

"Patrick Henry is a patriot, Lord Wellington. His views may be different from yours, but they are not treasonous. He is merely expressing concern for the future of the colonies," Alexandra said. The words were out of her mouth before she realized she had spoken them. Casting a sidelong glance at Nicholas, she braced herself for the angry glare she was expecting and was quite surprised to find him nodding in agreement.

"I think Alexandra is correct, Frederick. I have met Henry on several occasions, and though his method of voicing his opinions may be wrong, I think his words stem from concern, not treason," Nicholas said.

Alexandra was both shocked and gladdened by Nicholas's statement. Her heart swelled with gratitude. He had just defended one of the most blatant radical orators of Virginia to one of his own countrymen. The smile she bestowed on him was filled with warmth.

"My dear," Johanna said, "this talk of politics is boring me. Would you mind accompanying me upstairs? I need to freshen up."

Smiling sweetly, Alexandra replied, "Of course, Lady Wellington. Won't you excuse us, gentlemen?"

Alexandra had to lengthen her steps to keep up with Johanna Wellington's commanding stride. The woman walked as if she were heading a regiment of British Regulars instead of strolling leisurely through the palace. When they reached the upstairs bedroom that had been set aside for the ladies, Alexandra paused to catch her breath, taking a seat on the settee.

Observing Alexandra's flushed face, Johanna became alarmed. "I'm so sorry, my dear. I have a tendency to walk too quickly. I hope I haven't tired you."

"Not at all," Alexandra replied, taking a deep breath. "My maid cinched my stays too tightly. I'll be fine in a moment."

"Thank God, I do not have to suffer the torture of those things anymore. After I married and had children, I decided it wasn't worth putting myself through all that misery."

Noting Lady Wellington's rather thick waist, Alexandra smiled to herself. At least the woman wasn't pretentious, like some of Nicholas's other friends. "I believe you are quite sensible, Lady Wellington. I assure you, I only wear the blasted things when attending these types of functions. Normally I forgo them altogether."

"Please call me Johanna, my dear. Lady Wellington is so terribly formal, and things are much more relaxed here in the colonies than they are in England."

"What is it like being a duchess?" Alexandra asked, surprised at herself for wanting to know.

Turning from the mirror, her comb held in midair,

Johanna looked startled. "What an odd question. I don't think anyone has ever asked me that before."

"I'm to marry a duke; I have no idea what is expected of me," Alexandra replied, a miserable expression on her face.

Sitting down next to the young woman, Johanna smiled, patting her hand. "My dear, you will do just fine. Be yourself. That is the best advice I can give you. I have found that false fronts show through, while honesty is always appreciated."

Sighing, Alexandra shook her head. "Not in my case, I'm afraid. Nicholas prefers that I stifle my natural tendencies. He doesn't think they are becoming to a duchess."

"Poppycock! It would serve the fool right to be saddled with that empty-headed chit he was seeing back in London." At Alexandra's sharp intake of breath, Johanna continued, "I see by your expression you are unfamiliar with Nicholas's former mistress."

Alexandra felt like the wind had just been knocked out of her. Nicholas had a mistress. Why should she be surprised? Most men of quality did. But why did the idea of him holding another woman, kissing her, making love to her, make her feel like being sick?

"Nicholas was involved with a woman by the name of Sabrina . . ." She paused, tapping her finger against her chin. "Sabrina Montague, something like that. Anyway, rumor has it that he was quite enamored of her. She was a conniving thing, but very beautiful. I met her once. It was at Lady Ashford's ball. Yes . . . that's right. She was wearing a gown cut so low it was positively indecent. She looked like a cow in need of a good milking . . . if you get my meaning." The duchess winked.

Alexandra couldn't help but smile at Johanna Wellington's outrageous comment. "I assume since Nicholas's mistress didn't accompany him, they have called it quits."

"Never assume anything, Alexandra. Not when it comes to as conniving a woman as that Sabrina. She had her heart set on becoming Nicholas's duchess. She made no bones about saying so to everyone who came in contact with her. I think Nicholas was the only one who didn't realize it. Men can be a doltish lot, can't they? Well, we'd best be getting back before Frederick sends out a search party."

The words Johanna spoke stuck firmly in Alexandra's mind as she sat at the long mahogany table in the supper room. Her gaze strayed to Nicholas, who was seated across from her. Did he miss the beautiful Sabrina? she wondered. The thought cut into her like a knife. Nicholas smiled when he caught her gaze upon him, causing a hunger within her that had nothing to do with the supper set before her. She was, therefore, relieved when he bent down to listen to something Lady Dunmore was relating.

Deciding to take her mind off Nicholas, Alexandra let her gaze wander about the room. She was impressed by the beauty of her surroundings. The room had a definite oriental influence. There were ornate Chinese key moldings on the ceiling and pagoda-type arches above the double doors at either end of the room. On the far wall stood an exact duplicate of the black coal stove she had seen in the ballroom. The walls were painted a warm saffron color that seemed to glow in the radiance of the candles which burned in the crystal chandelier overhead.

Spearing another piece of grouse off her silver plate, she turned her attention to Lord Dunmore, who was seated at the head of the table.

"I am so pleased all of you were able to come this evening," the governor said. "As you know, my wife has just arrived from England. She has just presented me with the news that we are to have another child."

A boisterous round of applause ensued. Nicholas stood, raising his wineglass. "To Lord and Lady Dunmore. May your child be blessed with health and happiness."

Alexandra hesitated a moment before raising her glass. Then, deciding that an innocent child really wasn't to blame for any of the colonies' troubles, she joined in and made the toast. Her action elicited the most dazzling of smiles from Nicholas, and it caused a definite quickening of her heartbeat.

A short time later, Alexandra stood in the far corner of the room staring absently out the open window. The sounds of the tree frogs and crickets made an interesting accompaniment to the tinkling tones of the harpsichord.

"Are you having a good time, my sweet?"

Startled, Alexandra spun around; the champagne in her glass sloshed over, spilling onto Nicholas's satin frock coat. Her eyes rounded in horror at the wet stain spreading over his jacket. "I'm terribly sorry; you frightened me."

His smile was reassuring. "I didn't mean to scare you. Are you all right?" he asked, taking hold of her arm and leading her out the door that led to the garden.

Pleased by the look of concern she caught in Nicholas's eyes, she returned his smile. "Yes. I'm fine. Did you wish to speak to me about something? Is that why we have come outside?"

Guiding her down the path, Nicholas replied, "I felt the need for a bit of fresh air. I was hoping you'd join me."

Strolling past the grape arbor, they didn't stop until they reached a secluded area of the garden. Staring back at the mansion, which was now a good distance away, Alexandra felt a moment of uneasiness. "It was getting rather warm inside," she said, taking a seat on the stone bench that rested beneath a towering magnolia tree. She hoped her comment would explain away the sudden flush covering her body.

151

"Have I told you how beautiful you look tonight?" Nicholas asked, sitting down next to her.

Smiling shyly, she replied, "I believe you did, but thank you again. A lady never tires of hearing a compliment."

"I was very proud of you tonight. You handled Lord Wellington very diplomatically."

"I can be tactful at times, though not very often," she admitted. "And since you are handing out compliments, I feel it is only fair that I hand out one of my own." She saw his eyebrows rise inquiringly. "It was very good of you to stand up for Mister Henry. I wanted to thank you."

Picking up her hand, Nicholas placed a kiss on Alexandra's palm. "I think the time has come to view the other side, don't you? There are always two sides to every situation; I like to think that I am open-minded enough to consider both of them."

It was hard to concentrate on Nicholas's words when his lips were leaving a trail of fire up and down her arm. "Yes," she managed to choke out, "of course."

Drawing her into his embrace, Nicholas placed featherlike kisses up and down her neck. "I think it is time we called a truce. What do you think?"

How could she think when her heart was thudding wildly? Rather than reply, she turned her head, covering his mouth with her own. She heard his groan of pleasure as he tightened his hold, deepening the kiss. Boldly, Alexandra thrust her tongue into his mouth, savoring the brandy taste of him; his joined hers in a wildly erotic mating.

She didn't resist when his hands reached into the bodice of her gown, freeing her breasts. Her nipples hardened instantly. Gently, he massaged the aching globes until she thought she would die from desire, and when his lips replaced his hands, and his hands slipped under the skirt of her gown, she didn't protest.

Slowly his hands moved up her thighs, inching closer

and closer to the center of her being. The feel of his fingers on her bare flesh was titillating. Never before had she been touched as intimately as this. She arched up, her body craving release. Tenderly, he rubbed her woman's mound, kneading the tiny bud of passion until it pulsated with a life of its own. "Please, Nicholas," Alexandra cried, "I can't take anymore. Please."

He could take her now, Nicholas thought. She was ripe, ready for him. His manhood throbbed with the need of her. But he wouldn't. He didn't want her first time to be a tumble in the garden. When he made love to Alexandra, he wanted it to be perfect, glorious, fulfilling. "Alex, my sweet, just relax. I'm going to give you your woman's pleasure. Trust me," he crooned.

Beads of perspiration dotted Nicholas's upper lip as he tried to control his own body's needs. With gentle hands, he stroked the quivering flesh until it became pebble hard. Alexandra's shallow breathing quickened as she reached for fulfillment. "Let go, my sweet, let go," he urged. Suddenly, her body shuddered; his hands became wet with her passion. He smiled, pleased that he had been the first to give her such pleasure.

"Oh, Nicholas," Alexandra cried, her breathing slowly returning to normal, "I never realized anything could be so wonderful."

He planted a tender kiss on her lips. "There is much more to come, my sweet. That is, if we have declared a truce." His smile held a wealth of promise.

"I suppose we should seal this truce with a kiss," she suggested brazenly.

Kissing her again, Nicholas squeezed her gently. "Let's go home, my sweet. It's time to go to bed."

"Do you mean to join me, my lord?" Her question was asked in jest, but if she were truthful, she did not find the notion at all displeasing.

Nicholas's eyes glowed with a hunger that seared a path into her heart, rendering her weak in the knees.

"Soon, my lady . . . soon."

# PART THREE

# BOUND BY LOVE

*Ah Love, let us be true*
*To one another! for the world, which seems*
*To lie before us like a land of dreams,*
*So various, so beautiful, so new,*
*Hath really neither joy, nor love, nor light*
*Nor certitude, nor peace, nor help for pain;*
*And we are here as on a darkling plain*
*Swept with confused alarms of struggle and flight,*
*Where ignorant armies clash by night.*

—Matthew Arnold,
"Dover Beach"

## Chapter Twelve

The warm, lazy days of June were quickly replaced by the hot, humid days of July. Alexandra knelt before a row of summer squash, cutting the long yellow gourds and placing them into her brown wicker basket.

Gardening had become therapy for her. Planting herself between rows of cucumbers, corn, and collards took her mind off the persistent questions nagging at the back of her mind. Nicholas . . . her heart leapt every time she thought of him, which was constantly. Not an hour of the day went by when the image of his handsome face and his soft sensual lips didn't come to mind. What did she feel for him? She had asked herself that same question a thousand times.

Since that night in the palace garden, her animosity and anger had melted into a simmering passion. Their truce had held. There had been no more amorous interludes, only polite smiles and small talk that held an underlying thread of sexual tension.

She felt her cheeks grow warm at the brazenness of her thoughts. It was true. She was tense, aching, unfulfilled. Her emotions were drawn so taut, she feared they would snap.

"Miss Alex," Chloe demanded, a fierce expression on her face, "is you going to pick dem beans or murder dem? Lordy be, look what you has done to those beans.'' She shook her head.

Alexandra looked up into Chloe's scowling face, then back down to the basket of vegetables she held. The long green beans had been snapped into hundreds of little pieces. She had been so preoccupied with thoughts of Nicholas, she hadn't realized that she'd worked her way from the squash to the other side of the garden plot, where the beans hung suspended from cedar poles.

Blushing, she smiled guiltily at Chloe. ''I'm sorry. I guess my mind's on other things.''

Crossing her arms over her chest, Chloe tapped her foot impatiently. ''Girl, you been in a daze for weeks. What's gotten into you? If I didn't know you better, I'd think you was fallin' in love.''

Jumping up, Alexandra brushed the dirt from her hands and gown. Her cheeks were as red as the beets at her feet. ''Don't be ridiculous! It's just the weather. I always get lethargic this time of year.''

''I don't know nothin' about dis heah lethargic, but I do know when someone's got a fever in their blood.'' At the look of denial on Alexandra's face, Chloe's tone softened. ''Chile, I used to be young once. I knows what it feels like to hanker for a man.''

Tears slipped unheeded down Alexandra's cheeks. ''I can't be in love with Nicholas,'' she protested. ''I'm not even supposed to like him.''

The black cook came forward, drawing Alexandra into the comfort of her bosom. ''Who says you ain't suppose to like the duke? He seems like a nice man to me.''

''He's an Englishman—a nobleman. He stands for everything I hate.''

''Chile, you can't tell your heart what to do. Your mind may want to hate him, but your heart feels different. Let your heart lead you; it won't steer you wrong.''

''Were you ever in love, Chloe?'' Alexandra asked.

The kind brown eyes got a faraway look in them. "Yes, I had me a man once. Children, too. Two babies, a girl and a boy."

Alexandra couldn't withhold her shocked gasp; her eyes widened in surprise. "What happened? Did they die?"

A look of such intense sorrow crossed the black woman's face that Alexandra felt ashamed she had brought up the subject.

"They as good as dead, Miss Alex. They was sold away by the hateful master who used to own me."

"I'm so sorry, Chloe. I never realized."

"It was a long time ago, another lifetime. I carry their memory here." She placed her hand over her heart. "They can never be taken from there."

Tears misted Alexandra's eyes. "Thank you for sharing that with me," she said, hugging Chloe to her.

"I tell you so's you know. Life be too short. We have our love for so little a time, then it's gone. Just like that." She snapped her fingers; the sound reverberated loudly against the still morning air. "There's no shame in lovin' a man. The shame is when you deny it."

"Alex, dear." Her mother wore her usual anxious expression when addressing her. They were seated in the parlor discussing the merits of the annual family trip to Richmond.

"Are you certain you don't want to go to Richmond with us? We could shop and visit with your father's Aunt Patsy. It might be fun." Catherine looked expectantly at her daughter.

Alexandra repressed the grimace that threatened to surface at the mention of Aunt Patsy's name. If there was one thing she didn't need in her life right now, it was an eighty-year-old, partially senile, interfering busybody. She smiled to mask her feelings. "I'll be

159

fine. I have Betsy and Chloe to keep me company, and Ben won't be that far away."

Ben had been living with George Wythe since Nicholas had been quartered in their home. He had never been able to hide his dislike for Nicholas, and it probably was for the best, but she missed him terribly. Ben's teasing, friendly manner had always been able to lift her spirits, which definitely had been lagging of late.

"I'm not sure that it's entirely proper leaving you alone in the same house with Nicholas. Betsy is so preoccupied with that snooty valet, I don't think she'll be much of a chaperon."

"Really, Mother! Nicholas and I are engaged to be married, and in case you have forgotten, we don't get on all that well."

"Yes. But just the same . . ."

"Catherine!" Samuel bellowed from the hallway. "The carriage is waiting, and Alicia is chomping at the bit like a racehorse. Are you ready?"

Catherine looked anxiously from her daughter to the hallway. "Yes, dear, I'll be right along." Placing a kiss on Alexandra's cheek, Catherine's eyes filled with tears. "I'll miss you. This is the first time we all won't be together."

Wrapping her arm around her mother's waist, Alexandra guided her to the front door. Observing her father pacing back and forth in front of the house, she waved. "Have a wonderful time, and don't worry about a thing. Ben and I will be just fine."

As she watched the carriage pull out of sight, Alexandra was assailed by a feeling of melancholy. A lump rose in her throat as she thought of her mother's words: *This is the first time we all won't be together.*

She was growing up. Soon she would be married, and so would Ben. The close-knit family she had always relied upon would unravel to go their separate ways. She swallowed, blinking back the tears that clouded her vision. Turning, she walked back into the house, closing the door behind her. Leaning heavily against the wood panels, she heaved a sigh.

"Alexandra, what is it? Is something wrong?"

Nicholas was standing on the bottom step; a worried expression marred his smooth features. Seeing him look so concerned, so caring, Alexandra flung herself into his arms, almost knocking him backward in the process.

"Oh, Nicholas," she sobbed, "I just realized that nothing is every going to be the same again. After we're married, I won't be a part of this family anymore."

Tipping up her chin, Nicholas looked into Alexandra's eyes, the watery blue reminding him of an ocean at calm. He smiled tenderly. "Nonsense, my sweet. Just because you marry doesn't mean you give up your place in your family. You'll just have two families. After our children are born . . ."

"Children!" Alexandra shouted, her eyes wide and surprisingly dry. "You want children?" She had never considered that possibility.

"Of course, don't you?" The blush that rose to her cheeks was most becoming; it nearly matched the rose of her dimity gown.

"Yes! But I didn't think you would. You're so stern, so . . . so proper. I can't picture you rolling in the grass with a bunch of babies." The image that suddenly flashed through her mind brought a smile to her lips.

Still holding her within his embrace, Nicholas replied, "Well, if the truth be told, I'd much rather roll in the grass with you."

"Nicholas!" she chided, covering his mouth with her hand, "Ssh . . . someone might hear you."

His chest rumbled, laughter pealing out into the room when Alexandra removed her hand. "Do you know what I would love to do at this very moment?" he asked, watching her cheeks glow again.

She shook her head, her heart racing madly as she

waited for Nicholas to speak. She thought she knew what he wanted, but she wasn't bold enough to express it.

"I want . . ." He kissed her gently on the lips, eliciting a moan of pleasure. "To . . ." He kissed her again, more thoroughly this time until her body went limp against him. "Go on a picnic!" He laughed at her shocked expression.

Alexandra's mouth dropped open. Of all the things she had expected him to say, that wasn't one of them. "A picnic! Whatever for?" She tried to act nonchalant, wanting to hide the fact that her heart was ready to burst inside her chest.

Nicholas's smile was incredibly erotic. "Why, so we can roll in the grass, of course!"

"But, don't you have work to do?"

"Lord Dunmore is leaving first thing in the morning to lead an expedition into the Ohio River Valley against the Shawnee. I expect he will be gone quite a while. I will have plenty to do in his stead. So today I am going to play . . . with you, if you'll let me." He winked.

Alexandra was mesmerized by the sudden change in Nicholas's behavior. Where was the stuffy, proper Englishman she had grown so used to? Perhaps she had misjudged him. This new side of Nicholas was definitely intriguing—definitely more appealing. "Do you have any particular games you wish to play?" she asked, smiling seductively.

"Most definitely! But first, I think we need to talk Chloe into fixing us some lunch. I cannot play on an empty stomach."

Alexandra laughed, shaking her head. "Why is it that men always think about their stomachs?"

"I have a huge appetite, my sweet." He brought Alexandra's hand to his mouth, nibbling the fingers one by one. Observing the gooseflesh on her arms, he smiled knowingly. "I can see by your reaction, you have quite a hunger, too."

\* \* \*

The late afternoon sun beat down on the couple who rested in the shade of the huge linden tree. Their picnic lunch completed, Nicholas and Alexandra relaxed on the soft mat of grass growing on the banks of the James River.

Staring out at the water, her knees propped under her chin, Alexandra observed the changing color and mood of the tide and thought about how she had changed in her feelings toward Nicholas.

The day they shared had been glorious. Nicholas had confided many things about his childhood: his life in England, his schooling at Oxford. She had relived, through his words, the important events that had taken place in his life.

When he told her of his father's death, she could see by his expression that he had been deeply saddened by the loss. She now understood what had motivated him to carry on his family name.

Nicholas had also touched briefly on the fact that he had a brother. She had sensed a measure of animosity in his voice when he spoke of him, but she didn't want to delve into matters that were of no concern to her.

Looking over to where he slept, her heart filled with love. It was true. She could deny it no longer. She loved Nicholas Fortune.

Suddenly Nicholas's eyes flew open, and he grinned. "If you keep staring at me like that, I won't be responsible for my actions."

Alexandra's cheeks flooded with color. She felt transparent, as if Nicholas could read her mind. "Maybe I don't want you to be responsible," she replied boldly.

Nicholas groaned, reaching out to pull Alexandra down beside him. "My sweet, do you know what you are saying?"

"Nicholas, I ache for you. Ever since that night in

the garden, I can think of nothing else." She covered her face. "What is wrong with me?"

Gently pulling her hands down to her sides, Nicholas stared into her eyes. He saw innocence and something else he couldn't understand. "Nothing is wrong with you. You have a woman's needs. I am pleased that you enjoyed our lovemaking."

"But I didn't want you to stop." She wrapped her arms around his neck, drawing him closer. "Make love to me, Nicholas."

The words produced an instantaneous hardening of Nicholas's manhood. He stared intently into Alexandra's face. Desire was clearly written there. He breathed in the heady, musky scent of her passion and was powerless to resist her plea. Slowly he covered her mouth and body with his own.

When Nicholas's tongue entered her mouth, a delicious shudder heated her body. She abandoned herself to his kiss; the hot tide of passion raged through her as uncontrollably as a river. The sudden rush of cool air against her skin made her aware that Nicholas was removing her gown. His hands were warm as they caressed her naked breasts. His lips were hot as they seared her skin, traveling down her neck and her breasts, and finally coming to rest on her hardened nipples.

Boldly reaching into the waistband of Nicholas's breeches, she drew out the white linen shirt to run her hands over his naked flesh. The feel of his muscular chest sent her senses spiraling. It was like smooth marble beneath her fingertips. She heard his moan of pleasure.

"I want to touch you," she whispered. She drew his head down to hers once more. When she felt his hands on the bare flesh of her legs, her stomach knotted in wild anticipation. Her heart thudded madly as his fingers gently massaged the mound of her womanhood, separating the folds that hid her very essence. She experienced a moment of unease when Nicholas's mouth left hers. The heat rose to her cheeks when he lifted her gown, baring her body to his view.

"Just relax," he said. "I want to look at you—savor the beauty of your perfection."

She couldn't control the wetness that flooded the apex of her thighs when Nicholas's head bent down to place tender kisses there. She knew it was wrong, sinful even, but she couldn't bring herself to tell him to stop the delicious torment his tongue was creating as it darted in and out of her body.

Her reaction was so intense, she thought she had exploded with the joy of it until she felt the first drops of rain hit her face and realized it was thunder she was hearing. Please, God! she cried silently. Not now!

"My sweet," Nicholas choked out, "I'm afraid we had better depart. The lightning is striking too close for our comfort." He pulled down her dress, helping her to her feet.

Picking up the quilt and the remnants of their lunch, they hurried to the shelter of the waiting carriage. Alexandra's tears of frustration mingled with the rain on her face. She chanced a look at Nicholas when they were finally seated. His look of pain spoke volumes about how he felt. She opened her mouth, about to suggest that they complete what they had started, but then she shut it again. She didn't want Nicholas to think she was some kind of wanton. Although, after the way she had behaved, what else could he think?

They traveled in total silence save for the sounds of an occasional boom of thunder and the heavy rain pelting against the roof of the carriage. After a few moments, Nicholas drew the carriage to a halt and turned to face Alexandra. "I am sorry, my sweet. I wanted everything to be perfect for you."

Squeezing his arm, a warm flush suffusing her body, she replied, "It was perfect. The whole day. Thank you."

The kiss Nicholas placed on her cheek was filled with incredible tenderness. "It was my pleasure," he replied.

Suddenly, a flash of lightning split the sky. The roar of thunder was deafening. A huge oak limb, creaking and groaning, finally crashed to the ground near the carriage. The horses shied, prancing nervously about.

"Easy, boys," Nicholas said, uttering words of calm encouragement to quiet them down.

When the horses had settled once more, Nicholas turned to face Alexandra. "We have angered the gods with our impetuous behavior. It is a sign that we should wait until we are married."

"Do you think we can?" she asked, sighing deeply.

"No," he said, smiling ruefully, "I don't."

The following day found Alexandra flying about the house, issuing orders to a very distraught trio of servants in preparation for her parents' homecoming.

The fact that the Courtlands weren't due back for another week didn't seem to faze her one bit. She was bound and determined to keep busy—to exorcise the demons of lust that had consumed her body.

Bending before the hearth, broom and shovel in hand, Alexandra thought about the decision she had made last night. She had come to the conclusion that Nicholas was right. It was wrong to tempt Fate where their relationship was concerned. True, she loved Nicholas, and she certainly desired him, but she wasn't entirely convinced that a marriage between them was going to work. She had doubts: doubts about adapting to her life as a duchess; doubts about her and Nicholas's conflicting political beliefs; and finally, doubts that Nicholas would ever grow to love her.

"What shall we do with the rug, madam?" Habersham's clipped tones alerted Alexandra to the fact that she was no longer alone. Turning to look back over her shoulder, she contained the smile threatening to spill at the annoyed expressions Nicholas's valet and Betsy were exhibiting.

They stood on either end of the long rolled Oriental carpet, their faces flushed from the exertion of hauling it down the stairs.

"It's rather heavy, Miss Alex," Betsy reminded the gawking woman. Miss Alex had no reason to look so smug, Betsy thought. Not the way she looked at the moment. Her hair, supposedly secured by a white cotton mobcap, was falling about her shoulders in disarray. She had soot over her nose and cheeks, and her blue-and-white India calico dress was covered with grime.

"Take it outside and hang it over the fence. It needs to be beaten thoroughly," Alexandra ordered, nearly laughing aloud at the look of horror on Habersham's face. It was one thing for the cocky valet to help Betsy with her housework when he knew no one else could see him, but for him to have to venture into public carrying a rug! It would definitely be a humbling experience for him, Alexandra thought.

"But, Miss Alex," Betsy protested, "it's nearly dinner time. His lordship will be home soon to have his afternoon meal."

Alexandra sighed, throwing the iron utensils in the bucket. She stood, about to issue another order, when the door knocker sounded. "You two go hang the rug over the fence. As long as it doesn't rain, we can leave it until later this afternoon. I'll get the door." The knocker sounded again.

Hurrying to answer it, Alexandra pulled open the door to find two impeccably dressed strangers standing on her steps. "May I help you?" she inquired.

The man stepped forward, covering his nose with his handkerchief to show his disdain for the filthy urchin before him. "Tell your master that Basil Fortune has arrived from England."

Alexandra's mouth dropped open. She stared at the rotund man, unable to believe that this ugly individual was actually related by blood to her darling Nicholas. Her eyes then traveled to the exquisite creature standing next to him. She was dressed regally in a purple satin gown, totally unsuitable for the humid weather of Virginia. On her head, she sported a matching silk hat with plumes and ribbons cascading from it. Probably his wife, Alexandra thought disdainfully. A fortune hunter, no doubt. She smiled to herself at the cleverness of her pun.

"I beg your pardon," she finally replied. "Did you say your name was Fortune . . . as in Nicholas Fortune?"

"Really, young woman. Are you colonials so ignorant that you cannot understand a simple statement?"

Alexandra's eyes narrowed. Clenching her fists at her sides, she replied, "I am Alexandra Courtland, Nicholas Fortune's betrothed." She glanced over at the blonde-haired woman who had been unable to stifle her gasp of surprise.

"You are Nicholas's betrothed?" Sabrina asked, her eyes taking in the disheveled appearance of the woman before her. She didn't bother to disguise the smirk that rose to her lips.

Pretending not to notice, Alexandra replied, "Excuse my appearance, but I was in the process of cleaning. Won't you come in and have a seat in the parlor?" She ushered the haughty duo into the front room, closing the door behind her.

"Please forgive our rudeness, Mistress Courtland," Basil Fortune stated, taking a seat next to Sabrina on the settee. "We had no idea that Nicholas would be residing in the same house as his intended bride."

Alexandra felt the heat rise to her cheeks at the implication of Basil Fortune's words. "Nicholas is quartered here by order of the governor," she stated. Assuming a smile to cover her animosity, she then con-

168

tinued, "If you will excuse me for a moment, I shall take my leave to go upstairs and change. I will instruct my maid to bring refreshments." With that, she turned and fled the room, seething with indignation at the rudeness of her guests.

"This is going to be easier than we thought, Basil darling?" Sabrina cooed, turning to face her lover. "Did you see how dowdy the woman is? Why, I'll have Nicholas eating out of my hand in no time."

Leaning over, Basil placed his hands on Sabrina's breasts. "It isn't your hand my brother is going to want to feast on, my dear." He squeezed playfully.

Covering his hands with her own, Sabrina replied, "Soon we shall have it all, my darling. Soon, we will have all that we've ever desired."

# Chapter Thirteen

Entering the house a short time later, Nicholas paused outside the closed door to the parlor. He could discern Alexandra's voice coming through the door but was uncertain of the identity of the male voice he heard. A sudden pang of jealousy surfaced as he placed his hand on the brass handle. Whoever it was sequestered alone in the house with his betrothed had better have a damned good reason for being here, he thought, pushing open the door.

He came to an abrupt halt, surprise lighting his features at the sight of his brother and former mistress seated in Alexandra's parlor as if they visited with her every day. "Sabrina, what the devil . . ." Nicholas shouted, staring at the perfectly sculpted features he knew so well. He gave a cursory glance at his brother.

"Nicholas, darling," Sabrina effused, jumping up from her chair to fling herself into Nicholas's arms. "How wonderful it is to see you again!" She pressed her ample form into the solidity of his chest.

Alexandra's gasp was audible when she heard the woman's name on Nicholas's lips. Sabrina . . . the woman Johanna Wellington had warned her about. This was Nicholas's mistress, not Basil's wife, as she had originally thought. She couldn't control the sudden tightening of her stomach. How many times had he whispered her name in a moment of passion? The thought sent a jolt of piercing pain into her heart. The woman was beautiful, and it appeared she still had feelings for Nicholas. How on earth could she ever hope to compete with her? she wondered.

Removing Sabrina's arms from around his neck, Nicholas cast a quick glance at Alexandra, whose look of shock and dismay was clearly written on her face. "How nice to see both of you again." Escaping Sabrina's grasp, he walked over to where Alexandra was seated and bowed. "Good afternoon, my sweet. I assume you have already been introduced to my brother and his lady friend."

Taking a calming breath, Alexandra returned his smile. "Yes. We've been having a delightful chat about the socially inferior position of the colonials here in Virginia."

Nicholas almost laughed aloud. My God! Of all the people to choose to expound his supercilious views on, Basil had to choose Alexandra! And judging from the tautness about her mouth, she hadn't let him in on her true feelings, yet. He was proud of her restraint. "Is that so?" he said, taking a seat next to her on the loveseat.

Alexandra was having a difficult time breathing. She listened to the exchange going on between Nicholas and his brother, while watching his mistress fawn over him like a cat in heat. What was she going to do? Why did his mistress have to show up now? Just when everything was starting to go smoothly between them.

True love never runs a smooth course, her mother always counseled. Hah! The course she had been on was filled with enough twists and turns to confuse even the sanest of minds. She turned her attention back to the conversation at hand.

"How do you stand living here in this provincial place, Nicholas?" Sabrina asked. "Good heavens, it must be simply dreadful for you."

172

"I am adjusting quite well. Wouldn't you say so, Alexandra?" Nicholas asked, trying to draw his usually outspoken but now quiet betrothed into the conversation.

"You have done admirable, my lord," she replied.

"I'm afraid I would have to agree with Sabrina. These colonials are a bit too rustic for my taste," Basil said, straightening the ruffles on his sleeve. "Not to change the subject, Nicholas, but I would have thought you and your charming bride-to-be would be married by now."

Nicholas felt Alexandra stiffen beside him. Reaching over, he took her hand, rubbing it absently with his thumb. "We decided to wait awhile. We wanted to get to know each other better."

"And have you . . . gotten to know each other better?" Sabrina asked.

It took all of Alexandra's restraint to keep from jumping out of her chair to slap the stupid, nasty smirk off Sabrina's face. Using a more subtle method of attack, she replied, "Nicholas and I are very well acquainted." Turning her head in Nicholas's direction, she bestowed a dazzling smile upon him and was rewarded with a wink.

Nicholas squeezed her hand. He wasn't sure why Alexandra wanted to mislead his brother and Sabrina, but he wasn't going to contradict her in front of them. "Yes," he replied, "we find the differences that once separated growing smaller with each day that passes."

Alexandra's heart warmed at Nicholas's admission. Glancing over at Sabrina, she smiled sweetly, delighting in the look of annoyance the woman wore on her face.

Rising to her feet, Sabrina tugged on Basil's hand. "How wonderful to hear you two are getting on so well. We'd really love to stay and chat, but we're not quite settled in our lodgings. Isn't that right, Basil?" She looked over at her companion for confirmation.

"Indeed. Our rooms at the Raleigh should be ready by now. We must take our leave. Thank you so much for your hospitality, Alexandra. I hope I may call you that, since we'll be related soon."

Inclining her head, she stood when Nicholas did, escorting the obnoxious pair to the door. Once they had departed, Alexandra followed Nicholas into the study, closing the door behind her.

"Why has your brother come to Virginia, Nicholas? You didn't mention that he was expected."

Nicholas shrugged, taking a seat behind the desk. "He wasn't. Apparently Basil was curious to find out more about the colonies. He says, since he won't be inheriting the title, he might as well carve out a new life for himself. Personally, I think it's a splendid idea. The two of us never did get on all that well."

"And Sabrina?" she asked, holding her breath, fearful of the answer that was coming.

"Sabrina Montgomery and I were acquainted in London. She was a friend."

A friend. Men didn't have *friends* who looked like Sabrina. They had lovers. "It appears Miss Montgomery is also quite *friendly* with your brother," she said, unable to keep the sarcasm out of her voice.

"Just what is it you are implying, Alexandra?" Nicholas demanded, pursing his lips in an affronted expression.

"I'm not stupid, Nicholas. I happen to know that Sabrina Montgomery was not your so-called "friend," but rather your mistress. I don't know why you are trying to hide the fact." Crossing her arms over her chest, she waited for him to deny it.

Pushing himself out of the chair, Nicholas came to stand before her. "Who told you that?"

"That is not important. What I want to know is why you didn't admit it."

Rubbing the back of his neck, he sighed. "All right, it's true. Sabrina was my mistress, but I broke off with

174

her before I sailed for Virginia. I told her I was planning to marry.''

Relief flooded through her at Nicholas's admission.
She wanted to believe him, needed to believe him, but
some small part of her still couldn't quite accept that a
man would not want to resume his relationship with a
woman as alluring as Sabrina. ''Judging from the way
she was drooling all over you, I don't think Miss
Montgomery believes you.''

He smiled. ''You are starting to sound like a jealous
wife.''

She laughed to cover the truth of his words. ''Don't
flatter yourself. I am merely curious to know the extent
of your relationship. After all, since I'm to become your
wife, I think I have the right.''

Pulling her into his embrace, Nicholas nuzzled her
neck. ''My sweet, you needn't worry that I'm going
to resume my relationship with Sabrina. Why would I
want any other woman when I have you?''

Why indeed! Alexandra thought.


Situated in her small room at the Raleigh, Sabrina
paced nervously across the pine planks of the floor. She
was as edgy as a tomcat on the prowl about Nicholas's
infatuation with the colonial, Alexandra Courtland.

What he saw in that plain little wren was beyond her
ken. She was passably pretty, but that figure! She had
seen larger breasts on a fleshy man. Stopping in front
of the looking glass, Sabrina pulled down the front of
her gown, baring her breasts to her view. Holding them
up for inspection, she smiled. Nicholas always told her
that she had the perfect pair. The large, dusky nipples
hardened into stiff peaks when she thought of Nicholas
taking them into his mouth once again. Damn! She
had to get him back in her bed. Once he was reminded
of what he was missing, she knew he would want to
resume their alliance.

Stepping out of her gown, she drew on her white silk robe. She had just tied the sash when the door opened and Basil stepped into the room.

His eyes were immediately drawn to the dark round points on Sabrina's chest that were clearly visible beneath the transparent robe. Staring at the hardened nubs, Basil's brown orbs glowed with a lust he did not bother to conceal.

"I can see you have been thinking of me, my dear," he said, smiling lewdly. Crossing over to where she stood, he untied the robe, taking the heavy mounds of flesh into his hands. "My darling, why didn't you call? I would have hurried with my unpacking." He took the nipples between his thumb and forefinger, twirling them repeatedly. The twin peaks beckoned his tongue; he laved them over and over until Sabrina's moan of pleasure brought a self-satisfied smile to his lips.

Sabrina was powerless to resist. Although she despised the weasel, her thoughts of Nicholas had created a hunger in her loins that needed appeasement. Leading Basil to the bed, she spread herself to his gaze, watching his eyes darken at the offering she made. "Do with me what you will, my darling. I'm wet and ready for you." She arched her back enticingly, smiling in satisfaction when she saw him kneel on the bed at her knees.

An hour later, Sabrina leaned back against the headboard, observing her lover, who was fast asleep. How disgusting he was, she thought, screwing up her face at the sound of his deep rumbling snores. At least he had improved in bed. She had actually achieved a small measure of satisfaction today; she stretched contentedly.

Easing herself out of bed, Sabrina walked to the window, drawing open the wooden louvers. It was not quite dark yet. Her window faced the street; she felt a small thrill run through her at the possibility that someone might observe her nakedness.

Pushing open the window, she peered out. A virile-looking blond man with wide shoulders and trim hips stood on the street below. As if by will, he turned, staring directly up at her window. She saw the shocked look on his face before he smiled and winked. She blew him a kiss then stepped back from the window.

"Sabrina, are you crazy? Get away from that window. Someone might see you," Basil shouted at her from the bed.

Someone had seen her, she thought, and it shouldn't be too difficult in a town this size to locate him. Pasting a pout on her lips, she replied, "It's terribly hot in this little room, Basil. I was merely opening the window for some fresh air."

"Well, put on a robe, for God's sake. I don't want these local yokels viewing what is mine." He watched as she did what he instructed, then added, "I hope you are not going to continue to complain about the room. You know how difficult it was to persuade the proprietor to let you stay here. It cost me a goodly sum. He could put four or five men in that bed you are occupying by yourself."

Seating herself on the bed, Sabrina grabbed onto Basil's hand, rubbing it against her cheek. "You are so good to me, darling. I'll try not to complain, but I would like to know what you are planning to do about Nicholas and his betrothed."

Basil smiled sinisterly. "It seems we have arrived too late to prevent their engagement, but there is plenty of time to ruin their marriage plans."

"What are you suggesting?"

"A party, my dear. We are going to throw a party for the happy couple."

"A party!" Sabrina shouted, clearly annoyed. "What good will that do, except drain our pockets of more money? I refuse to part with any more of my jewelry, Basil." She had already sold the fabulous diamond brooch Nicholas had given her the previous Christmas.

"My dear," he crooned, reaching out to pull her down next to him. "I know, you want their marriage plans to fail, just as I do."

"Well . . . yes. But I can't afford . . ."

"Tsk, tsk," he chided, placing his fingers over her lips. "Success never comes cheaply, my dear. We all must pay a price: you must part with your jewels; I must part with you while I let my brother make love to you; and Nicholas will pay dearly for everything we suffer. That is a promise."

Standing on the palace green beneath the shade of a towering catalpa tree, Alexandra stared at the Georgian residence of the governor. She knew Nicholas would be working in the right wing that flanked the center structure where Lord Dunmore kept his office.

Biting her lower lip, she tried to decide if he would welcome an intrusion into his afternoon. He had kept his political activities to himself, rarely discussing the current events of the day with her. Perhaps he would view her visit as too presumptuous. After all, he had explained to her only this morning that he would be tied up in meetings most of the day.

Looking down at the wicker basket she held in her hand and then back up at the palace, she decided to chance it. She had to see him. The unexpected arrival of his former mistress yesterday had left her more shaken than she would like to admit.

"Alex."

She turned to find her brother striding toward her across the grass. Smiling, she waved. Seeing Ben reminded her of how much she had missed him these past few weeks.

"Hello. What brings you away from your studies? You're not shirking your lessons today, are you?"

Ben laughed, tweaking his sister's nose. "I might be. But it just so happens I'm on an important errand for Mister Wythe." Looking about to make certain they were alone, he lowered his voice. "Big things are happening, Alex. The non-importation agreement will be announced any day. There's been a meeting in Alexandria which General Washington presided over. Resolutions have been drafted calling for a Continental Congress."

Excitement and fear shone in the bright blue eyes. "The Crown will not ignore these steps, Ben. There is going to be retaliation."

"That is why you mustn't tell a soul, especially not your duke. I must go. I ride to Monticello with missives for Jefferson." Bending over, he kissed her cheek, something he hadn't done in a very long time. "I've missed you, shortcake."

Alexandra's eyes misted at the familiar endearment Ben had used since they were children. "And I you. Promise me you will come to dinner when you return."

"Alex, you know how I feel about the duke."

Grabbing onto Ben's arm, she looked beseechingly into his eyes. "Nicholas isn't so bad once you get to know him. I think you may grow to like him."

Returning the smile she offered, Ben tweaked her nose again. "I find that highly unlikely, but I'll come to dinner Thursday night."

"Be careful," she whispered, waving as she watched him walk away. She was worried something terrible was going to happen. If any of the governor's men were to find out what Ben was up to. . . . She trembled despite the warmth of the day.

Clutching the basket, she crossed the short distance to the palace. As she approached the black wrought-iron gate, the distinctive odor of osage orange drifted down from the branches overhead to fill her senses with

179

sweet fragrance. Inhaling deeply, she fortified herself with the courage to proceed.

Pausing on the steps of the building, she smoothed down the folds of her blue calico dress, adjusted the satin ribbons of her wide-brimmed straw bonnet, and entered.

Expecting to find a house full of people, she was surprised to find no one lurking about. It was strangely quiet. Walking further down the hall, she heard the unmistakable sound of a woman's laugh followed by Nicholas's hearty chuckle. A sick feeling centered in the pit of her stomach. She didn't need to be told who the owner of that high-pitched giggle was. Throwing open the door, she found Sabrina perched provocatively atop Nicholas's desk, showing a great deal more leg than was seemly.

Nicholas rose as she entered. Sabrina stood also, smiling spitefully while she adjusted the skirts of her gold satin gown. Doesn't the fool know that it's much too hot to wear satin? Alexandra wondered. Perhaps she would suffer a heat stroke and expire. That thought brought a smile to her lips. "Good afternoon. I hope I'm not intruding."

Sabrina's smile turned into a smirk. "Not at all. I was just leaving."

"Don't let me keep you," Alexandra said. "I'm sure you have a million things to do." The woman nodded and strode to the door, pausing before it.

"See you Saturday, darling," Sabrina said. "And do be on time, Nicholas. You know how I hate to be kept waiting." Flashing Alexandra another nasty smile, she departed.

Clenching her fists, Alexandra bit the inside of her cheek to keep from screaming vulgarities at the woman. How dare she arrange a clandestine meeting with Nicholas? And right under my nose! I'll tear her hair out . . . I'll scratch her eyes out, she raged silently.

"Are you all right, my sweet? You look as if you're

ready to burst a blood vessel. Has something upset you?''

The look of innocence on Nicholas's face astounded her. Was he jesting with her? She took several deep breaths to calm herself. ''You mean beside the fact that I find the man I'm supposed to marry snuggling up to his former mistress when he is supposed to be inundated with work?''

Nicholas's eyes hardened. ''I don't like what you are implying, Alexandra. There is a perfectly reasonable explanation for Sabrina's visit, if you would care to listen.''

Setting the basket down on the desk, she crossed her arms over her chest. ''Go on.''

Nicholas bit back a smile at the ferocity shining in Alexandra's eyes. He was reminded of a jealous she-cat; his feisty kitten had claws. ''Sabrina and Basil are hosting a party in our honor Saturday night.''

''This Saturday night? That's only five days away. I can't possibly be ready. You'll have to decline the invitation.'' The prospect of spending an entire evening in the company of that overblown hussy was more than she could bear.

''I've already accepted.''

''What!'' She advanced on him, placing her finger squarely in the center of his chest. ''How dare you accept without consulting me?'' Each word was accentuated with a poke of her finger.

Grabbing onto her hand, Nicholas brought it to his lips, kissing the tips of her fingers. ''You forget, I make the decisions in this relationship, my sweet. I need not consult you . . . merely inform you.''

She pulled her hand away, ignoring the tingling sensation that shot up her arm. ''I won't go!''

''Yes you will, or I will go to the governor about your brother.''

Alexandra's eyes narrowed into thin slits. ''How long do you intend to blackmail me? Haven't you got what you wanted? Your mistress is back. You have no need to vent your lust upon me."

"Vent my lust! Is that what you call it? I seem to remember you doing a great deal of *venting* yourself."

Raising her hand, she slapped him full across the face. The sound reverberated off the walls, reaching into the far corners of her heart. She stared wordlessly at the red imprint on Nicholas's face until the implication of what she had done registered on her brain. "Nicholas, I . . ."

"Say no more." His voice was harsh, his words encased in ice. "I was under the impression that you welcomed my advances. It appears I was wrong. You needn't worry. In the future, I shall find someone else to vent my lust upon. As you say, my mistress is back."

Choking back a sob, Alexandra ran for the door, fleeing from the hateful words Nicholas threw at her.

Dropping down into his chair, Nicholas banged his fist on the desk, upsetting the wicker basket that Alexandra had left in her haste to depart. Two plump green pears rolled out, laying side by side to form a heart. He frowned.

What else was in the basket? he wondered. His curiosity aroused, he reached in, extracting two crystal goblets and a bottle of Madeira. He smiled wistfully, thinking back to the night he had proposed. Reaching in again, he pulled out the patchwork quilt they had used on their last picnic. A dull ache formed in his chest.

"Damn it, Alexandra!" he shouted. "Why do you have to be so damned stubborn!" He threw the bottle of wine across the room, watching it bleed down the white plaster walls. "Why do you have to be so damned wonderful?" he whispered.

# Chapter Fourteen

The day of the party dawned dark and dreary, matching Alexandra's mood exactly. She could hear the thunder in the distance splitting the air like cannon fire. Every boom that shattered the stillness shattered her heart as well, for it brought to mind the joyful time she had spent in Nicholas's arms.

Sighing, she pressed her forehead against the glass. It felt cold—cold and hard, like her heart. Only it wasn't *her* heart that was cold; it was Nicholas's.

Moving away from the window, she walked toward the wall adjoining their rooms. It was quiet. Nicholas was still asleep. If she wasn't so damn prideful, she would march next door and climb into bed with him. God! If only she could. If only she could take back everything she had said in her moment of anger and jealousy.

Fool, she chided herself, you've pushed him toward the very person you wanted him to stay away from. Go to him—tell him you're sorry.

Picking up her robe, she slipped it on, tiptoeing out the door. Pausing in front of Nicholas's room, her hand on the knob, she took a deep breath. Do it, she told herself. Open it before you chicken out.

Just as she was about to turn the knob, it was wrenched out of her hand when the door was flung open. Nicholas stood there, fully dressed, a surprised expression on his face.

"Do you need something, Alexandra?"

His tone was achingly polite. There was no trace of friendship or warmth in it. What did you expect, you dolt! she castigated herself silently. You treated him badly.

She stood there for an eternity, staring up at him. He looked so handsome, but terribly remote. The words she longed to say died in her throat. She said instead, "I . . . I came to find out when you wished to leave for the party."

Nicholas quirked a questioning eyebrow at her. "I believe I told you eight o'clock. Don't you remember?"

"Yes," she replied, blushing furiously, "of course. How silly of me." Her explanation sounded hollow to her ears.

Nicholas took in her scanty attire and flushed cheeks. The sight of her all warm and tousled from sleep was doing queer things to his insides. "Is that all you wanted?" he asked, his tone harsher than he had intended.

No! her mind screamed. I want you. But aloud she replied, "Yes, thank you." She turned to leave.

"Alexandra," Nicholas called, grabbing onto her arm.

The sound of her name on his lips was a caress; his touch scorched her skin like a hot iron. Turning back, she looked up at him. "Yes?" she said, looking for a sign that he wished to end the hostility between them. They hadn't spoken more than a few words in days, and now they acted like polite strangers.

Nicholas gazed longingly at the lovely creature before him. He recalled every detail of the body that was hidden beneath the thin night dress: the way her velvet flesh felt beneath his hands, the taste of her passion upon his lips. His crotch tightened painfully; he shifted his stance to hide his discomfort.

"Have a pleasant day. I'll see you tonight," he said with a strange hoarseness to his voice.

There was no kiss of farewell, only a tight-lipped smile that seemed forced between his teeth, as if the very action caused him pain. As she watched him walk away, a feeling of desolation swept over Alexandra. Dragging herself back to her room, she plopped down on the bed and proceeded to cry her heart out.

Tapping his foot while he waited impatiently at the bottom of the stairs, Nicholas pulled out the gold pocket watch that had belonged to his father. Poor father, he thought, staring pensively at the timepiece. No one deserved to die such a painful death as he had. He missed him. For all his gruff manner and polite exterior, his father had loved him. He could even forgive him for the officious manner in which he had arranged his life.

Perhaps marriage to Alexandra would not be the dreaded life sentence he had originally thought it would be. If only. . . . Snapping the lid shut, he stuffed it back into his waistcoat, not liking the direction his thoughts were taking. He didn't have time to entangle himself in sentimental claptrap. He was here for a purpose: to fulfill his marital agreement and return to England with his estates and fortune intact.

The sound of footsteps on the stairs interrupted his train of thought. Looking up, he felt his breath catch in his throat at the sight that greeted his eyes. Floating down toward him was the most angelic vision he had ever seen. He stared, mesmerized.

Observing the look of awe plastered on Nicholas's face, Alexandra smiled. She felt beautiful. Betsy's choice of the white silk gown over a white lace petticoat had been perfect. She had fashioned her hair into a crown of curls which cascaded down over her left shoulder; her only adornment was a perfectly matched string of white pearls nestled at the base of her throat.

With Nicholas attired in his usual black, the contrast between them was striking. They were certain to turn many a head when they walked into the tavern this evening.

"Good evening, my lord," she said, dropping into a curtsy. "I hope I haven't kept you waiting."

"It was well worth it, I assure you, my sweet. You look beautiful."

Had Nicholas forgotten the animosity between them? she wondered. She certainly hoped so. When he took her hand and brought it to his lips for a gentle kiss, she flashed him a brilliant smile. Her heart fluttered madly as she observed the unguarded look of wanting reflected in his eyes before he shuttered them closed. Placing the mantle over her shoulders, he guided her out the door and into the black velvet night.

The walk to the Raleigh was brief. Alexandra's apprehension increased as they neared their destination. She didn't know what to expect tonight, but she was bound and determined to fend off Sabrina's calculated attempts at seducing Nicholas. She might not be as beautiful or full-figured as his mistress, but if love counted for anything, she had a lot more of that to offer.

Unconsciously, she tightened her hold on his arm, producing a reassuring squeeze from Nicholas. "Smile, my sweet. I know we are going to have a good time. Basil and Sabrina can be tiresome but that needn't prevent us from enjoying ourselves."

Alexandra was instantly buoyed by his comments. Perhaps her jealousy had been unfounded. Nicholas didn't seem to be as enamored of Sabrina as she had thought. Taking a deep breath, she entered the tavern with a tremulous smile and a trembling heart.

The Apollo Room glowed with the light of a hundred candles, sparkling and sputtering in the breeze that drifted in through the open windows. The room was warm owing to the dozens of bodies pressed together in close proximity.

Glancing about the large room, Alexandra observed many of the same faces she had previously seen at the Governor's Palace. Tories, of course! Sabrina and Basil would surround themselves with the loyal English faction of the colony.

Recognizing the Arnolds and Thaddeus Pembroke engaged in conversation in the far corner of the room, she grimaced. This night was going to be far more boring than she had originally feared.

"Shall we greet our hosts, my sweet?" Nicholas asked.

She followed his gaze. There by the window stood Sabrina and Basil talking with Lord and Lady Wellington. Thank God, Johanna was here! Alexandra thought as Nicholas propelled her forward.

The conversation ceased when the guests of honor arrived. Johanna smiled warmly, genuine pleasure lighting her eyes. "Alexandra, my dear, how lovely to see you again! You look absolutely dazzling this evening."

As she prepared to offer her thanks, Alexandra's eyes widened in shock and disbelief at the sight of Sabrina flinging herself into Nicholas's arms.

"Darling, how nice it is to see you," Sabrina cooed, planting a kiss on his lips. She ignored Alexandra completely.

Observing the look of approval on Nicholas's face when he took in Sabrina's costume, Alexandra felt her stomach clench. His eyes glowed with unconcealed lust as they lighted on the large expanse of bosom so provocatively displayed by the low neckline of her red satin gown.

He didn't seem to mind one whit that her nipples were sticking halfway out of her gown, or that she looked like a painted harlot with her red-tinted lips and kohl-darkened lashes. It was perfectly fine for him to drool over his mistress who looked like a whore as long as his future duchess didn't exhibit anything that could be remotely considered sensuous.

Looking down at her own gown, she frowned. Virginal, that's what she looked like—a stupid little virgin. Her breasts looked like peaches compared to Sabrina's watermelon-sized appendages, which at the moment were being pressed into Nicholas's chest.

"Nicholas." Alexandra suddenly blurted, "would you mind fetching a glass of champagne for me? I find that I'm quite parched." She almost choked on her words when she heard Sabrina offer to accompany him. That shameless hussy! How *dare* she throw herself at Nicholas that way!

Basil was quite pleased at how the evening was progressing. Nicholas seemed to be playing right into their hands. Alexandra was jealous. If looks could kill, his brother was a marked man. A few more hours in Sabrina's capable hands and the engagement of Nicholas and Alexandra would be history. Putting on an affable posture, he approached the dark-haired beauty.

"Sabrina and I were terribly happy you were able to come to our little gathering tonight, Alexandra. I did so want to do something nice for my brother and his betrothed," Basil said, taking the vacated spot next to her.

Alexandra forced a smile, noting the commiserating look on Johanna Wellington's face. "I wouldn't have missed it for the world. It was very thoughtful of you."

"I hope you will save a dance for me. I would deem it an honor to twirl such a beautiful woman around the dance floor."

"Of course," she replied, trying to hide the look of distaste that crossed her lips as she watched him walk away.

"I don't like that little toad," Johanna remarked. "He has shifty eyes."

Alexandra was grateful that Frederick Wellington had departed with Basil, leaving Johanna and her alone. "I'm afraid I would have to agree with you," she replied. "As a matter of fact, I don't particularly care for either one of them."

" 'Tis a great pity one can't pick their relatives. It would make life so much easier."

Alexandra smiled at the truth of Johanna's words. The more she got to know the outspoken duchess, the more she found she liked her. "You were right about Sabrina. She hasn't given up hope of ensnaring Nicholas. Look at the two of them. They look as if they're the only two people in the room."

Staring in the direction Alexandra indicated, Johanna's lips thinned. She had to agree. Nicholas was making an utter fool out of himself over that big-breasted harlot. "I'm sure they are just catching up on old times, my dear. She doesn't hold a candle to you, and I'm certain Nicholas realizes it," Johanna pronounced with far more confidence than she felt.

"Well, I intend to enjoy myself this evening. If Nicholas wants to flirt and carry on with his so-called *former* mistress, I can find plenty of men to occupy my time."

But as the evening progressed, Alexandra's time was not occupied with other men but in the constant surveillance of Nicholas and his paramour. Standing in the corner, she observed the couple, noting that Nicholas was drinking far more than usual.

In all the evenings she had spent out with him, he had always been able to hold his liquor. There had been no instances of slurred words and exaggerated motions such as she'd witnessed tonight. Perhaps he was intoxicated by the beauty of Sabrina, she thought, clenching her hands into fists.

Why was she standing here cowering in the corner when she should be fighting for the man she loved?

Drawing herself up to her full height, she marched across the room in Nicholas's direction.

"Nicholas," Alexandra said, tugging on his sleeve, waiting for him to turn around, "I believe this is our dance."

Nicholas lowered his head close to her ear; she grew lightheaded at the power his sensual smile had over her senses.

"Have I been neglecting you, my sweet?" His words were slurred; his breath smelled of brandy. Pulling her close, he planted an intoxicating kiss upon her lips.

Ignoring the malevolent look Sabrina shot at her, she pressed herself into him. "I've felt terribly neglected, Nicholas. Come . . . let's dance." She led him onto the dance floor, reveling in her nearness to him. Sabrina wasn't the only femme fatale in the room, she thought smugly.

Even in his drunken state, Nicholas was a marvelous dancer. As they glided across the floor, her feet seemed to float as if they had wings.

"Are you having fun?" he asked, twirling her about.

"Not nearly as much as you," she replied, unable to resist the dig.

Nicholas's grin was boyish, reminding her of a youth who had been caught tippling his father's cider. "I really don't understand how I could have imbibed so much in such a short time. I had only a couple of glasses of champagne and a shot of brandy," he confessed.

"Perhaps you were so infatuated with your companion that you lost count."

He grinned again. "Is jealousy rearing its evil head, my sweet?"

"Should I be jealous, Nicholas?"

Shrugging his shoulders, he replied, "Sabrina is a beautiful woman; she makes a man feel wanted."

The words pricked her skin like a thousand tiny pins. "And do you want her?" She held her breath, not really wanting to know the answer, afraid that she already did.

The look he gave her was unsettling. "I . . ."

"Alexandra, my dear," Basil interrupted, tapping Nicholas on the shoulder, "you haven't forgotten our dance, have you?"

Nicholas's expression was unreadable as he surrendered Alexandra into Basil's arms. What had he been about to admit? she wondered, cursing Basil under her breath for interrupting their conversation.

She listened with half an ear as Basil regaled her with the latest news from England. Her attention was focused on Nicholas, who was having another drink with Sabrina in a dark, secluded corner.

"Have you set a date for the wedding?" Basil asked.

Looking into his flaccid face, she was reminded of an old hound dog her brother once had. The dog had folds of excess skin that hung down from his cheeks and neck very much like Basil's—only the dog was much more appealing.

"The wedding?" she repeated, trying to pick up the thread of the conversation. "Probably December. I've always wanted a winter wedding."

Alexandra breathed a sigh of relief when the french horns and violins ceased their play and Basil departed, leaving her alone at the refreshment table. Quickly scanning the room for some sign of Nicholas, Alexandra spotted Johanna talking with Lady Dunmore. She approached the pair, apologizing to the governor's wife for spiriting Johanna away.

"Have you seen Nicholas, Johanna?" Alexandra asked, alarmed by the sudden flush that crossed over the older woman's face.

"Alexandra, I . . ." Johanna hesitated, slapping her fan nervously against her palm.

"What is it? I have a right to know." A shiver of apprehension darted through her.

The pity that entered Lady Wellington's eyes could

not be disguised. "I saw Nicholas depart a while ago; he was with Sabrina."

Alexandra's blood flowed like ice water through her veins, creating a chill over her entire body. A brief silence ensued before she found the courage to reply. "Did you see which way they went?" Her heart thudded painfully in her chest; her throat closed, blocked by a large lump of fear.

Johanna nodded. "I was curious; I followed them. They went . . ." She stopped, afraid to continue when she noticed how pale Alexandra had become.

"Please, Johanna. If you know, then tell me. I am not a child."

Johanna's cheeks turned an uncharacteristic shade of crimson. "They went upstairs."

"Upstairs?" Alexandra mouthed stupidly. Upstairs, where Sabrina had a room. Taking Johanna's hand in hers, she patted it reassuringly. "Thank you for telling me. Now you must go and speak to no one about this. I will take care of it."

A loud gasp arose from Johanna Wellington's throat. "You can't mean to follow them!" she cried, grabbing onto Alexandra's arm. "I won't allow it. They could be engaged in . . ." She paused, groping for the right word. ". . . In sordid behavior. It would only upset you."

Drawing on more courage than she realized she possessed, Alexandra calmed the older woman's fears. "If Nicholas has chosen to betray me with that conniving slut, he will be the one to be upset. I can assure you of that, Johanna. Now go. I don't want you involved anymore than you already are."

Watching the stately duchess walk away, Alexandra did not see the satisfied smirk on Basil's face as he watched from his post across the room. The look in his eyes was feral as he observed Alexandra leave the room and head for the stairway.

Alexandra's feet were leaden as she took the steps

# MORE PASSION AND ADVENTURE AWAIT... YOUR TRIP TO A BIG ADVENTUROUS WORLD BEGINS WHEN YOU ACCEPT YOUR FIRST 4 NOVELS ABSOLUTELY *FREE* (AN $18.00 VALUE)

Accept your Free gift and start to experience more of the passion and adventure you like in a historical romance novel. Each Zebra novel is filled with proud men, spirited women and tempt(uous love that you'll remember long after you turn the last pag)

Zebra Historical Romances are the finest novels of their kind. They are written by authors who really know how to weave tales of romance and adventure in the historical settings you love. You'll feel like you've actually gone back in time with the thrilling stories that each Zebra novel offers.

## GET YOUR FREE GIFT WITH THE START OF YOUR HOME SUBSCRIPTION

Our readers tell us that these books sell out very fast in book stores and often miss the newest titles. So Zebra has made arrangements for you to receive the four newest novels published each month.

You'll be guaranteed that you'll never miss a title, and home delivery is so convenient. And to show you just how easy it is to get Zebra Historical Romances, we'll send you your first 4 books absolutely FREE! Our gift to you just for trying our home subscription service.

## BIG SAVINGS AND FREE HOME DELIVERY

Each month, you'll receive the four newest titles as soon as they are published. You'll probably receive them even before the bookstores do. What's more, you may preview these exciting novels free for 10 days. If you like them as much as we think you will, just pay the low preferred subscriber's price of just $3.75 each. *You'll save $3.00 each month off the publisher's price.* AND, your savings are even greater because there are never any shipping, handling or other hidden charges—FREE Home Delivery. Of course you can return any shipment within 10 days for full credit, no questions asked. There is no minimum number of books you must buy.

one at a time. What would she find when she reached the top? she wondered, knowing the answer full well.

When she reached the landing, she paused, listening to the various sounds coming from the rooms. She heard Sabrina's high-pitched giggle floating down the hall from the door to her right. Slowly she approached. Her heart felt heavy in her chest, making it difficult to breathe.

Pausing outside the room, she pressed her ear to the door and listened. "Oh, Nicholas, how I've missed you, my darling." The pain of betrayal cremated her heart, leaving only ashes where cinders of love had once burned.

Taking several deep breaths to stem the rising heat that threatened to make her faint, she placed her hand on the knob and turned. Opening the door, she found her suspicions instantly confirmed.

Sabrina lay sprawled completely naked on the bed. Nicholas lay beneath a sheet, his eyes closed in relaxed slumber. No! her mind screamed. It wasn't true! But it was. It was!

At the sound of the door opening, Sabrina looked up, smiling maliciously. Her green eyes glowed with the thrill of victory. "My dear, you should have knocked." Her laughter was spiteful, filling the room with venomous sounds.

Alexandra slammed the door, shutting out Sabrina's triumphant laughter and the sight of Nicholas in her bed. With tears streaming down her face, she fled the tavern, leaving behind the man she would marry and the love that had become just a painful memory.

Sabrina hadn't felt so wonderful in months. They were going to win, she just knew it. Leaning over, she placed a passionate kiss on the man who lay by her side. There was no response; Nicholas was out cold.

Jumping off the bed, she grabbed her robe and ran to answer Basil's signal. Throwing open the door, she pulled him in, smiling smugly at his questioning gaze.

"Everything went perfect, just as you said." She threw her arms around him.

"She found you in bed together?"

"Yes. The poor little fool didn't bother to look closely enough to see that her darling Nicholas still had his breeches on."

They kissed, their tongues mating wildly as the victim of their scheme slept soundly in the bed. "Sabrina, my dear, I crave your lovely body." He ran his hands inside her robe, fondling her naked breasts.

"Basil, we mustn't. We have to get Nicholas dressed and out of here."

Basil's laughter sent a chill up her spine. "The opiate you put in his drink has done the trick. He will be out for hours." Leading Sabrina by the hand, he laid her down on the bed next to Nicholas.

The idea of bedding Basil while Nicholas slept near them sent a rush of moisture to the apex of her thighs. "What a delicious idea, my darling," she whispered, moving to accommodate her lover. While Basil grunted and groaned his enjoyment, Sabrina closed her eyes, pretending it was Nicholas that filled her body with pleasure.

# Chapter Fifteen

The temperature, as well as the political climate, sizzled during the blistering days of August.

Seated in the rear yard beneath the cool shade of the grape arbor, Alexandra listened while her father and Ben discussed the latest developments in the colony. The Virginia convention had met last week to adopt the resolves forbidding importation of British goods and slaves.

"I'm pleased with the selection of Washington, Henry, Randolph, and the others who have been chosen to represent us at the Congress next month," Samuel declared, eyeing his eldest daughter with concern. Something had happened to Alex while he and Catherine had been in Richmond. She was withdrawn, not at all like her usual self. "What is your opinion, Alex?" he asked, seeking to draw the sullen woman into the conversation.

Sipping slowly on her lemonade, Alexandra paused to consider the questions. "They're a good choice," she concurred. "I was sorry Mister Jefferson was too ill to attend the convention. I'm certain he would have been elected to go."

"Aye," Ben agreed, shaking his head, "his absence will be sorely felt, but the others who have been chosen will perform admirably."

"What does Nicholas think of all this, Alex?" Samuel asked."

Staring into her lap, she avoided the penetrating look her father directed at her. What could she say? That she and Nicholas hadn't spoken more than a few polite words to each other in weeks. That just the mention of his name had the power to wound. She tried to mask her hurt with an air of indifference. "We don't discuss items of a political nature."

"That's probably wise," Samuel said, patting her hand before standing to leave. He hadn't missed the raw hurt glittering in her eyes at the mention of Nicholas's name. What the hell had happened? he wondered. "I'll leave you two children to yourselves. I've got a pile of ledgers on my desk to catch up on," he added before disappearing into the house.

"What's troubling you, shortcake? I thought the news of the Continental Congress would make you euphoric," Ben probed. He suspected something was going on between his sister and the duke, but Alex was closemouthed when it came to Nicholas Fortune.

She smiled wanly. "I'm fine. Just hot. This heat could melt the largest of glaciers."

"And the coldest of hearts?"

Alexandra's head shot up. "What are you saying?"

"Come now, Alex. I'm not blind. I can see things are not going well between you and the duke. It wouldn't have anything to do with the buxom blonde I've seen him with all over town, would it?"

"Don't be ridiculous. I couldn't care. . . ." Quite unexpectedly, the dam that held a flood of tears broke. Alexandra covered her face, sobbing into her hands. Jumping up, she ran for the safety of her bedroom, nearly colliding with Nicholas, who had chosen that particular time to exit the door.

"Alex, wait!" Ben shouted.

"What's wrong?" Nicholas asked, staring at the re-

196

treating figure who darted past him as if the fires of hell were on her heels.

Ben's eyes narrowed; Nicholas's concerned expression irritated him. "Why don't you tell me, Englishman. I'm sure you have a pretty good idea." With that, Benjamin stalked across the yard, exiting by the side gate.

Staring at Ben's retreating back, then to the door that Alexandra had disappeared into, he shook his head. "What in bloody hell is going on?" he said, easing the tension out of his neck with the palm of his hand.

It had all started the night of Basil's party. Christ! He hadn't remembered being that drunk in years. Basil had explained how he had brought him home and deposited him with his valet; Habersham had verified the story.

Alexandra had treated him like the plague ever since that night. He had admitted to drinking too much and had apologized profusely for the fact that he had been too drunk to see her home. But would she accept his apology? Would she offer a little compassion and understanding? Hell no! She had sat in judgment on him and found him guilty. There was not an ounce of forgiveness in her stubborn hide.

Why couldn't she be more understanding, like Sabrina? Sabrina had never chastised him when he had come to her drunk. Instead she had rubbed his temples and other throbbing parts, offering words of consolation.

His member swelled hard and thick like the trunk of an oak tree. It had been a long time since he had lain with a woman . . . too long! Those passionate moments in Alexandra's arms had brought him to the brink of insanity. Christ! He was no saint; he needed a woman.

Sabrina had made it obvious that she wanted him. She had rubbed her breasts in his face, touched him intimately when they were alone, done everything but pull down his breeches and rape him. What the hell was keeping him from taking her up on her offer?

The image of Alexandra's tear-stained face suddenly surfaced. Bloody hell! I'm damned if I do and damned if I don't—so why not do it and enjoy it? he rationalized. He wasn't married yet; he had no vows to honor. He needed a woman, he needed release, and he knew just where he could find them.

His mind made up, Nicholas hastened to the Raleigh. He wasn't going to waste time by castigating himself over his decision. He was going to do it and be done with it. This was for Alexandra's good as well as his own, he told himself, climbing the steps to the tavern door. If things remained unaltered, he would not be able to prevent himself from taking her before their wedding. Yes, he decided, he was doing the right thing.

Once inside, he caught sight of his brother in the dining room. Basil was bent over a table arrayed with various dishes of meat, fowl, and fish. There was enough food on his plate to feed an army, Nicholas thought, shaking his head in disgust. Climbing the steps to the second floor, he checked the time. It was half past two. At the rate Basil was eating, he would be occupied for at least another thirty minutes.

Standing before Sabrina's door, he knocked, waiting but a moment before the door was flung open. Sabrina stood there clad in only her chemise. The sight of her full breasts and long limbs produced an instant response below his waist. He could feel his palms sweat in anticipation of touching those pendulous globes.

"Nicholas, darling! What a pleasant surprise. I thought it was Basil at the door," she said, smiling at the sight of the bulge in his breeches. Licking her lips, she felt triumphant, knowing she had won. Nicholas wanted her, and he was going to have her.

Smiling, Nicholas stepped into the room. "Do you always greet your callers dressed like that?" His eyes devoured her like a hungry man at a banquet. He threw his tricorn on the bed.

Pressing herself into him, Sabrina smiled at him sensually. "Only when I'm hot, darling." She ran her hand down his leg, noting the sheen of perspiration forming on his upper lip. "And I'm very hot right now, Nicholas."

Grabbing her, he thrust his tongue into her mouth, raping it, devouring it with an intensity that surprised him. Inserting his hand into her chemise, he ripped it away, exposing her milky white flesh to his view.

Raising his head, he stared at the silver-headed vixen. She was smiling provocatively, guiding him toward the bed, whispering promises of exquisite pleasure. The sight of those red-painted lips made him stop. Alexandra's sweet smile of innocence rose up to cloud his mind. Christ! What was wrong with him?

Staring at Sabrina, who was laid out before him like an offering from the Gods—the white, pink-tipped confections held up for his scrutiny, he swallowed. It was no use. She was not Alexandra—could never even come close to his fresh-faced virgin. "I'm sorry, Sabrina. I shouldn't have come here."

"Don't be silly, darling. I want you. I've always wanted you."

"But I don't want you." The words were final, his meaning clear. Nicholas picked up his hat, mumbled another apology, and fled out the door.

A rage such as she had never known came over Sabrina. Taking the pewter candlestick from the night stand, she threw it at the door. The metal clanged, hollow like her heart, dropping unbroken to the floor. "You bloody bastard!" she screamed. "If it's the last thing I do, I'll get you for this."

Nicholas heard the crash but did not break his stride. His thoughts were of Alexandra. He had to make things right with her; he needed her. There would be no waiting until they were married. He meant to have her this day.

Bending down over the long row of strawberries, Alexandra picked the plump red fruits, dropping them into her basket. For every five berries she picked, she couldn't resist popping one into her mouth. They were sweet and juicy; she licked her fingers, savoring the taste. Chloe had promised to fix shortcake for dinner tonight . . . to cheer her up, she had said. Frowning, Alexandra crushed the berry she held between her thumb and forefinger. There was nothing short of murder that was going to cheer her up.

A shadow crossed her path. She looked up to find Tom looking down at her. Rising to her feet, she found herself unable to contain the surprise she felt at seeing him. Why had he come? She had not seen or spoken to him since the day of the duel. She knew Alicia had been seeing him regularly, but Tom had not called at the house . . . not until today.

"Hello, Alex," he said, looking more ill at ease than she had ever seen him.

As she stood staring at Tom's face, all her childhood memories came rushing back to her. His nose was lightly sprinkled with freckles, and she remembered how she used to tease him about being kissed by the sun. Her eyes misted at the memory. Wiping her sticky hand on her apron, she held it out to him. "It's good to see you again, Tom. I've missed you," she said, realizing as soon the words were out of her mouth that she meant them. She had missed him. Even with everything that had happened, he was still Tom.

He smiled sheepishly. "I was hoping we could talk. I have something I need to tell you."

Brushing the dirt off her dress and straightening her straw bonnet, she took his arm, leading him to the porch at the rear of the house. A fresh pitcher of lemonade waited on the table. She poured two glasses, handing him one.

"What is it you wish to speak to me about?" Alexandra asked, trying to put him at ease. She could see that he was nervous by the tell-tale flush that covered his arms and neck. Tom always broke out in a rash when he was embarrassed about something.

"I've treated you badly. I've come to say I'm sorry. I was wrong to take out my anger and jealousy on you. I've acted dishonorably." He hung his head.

Reaching out, Alexandra touched his arm. "I forgive you, Tom. We've been friends a long time. I'd like us to be friends again."

"Do you mean that?" he asked, looking up, an uncertain smile on his face. "It's more than I had hoped for."

Returning his smile, she nodded. "We will talk of this no more. It's in the past . . . forgotten. Now tell me what you have been doing."

Looking about to make certain they were alone, he leaned forward. "I've been riding with Ben for the committee. They need every able-bodied man they can find."

"I'm relieved to know my brother has someone he can trust. I know, I don't need to remind you to be careful. What you do is dangerous and mustn't be taken lightly."

"Listen to you. Always mothering me and Ben, even though you're years younger."

"Speaking of younger . . . ." Alexandra paused, uncertain how to broach the subject. "Are you seeing Alicia?"

Tom's blush confirmed her suspicions. Alicia had been reticent about talking of Tom and of her feelings toward him. She was certain her sister had been seeing him, but they had never discussed it.

"Do you mind?"

Sipping thoughtfully on her lemonade, she teased the

rim of her glass with her tongue. "No. Not as long as you realize that she is in love with you."

He smiled. "I know. I love her, too. I've come to ask your father's permission to court Alicia."

The radiance of Alexandra's smile could not be contained. Jumping out of her seat, she threw her arms about the burly cooper. "That's wonderful. I'm so happy for both of you."

Neither of them noticed the dark-haired man who stood just inside the gate, witnessing their expression of mutual affection.

Raw jealousy surged through Nicholas at the sight of Alexandra embracing her former suitor. Clenching the book of sonnets he had purchased for her, he dug his nails into the soft leather. Striding forward, he paused before the porch. "Alexandra." His tone lent a chill to the humid air.

Taking a step back, Alexandra turned to find Nicholas standing a few inches away. He stood staring at them, his face a mask of stone—hard and unyielding. What brings you home so early?" She tried to keep her tone light, unwilling to let him know how his sudden appearance had flustered her.

"It appears I've arrived just in time," he said, staring meaningfully at Tom, who merely nodded in greeting.

"Tom has come to pay court to Alicia. He is here to see my father," she said, unsure of why she felt it necessary to explain anything to her faithless husband-to-be. It was obvious from Nicholas's look that he didn't believe a word she was saying. She was, therefore, grateful when Tom rose and prepared to leave.

"I shall see your father another time, Alex. Please tell him I will return this evening." Tom bowed over her hand, placing a courtly kiss upon it. Turning to face Nicholas, he nodded once more. "My lord." He inclined his head and strode casually away.

"I would like to speak to you, Alexandra," Nicholas

202

said. "Would you please come upstairs with me? I feel the need for some privacy."

She masked the sudden panic his words evoked. "That wouldn't be seemly, my lord. After all, we are not married, yet." Crossing her arms, she refused to budge.

"Don't be obstinate, Alexandra. I am not in the mood. If you will not come of your own free will, I will be forced to carry you. And quite frankly, my sweet, it is too bloody hot for that." Holding open the door, he waited.

Hostility written on her face, Alexandra marched into the house and up the stairs to the room that Nicholas occupied. As she entered, Betsy, who was in the room dusting, looked questioningly at her. "Miss Alex, what are you doing in . . ." Betsy's words trailed off as she caught sight of the duke following close on Alexandra's heels.

"Nicholas wishes to talk with me, Betsy. Perhaps you can finish up in here later."

"That's right, Betsy. Alexandra and I need a bit of privacy. You understand, don't you?" He winked at the maid, who blushed in response.

"Yes sir! I'll see that you're not disturbed."

Closing the door, Nicholas leaned against it, his arms crossed over his chest. "What was Farley doing here? I forbid you to see him again."

Alexandra smiled, picking up a small porcelain figurine of a horse that rested on the pie-crust table. "I'm afraid that's impossible. As I told you, Tom will be paying court to my sister."

"Just make sure that it's your sister he's coming to see, and not you."

"Why, Nicholas, are you jealous?"

A small throb started to pulse in his neck; he placed his hand over it. "I told you once, you belong to me."

The blue of her eyes darkened to midnight. "But

you don't belong to me, is that it?'' she countered, placing the figurine back down on the table.

"What are you talking about? We're to be married.''

"I am quite aware of that fact, my lord. It is too bad you chose to forget it.''

Coming forward, Nicholas dropped the book, grabbing onto Alexandra's arms. "Don't play games with me. If you have something to say, come out and say it.''

Taking a deep breath, Alexandra wrinkled her nose, noting the distinctive scent of lavender that she had smelled before. Her eyes narrowed. "How dare you come to me with the smell of your whore still on your person.'' She tore out of his embrace, crossing to the other side of the room. "You are vile—immoral. Have you no honor?''

Blushing a deep crimson, Nicholas rubbed the back of his neck. He could not deny the accusation; he had acted dishonorably—in thought if not in deed. "You are jumping to conclusions.''

"Do you deny that you were with Sabrina this afternoon?'' Alexandra waited, holding her breath for the answer she knew was coming.

"It isn't what you think. It's true I saw her today, but we did nothing.''

"What's the matter? Was your brother in the way?'' she challenged, walking toward the door. Guilt was written all over Nicholas. Nothing he could say would make her feel differently.

Advancing on her, Nicholas pulled her into him. "Alexandra, I'm telling you the truth. I could have had Sabrina. She's thrown herself at me often enough, but I don't want her. It's *you* I want.''

Liar! she screamed silently. Liar! Liar! Liar! Pushing at his chest, she extricated herself from his embrace. "At least your mistress is honest in her

204

affections. Perhaps you should take some lessons from her, Nicholas," she said, slamming out of the room.

Nicholas stood transfixed. The book of sonnets he had purchased lay forgotten at his feet. How could Alexandra have known what went on today? he wondered. It was impossible. He had been discreet. What, then, was she accusing him of?

Dropping down on the bed, he held his head within his hands. "I have been accused, found guilty, and sentenced, and I don't even know what I have done."

Marching into her bedroom, Alexandra slammed the door as hard as she could. The vibration sent the sampler over the fireplace crashing to the floor.

"I hate him," she screamed, crossing over to pick up the cherished needlework she had spent so many hours on. She ran her hand over the crudely fashioned letters, tracing each one reverently. If only life could be as simple as it was when she was twelve, she thought, sighing. She put the embroidery back in its place.

A moment later a soft knock sounded. Her stomach knotted until she heard her mother's soft voice floating through the door. "Alex, dear, may I come in?"

She faced her mother across the threshold. Catherine's tender smile was the key that unlocked the anguish in Alexandra's heart. Throwing herself into her mother's arms, she wept for all the shattered hopes and dreams that were no more.

Wrapped up in their grief and consolation, neither woman observed Nicholas, who had just entered the hall. He stood, mouth agape, unable to believe the scene he was witnessing. When the door to Alexandra's room closed, he stared at it for a moment, pondering the complexities of the female mind. Shaking his head, he decided that running the colony in Governor Dunmore's absence was not the biggest or the most difficult challenge facing him at the moment. He proceeded down the hall.

"My dear, what is troubling you? I have never seen

205

you so distraught." Catherine held her daughter at arm's length, waiting for her to confide her sorrow. Samuel's instincts had been correct: something was very wrong with Alexandra. Tipping up the tear-stained face, Catherine asked again, "What is wrong, my dear?"

Breaking free of her mother's embrace, Alexandra flung her arms in the air, pacing across the floor. "Everything is wrong, Mother. I am wrong. Nicholas is wrong. This whole idea of a marriage is wrong. It will never work."

"Please sit down here by the hearth and explain what has happened," Catherine said, taking a seat. She patted the space next to her.

Dropping down into the chair, Alexandra swung her head from side to side. "I can't tell you."

Picking up her daughter's hand, which felt as cold as her eyes looked at the moment, Catherine studied the pale face. Dark circles that hadn't been there before shadowed her eyes. Alexandra looked spiritless—defeated. Alarm filtered through her. "Alex, you must know that I will keep your confidence. If you have acted indiscreetly with the duke, there will be no admonitions on my part. I am hardly the one to pass judgment after the mistakes I have made in my life."

Observing the pain glistening in her mother's eyes, Alexandra sought to comfort her. "It is nothing I have done, Mother. It is Nicholas."

A knowing light came into Catherine's eyes. "Does this have something to do with that blonde creature I have seen about town?"

Alexandra's eyes widened. "You know?"

"My dear, I may be your mother, but I am still a woman. I am not immune to what goes on around me. When I first laid eyes on that vixen, I smelled trouble brewing. Why, even your father has cast a sly glance in her direction." At the look of misery on her daughter's face, she added, "Always remember, Alex, even though men find women like that attractive, they don't marry them.''

Small consolation, Alexandra thought. They don't marry them, but they still bed them. The Sabrinas of the world get all the pleasures of marriage with none of the headaches. ''She is Nicholas's mistress.''

''Is?'' Catherine's eyebrow shot up. ''It was my understanding that she was his former mistress.''

''That was my understanding, too, until circumstances taught me differently.''

''My dear, loving a man is the hardest thing you will ever do in your life. There will be times when you must look the other way and believe only what your heart dictates. Nicholas reminds me a great deal of Charles. He is a man of passion but also honor. Things are not always what they seem, Alex. Let your heart guide you.''

''Now you sound like Chloe.''

''Chloe's a smart woman. She has suffered a great deal of heartache in her life, but it never held her back.''

''But Nicholas betrayed me!''

''I know how difficult it is to love someone when your mind tells you it's wrong but your heart doesn't listen. I was lucky, Alex. I had a second chance at finding another love. Your father and I have been very happy together. But a love like ours is rare. If you love Nicholas, you must decide if you will listen to your heart or heed the warnings in your head. The decision must be yours. But if you make the wrong one, be prepared to suffer for it the rest of your life.''

Alexandra sat staring into the fireplace long after her mother departed. It was cold and empty, just like her heart felt at the moment. Why couldn't there be a simple answer? she wondered, picking at the colorful pieces of cloth that made up the braided rug beneath her. Up until now, life had been logical. There was right and there was wrong. You chose independence or subjugation. There was no gray, only black and white. Now everything was different. Nicholas had made it so. She was being forced to reevaluate everything she had been taught—everything that she believed in.

If only she didn't love him. If only he hadn't come here. But she did, and he did. And now she must decide.

# Chapter Sixteen

Like a flame smoldering in a bed of dry autumn leaves, the increasing hostility between Virginia and England continued to ferment. Governor Dunmore returned in October to find the seeds of dissent that the Continental Congress had germinated the month before in Philadelphia falling over Virginia as well as the other colonies.

Dunmore faced Nicholas across the tapestry-covered table in the council chamber, a grave expression on his face. Lord Wellington, advisor to the governor, sat to Nicholas's right. Basil Fortune, who had offered his unwavering loyalty to the Crown, sat on his left.

"We are faced with a difficult situation, gentlemen. Virginia views herself as an independent state, unaccountable to a superior power. This Congress that has taken place has only served to fuel the fires of discontent."

Nicholas listened inattentively as the governor droned on about the difficulties in the colonies. He had his own problems to contend with at the moment. He still had not been able to smooth matters over with Alexandra. Praise and compliments had fallen on deaf ears. Although she now spoke to him and acknowledged his existence, she still refused to allow any intimacy between them. A chaste kiss on her hand was as far as he had gotten these past few months. Celibacy had become a way of life for him. He might as well have become a monk for all the good his title and fortune had done him, he thought, snorting.

"Did you wish to offer a comment, Nicholas?" the governor asked, pausing in his diatribe.

Nicholas looked up, the heat rising up his neck. He shifted in his seat, trying to refocus his attention on the matter at hand. "Perhaps some of the grievances the colonies make are justified, my lord. Maybe we should seek a means to arbitrate their demands."

The governor stood, anger evident in the red flush covering his face. "Never!" he shouted, banging his fist on the table. "Great Britain will make no concessions to these insurrectionists. They will bend or break."

"I quite agree," Basil interjected, turning to face his brother. "I'm quite surprised at your position, Nicholas. You are, after all, a lord of the realm, sworn to uphold the dictates of the King. How can you take the colonists' part?"

Nicholas eyed his brother with contempt, wondering what Basil, who had never had a political opinion in his life up until now, was trying to prove. "I have tried to keep an open mind. Might does not always make right. We must be tolerant or suffer the consequences."

"You talk as if you know something we do not, Lord Blackstone," Frederick Wellington said. "Have you specifics to back up your dire predictions?"

Shaking his head, Nicholas replied, "No, my lords, I do not. But if there is no remedy to contain the disease of discontent, it will spread like an epidemic throughout the colonies."

His words produced rumblings of displeasure throughout the room. Nicholas sat back, crossing his arms over his chest, listening to the harsh words of censure directed at him. Who would have thought he would be compared to the likes of Patrick Henry? He smiled inwardly, realizing the comparison didn't bother him at all.

Fools, Nicholas thought, as he made his way to the Courtland home. Why should he waste his time worrying about the Crown's problems with the colony? They never listened to anything he had to say. He had more important things to think about, such as trying to figure out a way to salvage his union with Alexandra. He kicked at the decaying red and gold leaves at his feet. Decaying. An apt word to describe his relationship with Alexandra at the moment. There must be a way to reach her. He had to find out what was bothering her. Determination dogging his steps, he hurried home.

The object of Nicholas's concern was seated in the kitchen, watching Chloe prepare apple pies for supper. With her head propped up between her hands, Alexandra inhaled the spicy scents of nutmeg and cinnamon permeating the room; her stomach growled.

"Mercy, chile, ain't you eaten today? You sounds as if you plumb empty inside."

Smiling at Chloe's remarks, Alexandra picked off a piece of leftover crust, stuffing it into her mouth. "I have a big appetite," she replied. But the truth was, she hadn't been eating well at all. Her dresses hung on her, and if she wasn't careful, the little she had up on top was going to disappear altogether.

Try as she might, she still hadn't been able to reconcile her feelings for Nicholas. She loved him; there was no doubt about that. But how could she forgive a man who had betrayed her with another woman? Every night when she sat across the table from him at supper, her appetite vanished. All she had to do was conjure up the scene of Nicholas lying in Sabrina's bed, and she was unable to eat a bite.

"A woman can't live on love alone, chile. You had best eat so you can fill out that dress of yours."

"I just haven't been that hungry lately, Chloe."

"Hmph! If my man had his eye on another woman, I sure as heck wouldn't be moping around, turning into an old scarecrow. I'd do everything in my power to look beautiful so's I could win him back." She glanced at the mournful child out of the corner of her eye, trying to gauge her reaction.

Alexandra tilted her chin defiantly, her cheeks flashing as red as the apples in the earthenware bowl. "Maybe, I don't want to win him back."

Shoving a piece of hot apple pie and a glass of milk under her nose, Chloe retorted, "Well, just in case you have a mind to, I'd start by sweetening up that disposition of yours. A man don't like to come home to a grumpy woman. Especially after he's had him a hard day of working."

A twinkle entered Alexandra's eyes as she stared at the mock expression of disapproval on the black woman's face. Chloe could always be counted on to render an opinion, whether it was asked for or not. Taking a bite of the pie, she savored its tartness before remarking, "You know, for an old woman, you have some pretty sound ideas."

Admonishing Alexandra with the threat of her rolling pin, Chloe snorted. "Who says I'm old? There's plenty of spark left in this black hide. Why, I could put you younguns to shame, iff'n I had a mind to."

Smiling at the cook's indignation, Alexandra felt her heart lighten and her appetite increase. Pushing her plate forward, she winked. "I think I'd like another piece of pie."

The next morning at breakfast, Alicia was atwitter over the fair that was going to be held the following week. Between bites of buttermilk pancakes and sau-

212

sages, she regaled Nicholas and the rest of the Court-lands with news of the event.

"It's going to be ever so much fun, Alex. Are you and Nicholas planning to go?" Alicia asked.

Unwilling to face the black eyes boring into her as she bent over her meal, Alexandra concentrated on the food before her. "I don't think so," she mumbled under her breath.

"What did you say, Alex?" Alicia persisted. "Father says he won't let me go with Tom if you and Nicholas aren't there to chaperon."

"That's true, dear. You're much too young to be traipsing off by yourself with a man," Catherine said, smiling indulgently at her youngest child.

Alicia stuck out her lower lip but said nothing.

When Alexandra finally raised her head to look about the table, she was confronted with four innocent smiles. A feeling of suspicion was beginning to take root and grow. Looking into Nicholas's eyes, which twinkled like wet obsidian, she felt a conspiracy forming.

"I'm sure Nicholas has far more important things to do besides attend a silly fair." *A silly fair* . . . had she really said that? The annual fair held every autumn had been the highlight of her youth. She could recall every puppet show, every horse race and fireworks display that she had ever witnessed.

Setting down his cup of sassafras tea, Nicholas appraised the woman before him. Alexandra's wan appearance bothered him. Her eyes no longer sparkled in mischief; her lips no longer smiled in joy. He was aware she had been trying to avoid him. This was the perfect opportunity to breach the wall she had erected between them.

"On the contrary, Alexandra—I believe I would enjoy attending such a function. Part of my role here as aide to the governor is to experience as many of the local customs as I can."

"See, Alex," Alicia blurted out, "you have no excuse. You and Nicholas can accompany Tom and me. What do you say?''

Four pair of eyes waited eagerly for her answer. Her parents' smiles were encouraging, Alicia's hopeful, but it was Nicholas's smile that captivated and intrigued her. It was filled with such blatant sexuality and promise, a twitter of excitement ran up and down her spine, landing like a swarm of locusts in the middle of her stomach. His eyes held her spellbound until she heard her sister's entreaty.

"Come on, Alex, are we going?''

Tearing herself away from Nicholas's gaze, a warm flush dusting her cheeks, Alexandra smiled at Alicia, whose eyes held the look of youthful expectancy. "Far be it for me to spoil anyone's plans. I will go.''

Alicia's excited giggles produced a loud chuckle from Nicholas. Like a magnet unable to avoid the pull, Alexandra's eyes were drawn to his smiling lips, lips she remembered so well: lips that promised, lips that pleasured, lips that lied. Throwing down her napkin, she excused herself and hurried from the room.

Nicholas stared at Samuel, who could only offer a shrug and a shake of his head.

"Give her time, Nicholas,'' Catherine offered. "Time heals all wounds.''

"But what have I done?'' he asked, hoping to finally find out the answer to this dilemma he'd been thrust into.

Wiping her lips on the white linen napkin, Catherine smiled sympathetically. "That is between you and Alexandra.'' Turning to face her husband, she said, "Come, Samuel, you promised to help me bring down those chairs from the attic today.''

Watching the couple depart, Nicholas felt more confused than ever.

"Are you and my sister having a disagreement?'' Alicia asked.

Turning his head, Nicholas found a pair of bright

blue eyes disturbingly enough like Alexandra's to be disquieting staring up at him. "It's just a small misunderstanding. Nothing for you to worry about."

"If that's true, why do I hear Alex crying all the time? What did you do to her?" The look she directed at him was full of accusation.

Shaking his head, a miserable expression on his face, he replied, "I wish I knew, Alicia."

"Well, why don't you ask her, for heaven's sake! When two people love each other, there shouldn't be any secrets between them." Pushing herself out of her chair, she gave Nicholas one long look of disgust before exiting the room.

Love. Was it possible Alexandra was in love with him? No. She couldn't be. She had given him every indication that she hated him, despised him. Still, if she was in love with him, that would explain her erratic behavior of late. Women were such fanciful creatures, giving themselves over to all sorts of sentimental notions.

Perhaps if he played his cards right, everything would work out after all. When he married, he would retain his estates and fortune and gain a woman who was madly in love with him. The thought produced a grin as wide as the James River.

Rising from the table, Nicholas felt better than he had in weeks. Heading for the door with a jaunty spring in his step, he suddenly skidded to a halt. The smile he wore turned upside down; he rubbed his chin thoughtfully. Why should the thought of Alexandra loving him make him happy? he wondered, shaking his head. This was to be a marriage of convenience, not a love match.

Unless, of course, he was in love with her, too. He froze, his stomach dropping down to his feet. Impossible! The thought was too absurd to consider. Or was it?

* * *

The main street of Williamsburg was crowded as the four fairgoers made their way to the courthouse green. The afternoon air held a slight chill, owing to the absence of the sun. The autumn leaves littered the ground like a brown and gold carpet, crunching noisily beneath the soles of eight impatient feet.

Nicholas and Tom shared a smile as they watched the two Courtland sisters race ahead to catch the start of the puppet show.

"They're something, are they not, my lord?" Tom asked, chuckling and shaking his head. "Alex hasn't changed a bit since she was knee high to a ground hog. She's still full of gaiety and mischief."

"She's a handful. I'll grant you that. She'd led me a merry chase since my arrival."

Taking hold of Nicholas's arm to halt his stride, Tom's expression grew serious. "I owe you an apology, my lord."

"Nicholas," he corrected.

Tom smiled gratefully. "Nicholas, my conduct has been unforgivable. I hope you will accept my apology. I've already given it to Alex. Those things I said . . . they weren't true."

"Alexandra forgave you soon after you uttered them. She knew your words stemmed from hurt and not hate."

"She has a kind heart," Tom said.

Nicholas's look was wistful. "Aye, she does." Though he hadn't been the recipient of much of her kindness lately. "Shall we rejoin our two ladies?" he suggested. "We don't want them to have too much fun without us."

Grinning, Tom slapped Nicholas on the back. "You know, for an Englishman, you're not half bad."

Arching his brow, Nicholas replied, "Coming from

216

a colonial and a Virginian at that, I take your admission as a compliment.''

They were laughing loudly when they rejoined the sisters. Alicia and Alexandra stared in amazement at the duo.

"What do you make of those two?" Alicia whispered, observing the two former rivals who were engaged in easy comaraderie.

Shaking her head, a disapproving look on her face, Alexandra stared at the two grinning faces. "They've probably been in the hard cider.''

The two girls looked at the men and then at each other and burst out laughing.

"Might I inquire as to what you lovely ladies find so amusing?" Nicholas asked, slipping his arm around Alexandra's shoulders. He felt her stiffen but ignored her response.

"Why, the puppet show, of course!" Alicia volunteered, smiling impishly to reveal two charming dimples.

The puppet show the girls took such a delight in bordered on the edge of irreverence to the Crown. The puppets, dressed as proper English members of the nobility, were made to look like buffoons.

"Well, if you're finished watching those puppets ridicule us Englishmen, I'd like to get something to eat,'' Nicholas said, his smile belying the indignation that his words implied.

"Eat!" Alexandra exclaimed. "We just finished dinner an hour ago.''

"You know what an enormous appetite I have, my sweet,'' he replied, nibbling her ear.

Every nerve ending in Alexandra's body tingled at Nicholas's bold advance. Grabbing hold of Alicia's arm, she extricated herself from his embrace and yanked her sister toward Duke of Gloucester Street. She was not going to fall into Nicholas's arms this time.

She needed to keep her distance—needed to keep her wits about her.

"Alexandra!" Alicia shouted, grinding to a halt. "What are you trying to do? I want to walk with Thomas, not with you." She looked back to see the object of her affection coming toward them.

"Alicia!" Alexandra pleaded, noting that Nicholas was closing in on them.

"I wish you and Nicholas would stop acting so childish. I want to have a good time, and you're being a stick-in-the-mud."

When Tom and Nicholas finally caught up with them, Alicia latched onto Tom's hand, hauling him off.

Seeing Alexandra's look of dismay, Nicholas laughed. "What's the matter, my sweet? Did your reluctant companion desert you? Well, no matter, we'll just strive to have fun by ourselves." Pulling her by the arm, he led her in the direction of the food vendor.

Alexandra shot Nicholas a venomous look until the odor of hot cider and shrewsbury cakes overcame her resistance. "Hungry, my sweet?" he asked, holding up an enticing sweet cake.

Her eyes lit up; her stomach rumbled. Blushing, she inclined her head.

"How about trading this cake and a cup of hot cider for a smile?"

Uncertain blue eyes darted nervously between the tempting sweets in Nicholas's hands and the tempting smile on his lips. Unable to resist his persuasive bribe, Alexandra nodded, flashing him a heart-stopping smile.

"Basil," Sabrina whispered, grabbing onto her companion's arm. "Nicholas and Alexandra are over by the gypsy's wagon."

Tearing his eyes away from the cockfight in progress, Basil gazed in the direction Sabrina indicated and shrugged. "I have a lot of money riding on these matches, my dear. I can't worry about those two at the moment. Now be quiet and watch the contest like a good girl. As soon as it ends, we'll discuss what's to be done."

Flashing Basil a malevolent look, Sabrina turned to stare into the cockpit. Although the matches were held outside on the Courthouse Green, she still couldn't abide the horrible odor that permeated the air. Dozens of men and women were pressed in close proximity, watching the gruesome event. Wrinkling her nose at the smell of death mingled with the unwashed bodies that surrounded her, she lifted her handkerchief to her face.

As the next match prepared to get under way, she stared in revulsion at the two feathered combatants who were ready to engage in a battle to the death.

The cocks were armed with long, sharp, steel pointed gaffs which were attached to their natural spurs. Much to her dismay, Basil had meticulously explained every disgusting detail to her prior to the event.

The birds stepped about the ring, full of pride and dignity, circling each other to gauge their opposition. Suddenly they flew at each other, screeching and gawking, attempting to drive the deadly gaffs into each other's bodies.

As the first blow was struck, Sabrina covered her mouth, stifling the scream that rose to her throat at the sight of the blood spurting from the now lifeless bird on the left.

Casting a quick glance at Basil, who was smiling, she shivered. No doubt he had won his wager, she thought.

"Did you see how that cock took the other down in one blow? By jove, it was magnificent!" Basil said, taking Sabrina by the arm and guiding her away from the crowded area. They paused by the courthouse steps. "What did you wish to talk to me about?"

Shaken by the terrible scene she had just witnessed, Sabrina almost forgot what had caused her original dismay. "Nicholas is here with Alexandra."

Frowning, Basil scanned the area until his eyes landed on the laughing couple who waited outside the gypsy's wagon. "It would appear my brother has been successful in convincing the mindless chit of his fidelity. He always was a smooth talker. Perhaps it is time to go over and pay them another visit."

Sabrina's expression was doubtful. "Nicholas made it quite clear that he wasn't interested in resuming our alliance. I told you that." God, how humiliating his rejection had been. She had told Basil everything except that fact.

"Alexandra doesn't know that. It's up to you to make her think otherwise."

Sabrina's green eyes glittered dangerously as they fell on the happy couple; she was unable to stem the rising jealousy in her breast. Smiling vindictively, she nodded.

"Do you wish to have your fortune told, my sweet? I believe it is our turn," Nicholas offered.

Staring at the garishly painted yellow wagon decorated with stars and moons, Alexandra rubbed her hands together, pondering her decision. She had promised herself each time the fair came to town she would seek out the gypsy and have her fortune read. But each year she had made an excuse; she had not had the courage to enter the gypsy's wagon. This time, she was going to do it.

She nodded. "I've never done this before."

"There are a few things you've yet to experience, my sweet. All the more reason to savor each as they are presented and learn from them."

Flushing at Nicholas's words, Alexandra felt the familiar bud of desire blooming within her. Swallowing, she climbed into the wagon with Nicholas following right behind.

Entering the dark interior, she paused, letting her eyes adjust to the dimness.

"Come in, come in," the foreign accented voice directed. "I am Madame Olga. Do you wish for me to tell your fortune?"

Alexandra nodded, taking a seat on the narrow bench next to Nicholas.

"Good . . . good. Give me your hand, Alexandra."

Gasping, Alexandra clutched her throat. "How do you know my name?"

The old woman cackled, the sound reminding Alexandra of dried twigs being crushed beneath a wagon wheel.

"It is my business to know. Now, give me your hand."

Placing her hand in Madame Olga's gnarled one, Alexandra waited, studying the wrinkled face of the ageless woman. She had a swarthy complexion. Her white hair flowed down straight, hanging about her shoulders like a mantle of rabbit fur. She wore a red silk scarf tied about her head and two gold hoops in her ears. Her eyes were the palest of blues. They were almost transparent, as if one could see all the way into her soul.

"You are very perceptive, Alexandra."

The words made her jump.

"I see a wedding in your future. Am I right?"

Alexandra looked at Nicholas who winked. She nodded.

"Ah, yes," Madame Olga added, casting her gaze in Nicholas's direction, "this is the lucky man. He has traveled a great distance to wed you. You are troubled by this man. You think he does not love you, but you are wrong. His destiny and yours were made many years before you were born. You are bound together for eternity."

An intense heat covered Alexandra's entire body. She felt faint, numbed by the words the gypsy uttered.

221

Ripping her hand away, she laughed to cover her nervousness. "Now you must read Nicholas's fortune," she said, expecting to find an amused smile on Nicholas's lips. But when she glanced over to where he was sitting, he was staring at her with an odd unfathomable light in his eyes. Shivering uncontrollably, she moved to the rear of the wagon.

Madame Olga took Nicholas's hand and squeezed it; her face shadowed with fear. "Take care, my son. You have enemies."

Nicholas smiled, thinking of Sabrina's recent threats and Alexandra's surly moods. "You're probably right," he agreed.

The old woman shook her head. "You will be tested; you will have pain." She closed her eyes, rocking back and forth. A moment later, she stopped. "You are a man who keeps his feelings hidden. I cannot delve too deeply into your spirit. This is all I can tell you."

Reaching into his waistcoat, Nicholas extracted a gold coin, pressing it into the old woman's hand.

"Take care, Nicholas and Alexandra," the gypsy said. "Trust in each other. It will be your salvation."

The fortune teller's words sent shivers of apprehension coursing through Alexandra's body as she stepped down the narrow steps at the back of the wagon. When Nicholas alighted, she grabbed onto his arm, unable to mask the fear and worry on her face. "I'm scared, Nicholas. Do you think what she said was true?"

Taking her hand, which was now cold and clammy, he squeezed it, trying to make light of her fears. "Which part?" he said, grinning.

Two circles of red dotted her cheeks as she realized the implication of her question. "Never mind. I'm just being fanciful. I don't believe in fortunes . . . of any kind."

Nicholas smiled. "Well, the old woman may be right about mine. Here comes a large dose of bad luck."

Glancing in the direction Nicholas was staring, she

observed Sabrina and Basil coming toward them. Bile rose in her throat as she took in the triumphant smile on Sabrina's lips. She would never forget that look as long as she lived.

"Nicholas, my darling. I . . ."

"Excuse us, won't you?" Nicholas interrupted, grabbing Alexandra's hand. "Alexandra and I are late for an engagement." Ignoring the strangled cries of indignation emanating from Sabrina's throat and the shocked expression on Basil's face, he strode quickly away, pulling Alexandra with him.

When they reached the grounds of the Governor's Palace, Nicholas finally slowed his pace. "Forgive me, my sweet. I didn't mean to tire you," he apologized, guiding her to a bench.

Taking a minute to catch up, she inhaled deeply, her breath visible in the chill that descended on the early evening. "It wasn't necessary to avoid talking with your brother and your friend on my account," she said.

Nicholas smiled, taking a seat next to her. "You should know by now, Alexandra, that I do only what suits me. I have no desire to converse with either my brother or Sabrina. I'd much rather spend my time with you."

His words warmed her heart. A tiny spark of hope ignited in her breast, flaring into a burning flame at the sincerity she saw in his eyes. The words the gypsy woman spoke came back to haunt her: *Trust in each other. It will be your salvation.* She decided to heed the woman's advice.

"I am flattered to hear that, my lord," she said. Their faces were only scant inches apart, and she knew he was going to kiss her. When he pulled her into his embrace, she didn't resist, letting her heart and not her head rule her emotions.

# Chapter Seventeen

The days were turning colder. Frost iced the pumpkins that remained in the garden. The leaves had fallen, scattered by the chill November winds that tugged them off their branches, sending them swirling into space.

Staring out her window, Alexandra watched as the more tenacious leaves clung to their limbs, refusing to give in to the force of the wind. She knew how they felt. It was how she had acted for so long with Nicholas. She had fought against the inevitable—her marriage, her love. But now she had surrendered, given in to her heart's desire. She had taken a chance that her fragile love would not be torn asunder and scattered like the leaves.

The meeting with the gypsy had changed everything. Alexandra sensed a new maturity within herself. Her feelings for Nicholas had grown stronger, more intense. She had learned to forgive his affair with Sabrina; she would never forget, only accept, as she must to go on.

She sensed a change in Nicholas as well. It was as if he were seeing her for the very first time. He treated her with a reverence and respect that was maddening. She would have given in to him on more than one occasion these past few weeks. It had only been his strength, his willpower to resist her, that had kept her virtue intact. She had no self-control when it come to loving him. She didn't know how she would survive the remaining three weeks until their wedding.

"Miss Alex," Betsy said, sticking her head in the door. "Miss Alex," she said again, louder this time.

Spinning about, Alexandra's eyes widened as she caught sight of Betsy framed in the doorway.

"Sorry to disturb you, but I've brought the wedding gown for you to try on. Your mother is a bit taller, so we might need to take up the hem a bit."

"Come in, Betsy. I've just been daydreaming," Alexandra admitted, stripping off her red wool gown in preparation for the fitting.

Taking the white satin gown from Betsy's outstretched hands, Alexandra held it up in front of her, gazing at her reflection in the looking glass. It was a lovely gown, robe à la Française embroidered with tiny white silk rosebuds. The petticoat, also white, was deeply flounced with rows of lace and quillings. Staring wistfully at her reflection, she tried to imagine what her mother had looked like on her wedding day.

"You'll make a beautiful bride, Miss Alex," Betsy said, dabbing at her eyes.

The quiet weeping of the housekeeper drew Alexandra's immediate attention. "What's wrong, Betsy?" she asked, throwing the gown on the bed as she approached. "I thought you'd be elated to finally get rid of me. You should be happy for me, not sad."

"I'm just a sentimental old fool. It hasn't been that long ago that I changed your linens and kissed your hurts. Now you're all grown up."

Giving Betsy a hug, her own eyes starting to fill, Alexandra replied, "I'm going to miss you, too."

"I'm afraid you won't get much of a chance, miss."

Bewildered by the statement, Alexandra's eyebrow crinkled. "Why not?"

"Will and I are getting married. We'll be living with his lordship . . . if that's all right with you."

"Married! All right? Of course it's all right. Oh, Betsy, I'm so happy for you. Does Nicholas know?"

"I daresay he does by now. Will was going to break the news to him right after dinner."

Alexandra smiled. *Will*. Somehow she would never be able to call the redoubtable Habersham "Will."

"We must inform mother. We'll have to have a small engagement party to celebrate." Rushing to the door, she was just about to turn the knob when Betsy's voice halted her in midstride.

"Miss Alex!" Betsy shouted.

Turning impatiently, Alexandra frowned. "What is it? I must hurry."

Betsy's smile was full of tenderness. "Don't you think you should get dressed first? It wouldn't do to tempt his lordship so close to the wedding."

"Nicholas, don't forget to fetch those items on the list for the party tonight, especially the silver salts from the Golden Ball. Mister Craig is supposed to have the engraving done by this afternoon."

Nicholas listened attentively as Alexandra rattled off the articles she would need in preparation for this evening's celebration. It was amusing, in a perverse sort of way, to think that he, a duke, was actually shopping for his valet. He couldn't help the grin that covered his lips as he studied Alexandra seated behind her father's massive desk. She was a pint-sized despot, flinging orders that would have made her General Washington proud.

Thinking of Washington wiped the smile off his face. Matters were heating up in Virginia. He didn't like the road these colonials were traveling.

Only the week before a group of irate Yorktown citizens, mimicking their brethren to the north, had held a tea party of their own. They had boarded the ship *Virginia,* dumping into the York River two and a half chests of tea that had been shipped from London to John Prentis in Williamsburg.

In addition, two days after that incident, nearly five hundred merchants had gathered to sign the Continental Association, prohibiting the importation of British goods. The embargo was to take effect the first day of December.

Didn't these Virginians realize what their actions would instigate? The Crown would retaliate with a punishment so severe, these ill-equipped farmers and merchants would have no protection against it.

"Nicholas! Are you paying attention?" Alexandra chided, rising from her chair behind the desk with another piece of parchment. She smiled apologetically, handing him her list. "I've thought of a few more items."

"Good God!" Nicholas shouted, reading over the list. "I'll be out all afternoon doing your bidding. Is there no one else you can send?"

She shook her head. "You know there isn't. Everything must be perfect for Betsy's party. Please!" she implored.

Grabbing her about the waist, Nicholas pulled her into him. "You're turning me into a henpecked husband, and we're not even married yet."

Draping her arms about his neck, she pressed herself into him. "Perhaps I can offer you a reward for your sacrifice." She covered his mouth with her own, plunging her tongue between his lips. She kissed him passionately, wantonly, until she heard his groan of pleasure. Lifting her head, she saw the flames of desire burning bright within his eyes.

"Nicholas, let's sneak over to our new house. We can be alone; no one will disturb us there." They had rented the Widow Palmer's house on Nicholson Street only last week. It was fully furnished, complete with a large tester bed in the upstairs master suite. "It's silly to wait. I'm tired of waiting. I don't want to wait anymore.''

"Alexandra, lower your voice. Someone might hear you.''

"I don't care. We're to be married. Is it a crime to desire your future husband? Oh, Nicholas, please. I ache for you.''

Wiping the perspiration that formed on his brow, Nicholas shoved the handkerchief back in his pocket. "My sweet, your words and kisses torture me. I'm trying to be strong for both of us. We only have a short time left until our wedding." He kissed the tears that slid down her cheek. "Have you forgotten Betsy and Habersham's party? They would be terribly disappointed.''

Nicholas couldn't believe he was actually throwing away a chance to bed his beautiful bride-to-be. He must be crazy, he thought, trying to get his emotions under control. He had promised himself that they would wait until after the ceremony. He wouldn't pray on Alexandra's innocence or lack of experience. He owed her that much. To think he had almost sullied their union by succumbing to Sabrina's wiles. This was his self-inflicted punishment. He deserved to suffer, and by God, he was suffering.

The nagging suspicion that hid at the back of Alexandra's mind suddenly surfaced with a vengeance. Breaking free of Nicholas's embrace, her face full of accusation, she confronted him. "Do you desire someone else? Is that why you won't make love to me?''

"No, for Christ's sake!" he yelled so loudly that she jumped back a step.

Nicholas was filled with anger, frustration, and pent-up desire. "Do you know how long it has been since I've made love to a woman?" He didn't wait for her answer. "Almost eight months. Eight long, frustrating months. Does that sound like a man who desires another woman?''

Pulling her into him, he grabbed her hand, placing it on his hardened shaft. "Feel what you do to me. You are not the only one suffering, my sweet. I ache to fill your needs."

"Oh, Nicholas," she wailed, caressing his cheek, "I'm so sorry. Can you ever forgive me?"

"For desiring me, never! For being impatient, yes. Now go and prepare this evening's fete. And remember, every time I look at you, I undress you with my eyes . . . I bathe your body with my tongue . . . I fill you with my seed."

Every word Nicholas whispered into her ear pulled the strings of Alexandra's emotions tighter and tighter. His words stroked her as effectively as his hands. When he insinuated his hand between them, covering her mound through the voluminous folds of her skirt, she pressed into him.

"This is a treasure to be savored slowly," he said, pressing the palm of his hand into her. "I want to unfold you . . . unwrap the prize you hide within."

The tauntness between Alexandra's legs snapped. She grew wet, convulsing against his hand as he spoke. "My love, my love," she crooned, thrashing her head back wildly.

Nicholas cradled her within his arms. "It won't be long, my sweet, until I can make you mine."

After a few moments, her breathing returned to normal. Looking up, she blushed at the self-satisfied grin she saw on Nicholas's face. "You must think me a terrible wanton," she said.

Kissing her nose, Nicholas smiled knowingly. "Not wanton, my sweet, only wanting. There's a big difference."

Straightening his coat and stock, he brushed back the unruly strands of hair that had escaped his queue. "I'll see you later this afternoon when I'm done with my assignment." Holding up his lists, he blew her a kiss and exited the room.

Staring transfixed at the door, Alexandra smiled in satisfaction. Hugging herself, she warmed at the thought of what had just transpired. Whatever uncertainties marriage to Nicholas might hold, she would never doubt his desire for her again.

Positioned across the street from the Courtland house, Sabrina shivered within the folds of her woolen cloak as she observed the normal routines of the occupants within.

She had maintained a vigil these past two weeks, determined to find a way to exact her revenge on Nicholas and Alexandra.

The activity in the house had increased the past two days. She had learned from the milliner, Missus Hunter, that a party was being planned.

She sneered. How coarse and common these people were to actually entertain the idea of giving a party for a couple of servants! Basil had laughed when she'd told him, deriding Nicholas for stooping to the level of these colonials, pointing out how unfit he was to hold the title of duke.

Although she had told Basil of the party, she mentioned nothing of her plans. Basil would never approve of what she was going to do. She smiled, rubbing her hands together to ward off the chill. Revenge was going to be sweet. She didn't need Basil to end Nicholas's marriage plans; she had a few ideas of her own.

"Something sure smells good," Alexandra said, taking a deep breath as she entered the kitchen. "That wouldn't be sweet potato pie I smell, would it?"

Chloe turned, her teeth flashing white against her black face as she caught sight of the inquisitive girl sniffing at the pie pantry. "It surely is, and you'd best

231

keep your nose and fingers out of it. It's for the party tonight.''

"Is everything about ready?" Alexandra inquired, lifting the heavy cast iron lid to peer into the pot hanging over the fire.

"Don't you be messin' with my Brunswick stew, you heah? Everything be about done. I'm just waitin' on that worthless Habersham. Why Betsy wants to hitch herself up to that skinny excuse of a man is beyond me,'' Chloe said with a shake of her head. She had told the foolish white woman as much only this morning.

Shrugging her shoulders, Alexandra replied, "To each his own, I guess. I wouldn't expect any help from the lovebirds. They went to the jewelers to pick up their rings and haven't returned yet.''

Hands on her hips, her eyes flashing fire, Chloe snorted. "Well, I declare! That man was supposed to fetch me a ham from the smokehouse. Now what's I supposed to do?''

Throwing on her cape, Alexandra gave Chloe a reassuring smile. "Don't worry. I'll run out and get it. I've done it before. There's a stool in the shed I can use to stand on.''

Chloe's look was apprehensive. "I don't know if you should, Miss Alex. What if you was to fall?''

"Oh, posh! I'll be back before those biscuits you're baking are out of the oven,'' she said, closing the door behind her.

Alexandra walked along the shell-covered path toward the brick smokehouse, which was situated on the northernmost end of their lot. Tugging her woolen cardinal tight about her, she trembled as the cool late afternoon temperature chilled her bones. "Winter's coming, that's for sure,'' she muttered to herself.

Hurrying to reach the warmth of the smokehouse, Alexandra failed to notice the pair of emerald eyes that followed her movements.

As she entered the dark interior of the building, the smell of hickory smoke rose up to greet her. A dozen hams, smoked the month before, hung from wooden rafters. Placing the stool she had procured from the shed under the ham nearest her, she climbed up.

A moment later a loud crash caught her attention. Looking down, she noticed the smokehouse door had slammed shut. Damn! she thought. The wind must have blown the door closed; she would have to get down and open it to let in more light.

Pushing on the door, she found it wouldn't budge. Pushing harder, she realized it must have been locked from the outside. Smiling to herself and shaking her head, she thought of her sister. This was a prank the two sisters liked to engage in as children.

"Alicia, this isn't funny. Now open the door." When a moment passed and the door wasn't opened, Alexandra shouted again. "Alicia, I'll skin your hide. Now open this damn door!"

Suddenly the strong odor of smoke alerted her senses. Sniffing the air, she looked behind her to make certain that the fire inside the building was extinguished. Soon the smokehouse filled with smoke. Fear darted through her as she realized the smoke was coming in from the outside. Banging frantically on the door, she screamed loudly. "Help me! Somebody help me!" Someone would come. She had to stay calm. Chloe knew she was out here.

She brushed at the tears clouding her eyes. She could barely see; the smoke was as thick as morning fog. Coughing, she tried to clear her lungs of the harmful vapors. Lying face down on the dirt floor, she positioned her head close to the floor, near the door, inhaling the small amount of air that floated in through the tiny crack at the bottom.

The heat grew more intense; beads of sweat covered her face and body. Wiggling out of her cloak, she threw it off. It was getting difficult to breathe. Just the effort

233

of inhaling caused pain deep inside her chest. Oh, God! Why doesn't somebody come? She didn't want to die. Not now. Not when she had everything to live for. "Nicholas," she gasped before the blackness overcame her.

She was floating on a soft white cloud. There were voices, voices that called her name. She struggled to reach the voices; they sounded far away.

"Is she going to be all right, Doctor Martin?" Nicholas asked, taking the plump physician aside.

"If she regains consciousness, she should be fine. She'd breathed in a good deal of smoke. Her lungs are congested. I recommended bleeding her to let out the poisonous gases, but Missus Courtland wouldn't hear of it," he replied, putting on his greatcoat.

Thank God for that, Nicholas thought, eyeing the disgruntled looking physician with disdain. As he turned back toward the bed, his gaze fell upon Alexandra's still form. She was as white as the sheet beneath her. Catherine was seated on the bed, crying softly; Samuel was next to her, patting her back to comfort her.

How the hell had this happened? he wondered. If he hadn't seen the smoke when he had, Alexandra would be dead. He looked down at his bandaged hands, badly burned from the fire.

"Nicholas." The cry was barely audible.

Nicholas exchanged relieved glances with Catherine and Samuel before rushing to the bed. Kneeling beside it, he took hold of Alexandra's hand. "I'm here, my sweet. Can you hear me?"

The black eyelashes fluttered madly before opening to reveal two red-rimmed blue eyes. "Nicholas," Alexandra asked, "what happened?" Her voice was hoarse, the words barely discernible, but to the group gathered in the bedroom, they were the sweet sounds of life.

"Thank God!" Catherine said, sobbing into Samuel's chest.

"Let's go and leave Nicholas and Alexandra alone for a while, dear," Samuel said. "We need to escort Doctor Martin downstairs and tell the others that Alex is going to be all right."

Smiling wanly at her parents, Alexandra watched them depart the room. Turning to face Nicholas, she asked, "What time is it? I need to get ready for the party."

Kissing the hand he held so tenderly, Nicholas smiled. "My sweet, the party has been put on hold until you're feeling better." At the protestation forming on her lips, he added, "Betsy and Habersham insisted."

Nodding in concession, Alexandra squeezed Nicholas's hand, noting immediately that something was terribly wrong. Alarmed by the look of pain on his face, she looked down to discover that his hands were wrapped in bandages. "You've been hurt."

" 'Tis nothing," he assured her, "just a few burns."

"It was you who rescued me?"

At his nod, Alexandra's eyes filled with tears. "Nicholas, someone locked me in the smokehouse."

Seating himself on the edge of the bed, he felt his features turned harsh. "Tell me everything you can remember, and don't leave anything out."

Nicholas listened attentively, his eyes narrowing, the anger inside his breast building as Alexandra recounted her narrow escape with death. He had his suspicions, but he wouldn't voice them yet. If what he suspected was true, the perpetrator of the crime would pay dearly.

"Why would someone do such a thing, Nicholas? I could have been killed."

"It was probably just some childish prank that got

235

out of hand," he said, smoothing the wrinkles off of her brow. "Now you rest. I'll be back later to check on you."

Alexandra broke into a small smile. "This isn't exactly how I thought we'd end up in bed together."

Chuckling, Nicholas placed a kiss on her lips. "My sweet, I'm going to speak to your mother and father. I want our wedding date pushed up." He would not take the chance of exposing Alexandra to anyone's jealous hatred again. Once they were married, she would have the protection his name would afford. No one would dare strike out at a member of the nobility.

Beaming as brightly as the flaming candle next to the bed, Alexandra brought Nicholas's hand to her lips and pressed a tender kiss upon it. "That would make me very happy, Nicholas. I know we've had our differences, but I would strive to make you a dutiful wife."

Nicholas couldn't suppress the laughter welling up inside of him. "My sweet, you will never be a dutiful wife. I've already reconciled myself to that fact. But you are kind and loving, and I deem myself fortunate to have found such a treasure as you." He kissed her again, more deeply this time.

Tears clouded Alexandra's vision as she looked into the face of the man she loved. Taking a deep breath, the effort making her cringe in pain, she caressed his face. "I love you, Nicholas."

Nicholas stared in astonishment, unsure if he had heard her correctly. Seeing the love shining brightly in her eyes, his bewilderment turned to joy. Splitting into a wide grin, he drew Alexandra to his chest. "Your declaration pleases me more than I can say, my sweet. I only hope I can be worthy of your love." He placed a kiss atop her head.

Nicholas's admission wasn't exactly what she was hoping to hear, but it would do for now. Nicholas cared for her. She knew deep in her heart that he did. And if the old gypsy was right, his love for her existed whether he realized it or not. She would wait. They had their whole lives ahead of them. After all, they were bound for eternity.

# PART FOUR

# BOUND FOR ETERNITY

*True love's the gift which God has given*
*To man alone beneath the heaven:*
*It is not fantasy's hot fire,*
*Whose wishes, soon as granted, fly;*
*It liveth not in fierce desire,*
*With dead desire it doth not die;*
*It is the secret sympathy,*
*The silver link, the silken tie,*
*Which heart to heart and mind to mind*
*In body and in soul can bind.*

Sir Walter Scott

# Chapter Eighteen

"I can't go through with it!" Alexandra cried, raising her hands in supplication toward her mother. The fire roared in the hearth, illuminating the uncertainty that shadowed the young bride's face.

Catherine's eyes filled with tears as she stared at the lovely vision before her. Framed by the large stone fireplace, Alexandra was a portrait in grace and beauty. The satin wedding gown flowed regally about her; she looked like a princess on her way to meet her Prince Charming. Catherine couldn't help feeling nostalgic as she studied her daughter in her old wedding gown. Memories surfaced to cloud her mind with feelings she'd thought long forgotten.

"You're just having prenuptial jitters. All brides experience them," Catherine assured her.

"Even you?"

The question caught Catherine off guard. Turning, she walked to the window, unwilling to let Alexandra see her so maudlin on an occasion that should be filled with happiness and joy. Peering out at the street below, Catherine didn't notice the light snow that had fallen, caking the road with a fine white powder. Her mind had drifted back to another time, another wedding long ago, where the bride was as full of doubt as Alexandra.

Catherine had married Samuel Courtland knowing

full well that she loved another man. She had gone to her marriage bed out of duty, not love. She had played Samuel false, deceiving him as a wife and a lover. And in return, he had given her everything—his love, his patience, his friendship.

When did her feelings for her husband change? She didn't know. But the seeds of love and trust that Samuel had planted in her heart and nurtured with his kindness, had blossomed. She loved Samuel with all her heart. There would always be a special place in her heart for Charles—he was her first love, but Samuel was her life. It had taken her a long time to realize that. She prayed Nicholas and Alexandra would not waste the time she had, resisting what was always meant to be.

Turning back to face her daughter's uncertainty, Catherine smiled, finally replying, "Yes, dear, even me."

"Am I doing the right thing, Mother?" Alexandra questioned, pacing nervously in front of the fire.

"Do you love Nicholas?" Catherine asked.

Alexandra stopped. There was no hesitancy in her answer. "Yes. With all my heart."

"Then there's your answer."

"But what if he doesn't love me?"

Coming forward, Catherine took both of Alexandra's hands in her own. She wanted to ease the fear of the unknown from her daughter's face, but only time could do that. "Love is like a fragile flower, Alex. If you care for the flower—nurture it, it will continue to grow stronger and more beautiful with every day that passes. If you neglect the flower, it will wither and die on the vine. The love between you and Nicholas will bloom, my dear. Give it time."

Standing next to her new husband, Alexandra waited impatiently as friends and well-wishers lined up to offer their congratulations. The wedding ceremony had ended an hour before. Reverend Price had pronounced them man and wife at the altar of the Bruton Parish Church. Why not woman and husband? Alexandra wondered, stealing a peek at her new bridegroom out of the corner of her eye.

Nicholas was certainly handsome. The sight of his smile as he responded to something Frederick Wellington said made her heart flutter wildly. They had been standing in the receiving line for well over thirty minutes. Her feet ached, and her stomach was decidedly empty. Casting a look toward the end of the line, she breathed a sigh of relief: only three more couples to greet.

Her father had rented the Apollo Room at the Raleigh for the reception. The place conjured up memories best forgotten but difficult to put aside. It had taken all her acting abilities to place a smile on her face and greet Sabrina and Basil when they came through the line a few moments ago. To think she'd had to entertain that harlot at her own wedding! She grimaced.

"My dear, whatever has put such a scowl on your face on such a joyous occasion?"

Alexandra looked up to find Johanna Wellington standing before her. The older woman's concerned expression warmed her. Grabbing hold of her hand, she smiled at her dear friend. "I was just thinking of something you said, about not being able to choose ones relatives," she whispered.

A knowing look crossed the duchess's face. "Don't let them spoil your big day, my dear. They aren't worth it," Johanna said, giving Alexandra a peck on the cheek.

"You needn't worry, Johanna. I've wasted enough time and tears on that painted whore. She'll not spoil my day."

True to her word, Alexandra threw herself into her wedding festivities with wild abandon. If anyone

243

thought her behavior odd, they kept it to themselves, chalking it up to the champagne punch. She avoided Sabrina and Basil like the plague, keeping Nicholas by her side throughout the afternoon.

Pausing at the refreshment table, Nicholas handed Alexandra another glass of punch. "I really shouldn't let you have any more. I don't want you foxed when we enter our bridle chamber."

Alexandra giggled, taking another sip of the fruity punch to sooth her parched throat and frazzled nerves. "I'm having a wonderful time, Nicholas. I never realized being married could be so much fun."

Kissing her lips, Nicholas smiled. "We haven't begun to have fun yet. That comes later." He winked.

Blushing furiously, Alexandra grabbed onto his arm. "Let's dance again. I find I'm not able to stand still for a minute."

"Just don't use up all that energy, my sweet. I intend to put it to good use later," he replied, laughing loudly when he observed the scarlet color on Alexandra's cheeks.

"Look at those two lovebirds," Sabrina remarked, unable to keep the spite out of her voice as she eyed Nicholas with his new bride out on the dance floor. "You'd think Nicholas was actually in love with the little wren, the way he fawns all over her."

Basil gave Sabrina a calculating look. "Jealous, my love?"

"Of course not!" she protested a bit too vehemently. Taking a sip of her champagne, she tried to cover her mistake. "I'm angry that all our plans have been ruined. We were not able to stop the wedding, and now Nicholas will inherit everything."

"Lower your voice," Basil said, pulling the pouting woman to a secluded corner of the room. "Nicholas is not without influence. If he suspects anything, we are done for."

"It seems to me we are done for anyway," Sabrina insisted.

Brushing a spec of lint off his silver brocade coat, Basil smirked. "Not quite. I have a few more cards up my sleeve."

Sabrina eyed him suspiciously. "Do you mean to kill the Courtland wench?" she asked, trying to mask the hope in her voice. She would have succeeded in her plan to rid Nicholas of his betrothed if only he hadn't shown up when he did. When that black cook had left to fetch something at the main house, she had laughed in triumph, knowing victory was near, until Nicholas had arrived unexpectedly. Just a few more moments and the stupid little bitch would have suffocated to death.

"Nothing so droll as that, I assure you," Basil replied. "What I have in mind for my brother is much more devious, much less obvious than murder. Only a fool would resort to murder. It wouldn't take a genius to figure out who had the most to gain from Alexandra's death. I don't intend to swing from the end of a rope."

Rubbing her throat in an unconscious gesture, Sabrina took another swallow of champagne. "What do you intend?"

Basil eyed Sabrina's ample breasts, which were deliciously displayed by the low cut of her gown. Licking his lips, he ran his finger just inside the rim of the bodice, smiling when her eyes darkened.

Nicholas always did have good taste in women. He had to give him that. The little colonial was a striking beauty. He wouldn't mind having a taste of Alexandra's lush little body. He felt himself harden. Why not? he thought. Why not take everything Nicholas treasured? Sabrina was getting a bit jaded. A taste of that sweet young morsel was just what his palate craved.

"Let's go upstairs, my love," he whispered. "I have need of you."

Sabrina smiled, trying to hide the disgust that she felt. Basil's insatiable appetite was beginning to bore her. "I really would rather stay here and enjoy the party, darling."

His eyes narrowed. "Do you really think I care what you would rather do? Get upstairs and strip. I shall wait a few moments and join you." At the defiant look on her face, he added, "Don't be disobedient, Sabrina. You know I won't stand for any of your tantrums."

Basil watched Sabrina depart. He hadn't missed her malicious look; she would suffer for it later. How wonderful to be in control of those less fortunate, he thought, smiling in satisfaction. When he had control of Blackstone, those who had scorned and mocked him in years past would pay; they would pay most dearly.

The gentle tingle of sleigh bells kept rhythmic time to the fluffy flakes of snow falling silently from the sky. Alexandra huddled beneath the fur lap robe, snuggling closer to Nicholas in an attempt to keep warm during the short ride to their new home.

The two-story house came into view as soon as the sleigh made the turn onto Nicholson Street. The shutters were newly painted, the slate-blue color offering a pleasing contrast to the white clapboards surrounding them.

Shivering, Alexandra pulled her new wool cape, a gift from Nicholas, close about her. The cold weather, added to her own nervous tension, created tremors of icy fingers that gripped her knotted stomach.

"Are you cold, my sweet?" Nicholas asked, reigning the dappled gray mare to a halt. "I'll have you warmed up in no time."

The smile and wink Nicholas bestowed upon her quickly thawed whatever apprehension Alexandra felt. Returning his smile with a tremulous one of her own,

246

she nodded, alighting from the sleigh with Nicholas's assistance.

"Go into the house," he said. "I need to get the horse into the barn before the storm worsens."

Following his instructions, Alexandra pushed open the white picket gate and made her way up to the door. Expecting to find the inside of the house as cold as the frozen exterior, she was pleasantly surprised to discover a cheerful blaze roaring in the brick fireplace of the parlor.

Rushing forward, she removed her gloves, holding her hands out to the warmth of the flames. Her fingers tingled as the numbness in her hands began to thaw. Untying her cape, she flung it over the chair to dry out. Turning about, she lifted the heavy satin skirt of her dress, warming her backside toward the fire.

The room smelled of beeswax and charred pine. Her critical eye took in the tattered ends of the faded gingham window curtains and frayed edges of the oriental carpet. Funny, she hadn't noticed how worn the furniture and accessories were the first time she had inspected the house. In her excitement to have a home of her own, she had overlooked the obvious flaws.

It didn't really matter, she thought dismally. This was just a temporary residence. Nicholas had made it quite clear that they would be leaving for England shortly after the new year. Sighing deeply, she shook her head. The thought of leaving all she held dear caused an ache deep within her chest. If only there were some way to remain! But she knew there wasn't. Nicholas was a duke; his title and his home meant everything to him. He would never stay.

The slamming of the front door alerted Alexandra to Nicholas's presence. She dropped her dress as he entered the room.

Nicholas smiled inwardly at Alexandra's sudden display of modesty. The sight of her long legs, however brief, brought a tightening to his loins. "I believe I can

247

warm you more effectively than that fire, my sweet," he said, striding purposefully into the room.

"Nicholas!" Alexandra felt her cheeks glow as red as the flames that burned so brightly in the hearth. She brushed the folds of her gown self-consciously, aware of her new husband's scrutiny.

Her eyes locked with his as he stripped his snow-covered greatcoat off. Impatiently his fingers worked at the buttons of his frock and waistcoat. He tugged at them, tossing the offending garments to the floor.

Coming forward, he drew Alexandra into his embrace. "Have I told you what a beautiful bride you are, my sweet?" His voice was as soft as the newly fallen snow that masked the ground outside. Lowering his head, he covered her mouth, drinking the honey from her lips.

Locking her hands about his neck, Alexandra pressed into the solid planes of Nicholas's body. Her heart quickened as the feel of his hardened bulge pressed against her. His lips devoured hers completely, sapping the strength from her body and soul.

As he lifted his head, Nicholas's eyes burned a path of desire straight to her loins. "Let's go upstairs, my sweet. The time for waiting is over." Sweeping Alexandra into his arms, he cradled her gently to his chest, climbing the steps to the second floor.

Alexandra's heart beat a cadence with every step Nicholas took. When they reached the hallway, he stopped, pausing outside the door to their room. "Tonight the final ties are bound. You are mine, now and forever."

The words pulled at the sensitive strings of Alexandra's newfound feelings of love. A symphony of ecstasy played within her. Pressing her lips tenderly to his, she whispered, "In your arms is where I want to be."

The whitewashed walls were bathed in the golden glow of firelight as they entered the bridal chamber.

The light of the candles flickered softly against the lengthening shadows of the day.

"As much as I enjoy holding you in my arms, my sweet, I want to get you out of that dress and into that bed," Nicholas said, setting her down gently.

Turning, she presented her back to him. "I want no barriers between us this night."

One by one, the hooks came apart under Nicholas's deft fingers. As each was loosened, he pressed his lips to the white skin presented to his view. His mouth scorched a burning path from neck to waist, until at last the final hook was undone. Spinning her about, he lowered the gown, exposing her thinly clad body to his view.

"You are perfection, my sweet."

Stepping out of her gown, Alexandra untied the ribbons of her chemise. Stripping out of the remaining garments, she stood naked before her husband. Nicholas's eyes darkened, glittering brightly like a starlit night as his gazed traveled over her nakedness. Her heart quickened. "Now it's your turn," she said, smiling seductively.

The sight of Nicholas's naked chest produced quivers of yearning between Alexandra's thighs. When he reached down to unfasten his breeches, she held her breath. Faint with desire, she stared mesmerized as Nicholas's clothes were discarded, revealing the thick evidence of his desire for her. A moment of panic overtook her as she realized that the moment of her awakening had come. Taking hold of Nicholas's outstretched hand, she followed him to the bed.

Gently he eased her onto the bed, covering her body with his own. The feel of his nakedness pressed so provocatively against her own sent a jolt of newfound pleasure rippling through her. His lips covered her nipples with tantalizing possessiveness. He lapped at the marble-hard tips, caressing the sensitive swollen points until her pleasure turned into painful wanting. His lips traveled down her breasts to her stomach; his hands explored her thighs, stroking and teasing until she was mindless with wanting.

Instinctively Alexandra's body arched toward him. Her hands massaged the roughened planes of his back and chest in gentle exploration. The feel of his skin and hair against her hands was wildly erotic to her senses. When his mouth covered her pulsating mound, she relaxed her legs, giving in to the sweet, sensual pleasure.

The tautness between her legs increased. She thrashed her head from side to side, bucking against Nicholas's mouth, urging him to provide the fulfillment her body craved. As she neared the crest, Nicholas raised up, positioning himself over her. Spreading her legs, he placed his swollen member at the entrance to her womanhood. "Relax, my sweet. I will try to make this as painless for you as possible," he whispered, before plunging into the depths of her desire.

Alexandra felt a moment of deep burning pain. It was over in an instant. The pain was soon replaced by a pleasure so intense, she felt her insides lighten and expand.

Their bodies became one, rocking in the age-old rhythm of lovers. Higher and higher they climbed the peak of their passion, until at last, reaching the top, they soared like wingless birds across the heavens.

Raising himself up, Nicholas looked down into Alexandra's relaxed features. He smiled tenderly, brushing back the damp curls that sprung around her face. Her blue eyes were filled with wonderment; she smiled warmly at him.

"I love you, Nicholas," she whispered, caressing his cheek.

Grabbing the soft hand in his own, he kissed it tenderly. "I love you, too."

# Chapter Nineteen

"I declare, Miss Alex, I can't recall ever seeing you dis happy. Marriage must be agreeing wid you," Chloe remarked as she stole a peek into the oven to check on the Sally Lunn bread she was baking for the Christmas holidays.

The preparations for the festive season had begun. The fruitcakes had been laid to rest in their brandy-covered containers, while the gingerbread dough waited patiently on the table to be transformed into whimsical figures of Chloe's active imagination.

Alexandra's mouth watered as the aroma of baking bread filled the kitchen. She smiled to herself at Chloe's preceptiveness. She was happy—deliriously happy. The three words Nicholas had uttered on their wedding night and every night thereafter had made her so.

She couldn't control the satisfied expression crossing her face when she thought of how wonderful married life had been these past two weeks. She felt her cheeks grow warm as the memories of her passion-filled nights in the big tester bed came to mind.

"Dat look on your face is purely indecent, honey. I guess you and dat handsome duke is getting along just fine."

"Chloe!" Alexandra scolded, covering her face in

251

mortification. The woman was just too perceptive for her own good.

"Well, it's true, ain't it?" Chloe asked, wiping the perspiration off her forehead with the edge of her snowy-white apron.

Alexandra smiled, rising to her feet. "Yes, it's true. Now quit being so nosy and show me how to prepare the batter for the bread. You *did* promise to teach me how to cook."

Chloe chuckled, shaking her head. "Why, you want to learn how to cook? Your husband got a passel of servants back in England. That snooty Habersham done told me so."

"Nevertheless, while we are living here, I wish to be a competent housewife. Betsy has been helping me make new curtains for the parlor, and I want you to teach me how to cook."

Handing Alexandra a wooden spoon, Chloe added a little more flour to the batter in the bowl. "Cookin's like making love, honey. You needs a gentle touch and a heap of creativeness." At Alexandra's reddening complexion, Chloe laughed. "You ain't going to find out how to please your man by learning what goes on in the kitchen. You needs to pay attention to what's being taught in the bedroom. What you learn in there is going to make your husband a whole lot happier. Making his blood boil is a lot more important than learning how to boil water."


Trudging through the freshly fallen snow, the white powder crunching beneath her boots, Alexandra thought of Chloe's sage advice as she traversed the short distance home. She certainly had become an apt pupil in the bedroom under Nicholas's ardent tutelage. It was the one part of marriage she found totally fulfilling. Her expertise in the kitchen was a little less exacting. Perhaps Chloe was right. Maybe she should concentrate her homemaking skills on what she was good at. They might starve to death from lack of food, but they would be filled to overflowing with love. Laughing to herself, she pushed open the gate at the front of the house.

She was greeted at the door by the droll figure of Betsy's new husband. Betsy and Habersham had tied the knot a few days after she and Nicholas had married. Habersham would not flout propriety by "living in sin" with Betsy, as he had put it, and had insisted that they marry right away. Only too happy to comply, Betsy married Will Habersham in the parlor at the Courtlands' with only the immediate family present.

Four newlyweds in the same house was definitely an experience. Especially when one presided over the small abode as if it were a grand estate.

"May I take your wrap, my lady," Habersham offered, stepping forward to take Alexandra's fur-lined cape.

Sighing, Alexandra nodded. It was useless to instruct the stuffy servant to call her anything but "my lady" or "your grace." Habersham was a stickler for formalities. "Has Nicholas arrived home?" she inquired, observing his rigid posture. They had a truce of sorts, neither of them quite forgetting his original animosity toward the other.

"No, my lady. His lordship has not yet returned."

"Please tell Betsy to prepare a pot of strawberry tea. I'll await Nicholas in the parlor."

Habersham bowed and took his leave. He was so terribly British and probably very indicative of what she would find if she ventured to England with Nicholas. *If,* she thought. Didn't she mean *when?* Frowning, she took a seat on the settee, running her hand absently over the frayed red brocade upholstery; she stared into the flames of the fire.

The subject of their leaving hadn't come up in conversation again. If only something would happen to prevent their leaving—to change Nicholas's mind. Why did things have to be so damned complicated? she wondered, blinking back the tears clouding her vision. She didn't want to move to England. It was a strange forbidding place.

As much as she loved Nicholas, she would never be comfortable in her role as the Duchess of Blackstone. She was too independent, too American.

"I've brought your tea, Miss Alex," Betsy said, setting the silver tray down on the mahogany tea table.

Brushing away her tears with the back of her hand, Alexandra looked up into Betsy's questioning expression and smiled wanly. "Thank you, Betsy."

"Why are you looking so glum, Miss Alex? I would have thought you'd still be walking on air . . . you being newly married and all."

Patting the space on the sofa next to her, she invited Betsy to join her. "I've just been thinking about us having to leave this place, Betsy. Have you thought about what it will be like when we have to travel to a strange land—live among strange people?"

Betsy's smile was sympathetic. "I've lived among strangers most of my life, miss. Being widowed and indentured at such a young age, I had to learn to do for myself. I was lucky to find such a fine family as yours to take me in."

"But don't you feel scared about going back to a land that is totally foreign to you? After all, you've lived in Virginia most of your life."

"I found that being scared doesn't change things. If you learn to adapt, life is much easier. You'll just make yourself and those you love unhappy if you don't accept your new set of circumstances."

"I guess you're right, Betsy," Alexandra conceded, patting the older woman's hand. "Thank you for listening."

Rising to her feet, Betsy smiled. "Don't you be fretting over something that hasn't happened yet. Things

254

have a way of working out.'' Giving Alexandra a pat on the cheek, she exited the room.

Observing the handcarved nativity scene on the mantel, Alexandra smiled. It was too close to Christmas to be this maudlin. This was the season for miracles. Perhaps if she prayed hard enough, she would be granted one of her own.


Alexandra was having difficulty concentrating on the Reverend Price's sermon. She fidgeted as anxiously as a small child, hoping the long-winded pastor would bring his oration to an end. It was Christmas Eve, and like every other year, the Courtlands and their servants were assembled in Bruton Parish Church for the traditional Christmas Eve services. Of course, this year it was the Courtlands and the Fortunes who assembled. Smiling to herself, she chanced a peek at Nicholas, who was seated beside her. She hoped he liked what she had bought him for Christmas. It had special, sentimental value.

''What are you grinning at, my sweet? You look very pleased with yourself,'' Nicholas whispered.

She was saved from replying by the organ's announcement of the last hymn. A hundred voices united in fellowship and goodwill joined in the strains of *Oh Come, All Ye Faithful.*


The sound of church bells, ringing as clear and crisp as the winter sky overhead, accompanied Nicholas and Alexandra as they strolled down Duke of Gloucester Street toward the Courtland house. A million sparkling stars lit the heavens, announcing to the world that this night had been singled out as special.

They shared amused glances at the antics of Alicia and Tom, who ran ahead to frolic in the snow. Alexandra's parents and the rest of the family, having decided against walking, had taken the carriage home.

"They look like they're having fun, don't they?" Alexandra stated wistfully, staring enviously at the happy couple. Although Nicholas's icy exterior had thawed a considerable degree since their marriage, she didn't think a lord of the realm would appreciate a romp in the snow.

"I think they might be having too much fun," he replied, picking up a wet handful of snow and forming it into a ball.

Alexandra's eyes widened. "You don't mean to throw that, do you?"

"Of course, my sweet. You'd better arm yourself. This fight could prove a messy one."

Clamping her hand over her mouth, Alexandra tried to stifle the giggles that threatened to erupt.

Nicholas's unexpected bombardment of the kissing couple brought a myriad of squeals and shrieks from Alicia and Tom, who soon retaliated, catching Nicholas in the side of the head with a clump of snow. Seeing her chance to get into the melee, Alexandra picked up a large handful of white flakes, rubbing it into the back of Nicholas's neck.

Nicholas jumped as the ice-cold liquid slid down his back. "You traitor!" he yelled. "You're supposed to be on *my* side." He tackled Alexandra to the ground, rubbing a handful of wet snow in her face.

"Stop, Nicholas," she cried, giggling hysterically. "I surrender." She laughed so hard, she thought her sides would burst.

Helping her to her feet, Nicholas wiped her face with his handkerchief. "That will teach you to think twice before waging war on an Englishman."

Suddenly an uncomfortable silence filled the air. Tom and Alicia's expressions grew somber. Nicholas's face reddened as he realized the implication of his words. It was Alexandra who finally lightened the awkward moment.

"You forget, my Lord Blackstone, I am now on equal footing with you. As a duchess, I have inherited the prowess you English claim to have on the battlefield. Careful you don't raise my ire," she teased.

Chuckling, Nicholas squeezed Alexandra's waist. "Your prowess is well known in other areas, my sweet. Careful you don't raise something else."

"Nicholas!" Alexandra cried, her reddened cheeks turning a deeper shade of scarlet.

Tom's booming laughter broke the stillness; the others followed suit. Walking hand in hand, their merriment ringing out against the dark quiet of the night, the four friends made their way home.

Standing in front of the long cheval mirror, Alexandra admired the exquisite diamond pendant Nicholas had given her for Christmas. It sparkled, flashing its brilliance in the light of the sun that shone through the window.

Yesterday's Christmas celebration had been wonderful. Filled with good food and good feelings, everyone had been joyful. She would never forget the surprised expression on Nicholas's face when he unwrapped the gift she had given him: a copy of John Locke's book. The smile and kiss he had given her, told her more than words, that he had remembered their original meeting.

Benjamin's surprise announcement of his engagement to Prudence had created quite a stir. Although Ben had acted pleased about his impending marriage, something had told her things weren't quite right with him. Therefore, it had come as no surprise when he had cornered her after dinner to say he wanted to speak with her today.

Running her hairbrush through her long ebony

tresses, Alexandra wound up her hair in a knot, stuffing it beneath a white cotton mobcap. Smoothing the folds of her cranberry wool dress, she went downstairs to wait for her brother.

She had barely reached the bottom stair when the brass door knocker sounded. "I'll get it, Habersham," she announced to the harried valet, who was approaching quickly from the rear of the house. He flashed her an indignant look, turned on his heel, and retraced his steps.

Opening the door, she found Benjamin waiting patiently on the porch. Smiling, she took his coat, hanging it on the hall tree in the entry. She ushered him into the parlor, seating herself next to him on the settee.

"It's good to see you again. I'm so happy about your engagement to Prudence. She's a lovely girl; she'll make you an excellent wife."

Ben's smile did not reach his eyes. "I only hope our marriage will be able to take place."

"What's wrong, Ben? I sensed something was bothering you last night. Don't you want to marry Prudence?"

"Prudence has nothing to do with it. It's the situation with England, Alex. Things are heating up to the point of no return."

Fear lodged in her throat at Benjamin's statement. "I thought things had quieted down. There's been nothing in the paper of late."

"South Carolina has had a "tea party." Word just arrived yesterday."

"Do you suppose Nicholas knows?"

Benjamin sneered. "I doubt it. For all their spies and connections, the British aren't all that well informed. Our lines of communication are much faster, much more reliable."

Pouring Benjamin a cup of hot chocolate, Alexandra handed it to him. "I know you have never cared for

258

Nicholas, but he is my husband. I must ask you to refrain from such snide remarks and gestures when you are in my home."

Benjamin stared thoughtfully at his sister. "There is more at stake here than my dislike of your husband, Alex. I believe the colonies and England are heading for war."

"War!" She mouthed the word, her face turning white. She never wanted it to come to this. She should have known England would never give up her colonies without a fight. How naive she had been to think otherwise.

"I need your help, Alex."

"My help! What can I do? Are the colonies recruiting women for their army?" she asked.

Ben smiled, tweaking his sister's nose. "No. Nothing quite that drastic . . . it has to do with your husband."

"Nicholas?"

Ben nodded. "Nicholas is privy to a vast amount of important information—documents and dispatches arrive daily from London."

Alexandra shook her head. "I don't understand. What does that have to do with me?"

"We want you to spy on your husband."

The cup of chocolate clattered to the floor. "Spy on Nicholas?" She shook her head. "That's impossible. He's my husband."

"He'll soon be your enemy. Your allegiance must be to Virginia's fight for freedom. You can't let your love for one man blind you to the justness of our cause."

"You don't know what you're asking. Nicholas loves me. He trusts me. I won't betray that trust."

Benjamin stood, heaving a sigh. "Your loyalty has always been an admirable trait, Alex. No one knows that more than I. But the time has come for you to choose sides. The freedom of our country is at stake.

Think about it. I'll speak to you again after you've had time to consider."

Alexandra's head shot up. "I don't need time to consider. I won't betray the man I love. America will have to win its independence without any help from me."

Crossing the room, Benjamin stopped, turning back to face his sister. The expression of pain on Alexandra's face touched him deeply. "I'm sorry, Alex. If there was any other way, I wouldn't have asked you." Blowing her a kiss, he exited the room.

Alexandra felt numb. She stared stupidly at the door, unable to believe what had just transpired. What Ben asked of her was impossible. She couldn't cast aside her role as Nicholas's wife as if it had no meaning. She had taken a vow; she loved him.

But what of her vow to help gain America's independence? What of her role as an American? What of her love for her country? She recalled the words she had spoken to Tom so long ago: *My marriage will not change how I feel about America. I am as true to the cause as I ever was.*

Bending over in anguish, she rocked back and forth, trying to stem the pain building deep inside her. Her tears slid silently down her cheeks, falling into her lap. She would never be able to choose between love of country and love of man. She shook her head. Never!

# Chapter Twenty

The faces of the men who sat around the tapestry-covered table in the governor's council chamber were somber. Word had just reached Lord Dunmore of South Carolina's treasonous activity against the Crown.

It had taken over a week for the news of the Carolinian's "tea party" to reach the shores of Virginia and the ears of the loyalist government's representatives.

Lord Dunmore, seated at the head of the table, faced the members of his council. "I don't mind telling you that these revolts against the King's authority have me worried. Parliament needs to take stronger action against these insurrectionists. If they had come down harder on those damned Bostonians, we wouldn't be faced with all this turmoil now."

"Samuel Adams should have been strung up long ago," John Randolph stated, pounding his fist on the table.

"Aye, and Patrick Henry right along with him," Thaddeus Pembroke interjected.

"Gentlemen," Nicholas said, rising to his feet, "we need to keep our anger in check and our opinions rational. Violence only begets more violence. These men you speak of, however outspoken or misguided, are still subjects of the King. They're entitled to the same rights and protection from King George that we are."

"There you go, defending these rabble-rousers again, Nicholas," Basil said, pushing himself out of his chair to face his brother. "One would think, to listen to you speak, that you have not only embraced a colonial to your heart, you have embraced their cause as well."

Nicholas's face was a glowering mask of rage. "How dare you cast aspersions on my loyalty—on my motives? If you were any man other than my brother, I would call you out for your remarks."

Basil's face turned ashen.

"Gentlemen, gentlemen," the Governor cautioned, "please sit down and calm yourselves. We have enough to worry about dealing with these malcontents without resorting to fighting amongst ourselves."

Nicholas did as requested, continuing to direct burning, reproachful looks at his brother. Small wonder their father had never had much use for Basil. He could remember clearly how the duke had classified his second son as a grave mistake of nature. A weakling, his father had called him.

Nicholas had always thought his father's attitude toward Basil a bit harsh. He had tried to compensate over the years, making excuses for Basil's behavior, covering his gambling debts when they became an embarrassment.

Shaking his head in disgust, he watched his brother cower in his seat. Basil was a born disgrace. Thank God he had not been born first. Nicholas shuddered at the thought. Had that been the case, there was no telling what might have happened.


Pacing across the small tavern room like a caged animal, Sabrina waited anxiously for the return of her lover. Basil had left over three hours ago to attend a political meeting at the Capitol. Why he felt his presence was necessary or wanted was a mystery to her. She didn't think he possessed the ability or expertise to sort out difficult matters of state. It was probably just another way he found to inflate his already overinflated ego.

Walking to the window, she peered down the street once again. The heavy rain had turned the road into a quagmire. She watched as two black men jumped down from their perch atop the coach they were driving and attempted to free the mud caked wheels that were stuck. Their muscles strained against the rain-soaked shirts plastered to their bodies. She felt a familiar tightening of awareness in her loins.

"Damn! Where was Basil?" she muttered angrily. It was just like him to leave her stuck in some dingy little room while he went off cavorting with his cronies. She would go mad if she had to spend another hour cooped up in this cubicle of a room. The innkeeper had made it quite clear that her presence would not be tolerated in any of the common rooms without the escort of her companion. How provincial these colonials were! Why in England, she went where she pleased and with whom she pleased, and no one ever said a word.

The sound of footsteps outside her door made her turn abruptly. Basil sauntered into the room, a worried expression creasing his brow.

"Whatever is the matter?" Sabrina asked, coming forward to take his coat. "You look lower than a whipped dog."

"Get me a brandy. I've had a rough day."

"*You've* had a rough day!" she shouted, throwing his coat on the floor. "*I've* been the one closeted in this room like a chicken in a coop. Don't tell me how difficult your day has been."

Basil shot her a malevolent look. "At least you

263

haven't had to contend with the vicious temper of my brother. He can be nasty when crossed.''

Sabrina smiled inwardly, remembering only too well Nicholas's occasional bad temper. Of course, she had always been able to restore his good humor. ''What happened?''

Taking a seat on the edge of the bed, Basil sipped his brandy thoughtfully, ignoring Sabrina's question. After a few moments, he looked up, a wicked smile lighting his features. ''I think I may have just discovered the key to our success.''

''Whatever are you talking about, Basil? I thought we had decided to pack up and leave this godforsaken place. I want to go home to England.''

''You shall, my love, you shall. But don't you want to go home wealthy beyond your wildest imaginings?''

Sabrina's eyes narrowed. ''I believe we've played out the cards up your sleeve. Why don't you just admit that we've been defeated and leave it at that. I want to go home.''

''Never!'' Basil shouted, rising to his feet. He crossed the room to stand in front of her. ''I will get what is rightfully mine. I told you, no one will stand in the way of my success. Not even you, my love.'' He grabbed her arm.

Sabrina grew fearful at the maniacal look in Basil's eyes. She should have known the man was demented; she never should have allowed herself to get involved in his schemes. ''You're hurting me, Basil,'' she said, pulling away from him.

As he ran his finger over her cheek, Basil's smile was sinister. ''It would be a pity to mar that flawless skin.''

Sabrina smiled, pressing herself into him. She knew how to tame the beast within the man. ''Darling, you know I want to help you in whatever way I can,'' she whispered, running her tongue along the sensitive ridges of his ear. She felt triumphant when she detected his hardened shaft against her leg. "Tell me your plan."

"My plan is simple," he said, taking her breasts into his hands. "We are going to discredit Nicholas in front of his peers." His eyes glowed with a strange inner light; he squeezed Sabrina's breasts painfully.

"You're hurting me, darling," Sabrina said, tears misting her eyes, a cold knot forming in her stomach.

Basil laughed. "Am I?" he asked, squeezing harder. "Pity, you don't give me the respect that I deserve, Sabrina. You and my brother have a painful lesson to learn. Nicholas's will have to wait a while longer; yours will begin now."

Staring thoughtfully at the lovely vision seated across from him at the dining room table, Nicholas watched in amusement as Alexandra devoured her second piece of pecan pie. She was beautiful—full of passion and life. As her tiny tongue reached out to lick a sweet morsel from her lips, his stomach tightened. Who would have thought his little sharp-tongued seditionist would possess such an ardent nature? Never in his life had he known such fulfillment in the arms of a woman. Even Sabrina's practiced charms didn't elicit the response he felt when he was encased in the velvet softness of Alexandra's body. His crotch tightened painfully; he shifted in his seat to hide his discomfort.

Frowning at the avenue his thoughts were traveling, Nicholas tried to clear his mind and concentrate on the matter at hand. Now was not the time to let his tender feelings for his young bride interfere with the immediate problem they must face.

As if sensing the turmoil dwelling within him, Alexandra looked up into his eyes and smiled. The radiance of that smile took his breath away.

"You're so quiet this evening, Nicholas. Is everything all right?"

Cradling the bowl of the wineglass in his fingers, he stared silently into the deep burgundy liquid as if it were a crystal ball that could reveal what Alexandra's reaction would be to the news he must tell her.

News of the increasing animosity between his country and hers would upset her. He realized, after today's heated discussion at the Capitol, the time for reason had come to an end. Soon there would be an outbreak of hostilities, and after that. . . . He shook his head. He couldn't bring himself to utter the word that was prevalent in everyone's mind: war. He had to tell her. They needed to make plans to leave for England as soon as possible. He did not want to remain in Virginia if war broke out.

"Nicholas?" Alexandra's voice was full of concern. "What is it? You look troubled."

Taking a deep breath, Nicholas looked up. "I think we should go into the parlor and have a talk. There is something that I need to discuss with you."

Tremors of apprehension surged through Alexandra's body. Nicholas's words and behavior, coupled with her brother's dire predictions of this morning, caused a tightening in the pit of her stomach. Nodding, she followed him into the front room.

The cozy warmth of the fire could not dispel the chill that suddenly permeated the parlor. Nicholas stood with his back to the blaze, his feet braced far apart, his hands clenched behind his back. Taking a seat in one of the wing chairs that flanked the fireplace, Alexandra waited for him to speak.

"I have come to a decision today, Alexandra," Nicholas said, his tone resigned. "Events are occurring here in the colonies which I am not at liberty to discuss. However, because of them I have decided it is imperative that we make arrangements to leave for England as soon as possible."

Alexandra stared wordlessly at Nicholas, stunned by his bluntness. She tried to let the words he uttered penetrate her numbed mind. The silence between them lengthened. The crackling and hissing of the logs seemed to magnify in the quiet. Finally she stood, facing her husband. The stubborn set of his jaw told her he would be unyielding in his conviction.

"I find it totally unacceptable and not the least bit flattering that you have chosen to exclude me from your confidence," Alexandra stated. "Do you propose to uproot me from the only home I have ever known without so much as a civil explanation?"

"I need not give you explanations, my sweet. I am your husband. It is your duty to honor my wishes—to obey, if you will."

Clenching her fists, she felt the heat of anger scorch her cheeks. "I am not an unreasonable woman. I knew one day we would have to return to England to attend to your estates, but I will not be treated like a second-class citizen just because I happen to be a woman and your wife. I demand to know what the events are of which you speak. Why is it so imperative that we leave now?"

Walking to the liquor cabinet, Nicholas poured himself a generous portion of brandy. "I can't tell you that," he stated, gulping down the fiery liquid.

"You can't tell me! I am your wife. Do you mean to tell me that you don't trust me?"

Banging the glass down on the table, Nicholas turned. "Of course I trust you. But these are matters of government. They do not concern you."

Remembering Benjamin's words of war, a sudden chill flowed through her. She rubbed her arms, trying to ease her fear. "Ben was right," she whispered, not realizing she had spoken aloud.

Nicholas stepped forward, placing his hands on her shoulders. "Ben was right about what?" he questioned. If anyone was privy to information about the

267

colonials' present position, it was Benjamin Courtland. "What did Ben say?" he asked again.

Twisting out of his hold, Alexandra crossed to the window. Her heart felt as frigid as the night air, her despair as black as the shadowed sky. "Nothing," she finally replied. "Ben said nothing."

"Alexandra!"

Turning, she found herself scant inches away from her husband's angry face.

"If you have information that could be beneficial to the Crown, it is your duty to reveal it. You are a duchess—a member of English nobility."

Alexandra's eyes flashed fire. "I am an American. Your loyalty may be to your King, but mine is to my country."

"And what of your loyalty to me?"

The question hung in the air, suspended by a fragile thread of trust and a newly found love.

"How dare you doubt my loyalty—demean my love!" she screamed, tears streaming down her face. "You are wilting our flower."

"What the hell are you talking about? What flower?" He threw his hands up in the air.

"Stupid Englishman!" she cried, running out the door and up the stairs.

"Alexandra, wait!" Nicholas shouted, reaching out for her as she flew by. Grabbing only thin air, he dropped his arms dejectedly.

"Damned stubborn woman!" he muttered, dropping dejectedly onto the settee. He flinched when he heard the bedroom door slam shut; it sounded painfully final.

What the hell was happening? he wondered. Had everyone become crazed, fevered by the uncertainty of the times? He shook his head. Would he ever know the peace and contentment he had once enjoyed in England? Was he doomed to live in a state of constant turmoil caused by a pint-sized termagant who had turned his well-ordered existence as upside down as the world they were living in?

Staring into the flames of the fire, he sighed deeply, knowing that the questions he asked had no answers. Only time could give him the answers, and time was running out.

# Chapter Twenty-One

"What do you mean by calling me a foolish American woman! The only foolish thing I've ever done is marry you." Betsy's shrill voice floated through the thin wall of Alexandra's bedroom. Rushing over to the partition, she pressed her ear against the plaster surface.

"Now, pumpkin, you know I wasn't referring to you."

Habersham's voice was fully of entreaty. Alexandra could well imagine who the imperious servant was referring to. Suddenly the sound of broken pottery made her jump back. Worried that something dreadful had happened, she donned her robe and flung open the door.

She gasped, her eyes widening in surprise, at the sight of Habersham standing in the hallway, the contents of a foul-smelling chamberpot splattered over his usually immaculate dress. Covering her nose at the offensive odor, she stared at the look of surprised outrage on Habersham's face. Taking pity on the stunned valet, she reached for a towel, handing it to him.

"Thank you, madam. If you will excuse me, I shall be back momentarily to clean up this mess."

Alexandra nodded, speechless that any human being could exert so much self-control. The man must have a steel spike for a spine, she thought. Closing the door, she leaned heavily against it. The discord between her and Nicholas these past few weeks was taking its toll on the other members of the household.

Nicholas . . . his name brought a queer ache to her heart. Sighing, she stared at the empty bed. They were living like polite strangers. The nights of passion had given way to silent, angry stares. Her relationship with him had become like the last remaining days of January—dark, dismal, and depressing.

Vowing to bridge the widening gap between them, she performed her morning ablutions in haste. Fastening the hooks on her serviceable gray wool morning dress, she decided to walk to the printer's and purchase the latest edition of the newspaper. She would then come home and cook a romantic supper for the two of them. Humming quietly to herself, she put the finishing touches to her hair. Donning her pattens to keep her slippers from sinking into the wet dirt, she hurried down the stairs.

The heavy rains had turned the road into a mire of mud. Her feet felt weighted down from the mud caked onto the bottoms of her pattens, making every step she took an effort. She sighed in relief as the print shop came into view.

Upon entering, Alexandra was greeted by Mister Dixon's friendly smile. She was about to offer a greeting in return when her gaze fell on the unwelcome presence of Sabrina Montgomery. Just my luck, she thought, trying to hide the loathing she felt behind a polite facade.

"Good morning," she offered, making the effort to be civil. "I wasn't aware you frequented the print shop, Sabrina."

"I usually don't, but Basil is in the back having something printed up," Sabrina replied, taking in Alexandra's bedraggled state; she eyed her dress disapprovingly. "How is Nicholas? I haven't seen him lately."

"Nicholas is fine, but terribly busy. I've been keeping him occupied of late." She lowered her lashes, letting the full import of her statement sink in. Smiling in satisfaction at Sabrina's angry glare, Alexandra was rewarded a moment later when the woman turned away in disgust.

"I have come for the latest edition of the *Gazette*, Mister Dixon. Is it ready?" Alexandra asked the proprietor.

"Indeed, Lady Blackstone," he said, lowering his voice, "and the news it contains is not good."

Alarmed by Mister Dixon's tone, she handed him her coin, took the paper he proffered, and hurried home.

Seated at the desk in Nicholas's study, Alexandra spread the newspaper out before her. She perused the pages, noting the usual birth and death announcements. She smiled, reading the "Rules for the Advancement of Matrimonial Felicity" that appeared on the second page. *"Never dispute with him whatever be the occasion. . . . And if any Altercations for Jars happen, don't separate the bed. . . ."* The author must have had her and Nicholas in mind when he penned the article, she thought.

As she turned the page her face paled. There in bold print was Lord Dartmouth's circular letter of October 19th, informing the governors of the colonies that the Crown was expressly forbidding the exportation of powder and arms from Great Britain to the colonies. Her heart began to pound as she read the words before her: ". . . *take the most effectual measures for arresting, detaining, and securing any Gunpowder or any sort of Arms or Ammunition which may be attempted to be imported into the Province under your Government."*

"My God, they must be mad!" The colonies would never stand for such actions. Benjamin was right. War was coming. She couldn't turn her back on the American fight for freedom, not with the alternative of British autocratic rule breathing down their necks. She had made her position clear to Nicholas. She only hoped that he would understand what she must do.

Grabbing hold of the brass handles on the top drawers of the desk, she slid them open. Searching their contents, she found only receipts of purchases and bills for goods rendered. Tugging on the handle of the right bottom drawer, she found it wouldn't budge. Thinking it was stuck, she pulled a little harder. It was locked. Her heart beat faster. There must be something terribly important inside if Nicholas kept it locked.

Remembering where her father had always hidden the key to his desk, she felt beneath the center drawer. She pushed on the wood until one of the panels popped open, smiling in satisfaction when a small brass key dropped into her hand. Clutching it tightly, she struggled with her conscience. The key felt as heavy as her heart.

Deciding she had no alternative, she placed the key in the lock and opened the drawer. Her eyes fell upon two official-looking documents; the gold wax seals were already broken. Swallowing hard, she lifted the pages, reading their contents.

Her eyes widened in surprise as she read about William Pitt's proposal in Parliament that the British withdraw their troops from Boston. She felt a moment of elation until she read further that the proposal had been defeated.

Scanning the second document, she gasped, a lump lodging in her throat. Stated plainly in black and white was the authorization from the Crown that General Gage was to use force to retain the loyal authority in Massachusetts. The letters blurred before her eyes as tears surfaced to cloud her vision. ''War.'' She breathed the word quietly. My God, what was going to happen now?

Shoving the papers carefully back into the drawer, Alexandra locked it once again, replacing the key where she had found it. She might have need for its use once again; she had decided to comply with Benjamin's request for assistance.

Entering the Courtland home a short time later, Alexandra was relieved to discover that her parents had gone out for the day. The new housekeeper, hired to replace Betsy, directed her into the study.

She found Ben seated at her father's desk, reading over some official-looking papers. "Hello," she said as she entered.

Benjamin looked up, his face paling slightly. Shuffling the papers before him into a pile, he stuffed them into a brown leather satchel. "Alexandra," he replied, smiling in greeting, "what brings you out on such a dreary day?"

Closing the door behind her, Alexandra approached the desk. "Have you read this morning's *Gazette?*"

Ben nodded, his mouth thinning in displeasure. "Aye, it was no more than we expected from our benevolent king."

Plopping down in the chair before the desk, Alexandra took a calming breath. "There's more," she said.

Ben's forehead creased in confusion. "More? More what?"

"Gage has been ordered to use force in Massachusetts if he deems it necessary."

Rising from his chair, Ben placed the flat of his hands on the top of the desk. He leaned forward and lowered his voice. "How do you know?"

"I have betrayed Nicholas."

"Did he tell you this information in confidence?"

Shaking her head, she proceeded to tell Benjamin about the events of the morning.

Noting the expression of misery on his sister's face when she finished her confession, Benjamin came forward, kneeling by the side of her chair. Taking hold of her hand, which was cold and clammy, he tried to reassure her. "You did the right thing, Alex. You must believe me."

A single tear slid down her cheek. "I have been disloyal to my husband. I have tarnished our vows of matrimony." She covered her face, sobbing softly into her hands.

"Nicholas understands loyalty to one's country. He would not condemn you for following your conscience."

Alexandra's head shot up. "He would despise me if he knew I had betrayed him. He is an honorable man. He lives by a strict code of ethics."

"Nicholas needn't find out you are passing information. If you discover anything important, relay the information to me. I will see that it reaches the proper channels."

"You're sure he won't find out?" She spoke in a broken whisper.

"Not unless you tell him. Take no risks, and most important, act no differently. Your own guilty conscience will give you away if you let it."

Act no different, Benjamin had said. How on earth was she going to do that? she wondered, checking her appearance in the looking glass one last time.

The blue satin gown was one of Nicholas's favorites. Surely he would know she was up to something when he saw her this evening. *Your own guilty conscience will give you away if you let it.* Damn! She had to get herself under control.

Pinching her cheeks to add a little color to her pale complexion, she tugged the bodice of her gown a little lower. It wouldn't hurt to use some feminine wiles to take Nicholas's mind off their disagreement and put him in a more receptive frame of mind.

She felt guilty enough knowing that she had betrayed Nicholas and would do so again if necessary. The least she could do was humble herself before him and try to make amends for her shrewish behavior of the past few weeks.

Dabbing a few drops of the rose-scented perfume Nicholas was particularly fond of into the cleft of her bosom, she took a deep breath and marched down the stairs to face her husband.

Nicholas was seated in the parlor, sipping slowly on a brandy, when she entered. He stared thoughtfully into the fire. Was he thinking about her? she wondered. The sound of her satin skirts rustling softly over the floor alerted him to her presence. She smiled when he looked up.

"Good evening," she said, pleased by the way his eyes traveled appreciatively over her body, landing on the seductive swell of her bosom. "I hope I haven't kept you waiting." He said nothing, but the lust in his eyes spoke volumes. He wanted her; her nipples tightened in response.

As if awakening from a pleasant dream, Nicholas blinked. "Not at all," he finally responded, returning her smile. "Would you care for a drink?"

"Yes, please."

The polite facade merely added to the tension building between them. Alexandra knew Nicholas wasn't interested in before-dinner drinks and small talk. His eyes stripped her naked every time he looked at her. The weeks they had been apart had left a hunger within them that no amount of food or drink was going to appease.

"Thank you," she said as he handed her the crystal wine glass. Their fingers touched; a tingle of yearning shot up her arm at the innocent gesture.

Sipping slowly on the rich burgundy, Alexandra let her eyes roam over every inch of Nicholas's masculine physique. They traveled up the white silk stockings that showed off his muscular calves. His thighs were encased in tight fawn-colored breeches, and there was no mistaking the hardened bulge that jutted forth beneath her scrutiny.

Looking up into Nicholas's fathomless jet-black eyes, she felt herself drowning. A warm flush suffused her entire body; her cheeks grew warm. She licked her lips, which suddenly felt dry.

"Are you hungry, my sweet?" Nicholas inquired, taking the glass from Alexandra's fingers and placing it on the table.

"I find I have built up an enormous appetite these past few weeks," she confessed.

"As have I." He stared at her intently. "Shall we adjourn to the dining room?"

"I think I would prefer to ease my hunger in the bedroom," she replied boldly.

The warmth of Nicholas's gaze wrapped her like a warm blanket. He smiled, pulling her into his embrace. "I have missed you, my sweet." His lips tantalized her mouth; his tongue teased and tormented until she felt her knees turn to jelly.

Taking his hands, she placed them on her breasts. Her nipples ached as his fingers played provocatively across the hardened nubs. A moment later her hooks were undone, and she felt her breasts burst free from their confinement.

"You are full of surprises tonight," Nicholas said, staring at her nakedness.

Alexandra smiled, pushing the gown down past her hips. From the look of intense pleasure on Nicholas's face, she knew her decision to forgo her underclothing had been a correct one.

"Now it's your turn."

"What if someone comes?"

Reaching for the buttons on his breeches, Alexandra released them one by one. "I'm hoping someone does!"

Pulling her hard against him, Nicholas cupped the soft flesh of her buttocks. "You are shameless. I was speaking of the servants."

"They have been instructed not to disturb us . . . for any reason."

Tipping up her chin, he looked into the brilliant blue flames of her eyes. "Did you plan this seduction?"

Insinuating her hands inside his breeches, she cupped his stiffened member, stroking it with tantalizing slowness. "Do you object?" she asked, noting the beads of perspiration forming on his upper lip.

"No!" he choked out. "God, no!"

Their joining was more frenzied, more fulfilling than any that had occurred before. Gazing into the relaxed features of her husband as they lay before the fire, Alexandra noted how serene he looked in slumber. She memorized every plane, every line of his face, imprinting them into her mind, her heart, her soul, where they could never be taken from her.

She had traveled down a dangerous path today. Where that road would lead her was anybody's guess. But like any road, eventually it had to end. She only hoped when it did, Nicholas would be there waiting for her.

# Chapter Twenty-Two

Basil had observed his prey carefully many times over the last few weeks. Not only had he paid particular attention to Nicholas's movements but to Nicholas's wife's as well.

Alexandra's activities were of particular interest to him. He had observed her on several occasions meeting with her brother and the cooper, Tom Farley. This evening was no exception. From his position across the street, he observed her leaving the house. He knew Nicholas wasn't at home this evening. He had seen him earlier at the palace in the company of the governor.

Following Alexandra the short distance to her parents' home, Basil waited. She didn't enter the house but crossed the street directly opposite it. A moment later, Benjamin Courtland arrived, alone. Basil stared in surprise as Alexandra reached beneath her heavy cape to extract some type of document. She looked around nervously before handing it to her brother. Courtland read it, shaking his head as if he was upset about something. Handing the missive back to his sister, he kissed her on the cheek and disappeared into the darkness.

Basil had no doubt where Alexandra had procured such a document. He knew the Courtlands were sympathetic to the colonial cause. It was only logical that she would be selected to aid in their objective. As the wife of an influential aide to the Governor, she had access to all of Nicholas's important papers.

Did Nicholas know? he wondered. He doubted it. Nicholas was far too honorable to betray the trust of his King, even for the love of a woman.

Permitting Alexandra to get a safe distance ahead of him, Basil followed her home.

Approaching the house on Nicholson Street, Alexandra quickened her steps. She couldn't shake the feeling that someone was watching her. Glancing nervously about in both directions, she was relieved to find it was only her imagination playing tricks on her. These meetings with Benjamin were getting too risky. Nicholas was certain to find out if she kept them up much longer.

Not bothering to remove her cape when she entered the house, she hurried into the study. She knew she wouldn't be disturbed. She had made it a practice to give Betsy and Habersham the night off whenever Nicholas was working late.

Lighting the candle on top of the desk, she unlocked the drawer, placing the sensitive documents back in their resting place. She breathed a sigh of relief, thankful that tonight's meeting had gone well. The news that the Crown was planning to increase troop strength here in the colonies was vital to the cause. Benjamin planned to leave immediately to carry the information to Jefferson. Blowing out the candle, Alexandra gave one last look around before leaving the study.

Basil smiled in satisfaction. Positioned outside the window of the study, he had been able to observe everything. Alexandra was very clever. He never would have guessed where the key to the desk was hidden. Now that he had that valuable piece of information stored away, he would be able to proceed with his plan.

Nicholas's reign as the Duke of Blackstone would soon be coming to an end.

Hurrying back to the Raleigh, Basil entered the taproom. The crowded, smoke-filled room was noisy with laughter and conversation. Several of the inhabitants were engaged in a spirited game of loo, while others tipped their tankards in a more libationary sport.

Searching the room, Basil was relieved to spy the drunken sailor he had befriended several weeks before. Davey Johnson was the poorest excuse of a seafaring man he had ever laid eyes on. His tall, husky frame sported a too-small head; his entire appearance was grossly out of proportion. Davey wasn't much to look at, and from the little he had learned about him, he wasn't much of a sailor; but he just might be the key to unlocking the door to his brother's demise.

"Davey, my good fellow, I was hoping to catch you in here tonight," Basil said, approaching the drunken man. He sniffed his nose in disgust at the smell of whiskey and cheap perfume that surrounded the sailor.

Two bloodshot eyes looked up, squinting at the familiar form before them. The gray eyes tried to focus in the direction of the well-modulated voice. "Is that you, Basil?" The speech was thick, the words slurred.

Basil smiled, taking a seat next to Davey on the bench. "Yes. I thought perhaps we might have a drink together," he said, patting the sailor on the back as if they were old friends.

It was a fortuitous day when Basil stumbled onto the likes of Davey Johnson. Johnson, it seemed, was some type of courier for the colony. His exact position was unclear; Johnson had been very closemouthed about his activities. It was Basil's guess that Davey wasn't carrying messages for the Crown. If that was the case, tonight could prove to be very profitable.

Setting a full bottle of rye in front of the intoxicated man, Basil smiled inwardly. It wouldn't take much to loosen the tongue of this blathering idiot. One thing he had learned while frequenting the taprooms and gambling halls of England: pitiful wretches loved to talk about themselves.

"You're all right for an Englishman," Davey said, pouring himself a drink. His aim was poor; the liquor sloshed over the table, spilling onto Basil's lap.

"I told you, Davey, I'm planning on making Virginia my permanent home," Basil said, dabbing at the mess with a napkin, trying to hide the annoyance he felt. "I've had enough of England and the unjust laws of the King."

Davey scratched the stubble on his chin. "You'd best be careful who you speak to about things like that. You could find yourself in a heap of trouble with the soldiers." He glanced about, hoping the two red-uniformed men hadn't heard Basil's treasonous remark.

Basil shrugged. "I'm not worried. My brother holds high office on the governor's staff." He noted the spark of interest that lit the red-rimmed eyes.

"You don't say," Davey said, pouring himself another drink. "Does this brother of yours have access to information?" The bloodshot eyes suddenly grew a little clearer, a little more assessing.

"Indeed he does. It wouldn't surprise me if Nicholas knew everything that went on here in Virginia."

Davey digested this piece of information. "I take it you and this brother of yours don't get along."

Shaking his head, Basil sneered. "Nicholas is a duke. He inherited the title from my father. I'm the second son—the castoff. I've come to the colonies to carve out my destiny—be my own man."

Davey smiled. If there was one thing he admired, it was a self-made man. Raising his glass in salute, he said, "Here's to your destiny. I'm sure you'll succeed in whatever it is you are planning to do. America is the land of opportunity."

"You can be sure of it. I plan to seize my opportunity as soon as it presents itself."

"And do you have a plan?"

"To be sure. I'm going to be a rich man." Noting the eagerness in Davey's face, he continued, "I could always use a smart man like yourself to help me." He poured another glass of whiskey, handing it to Davey.

Rubbing his chin, Davey shook his head. "I've got to do another job day after tomorrow." He lowered his voice. "It's sort of a secret mission."

"I knew you were the kind of man people put their trust into. I knew it the minute I laid eyes on you," Basil said.

Davey threw his shoulders back, his chest out. "I do what I can to help."

"Do you think I could be of some assistance on this mission? It would be a good opportunity for us to see how well we work together."

"I don't know . . . you haven't been cleared by the committee," Davey said, his look clearly skeptical.

"They wouldn't need to know. What harm could it do if I came along to keep you company?"

Scratching his whiskered cheek, Davey pondered the offer. "You'd have to keep your mouth shut about everything you see or hear. We want to avoid trouble."

"I'm well aware of what's at stake, my friend. Rest assured, I want this mission of yours to go smoothly. I'll know what to do when the time comes." Basil smiled reassuringly at Davey's puzzled stare, pouring his unsuspecting accomplice another drink. You can bet your life that I'll know what to do when the time comes, Davey old boy, Basil thought. I'll know just what to do.

Seated at his desk in the study, Nicholas pondered the importance of the document he held in his hand:

Dunmore had requested a contingent of Royal marines to be sent from England as soon as possible.

There would be no turning back the tide of events that was certain to drown the unsuspecting colonial insurrectionists. Parliament had already declared Massachusetts to be in a state of rebellion.

Shaking his head, Nicholas sighed, placing the document in the drawer of his desk and locking it securely. Returning the key to its hiding place, he stood and walked to the window.

He observed the naked branches of the dogwood tree that graced the yard. Tiny buds of new growth were barely visible on its limbs. Another month and spring would arrive, bringing forth new life to winter's dormant days. New life—new changes, most of which would not be kind to the inhabitants of Virginia.

He had planned to be gone by now—gone from the strife and unpleasantness of this country in turmoil—back to the serene, peaceful life he had missed back in England. He had stayed for two reasons: the governor's insistence that a replacement could not be found so quickly, and Alexandra.

Alexandra needed time to adjust to the changes that were taking place in her life. He didn't want to spoil the beautiful relationship that had blossomed since their reconciliation.

As if conjured up by his thoughts, Nicholas turned to find the object of his deliberation standing before his desk.

"Good morning, Nicholas. I hope I'm not intruding on your work," Alexandra said.

The sight of Alexandra's smiling face brought wildly erotic thoughts of last night's amorous encounter to mind. Gazing upon her prim attire, he mentally stripped it off of her, revealing the mounds of naked flesh he had held in his hands and mouth. Pulling his collar away from his neck, he loosened the tightness he felt. "Not at all, my sweet," he assured her, his voice strangely hoarse. "What can I do for you?"

Her brow wrinkling in puzzlement, Alexandra frowned. "You're not coming down with something, are you? You seem flushed to me." Walking forward, she placed her hand on his brow, relieved to find it was cool.

"I need only to be in your presence, and I find my blood boiling uncontrollably."

Alexandra laughed. "You say the most outrageous things. Now behave yourself. I've come to discuss the plans for my mother's birthday party tonight."

"It's tonight?" he asked, thinking about the sensitive document he needed to deliver.

"You haven't forgotten, have you? Oh, Nicholas! I told you father has been planning to surprise mother for weeks."

At the look of dismay on Alexandra's face, Nicholas smiled, placing a kiss upon her hand. "Of course, I haven't forgotten. What time is the party?"

"Eight o'clock. But we need to arrive a little early to set everything up. Is that all right?" She hoped that Ben would arrive early, also. She needed to talk to him—to tell him she had decided their secret meetings would have to end. After the other night's rendezvous, she hadn't been able to shake off the feeling that something was wrong. She would take no more chances with her and Nicholas's happiness. She had done her part for the cause. She would not betray Nicholas again. Benjamin would just have to understand.

Casting a furtive glance at the drawer of his desk, Nicholas frowned. There was no way he would be able to send the dispatch out today. There wasn't time to coordinate everything. He would wait until tomorrow. The governor's grand scheme for bringing the colonists to heel would just have to wait one more day.

"Of course, it's all right. I will stop at Mister Prentis's store and pick up a gift."

"But I've already purchased something."

"I know, but if it wasn't for your mother, my sweet, we might never have gotten married. I want to give her something a little extra special."

Putting her arms around his neck, Alexandra pressed a kiss to Nicholas's cheek. "You're so thoughtful, Nicholas. That must be why I love you so much."

Pulling Alexandra into his hardness, Nicholas nuzzled her neck. "Can't you think of a better way to express your love, my sweet?"

"Nicholas! You're insatiable!"

"Can I help it if my wife is irresistible? I find I cannot get enough of your sweet, little body." He nibbled her ear, trailing his tongue over the sensitive area of her neck.

The pulse at the base of Alexandra's throat skittered alarmingly; her skin prickled pleasurably. "Perhaps we should finish this discussion upstairs in our room," she suggested.

Nicholas smiled a slow, secret smile. "Perhaps we should, my sweet."

Perusing the shelves of the Prentis Store, Nicholas surveyed the sweet smelling soaps and bolts of brightly colored cloth that were attractively displayed next to porcelain figurines and candlesticks of brass and pewter.

He had spent the last twenty minutes trying to find the perfect gift for Catherine. He was just about to give up when he spied a hand carved, rosewood music box. Smiling in satisfaction, he picked it up, opening the lid. The tinkling tones played a lovely rendition of "Greensleeves." It was perfect. Catherine would absolutely love it. Handing the box to the shop clerk, he waited while it was wrapped.

"Are you buying a present for your charming wife?"

Nicholas turned to find his brother standing beside

him. Basil's smile was contrite—almost apologetic. It was just like Basil to try and make amends for his thoughtless remarks, Nicholas thought. " 'Tis a gift for Alexandra's mother," he finally replied.

"What's the occasion?"

"There's to be a surprise birthday party tonight."

Basil picked up a clay pipe, pretending to examine it. "Alexandra must be in a dither, getting ready for the party."

Nicholas shook his head. "The party is being given by her father. He has made most of the plans."

Basil could barely contain his excitement. There would be no need to lure Nicholas out of his house tonight as he had previously planned. Apparently he and Alexandra would be occupied most of the evening at the Courtlands'.

"Well, I pity you, old boy," Basil said, slapping Nicholas on the back. "I've never been one for family functions. I'd much rather spend my evenings with a good game of cards and a good-looking woman."

Taking the package from the clerk's outstretched hands, Nicholas looked disparagingly at his brother. "Someday you will find there is more to life than idle pursuits."

Yes. There is money and power, Basil thought. "Give me time, Nicholas. After all, you've had your chance to sow your wild oats. I should be afforded the same opportunity, and Sabrina is such a pleasant diversion."

"Careful your pleasant diversion doesn't prove your ruination. The woman is a fortune hunter."

"But I have no fortune, remember? She must be enamored of my many charms instead. She claims she has never bedded anyone quite like me."

Nicholas held his laughter in check. Basil's comparison was obvious. He wouldn't belabor the point. Basil would learn his lesson soon enough. "I wish you luck,"

Nicholas replied. "Now, I'd best be on my way. I have other matters to attend to this day."

Basil nodded, watching his brother depart. Nicholas had wished him luck. His smile widened. He didn't need luck. He had planned everything perfectly. To-night, the Duke of Blackstone would be in for a big surprise—a very big surprise indeed.

# Chapter Twenty-Three

"Surprise!" The chorus of merry voices shouted as Catherine entered the dining room.

She stood in the doorway, mouth agape, as her eyes fell upon the faces of each of her children who were seated around the mahogany table, grinning at her with undisguised pleasure. "Oh, my!" she said, throwing up her hands to halt the reddening blush that covered her cheeks.

"Happy birthday, my dear," Samuel said, giving his startled wife a kiss on the lips.

"Samuel, for heaven's sake, did you plan all this?" Catherine asked, directing an accusing look at her husband.

"Father planned it," Alicia confessed. "We all helped, even Tom and Nicholas. They hung the decorations, and Ben made the punch."

Ben smiled sheepishly, raising his glass in silent toast to his mother.

Gazing about the room, Catherine noticed the festive decorations for the first time. There were streamers and bows of pink satin ribbon strewn all about. The table had been set with her finest bone china and crystal. She smiled, her eyes brimming with tears of joy. "Everything is lovely. Thank you all."

"Come and sit down, Mother," Alexandra directed,

pulling out the chair at the head of the table. "Chloe has fixed a special meal of roast turkey and her famous cornbread dressing for this auspicious occasion."

After Catherine was seated, Samuel tapped gently on the rim of his crystal water goblet, waiting until everyone quieted. "I should like to propose a toast," he said, lifting his wineglass high in the air; he stared lovingly at his wife. "To the finest wife and dearest friend a man could ever hope to find." Directing his attention to the three men seated at the table, he added, "I pray that you gentlemen will be similarly blessed."

Tom, Ben, and Nicholas exchanged boastful glances and smiled at their respective mates.

"Hear! Hear!" Nicholas said, joining in the toast. He gave Alexandra an intimate smile and winked.

Returning Nicholas's smile with a dazzling one of her own, Alexandra felt as if her heart would burst with happiness. She was surrounded by the people she loved most in the world, and her joy knew no bounds. Everything was perfect. There was nothing that could mar this wonderful day.


Whistling a lively tune, Basil felt better than he had in weeks. He patted his stomach, feeling for the document hidden on his person. Nicholas was going to be in for a big surprise when he opened the drawer of his desk. The theft of the document had gone off without a hitch. It had been easier than stealing money from a blind beggar.

"Quit that infernal noise, will you?" Davey demanded. "We don't wish to draw attention to ourselves." He stared at the Englishman who sat awkwardly upon his horse and shook his head. He should never have let Basil talk him into accompanying him tonight. He must have been well into his cups the other night to have done so. The fool could jeopardize the entire mission. It was imperative he reach York-

292

town before his contact left. A message of grave importance was to be delivered to him tonight.

"How much farther until we reach our destination?" Basil inquired, glancing about the area, noting the thick copse of trees surrounding them. He needed to put his plan into action soon. Sabrina had managed to finagle a late-night supper invitation from Lady Dunmore and would meet him at the Governor's Palace.

"I'd say we have another six or seven miles," Davey replied.

"Hold up a minute," Basil said. "I think there might be something wrong with my horse." Dismounting, Basil walked around to the rear of his steed.

"I'd better ride on ahead. I can't afford to be late."

Pulling a pistol from beneath his coat, Basil aimed it at the chest of the startled man. "I'm afraid I can't allow you to do that, old man. Sorry. Now dismount."

"What's going on!" Davey shouted. "I knew I should never have trusted an Englishman."

Basil smiled. " 'Tis fortunate for me that you did. I'm sorry, Davey, but this is where we part company."

Davey stared at the pistol and then at Basil's face. "Why for heaven's sake!"

"Let's just say, I have come to the aid of king and country this evening and leave it at that."

"You Tory bastard!" Davey screamed, lunging forward. "I'll kill you for this."

Basil fired, watching his victim fall to the ground. "I really did like you, Davey," Basil said, kicking at the inert form to make sure he was dead. "Unfortunately, you are of more use to me dead than alive." Smiling, he thought of the governor's reaction when he presented the two pieces of tangible evidence that would implicate Nicholas in an act of treason: the stolen document, and the dead body of a man who rode express for the committee. A man who would be portrayed as Nicholas's partner in crime in performing treason against the King.

With Nicholas's outspoken defense of the colonists' rights, he shouldn't have any trouble at all convincing the governor of his guilt. Whistling a spirited tune, he mounted up.

The hour was late when Basil reached the palace. It had been necessary for him to go back to his room, remove his bloodstained clothes, and change into something more suitable for the occasion. Pulling at the bottom of his gold brocade waistcoat, he took a deep breath and entered the dining room.

Spying Sabrina, who was seated on the settee with a look of boredom on her face, he strode casually in her direction. "Good evening, my love," he said, smiling at her startled expression.

"Basil! I've been so worried. Did everything go as planned?"

"It couldn't have been more perfect. Is the governor still here?" He looked about, frowning when he noted his absence.

"Yes. He went to his office about ten minutes ago to take care of something. He should be back any minute."

"Excellent. I will go and speak with him. I don't want to drag this affair out any longer than necessary. The courier I told you about is strapped on a horse and tied up outside by the stables. I don't want someone else finding him and asking a lot of questions before I have a chance to speak to the governor."

"Shall I accompany you?"

Shaking his head, Basil took hold of Sabrina's hand, placing a kiss upon it. "No, my dear. This is too sordid for you to witness. I shall take care of everything. You are not to worry. By tomorrow, everything we have worked for will be ours."

Sabrina's heart pounded so loudly she was certain the other guests could hear it; she watched Basil exit the room. Placing her hand upon her breast, she tried to stifle the nervous tension beating within. Basil was actually going to pull this off, she thought, smiling to herself. The inept fool wasn't so useless, after all.

It was a pity the only way she could become the Duchess of Blackstone was to marry Basil. Nicholas would have been a great deal more preferable. Oh, well, beggars can't be choosers, she thought. A duchess was a duchess, no matter who was duke. Once she had the title, it would be easy enough to seek her pleasure elsewhere. She cooled her excitement with a wave of her fan.

Basil knocked softly on the door to the governor's office. A moment later he was bidden to enter. Lord Dunmore was seated at his desk, and mercifully, he was alone.

Lord Dunmore looked up, surprised to find Nicholas's brother striding through the door. "Hello, Basil. I wasn't sure you were going to come to our little gathering this evening. Miss Montgomery said something about your being delayed."

"I have come to see you on precisely that matter, your grace," Basil said, closing the door behind him. "I have grave news to report . . . news that will shock you as severely as it shocked me."

Indicating the Chippendale chair by the desk, Lord Dunmore replied, "Sit down and tell me what has happened. By the anxious expression on your face, I can see this must be serious."

Reaching into the waistband of his breeches, Basil laid the paper he had stolen from Nicholas's office on the governor's desk. He could tell by Lord Dunmore's surprised expression that he recognized the missive as one of his own.

"Where did you get this?" he demanded, his tone accusatory. "I could have you strung up for having possession of such a sensitive document."

Basil paled, surprised by the direction Lord Dunmore's thoughts were taking. "It is not I who should be strung up, your grace. I took this document off an express rider for the Committee of Correspondence.''

Rising from his chair, Lord Dunmore began to pace behind his desk. "An express rider. Where would he get such a document. I gave it to Nicholas only this morning.''

Basil nodded. "Precisely.''

"What are you saying! Do you realize the seriousness of that remark?''

Lord Dunmore, I have reason to believe that Nicholas is a traitor.''

"Say no more!'' the governor ordered, holding up his hands. "I won't listen to such rubbish. Your brother is one of the most honorable and loyal men I know.''

"Do you think this is easy for me? Nicholas is my brother. I am just as shocked as you to find that he has betrayed your trust in him.''

"Where is your proof? You cannot accuse a man of treason without proof. It is a serious offense.''

"The man I took the document from is tied up outside on his horse.''

"Well, bring him in here, for God's sake. I want to question him.''

"I'm afraid that's not possible. He's dead.''

Dropping into his seat, the governor poured himself a brandy. "You had better explain everything from the beginning. I wish to know all the details.''

Basil explained how he had come to make the acquaintance of Davey Johnson. He went on to tell Lord Dunmore how Johnson had incriminated his brother, Nicholas, by naming him as his contact in Williamsburg.

"Is the story from the lips of a traitor the only evidence you possess?'' the governor inquired.

"There is the document, your grace,'' Basil said, pointing to the paper on the desk. "Davey told me Nicholas gave it to him this afternoon with instructions to deliver it to Yorktown. That's where we were going when I shot him."

Lord Dunmore's eyebrows raised in disbelief. "You shot him! Why?"

"I tried to arrest him, to bring him back for questioning, but he came at me. I had no choice. It was my life or his."

The governor shook his head. "This is all so difficult to believe. I might have expected betrayal from other men, but not from Nicholas Fortune."

"I know you can appreciate how difficult this has been for me, your grace. Nicholas is, after all, my brother. I don't wish to destroy our relationship over this matter."

The governor studied the man before him. "What is it you wish me to do?"

"The final decision regarding Nicholas's guilt must be yours. I only ask that you leave my name out of it if you decide to bring charges against him. Nicholas may have betrayed his country, but I have betrayed my own brother." Covering his face, he wept.

The governor steepled his fingers in front of his face, pondering his decision. After a few moments he spoke.

"The charge of treason is too serious to overlook. I must act accordingly and have Nicholas arrested. Since it is your desire to hide the fact of your involvement from your brother, I will abide by your wishes. Go now and speak to no one about this. I want this matter handled as delicately as possible due to the sensitive position Nicholas occupies on my staff."

"My betrothed, Miss Montgomery, already knows, your grace. I wasn't able to bear such a terrible burden alone."

Frowning, Lord Dunmore stood. "See that this goes no further. Inform your intended not to speak about this to anyone. I will hold you personally accountable if word of this leaks out before I'm ready."

"Of course. You can rely on my discretion," Basil

said, turning to leave. Pausing by the door, he looked back at the governor, almost laughing at the look of pain the old fool wore upon his face. "If it's any consolation, your grace, I think you are doing the right thing."

"I wouldn't be in such a hurry to convict your brother, Fortune. He hasn't been tried of any crime yet. I like to think a man is innocent until proven guilty."

"You are a just man, my lord. I can see Nicholas is in good hands." With that, Basil exited the door, pausing to lean against the wall in the dimly lit hallway. He smiled. He had done it. He had succeeded in convincing Lord Dunmore of Nicholas's guilt. The old man could protest Nicholas's innocence all he wanted; the look on Dunmore's face when he spied that document was all the proof he needed. Nicholas was as good as hanged. When that happened, he would become the new Duke of Blackstone. Wouldn't father be proud, he thought. He never thought I would amount to much, but I showed him. I showed them all.

The dulcet tones of the music box filled the parlor with its sweet, harmonious sounds. Alexandra's eyes twinkled in merriment as they fell upon her mother and Nicholas dancing about the room in time to the music.

"Your mother seems to be enjoying herself," Samuel said, sitting next to his daughter on the loveseat.

Noting the look of pleasure on her mother's face, Alexandra smiled. "It was a wonderful party, Father. I'm happy everything turned out so well."

"From the thunderous expression on your brother's face, I'm not so sure it did."

Following her father's eyes, Alexandra glanced over at Ben, who was leaning up against the mantel, staring into the flames of the fire. "Ben's got a lot on his mind these days. He's deeply committed to the cause. I fear it has put an unfair burden on his relationship with Prudence. Their manner seemed a bit strained tonight."

Samuel lit his pipe. "I fear we shall all feel a bit strained in the coming months," he said, blowing the smoke into the air. "Have you and Nicholas made a decision about what you are going to do?"

"Yes. We didn't want to mention our plans and spoil mother's birthday, but we've decided to leave for England in the early part of April."

Taking Alexandra's hand, Samuel squeezed it reassuringly. "I know how hard this has been for you. I'm proud you have met your responsibilities so admirably."

"Loving Nicholas as I do has made my choice easier."

"You're a loyal daughter and a loyal wife. Nicholas is lucky to have you."

"Did I hear my name mentioned?" Nicholas asked, looking down on the somber pair before him.

"Father was just saying how lucky you are to have me. I quite agree," she said, a teasing smile lifting the corners of her mouth.

Before Nicholas could reply, a loud pounding sounded at the front door.

"I wonder who that could be at such a late hour," Catherine said.

Samuel stood, walking to the door. Before he could open it, the door was kicked in and a trio of red-uniformed soldiers burst into the room.

"What is the meaning of this? How dare you break into my home!"

"Get out of our way, old man. We've come on orders from Governor Dunmore."

Nicholas, Alexandra, and Ben rushed into the hallway.

"Father, what is it? Why have the soldiers come?"

Alexandra asked, fear twisting her stomach into a painful knot. It's Benjamin, she thought, looking over at him. They've found out that he rides for the committee.

Pulling out a sheet of parchment from within the breast pocket of his uniform coat, the dark-haired soldier read the order. "We have come to arrest Nicholas Fortune."

Alexandra gasped, clutching her throat. *"Nicholas."* She breathed his name under her breath.

Nicholas stepped forward. "There must be some mistake. I am Nicholas Fortune, aide to Governor Dunmore."

"There's no mistake. The governor signed this order himself."

"What's the charge?" Nicholas asked, throwing an comforting arm around his wife's shoulders.

"Treason. Treason against the Crown."

# Chapter Twenty-Four

Treason . . . treason . . . treason. . . . The words exploded like cannon fire, shattering Alexandra's composure. "My husband is no traitor," she said. "You have made a terrible mistake."

The soldier looked with disgust at the hysterical woman. "The mistake was your husband's, madam, not ours." Grabbing hold of Nicholas's arms, the soldiers pulled him toward the door.

"Nicholas!" Alexandra cried, running after him.

Ben reached out, pulling Alexandra to him.

"Don't worry, my sweet. I'm sure this can be cleared up by morning," Nicholas said, giving Alexandra one last reassuring smile before he was escorted into the night.

The governor's office was dimly lit when Nicholas entered a short time later in the custody of two grim-faced soldiers. A single candle flickered on the desk, illuminating the haggard features of John Murray, the Earl of Dunmore. He was bent over a sheaf of papers, affixing his wax seal to each of the official-looking documents.

Relief flooded through Nicholas at the sight of his old friend. Surely John would be able to shed some light on the disturbing events of the evening. "Thank

God you're here, John. Would you please tell these fools that they have made a terrible mistake.''

Setting down his quill and wiping the red wax off his ring, Lord Dunmore looked up, his expression grave. ''Leave us alone,'' he ordered the red-coated guards. Turning his attention to Nicholas, he indicated the chair in front of his desk. ''Be seated, Lord Blackstone.''

Doing as he was instructed, Nicholas felt more confused than ever by Lord Dunmore's attitude. A seed of fear was beginning to take root and grow within him. He waited but a moment for the governor to speak.

''It has been brought to my attention that you, Lord Blackstone, have engaged in treason against King George III of England.''

Nicholas jumped up, slamming his hands down on the desk. ''That's a lie! Who told you such filth? I am no more a traitor to the Crown than you. How can you think it after you have known me all these years?''

''I didn't want to believe it, Nicholas. In fact, I was hesitant to accept the word of such a. . . . Well, that's neither here nor there. The fact is, there is proof to support the accusation. Irrefutable proof.''

''What proof? I have no idea what you are talking about,'' Nicholas said, resuming his seat.

''Do you recall the document I gave you only this morning? The contents of which, I'm sure you will agree, would be devastating in the hands of the wrong people.''

''Of course I recall. It's locked in the drawer of my desk. I meant to dispatch it today, but it was my mother-in-law's birthday; I postponed its delivery until tomorrow.''

Lord Dunmore reached inside the top drawer of his desk, pulling out a cream-colored sheet of parchment. Handing it to Nicholas, he asked, ''Is this not the same document that you claim to have secured in your desk?"

Scanning the contents, Nicholas paled. "Yes, it's one and the same." He looked up to read the accusation in John Murray's eyes. "I don't understand how it could be in your possession. I placed it in my desk only this morning."

Holding out his hand for the missive, Governor Dunmore shook his head. "This document was found on the person of one Davey Johnson. A man who rode for the Committee of Correspondence—a man who claimed you were his contact here in Williamsburg.

Rising to his feet, Nicholas faced Lord Dunmore. "That's another lie. I've never heard of this Davey Johnson. Let me interrogate him. I'm sure he'll confess his perfidy in this matter."

"I'm afraid that's not possible, Nicholas. Davey Johnson is dead."

Momentarily taken aback, Nicholas quickly regained his composure. "I have no knowledge of this person. You must believe me. Who is this other person that claims I am involved? I have a right to face my accuser."

Standing up, the governor walked over to the door. "I'm sorry, Nicholas, I am not at liberty to divulge that information. Until this matter can be looked into further, I have no choice but to arrest you." He signaled to the guards who waited outside the door.

"Due to the seriousness of the charge and the position you hold on my staff, there will be a private investigation and hearing. I do not want our problems aired in public, giving more ammunition to our enemies. If you demand a trial by jury, I will have no recourse but to comply; but let me assure you, a jury of your peers will be much harsher in its judgment of you than I.

"Until such time as a decision is reached in this matter, you shall be incarcerated in the palace under heavy guard. I do this out of respect for our past friendship and the fact that you are a member of the nobility."

Nicholas was stunned. He stared in disbelief, listening to the words the governor spoke but not really hearing them. A thousand thoughts darted through his mind as he listened to Lord Dunmore's speech. Someone was out to frame him—to use him as a scapegoat. Someone wanted him dead, but who?

"Are you ready to go, Nicholas? The soldiers will escort you to your room. I'll send for your valet to bring your clothes and such."

Nicholas nodded, staring intently into Lord Dunmore's face. "I will go, but remember this, I am innocent. You have accused me unjustly. I don't know who stands to profit from my conviction, but rest assured, I intend to find out."

Alexandra paced the confines of her father's study while Benjamin and Samuel stood near the fireplace conversing in tones too low for her to distinguish. The clock on the mantel struck two. Her mother had long since retired, exhausted from the activities of the day and the added strain of Nicholas's arrest.

Nicholas had been arrested like a common criminal. God! How had it happened? Her father and brother had spent the better part of the evening debating that very question.

Approaching the two tired men, Alexandra noted how quickly their conversation ceased. A measure of alarm threaded through her. "What are you keeping from me?" she demanded, facing the pair of worried faces.

Samuel reached out, drawing Alexandra into his embrace. "We are discussing the possible reasons for Nicholas's arrest. Neither of us can figure out why he was singled out."

Alexandra shot her brother an accusing glance. "It's

my fault. If I hadn't helped Ben, none of this would have happened."

"You mustn't blame Ben, Alex," Samuel said. "He only did what his conscience dictated."

"I don't blame Ben; I blame myself." The tears she had tried to hold back, slid slowly down her face.

Ben came forward taking hold of Alexandra's hand. "I'm sorry, Alex. I promise you, I will find out who is behind Nicholas's arrest."

"Do you think they will let me see him?"

Both men exchanged sympathetic looks. Samuel squeezed Alexandra's shoulder. "Your political persuasions are well known, my dear," Samuel replied. "Do you know of anyone who might be willing to help?"

After a moment, Alexandra's face brightened; she wiped her tears with the edge of her sleeve. "Johanna . . . Johanna Wellington. Her husband is on the governor's staff. First thing tomorrow, I will pay a visit to her. If anyone can help me, it would be Johanna."

The next morning, Alexandra was ushered into the parlor of the Wellington house, which was situated on the Palace Green not too far from the Wythe house. She waited impatiently on the green velvet settee, casting nervous glances at the door while waiting for Johanna Wellington to appear.

The ornate brass clock on the mantel ticked off the minutes. The steady, repetitive sound kept time to the nervous beating of her heart. A freshly brewed pot of tea resting on the table before her sent billows of aromatic steam into the air. It was just too tempting to resist. Putting aside her staunch convictions, she picked up the bone china cup and poured herself some. The distinctive orange flavor had a calming effect on her nerves. As the clock struck ten-thirty, Lady Wellington floated through the doorway in a swirl of raspberry satin and white lace.

"My dear, I'm so dreadfully sorry," Johanna said, rushing forward to draw Alexandra into her embrace. "Frederick told me about Nicholas's arrest only this morning. I didn't believe a word of it. Imagine the fools thinking Nicholas a traitor." She shook her head in disbelief.

"Thank you, Johanna," Alexandra replied. "You don't know what your words mean to me."

"What can I do to help? I know you would not be wasting your time on social calls at such a difficult time."

Giving the older woman a hug, Alexandra blinked back her tears. "You are as perceptive as always. I do need your help. Habersham, Nicholas's valet, informed me this morning that Nicholas was being held at the palace under heavy guard. Habersham was allowed to drop off his clothes and other items of a personal nature but was not allowed to carry on any type of conversation with him. Because of my family's political views, I'm afraid they will not allow me to visit my own husband."

"That is shocking! Simply shocking!" Johanna replied. Tapping her cheek with her finger, she paused to consider Alexandra's predicament. "Frederick is not without influence with the governor, and I am definitely not without influence with Frederick. Let me see what I can work out. Unless my husband wants to carry this disagreement between the King and colonies into his bedroom, he will concede to my demands. You have my word on it, my dear."

Heaving a sigh of relief, Alexandra thought of poor Frederick. The man was up against insurmountable odds where Johanna was concerned. Her visit with Nicholas was almost assured.

Waiting nervously outside the door to the northeast bedroom of the palace where Nicholas was sequestered,

Alexandra avoided the callous sneers of the guards posted outside his room. She felt uncomfortable under their scrutiny. The insulting looks they had cast her way made her pray fervently that she would be ushered into Nicholas's quarters soon.

The sound of the door opening eased her apprehension. Looking up, she found Lord Wellington coming toward her. True to her word, Johanna had pressured Frederick into pleading her case before the governor.

"You may go in now, Lady Blackstone. Johanna has vouched for your integrity, so it will not be necessary to have you searched."

Alexandra's eyes widened, but she kept silent.

"Please keep your visit as brief as possible. The governor has already received censure from the other council members because of his lenient treatment of your husband."

"Thank you, my lord. I won't forget your kindness."

Pressing a kiss to her hand, Lord Wellington opened the door to allow her entry.

It took a moment for her eyes to adjust. She spotted Nicholas staring out the window; his forlorn expression made her heart ache. He looked tired, unkempt. His face was unshaven, and his eyes were red from lack of sleep.

Nicholas turned as the door banged shut, his eyes lighting with pleasure as they fell upon the lovely figure of his wife. "My sweet, I've missed you," he said, coming forward.

"Oh, Nicholas," Alexandra sobbed, "what are we going to do? How could the governor have made such a terrible mistake?"

Nicholas shook his head, patting Alexandra's silken tresses. "I've been set up, Alexandra. I don't know by whom, but someone is out to get me."

Basil's sinister smile flashed through her mind, but she refrained from speaking her suspicions. If Nicho-

307

las's brother was responsible for this, she would need proof. She would not be able to voice unfounded accusations. Masking her fears, she replied, "Do you suspect anyone?"

Leading Alexandra over to the settee, Nicholas pulled her down next to him. "Please don't be upset, but the only one I can think of who might be involved in my misfortune would be your brother Ben."

Alexandra paled; her hands started to shake.

"I knew my suspicions would upset you," Nicholas said, taking her hand. "I'm sorry."

Taking a deep breath, Alexandra tried to regain her composure. Although Ben had professed his innocence in the matter, she knew they were both guilty. By aiding Ben, no matter how unwittingly, they had brought this calamity upon Nicholas.

"Ben has assured me, none of his men had any knowledge or involvement with your arrest," she finally replied. "He has promised to look into the matter to try and discover the truth."

Squeezing Alexandra's hand, Nicholas smiled. "I'm glad. I know Ben and I have had our differences, but I find I like your brother."

Covering her face, Alexandra wept. The sobs wracking her body alarmed Nicholas. Drawing her into his arms, he said, "Don't cry, my sweet. You must be brave. Together we shall conquer whatever problems befall us. With you by my side, I know all will work out. I have implicit trust in you."

Alexandra could not bring herself to look up and see the love and trust she knew were shining in Nicholas's eyes. She had betrayed him—betrayed his trust—betrayed his love—betrayed their vows. What would happen if Nicholas were to discover the truth? She shivered at the thought.

# Chapter Twenty-Five

Humming a cheerful ditty, Basil adjusted the white silk of his stock before buttoning his green brocade waistcoat. Today was the day. Nicholas's hearing would be held in the private council chamber of the Governor's Palace at one o'clock. Only the immediate family and council members would be allowed to attend.

"You're certainly chipper this morning," Sabrina said, eyeing Basil's grinning face. He looked like a plump peacock all dressed up in his brocades and satins. At times like this, she wondered if the money was really worth it. Fortunately, her conscience only reared its head in short intervals. She knew that the money, and the position it would afford her, made everything she had to do worthwhile—even bedding Basil.

Eyeing Sabrina's reflection in the mirror, Basil smiled and turned to face her. "Today's the big day, my dear," he said, his tone euphoric. "Be certain you're dressed and ready to go when I return."

"How can you be so certain things will go your way? Perhaps the council will rule in favor of Nicholas."

Shrugging into his coat, Basil smiled confidently. "I don't leave things to chance. I've bent the ear of every member of the council these past few days, reminding them of Nicholas's defense of the colonists, how radical

309

his wife and her family are, and how poor Davey Johnson named him as his accomplice. He's as good as dead.''

Sabrina smiled. ''It seems you've thought of everything.''

''Yes, I've covered all the bases. The only thing left to do is pay a last visit to my brother to apprise him of his wife's activities.''

Sabrina's eyes lit up maliciously. ''The bitch will finally get her due.''

''All bitches deserve their due, my dear. In time, those that are deserving reap their just reward.''

The hairs on the back of Sabrina's neck stood on end as Basil blew her a kiss and left the room.


Nicholas paced back and forth across the red Turkish carpet of his luxuriously appointed cell. Although the room was one of the finest in the palace, it was still a cell, representing his lack of freedom.

Today he would learn his fate, and things did not look good. According to Frederick, most members of the council were leaning toward a guilty verdict.

He kicked at the cabriole leg of the Queen Anne table, upsetting the brass candlestick that rested on top. ''Bloody hell!'' he shouted. Because of a false confession by a dead man he didn't even know, he stood to lose everything—including his life.

The sound of the key turning in the lock made him start. Glancing up at the clock, he noted the time: ten o'clock. It was too early for the proceedings to begin. Then his gaze fell upon the unwelcome presence of his brother. He rubbed his neck in an agitated fashion. Basil was the salt in an already festering wound.

''Good morning, Nicholas,'' Basil said, tossing his hat onto the bed. ''I've come to offer my support in your hour of need.''

''How charitable of you, brother dear,'' Nicholas

310

replied, his voice laced with sarcasm. By the self-satisfied expression on Basil's face, Nicholas knew the insult had gone over his head.

"I've been terribly upset by the recent events, Nicholas. I want you to know, I've done everything in my power to convince the council of your innocence. Unfortunately, they have paid me little heed, owing to the fact that I have been here such a short time."

Basil's concerned expression touched him. Perhaps he had judged him a bit too hastily. "I appreciate your efforts, Basil. It's good to know I can count on my wife and my brother to stand by me."

"Of course I will stand by you, but as for your wife. . . ." He shrugged.

Nicholas's face reddened in anger. "What are you implying? I won't have you casting aspersions on my wife merely because of her political views."

"Even if those views have placed you under arrest?"

Crossing over to stand in front of his brother, Nicholas reached out, grabbing onto his arm. "Explain yourself."

Paling slightly, Basil took a deep breath. "I hesitated to tell you because of your present predicament, but I believe your wife may be responsible for your incarceration."

"That's ridiculous. How can you make such a statement?"

"I witnessed her treachery first hand."

Letting go of Basil's arm, Nicholas walked to the window, looking out at the grounds below. "Tell me."

"It is my habit to take a brief walk before bedtime. I never like to retire on a full stomach. While on two of these outings, I observed your wife in secret meetings with her brother."

Nicholas laughed. "That is your proof? Alexandra meeting with a member of her own family?"

"Let me finish. They met outside her parents' home, across the street, to be exact. She passed him some type of documents which he read and gave back to her. She hid the documents within the folds of her cloak and then hurried back in the direction of your house. I thought it odd at the time but didn't pay much attention to it until after your arrest. It is my opinion that your wife has been spiriting government documents out of your house and into the hands of the enemy."

A cold rage began to build inside Nicholas's breast. Everything Basil said made sense. If Alexandra had found out where he kept his papers, it wouldn't have been that difficult for her to obtain them and give them to her brother. By God, she has betrayed me! He clenched his fists.

Turning to face his brother, Nicholas masked the hurt and anger he was feeling. "I wish to ponder this information of yours in private. I would appreciate being left to keep my own counsel."

Basil inclined his head. "Of course. I'm sorry to have been the bearer of such news, but I thought you had the right to know." Seeing the desolation on Nicholas's face, Basil turned to depart, smiling inwardly. "I shall see you this afternoon, Nicholas," he shouted over his shoulder.

After the door slammed shut, Nicholas began pacing the room once again. Had Alexandra really betrayed him with her brother? The thought brought a searing pain deep in his chest. He remembered all the times she had vowed to get even with him. He also remembered how she had lain in his arms, professing her love in so many different ways. A lump rose in his throat, making it difficult to swallow. He brought his hand up to brush at the strange sensation tickling his cheek. The tears that filled his hand were new to him. He hadn't cried since he was a child, not even when his father died. "Alexandra," he choked out, "please tell me it isn't true. Please tell me our love was not a lie."

\* \* \*

Seated between her father and brother in the paneled council chamber, Alexandra sat quietly while the members of the council debated Nicholas's fate. The evidence they had presented was damaging. The confession of the dead man, Davey Johnson, had sealed Nicholas's destiny in the minds of many of the members. She could see it in the fierceness of their eyes, in the thinning of their lips.

Nicholas sat rigid, listening to his accusers. She had tried in vain to gain his attention, but he seemed intent on avoiding her.

The governor and the council stood, adjourning to the adjoining room to consider the evidence. Reaching over, Alexandra grabbed onto her father's arm. "What do you think this means?" she whispered. "This trial is unlike any I've ever attended."

Samuel patted his daughter's hand. "This is more of a hearing than a trial, my dear. The governor wishes to keep this sordid affair secret from most of the community. He's afraid the colonists might unite behind a man accused of aiding their cause."

"Why do they seek private counsel? Do you think perhaps they cannot reach a unanimous decision?" A spark of hope entered her eyes as she waited for her father's reply.

"I pray that is the case. Nicholas has many friends on the council. Perhaps they are speaking out in his behalf. We will just have to wait and see."

A few moments later the procession of men reentered the room and took their seats. The governor remained standing. The expression of sadness he wore on his face chilled Alexandra to the bone.

"Lord Blackstone, please rise and face the court," the governor directed.

Nicholas stood, his face a mask of stone as he turned toward the governor and the other members of the council.

"It is the decision of this hearing that you, Nicholas

Fortune, Duke of Blackstone, are guilty of high treason against King George III of England. I am, therefore, petitioning Parliament to strip you of your title, lands, and fortune."

Alexandra gasped, grabbing her throat.

Basil and Sabrina exchanged knowing looks.

Ignoring the murmurs and outcries of the onlookers, Lord Dunmore added, "Because of the fact that your accomplice, Davey Johnson, is dead and cannot confirm your guilt, you will be spared the punishment of death that usually accompanies such a crime. You will be free to go, but you will be afforded none of the privileges that were formerly yours by right. Do you wish to make a statement?"

Nicholas's eyes hardened into two pieces of obsidian. "I am innocent of treason. The only thing I am guilty of is trusting the wrong people," he said, looking straight at Alexandra.

Alexandra was taken back by the viciousness of Nicholas's gaze. He was looking at her as if he despised her. A shiver of apprehension ran up her spine, and she trembled. Her brother's hand closed comfortingly around hers. *He knows,* she thought. *Nicholas knows.* She didn't have long to wait for her suspicions to be confirmed. A few minutes later, Nicholas stood before her, holding out his hand.

"It is time to go home, Alexandra. There is much we need to discuss, is there not?"

Grabbing onto his hand, which was a cold as the black eyes that accused and condemned, she blinked back the tears, swallowing the fear that welled up inside her. "I am ready." Bidding farewell to her father and brother, whose expressions were filled with sympathy and pity, Alexandra followed her husband home.

The house was deathly silent when they entered. Habersham and Betsy were nowhere in evidence. Removing her cloak, Alexandra hung it on the peg in the hallway and hurried into the parlor. The welcoming fire that greeted her could not dispel the pall of gloom that hung over the room. A moment later Nicholas entered, wearing a look so glacial, no fire on earth could warm it.

"You have gotten the revenge you always said you would, haven't you, Alexandra?"

Shaking her head in denial, she placed her hand upon his arm. "You must believe me, Nicholas. What I did was not done for revenge, only for love of my country."

"So it's true . . . you *did* betray me."

Alexandra turned away, unable to face her husband's accusing glare. There was nothing she could say in her defense, nothing she could say that would make Nicholas understand why she did what she did. She nodded.

"Why, for Christ's sake? Why in bloody hell did you seek to destroy me? You said you loved me!"

Spinning around, she looked into Nicholas's eyes—eyes filled with sadness and anger. "I do love you, never doubt it. But I was torn between my love for you and my love for this land. I couldn't stand idly by and let King George's tyranny destroy everything good that this country stands for. I never would have done what I did if I thought you would be hurt by it."

"How did the governor gain possession of the documents that I had locked inside my desk, the ones Davey Johnson supposedly had on his person?"

Alexandra shook her head. "I don't know. I had nothing to do with any of that."

Nicholas grabbed her arm. "You're lying. Who are you protecting? Your brother, perhaps? Tell me, Alexandra . . . you owe me that much."

Trying to break free of the bruising grip Nicholas had upon her wrist, Alexandra twisted and turned. It was no use, Nicholas's hold was too tight. "I tell you, I know nothing about the documents you were accused of taking. Ben told me that Davey Johnson's mission was to ride to Yorktown to meet another express rider. There was no arrangement for a delivery of any document."

Nicholas released Alexandra suddenly, causing her to stumble back onto the settee. "Do you realize what you and your brother have cost me? Do you know what it means to be stripped of a title . . . to have the lands of my forefathers taken from me . . . to be reduced to a pauper because of some idealistic notion that you had? Nothing can ever replace what you have taken from me. You have used me, betrayed me, cost me everything that I held dear."

Shaking her head from side to side, tears streaming down her face, Alexandra held out her hands beseechingly. "Please, Nicholas. I never meant for any of this to happen. I'm so sorry. Please forgive me."

Nicholas laughed; the sound so demonical it sent shivers up and down her spine. "Forgive you? Forgive you for destroying me—for taking away my honor, my birthright? Never! May your life as my wife become the living hell that you have placed me into. Seek your forgiveness from the Almighty God. You shall never have it from me."

"Nicholas," Alexandra whispered, "I love you." But it was too late. Nicholas had exited the room, slamming the door to the room and to his heart as well.

# Chapter Twenty-Six

The four women who gathered in the Fortune parlor this chilly March evening wore faces more suitable to that of a funeral than a quilting bee.

Alexandra and Alicia sat across from their mother and Betsy in front of the crackling fire that warmed the parlor where they worked. The large wood quilting frame rested between them. Four pair of hands worked diligently to piece the squares of velvet, calico, and chintz together.

Beneath lowered lashes, Catherine eyed her two daughters carefully. The girls were a study in contrast. Alicia's eyes were bright—sparkling with life, her face reflecting the joy of her upcoming wedding to Tom. Alexandra's blue eyes were flat and full of pain. The drawn, pale appearance she had exhibited since the day of the hearing over two weeks ago brought a dull ache to Catherine's breast. There was no sign of the previous bliss that had existed such a short time ago.

To make matters worse, Alexandra had been left to her own devices of late. Betsy had divulged that Nicholas was rarely home anymore, and when he was, he was usually intoxicated.

Sighing, Catherine took another precise stitch in the material. The quilting had been the only excuse she and Betsy could think of to take Alex's mind off her troubles. Perhaps the exuberance of her younger sister would brighten Alex's mood.

"I think the quilt is going to be lovely, don't you, Alex?" Alicia questioned, biting off a white piece of yarn.

Smiling wanly, Alexandra nodded. "It will make a fine addition to your hope chest."

"I just pray that the hostilities between the colonies and England hold off long enough for Tom and me to get married. The way Tom's been talking, things are coming to a head."

Shaking her head, Catherine shot her youngest daughter a warning glance.

"It's all right, Mother. Alicia has a right to express her concerns," Alexandra said, spying her mother's fierce expression. "You needn't be worried that it will upset me. The war is inevitable. It just started sooner for me, that's all."

Taking hold of her sister's hand, Alicia gave it a gentle squeeze. "I'm sorry, Alex. How thoughtless of me to go on about Tom and I when you and Nicholas are having so many problems."

"I brought them on myself. I should have put my husband first. Instead, I chose to aid my country."

"You did what you thought was right, dear. Don't continue to chastise yourself," Catherine said. "Given the same set of circumstances, you would probably follow your conscience once again."

"Your mother's right, Miss Alex. Even Will, who thinks the sun rises and sets on his lordship, don't fault you for what you did. He says it took a lot of courage to stand by your convictions."

Alexandra couldn't suppress the surprise that Betsy's statement elicited. To think that Habersham had actually spoken out in her defense. She was deeply touched. She blinked back the tears, dampening her lashes. "Thank you, Betsy. That's high tribute coming from someone as loyal as Will."

The clock on the mantel chimed nine; Catherine glanced over in its direction. "Oh, dear! Is it that late already? I told your father we would be home early this evening."

Alexandra smiled. "Habersham will walk you home, Mother. He's waiting in the . . ."

"Well . . . well. What have we here?"

All heads turned toward the door to discover Nicholas leaning against the frame. Alexandra wrinkled her nose in disgust at the familiar odor of brandy. From the way Nicholas staggered into the room, it was obvious he was very drunk. Unfortunately, this wasn't the first time he had come home in this condition. He had followed a similar pattern of drinking and staying out late since the day of his hearing.

"Good evening, ladies," he said, bowing in an exaggerated fashion, his speech thick and slow.

Alicia and Catherine exchanged startled glances before offering Alexandra a commiserating look.

"Have you come to help my wife earn a living?" he asked, putting his arm about Alexandra's shoulders. "Are you taking in sewing to support the family, my sweet?" he added, leaning heavily against her.

"We are sewing a quilt for Alicia's wedding chest."

"Ah, yes . . . the wedding. Another victim entering the throes of connubial bliss."

"That's enough, Nicholas," Alexandra said, her voice edged in anger.

Bowing, Nicholas lost his balance and would have fallen to the floor had it not been for Alexandra's quick reflexes.

"Beg pardon," he slurred. "I'm sure you'll be as deliriously happy as Alexandra and I are. Isn't that right, my sweet?" He planted a wet kiss on her cheek.

"We really must be going, dear," Catherine said, rising to her feet. She pulled Alicia toward the door. "We'll see you tomorrow. Good night, Nicholas," she added before departing.

"Don't run off on my account," Nicholas said, falling heavily onto the settee, upsetting the quilting frame and knocking it to the floor.

Alexandra stared at the drunken man before her. She shook her head. Nicholas was out cold. Lifting his legs, she propped his feet onto the cushions and covered him with a quilt. He would be content to spend the night there. It was how he had spent every night the last two weeks: drunk and alone.

It was difficult to be angry with him. She knew he hadn't been able to face the loss of his title and ancestral home. She blamed herself. Nicholas was floundering like a fish out of water, trying to find himself. She only hoped he would come to terms with his situation before he drowned in his own self-pity.

Walking to the window, Alexandra observed Betsy and Habersham escorting her mother and sister home. Pressing her forehead against the cool pane of glass, she let the tears she had held in check, spill out to dampen her cheeks.

Was this how her life was to be from now on? Was this the living hell Nicholas had promised her? Looking back toward the settee, she wiped the tears from her eyes with the back of her hand. If this was living in hell, then surely Nicholas was the devil himself.

A few nights later, Nicholas sat in the public room of the Wetherburn Tavern having a pint of ale with two men he had just met. Now that his title and fortune were gone, he found he was readily accepted into the bosom of the local gentry—the local patriot gentry. The Tory faction—his so-called friends and fellow countrymen—treated him as if he were infected with the plague. The only friends who still remained from his pretrial days were the Wellingtons. Johanna and Frederick had proven themselves to be true and loyal allies.

Even his brother, who had vowed his undying support, was abandoning him. Basil had informed him yesterday that he and Sabrina would be leaving for England as soon as they could arrange passage. That stood to reason, Nicholas thought, sipping thoughtfully on his ale. With the title and fortune at large, it was only logical that Basil would wish to stake his claim to it. Nicholas shook his head. Basil as the duke . . . how preposterous—how terrifying! He banged his tankard down loudly, not realizing he had done so until the gentleman on his left spoke.

"What troubles you, friend? Your look is as black as the devil's own heart."

"Do you think the devil and King George might be one and the same?" Nicholas asked.

"Careful, friend. The words you speak are dangerous," said the gray-haired man who'd introduced himself as Joseph.

"What have I got to lose, gentlemen? The Crown has already robbed me of my birthright and fortune. All that is left for them to take is my life. And that isn't worth much these days."

"We've heard of your misfortune, Lord Blackstone," the younger of the two men stated.

Nicholas winced at the man's address. "Please . . . call me Nicholas. I no longer carry the title of duke."

The younger man looked about, making sure no one was listening. "Nicholas, perhaps now that you sit on the other side of the fence, you will begin to see as we have seen, how unjust the laws and dictates of the King are."

"Aye," Joseph said, nodding his head, "you have lost your land and fortune, but there are those of us who have worked by the sweat of our brows to make a living. We stand to lose as much or more than you. Over the years, we have been systematically robbed by one unjust tax after another. The King has squeezed us dry until the little we have left is not enough to meet our obligations.''

Nicholas listened to the complaints and grievances against the King. They were beginning to make sense to him. Had he not been similarly treated by the unjust laws of the King? Many of the arguments they voiced were the same ones he had heard before—the same ones Alexandra had ranted about.

Alexandra. Her smiling face haunted him. Why was she always in the forefront of his mind? Why did her bright blue eyes and ruby red lips have the power to torment him?

Taking a sip of his ale, he wiped his mouth on the edge of his sleeve. He would exorcise her from his subconscious—drown her image until she was only a blur, a figment of his imagination. Picking up his tankard, he downed the contents in one gulp, determined to do just that.

The future Duke of Blackstone, regally ensconced in the finest suite the Red Rose Tavern in Yorktown had to offer, lay with his arms folded behind his head, his back supported by the massive walnut headboard.

As Basil smiled in satisfaction, his eyes raked over the lush curves of Sabrina's nakedness as she performed her morning ablutions. He had just completed a most enjoyable tryst with his mistress. Sabrina certainly knew a hundred ways to please a man with her luscious body and teasing mouth. He felt himself harden and adjusted his weight to hide his discomfort.

He had no more time to devote to matters of the flesh. He had booked passage on a ship leaving Yorktown for England this afternoon. In a few short weeks, he would be back in London to claim the Blackstone title and fortune. He chuckled with delight at the thought.

"What is so amusing, darling?" Sabrina asked, catching sight of Basil's self-satisfied grin in the mirror. She almost laughed at the sight of him reclining on the bed like a pasha in a sultan's tent. Acquiring a title had certainly given Basil airs. He had had the audacity to rebuke her for not dropping into a curtsy and referring to him as "your grace" when he entered the room this morning.

"I was just thinking of our glorious lovemaking, my dear. You really are quite adept at your trade."

Bristling at the comment, Sabrina narrowed her eyes. "I do not appreciate being compared to a loose woman, Basil. You know how faithful I have been to you since we formed our alliance."

"Of course, my dear," he said, smiling. "Your motives have always been clear to me, but you should not be insulted to hear that you make love like a whore. Some of the best times I've had in bed have been between a whore's thighs. I meant it as the highest of compliments."

"How flattering," Sabrina smirked, setting down her hairbrush. She didn't doubt for a moment that the only women Basil could get to bed him before she'd come along were whores. Who else would want anything to do with the repulsive little weasel?

"Wipe that pout off your face, my dear. I'm in too grand a mood to have you spoil it. Have you forgotten what day this is?"

No, she hadn't forgotten, Sabrina thought . . . it was *all* she had thought of the past few weeks. Each time she had lain in Basil's arms, she had thought of her new role as the Duchess of Blackstone. It would be worth it in the end, she had told herself a hundred times. Once the title and fortune were hers, Basil could seek out as many whores as he wished. He was more than welcome to them!

"Are you listening, Sabrina? I asked if you knew what today was."

323

Sabrina smiled. "No, darling, I haven't forgotten," she replied, tying the ribbons of her chemise. "Don't you think you had better get dressed? I thought you were going over to the shipping office to purchase our tickets." Presenting him with her back so he could fasten her hooks, she added, "When did you say we would be leaving?"

Placing a kiss at the nape of her neck, Basil replied, "Tomorrow, my dear. By this time tomorrow, Virginia will have seen the last of me."

Sabrina hadn't given much thought to Basil's reply until the afternoon sun had been swallowed up by the lengthening shadows of evening and Basil had not returned. Glancing out the window one more time, she looked down at the darkened street below for some sign of him.

"Where could he be?" she muttered. Surely he should have returned by now. He needed to finish packing and. . . . A seed of suspicion began to grow. Searching the dresser for the key to Basil's room, she spied it among her powders and rouge. Pressing the cold brass tightly in her palm, she crossed the hall and let herself in.

She gasped. The room was empty. Walking over to the wardrobe, she flung it open. Empty . . . there was no sign of Basil's portmanteau, nor any of his possessions. The bastard had dumped her!

Fury almost choked her as she stalked back to her room, slamming the door behind her. Leaning her head against the door, she swallowed, trying to control the violent spasms overtaking her. Seating herself at the dressing table, she stared at her image in the mirror. "Fool," she berated herself. "You stupid fool," she screamed, knocking the cosmetics off of the dressing table with one fell swoop of her hand.

Jumping to her feet, she paced the room like a

wounded tigress. How dare he think to betray me, she thought, clenching her hands into fists, shaking them in the air. "That filthy bastard!" she screamed. "He'll pay for his treachery. By God, he'll pay!"

# Chapter Twenty-Seven

Standing in the rear of St. John's Church in Richmond, Nicholas listened with rapt attention to the words Patrick Henry cried out as he voiced his support of a resolution to put the colony into a position of defense. The second Virginia Convention had been summoned in response to the British man-of-war that lay in the James River dangerously close to Williamsburg. Henry had introduced his bill for assembling and training a militia. "Give me liberty or give me death," Henry shouted, raising the hairs on the back of Nicholas's neck.

Nicholas had come to Richmond against his better judgment at the insistence of his two cohorts, Joseph Walker and his son Jacob. The men had insisted that he needed to hear the words of Patrick Henry to really understand the quest for freedom that the colonies craved. He had to admit, what Henry said made a lot of sense. If war with England was as imminent as it seemed, a strong defense would surely be necessary to repel the forces of King George.

Did he really think that? he wondered. If so, he was truly guilty of the treason he had already been charged and convicted of.

Glancing about the church, he recognized many of

the upstanding members of the Williamsburg community. Alexandra's father, Samuel, sat in one of the rear pews to his right, and next to him was her brother Ben, with Tom Farley. All three men were probably responsible for encouraging Alexandra to participate in their game of intrigue. Could he really blame them? Would he have not done the same if it were his country's freedom at stake? He mulled over these disturbing questions in his mind, turning his attention back to the speaker.

After the fiery oration was over, Nicholas and the Walkers walked to the Dogwood Tavern to quench their thirst and rehash the events of the day.

Seated at the long trestle table, Nicholas spotted Ben Courtland striding through the door. He was alone. Their eyes met; Ben nodded in his direction. Nicholas returned the greeting, and Ben sauntered over.

"Nicholas, I am surprised to find you here in Richmond. Is Alex with you?"

The question caught Nicholas off guard; he felt his face redden. "No," he answered harshly, "your sister is still in Williamsburg. I have come with these two gentlemen, Joseph and Jacob Walker." He indicated the gentlemen seated on his right.

Ben smiled at the sight of the two familiar faces. He knew the Walkers well. They undoubtedly would be an excellent influence on Nicholas's distorted views on English government. "I was hoping to have a talk with you, Nicholas . . . privately, if Joseph and Jacob don't mind."

The two men rose, assuring Nicholas that they didn't mind at all and would see him later, back at the tavern.

"What is it you want, Ben? Haven't you done enough to interrupt my life?"

"That is precisely what I wish to discuss with you, Nicholas," Ben said, taking a seat at the table. "You

328

have cast the guilt for your misfortune in the wrong direction.''

Nicholas snorted. ''I find that highly unlikely. You and my wife were observed exchanging information on more than one occasion.''

''That may be true, but the information Alex passed to me had nothing to do with your charge of treason. Most of the information I gathered from your files was already known to the committee.''

''Why did you deem it necessary to use your sister against me? As my wife, she owed me her loyalty.''

Flipping the server a coin, Ben picked up the pewter tankard and sipped thoughtfully at its contents. ''Alex refused to help me when I first approached her. It was only after events began to worsen that she agreed to work for me. She told me the night of mother's birthday party that she would not risk losing your love by helping me any longer . . . no matter how serious the consequence might be for the colony.''

''The damage has been done,'' Nicholas said, his tone bitter.

''Not by Alexandra. Your charge of treason was trumped up by someone else close to you.'' At Nicholas's puzzled stare, Ben continued, ''Didn't you pause to consider who would have stood to gain the most by your death? It was certainly not your wife, who loves you more than life itself.''

The light of recognition came slowly to Nicholas's eyes. ''Basil,'' he muttered, shaking his head. ''Of course! Why was I so blind?'' To think his own brother had wanted him dead. The poor wretch was even more twisted than he had given him credit for. And Sabrina. She would have done anything to achieve the title of Duchess of Blackstone. That bitch had a lot to answer for, including, he was sure, setting fire to the smokehouse.

"Sometimes we see only what we wish to see," Ben said.

Jumping up, Nicholas upset his tankard of ale, spilling it onto the floor. "I'll kill him," he shouted, unaware that many had turned in his direction and were staring at him.

Tugging on his sleeve, Ben pulled Nicholas back down. "It's too late for that, Nicholas. He's gone. My sources tell me he left for England last week."

Nicholas grabbed the sides of his head; pain and anguish shadowed his eyes. "Bloody hell! Your sister must hate me for the way I have treated her these many weeks."

"Alex blames herself for your troubles. She has a forgiving heart. She forgave you for your little indiscretion with your former mistress, didn't she?"

Nicholas's head shot up. "Sabrina? What indiscretion? I committed no adultery."

" 'Twas before you were married. The night of the ball—the one hosted by your brother."

Nicholas's eyes narrowed. The night he had become so drunk, he could remember nothing. And after that evening, Alexandra would have nothing to do with him. "What is it I'm supposed to have done?" he asked finally.

"Alexandra claims to have found you and Miss Montgomery in bed together . . . naked."

"My God! Poor Alexandra. How she must have suffered to think that I had betrayed her."

"Exactly," Ben said smugly, "but she found it in her heart to forgive you because she loved you. Couldn't you do the same?"

"But I was innocent. I never bedded Sabrina willingly. I must have been drugged."

"You were used, just as Alex was. She doesn't deserve your condemnation."

"But I have lost everything!" Nicholas protested.

Ben rose to his feet. "You still have Alex," he said patting his brother-in-law on the back. "Think about it."

Nicholas did think about it. He thought long and hard after Ben had departed, through one tankard of ale and then another.

He thought about what he would do to Basil and Sabrina when he caught up with them.

He thought about kissing and fondling Alexandra, making passionate love to her until they were both fulfilled and fatigued.

And then, as his head lolled forward hitting the table, Nicholas thought no more. He had passed out.


Strolling leisurely through the garden, Alexandra paused to consider a new bud bursting forth on the branch of the dogwood tree. Yellow daffodils and tulips of red and pink bordered the edge of the white picket fence. Spring had finally arrived. She held her face up to the sun, enjoying the warmth as it radiated down over her cheeks. Perhaps the sun would restore a little color to her face, she thought. She hardly recognized herself in the looking glass this morning; she had become pallid—wan looking. The glow of her youth had disappeared, replaced by the harsh realities of life with a husband who hated her.

Nicholas had left for Richmond without a word. It was Habersham who had told her, apologizing profusely for his lordship's manner. A soft smile touched her lips when she thought of how protective Habersham had become toward her since her problems with Nicholas had arisen. Instead of the condemnation she feared at his lips, he had only words of consolation and kindness.

Why had she been so foolish to jeopardize her happiness—her husband's love? Her mother had been wrong. If she'd had it to do over again, she never would have risked losing Nicholas. Nothing was more important than his love. She realized that now, albeit too late.

Gathering up her wicker basket, which she had filled with a colorful array of daffodils and tulips, she turned back toward the house. She stopped dead in her tracks. Before her stood Nicholas, looking resplendent in a coat of black superfine.

He looked healthier than he had in weeks. His eyes were clear, no longer bloodshot; his face was tanned and achingly handsome. Perhaps his visit to Richmond had done him some good after all, she admitted grudgingly.

She couldn't control the way her heart raced as her eyes drank in the sight of him; she was a woman whose thirst had been denied too long. They stared at each other for several moments until Nicholas broke the silence.

"Good morning, Alexandra. Have you been working in the garden?"

Embarrassed to have been caught in one of her oldest gowns, she looked down at herself, her face full of the dismay she was feeling. "Yes. I was just cutting some flowers for the dining room table." Why was Nicholas looking at her so strangely? Why was he speaking to her at all? They hadn't had so much as a civil conversation in over a month.

"Did you have a pleasant trip to Richmond?" she finally thought to ask.

Nicholas smiled. "It was very enlightening. I apologize for not appraising you of my leaving."

Alexandra shrugged. "It was no matter. I hardly noticed your absence." Liar, she told herself. She had pined and bemoaned the fact that Nicholas had left as soon as she'd discovered his absence. In truth, she thought perhaps he wasn't coming back.

"I brought you something."

Her mouth dropped open. She was too surprised to do more than stare at him stupidly. "Whatever for?" she finally replied, trying to hide her pleasure.

Taking a step forward, Nicholas dropped a small, brightly wrapped package into her flower basket. "I hope you will wear this for me sometime." Giving her a smile warm enough to melt the hardest of hearts, he stuffed his hands into his pockets and strolled casually away.

Alexandra stared after him, more confused than ever. Reaching into the basket, she retrieved the gift he had brought her. Staring at the pretty package, she unwrapped it to find a small vial of French perfume. Removing the stopper, she took a whiff. Her nostrils filled with the smell of roses—her favorite scent. She couldn't help the quickening of her heart. What did this mean? Was Nicholas trying to make amends for his past behavior?

Replacing the stopper, she clutched the bottle of perfume, smiling to herself. Nicholas was willing to forgive her. Her heart filled with joy. Picking up the basket, she started forward, suddenly grinding to a halt. Frowning, she stared at the perfume again. He might be ready to forgive her, but was she willing to forgive him? He had made her suffer these many weeks. True, she had acted dishonorably, but her crime did not warrant the cruel and unusual punishment he had met out. Should she forgive him? Act as if nothing had happened? She shook her head. Smiling to herself and kissing the bottle of perfume, she decided a little taste of his own medicine wouldn't be out of the question.

When Alexandra entered the dining room later that afternoon, Nicholas was already seated at the dinner table. It seemed strange, facing him across the table again after so many weeks of eating her meals in solitary confinement.

Nicholas rose as she entered, noting the look of surprise she wore when he glanced down to find a long velvet box resting on her plate. He waited anxiously until she was seated, eager for her to open it. He was, therefore, quite disconcerted when she picked up the box and set it aside without comment.

"Aren't you going to open it?" he inquired, trying to keep the annoyance he felt out of his voice.

"Excuse me? Were you speaking to me?" Alexandra asked, a sweet smile of innocence on her face.

"You know very well that I am. I asked if you were going to open my gift to you."

Taking a bite of her crab cake, Alexandra paused, fork in midair, to consider the question. "No, I don't believe I am."

Nicholas's face reddened to the color of the beets on his plate. "Why ever not? I have presented you with a gift, and you have thrown it back in my face."

Slamming down her fork, the metal clanging against the china plate, Alexandra stood. "Like you have thrown my love for you back in my face." She stood.

"Alexandra wait!" Nicholas pleaded, rising out of his chair.

"I cannot be bought with pretty trinkets and sweet-smelling gifts, Nicholas. If you have decided that you want to patch things up between us, make amends for the hell you have put me through these past few weeks, I shall await you in the parlor."

Rubbing the back of his neck, Nicholas stood there, mouth agape, trying to figure out how Alexandra had managed to turn the tables on him again. He didn't know whether he should rage at her or laugh at her. The woman was quite infuriating—most extraordinary. She wanted him to beg forgiveness when he had been the wronged party. He threw down his napkin, staring at the empty doorway she had retreated through.

He knew he deserved some of her wrath. But by God! He had been pushed to the very brink of madness by her actions. Deciding that the only way to clear the air was by facing Alexandra and having it out with her, he followed her into the parlor.

"All right, let's have done with it. I'm tired of waging this battle between us," Nicholas said, entering the room. He stopped short at the sight of Alexandra bent in concentration over a cross-stitch sampler.

With the sun streaming in through the window to bathe her in a golden glow, she looked angelic. He noticed for the first time the dark circles under her eyes and the way her cheeks had hollowed from loss of weight. His anger instantly dissolved. Crossing the room, he knelt before her chair. "Can you find it in your heart to forgive me, my sweet? I find I am unable to live without your love."

"Oh, Nicholas," Alexandra cried, dropping the sampler and throwing herself into his arms. "It is I who should beg your forgiveness. I would rather die than lose your love."

Nicholas captured her mouth in a soul-searching, heart-healing kiss that seemed to go on forever. When at last he lifted his lips from hers, she stared through her tears to see his love shining at her like a beacon of light against a darkened sky.

"I love you, Alexandra," he whispered against her hair, cradling her body to his chest.

"As I love you. Make love to me, Nicholas. I thought I would perish these lonely nights without you by my side."

"Let's go upstairs to our bed. I find the thought of reclining on the settee a most distasteful one."

Smiling, Alexandra nibbled his chin. "Was it terribly uncomfortable?"

Nicholas nodded. "I find that my entire body could benefit from a gentle massage." He grinned wickedly, pulling Alexandra to her feet. "Of course, some parts need more attention than others," he added.

"Of course!" she replied, threading her fingers through his and leading him to the door.

Nicholas let his gaze wander over his wife's naked loveliness. Alexandra was asleep—exhausted from their arduous hours of lovemaking.

Pulling the sheets up over her, he placed a tender kiss upon her lips. She smiled in response but did not awaken. To think how close he had come to losing her. His heart twisted painfully.

Careful not to disturb her, he eased himself out of the bed and walked to the window. Dusk was descending, turning the sky a palette of purple and gray.

Catching sight of a gaudily dressed man in purple brocade who passed beneath the window, Nicholas narrowed his eyes. The man reminded him of his foppish brother, Basil.

Basil. How neatly he had played him for a fool, nearly getting him hanged, almost destroying his relationship with Alexandra. He clenched his fists. Bloody Christ! The bastard would pay someday. For now, he would have to bide his time until there was some way of proving his brother's treachery. Basil and Sabrina were out of reach for the time being . . . but someday. . . .

"Nicholas, is something wrong?" Alexandra whispered.

Closing the shutters to block out the unpleasantness

of the world, Nicholas padded back to the bed. "Nothing is wrong, my sweet," he said, climbing in next to the warm, willing woman. "Not anymore."

# Chapter Twenty-Eight

Taking her wrap from Frederick Wellington's outstretched hands, Alexandra leaned over, placing a kiss on his weathered cheek. Saying good-bye to Johanna and Frederick was far more difficult than she had expected. They had become dear friends in the short time she had known them. Unfortunately, with the rising hostilities between England and her colonies, the Wellingtons had decided it was time for them to leave. Tomorrow they would board a ship that would take them back to England. She and Nicholas had come to bid their friends good-bye.

Facing Johanna, Alexandra blinked back the tears that suddenly surfaced. "Thank you so much for everything, Johanna. I'm terribly upset that this will be our last evening together." She gave the older woman a hug.

Wiping the tears from her eyes, Johanna smiled. "We're going to miss you and Nicholas. I know in my heart that we will see each other again. Once these hostilities cease, you must promise to come to England for a visit."

Draping a comforting arm around his wife's thick waist, Frederick gave her a gentle squeeze. "Never fear, my dear, the King will have these miscreants under control in no time.''

Spoken like a true misguided Tory, Nicholas thought, trying to hide his skepticism. The Crown always did underestimate the opposition; this time such an attitude could prove fatal. "Whatever the future holds for all of us,'' Nicholas said, "we count it an honor to have been included among your friends.''

"God bless both of you,'' Johanna said. "I pray you will see justice served in the end.''

Waving farewell, Nicholas and Alexandra stepped out into the darkness of the evening. The warmth of the April day had carried into night, the temperature so pleasant, they decided to walk rather than take the carriage the Wellingtons had offered.

The smell of boxwood lent a distinctive odor to the air as the couple made their way down Duke of Gloucester Street. Alexandra inhaled deeply, filling her lungs with the fragrant smell of the dogwood and tulip trees that lined the road. "This is my favorite time of year,'' she declared, taking another deep breath. "Everything is so fresh and new—so alive.''

Nicholas laughed. "Only you would find the malodorous scent of animal droppings fresh and alive,'' he teased.

"Oh, Nicholas, you really must take the time to. . . .''

Suddenly there was a loud outcry coming from the direction of the powder magazine. Voices could be heard in angry protest.

The shrill cry of the night watch floated through the air. "Come quick. The marines are stealing the powder.'' The cadence of drums beat loudly, sounding the alarm.

Nicholas and Alexandra exchanged worried glances, hurrying their pace.

As they neared the magazine, Nicholas drew Alexandra to a halt. Dozens of angry men, carrying torches and lanterns, hurried toward the brick building. "We mustn't get any closer," Nicholas warned. "There could be danger; I don't want to take the chance of your getting hurt."

"But, Nicholas, I want to see what's going on," she protested.

Halting a young passerby, Nicholas asked, "Can you tell us what has happened?"

Taking a deep breath, the boy blurted, "The governor has sent marines to steal the gunpowder from the magazine."

"My God!" Alexandra cried. "Do you know what this means?" she asked, grabbing onto Nicholas's arm.

"Yes, my sweet. I'm afraid I do. Our illustrious governor has just brought war down around our ears."

Alexandra was shocked to hear the vehemence in Nicholas's voice. He sounded as if he were actually taking the side of the colonists. "Why do you suppose he has taken this action now?"

Nicholas shook his head. "It would be my guess that something up north has triggered this action. Let's go over to your parents' house. Perhaps Ben and your father will be able to shed some light on the situation.

Weaving their way through the angry mob, Alexandra and Nicholas reached the Courtland home without incident. Just as Alexandra had suspected, her father and Ben were not at home. Knowing them as she did, she suspected that they were at the magazine, in the thick of things.

Following her mother into the parlor, they took a seat on the loveseat. "Come in and have some tea. I've just had Sally brew up a fresh pot. With all this commotion tonight, I feared we would need something to keep us calm."

Alexandra and Nicholas waited while Catherine poured sassafras tea into china cups. "There you are," she said, handing them their tea. "Now tell me what is going on outside. I've never heard so much shouting and yelling in all my born days."

"You mustn't worry, Mother. I'm sure everything is under control by now. It seems Governor Dunmore has taken it into his head to seize the gunpowder from the magazine."

"How dreadful!" Catherine said, twisting the wedding band on her left hand nervously. "I hope your father and brother are all right."

A moment later, Samuel and Benjamin burst through the door. Their faces were flushed with excitement; their eyes burned with the fervor of retaliation. "We've just come from the market square," Samuel said. "I thought surely there was going to be violence after what happened. But Peyton Randolph and some of the others were able to persuade the crowd to handle their grievances in a more diplomatic fashion."

"Can you tell us exactly what happened?" Nicholas asked. "We have only a sketchy idea of the proceedings. I didn't want to expose Alexandra to any violence."

"You were smart to bring her here," Samuel said. "An unruly mob can become violent without much provocation."

Taking a seat in the wing chair, Ben poured himself a cup of tea. His face was fraught with tension. "The governor ordered a contingent of marines from the *Magdalen*, the man-of-war anchored at Burwell's Landing, to take the gunpowder from the magazine. Apparently they confiscated about fifteen half-barrels."

"What happens now?" Nicholas questioned.

"A delegation has been formed to enter a protest with the governor. They have gone to the palace to arrange an audience with him."

"Do you have any idea why the governor took this action?" Alexandra asked.

Benjamin's face went grim. "It would be my guess that General Gage up in Boston had something to do with it. We've had no official word yet, but mark my word, this is only the beginning."

Eight days later, word reached Williamsburg that a battle between British regulars and American militiamen had taken place in the countryside outside of Boston in the two small towns known as Lexington and Concord.

Scanning the latest edition of the *Virginia Gazette,* Alexandra read with rising dismay the words that reflected her very thoughts at the moment: *"The sword is now drawn, and God knows when it will be sheathed."* There would be no turning back now, she thought sadly. The bloodshed in Massachusetts would soon spill out over Virginia soil. She wiped at her tears with the back of her hand.

"What is it, Alexandra?" Nicholas asked, a worried frown creasing his brow.

Handing him the paper, she walked to the window. Everything looked as it should: the sun was shining, the trees were in bloom, the vegetables were beginning to sprout in the garden. But nothing was ever going to be the same again. War had come, and the world they had known would be lost to them forever. Feeling Nicholas's hands on her shoulders, Alexandra turned.

"I admit things look bad, my sweet, but you shouldn't give up hope that a peaceful settlement can be reached. I'm certain King George doesn't desire war any more than the rest of us. For one thing, I know he isn't in a position to afford it." He kissed the tip of her nose.

"I'm sorry to be so pessimistic. Especially when you have so many important things on your mind," Alexandra said.

"I'm afraid Basil and Sabrina, and my own troubles with the Crown, pale in comparison to the colony's."

"Have you had any luck with the inquiries you have made?"

Shaking his head, Nicholas frowned. "I'm afraid not. There is little that can be done unless I can find someone who knew of Basil's perfidy. Unfortunately, the only other person besides Basil and Sabrina who could have helped me is dead."

Wrapping her arms around Nicholas's waist, Alexandra nestled her head into his chest. "If it's any consolation, I would love you even if you were the lowliest beggar on the street."

"If we do not find evidence to prove my innocence, you may just be put to the test."

The heavily loaded hay wagon pulled to a halt in front of the Governor's Palace. The occupant of the wagon looked about, hoping no one she knew would recognize her. She pulled the brim of her wide-brimmed hat down over her face.

"Is this the place you wanted to be dropped off, miss?" the burly farmer questioned. Jumping down, he came around her side of the wagon to help his passenger alight.

Sabrina Montgomery nodded, brushing the bits of straw off her yellow brocade gown. "Yes, thank you. I shall be able to find my way from here."

"Well, then, I'll be on my way. Sure hope you're able to find that husband who ran out on you," he said, shaking his head. "I can't believe any man would run off and leave a pretty thing like you."

Sabrina's smile never reached her eyes. "How kind of you to say. Some men obviously have more taste than others. Good-bye, Mister Murdock."

Smoothing her silver tresses, Sabrina gathered up

344

her skirts and walked through the wrought-iron gate leading to the entrance of the palace. She had some very interesting facts to impart to Governor Dunmore, and when she was done, Basil Fortune would wish he had never laid eyes on her.

Following behind the majordomo, Sabrina was led to the upstairs middle chamber where Governor Dunmore was receiving his visitors this morning. Her eyes roamed appreciatively over the leather-covered walls and rich brocade window hangings. She had come so close to possessing such luxury herself. If only that bastard Basil hadn't tricked her.

"Miss Montgomery, I thought you had departed for England," Governor Dunmore stated, his voice reflecting his surprise. Walking forward, he took her hand, placing a courtly kiss upon it.

Dropping into a curtsy, Sabrina smiled. "That was the original plan, my lord, but I'm afraid I have been sorely used by that rascal Basil Fortune."

Indicating with a wave of his hand that she should be seated, the governor asked, "What has happened? How may I be of service to you?" He took the seat across from her.

Folding her hands primly in her lap, Sabrina took a deep breath. "I believe that I may be of service to you, my lord."

Lord Dunmore's eyebrow rose at her statement. "Please go on."

"I have information that could prove that Nicholas Fortune is innocent of the treason charge that was filed against him."

"What sort of information?"

"Before I reveal what I know, there are certain stipulations that I must ask of you."

Leaning forward, he replied, "Go on."

"I want your assurance that the information I'm about to reveal will not be used against me. In addi-

345

tion, I desire passage back to England on the first ship leaving Yorktown.''

"I take it you were involved in some sort of wrong-doing." His stare was searching, probing.

Squirming in her seat, Sabrina mopped her brow with her linen handkerchief. "I will not admit to anything until I have your word that I will not be prosecuted."

"If what you tell me can clear Nicholas Fortune's name, then you have it. Now please, start from the beginning."

When Sabrina was finished with her confession and assured of her immunity, she was shown to one of the bed chambers. She was to spend the night at the palace and depart for Yorktown first thing in the morning.

It was imperative that she leave Williamsburg as soon as possible. She had made that quite clear to the governor. Once Nicholas found out the part she had played in Basil's scheme, her life would be worthless. Although she was responsible for helping him gain back his title and lands, she doubted he would be thankful. Nicholas could be very vindictive when he set his mind to it. She shivered at the thought.

Lord Dunmore paced the confines of his chamber, trying to determine the best way to resolve the matter of Nicholas Fortune without looking like a complete fool. Deciding on his course of action, he summoned his secretary.

"I wish to call an immediate meeting of the council. Have the members meet me in the council chamber at the Capitol in thirty minutes."

It had come as no surprise to hear that Basil Fortune was behind Nicholas's problems. It was no more than he had suspected. Unfortunately, he had been powerless to do anything about it. The evidence had been too strong.

With luck he would be able to make things up to Nicholas. He just hoped Nicholas and his hot-headed wife were going to appreciate his efforts on their behalf. He had enough problems right now with all these damn malcontents. He didn't need two more to add to his list.

Standing sideways in front of the cheval mirror, Alexandra studied her protruding abdomen and smiled. She had suspected for several weeks that she might be pregnant; it was obvious from the evidence before her that her suspicions were correct.

Nicholas was going to be ecstatic when she told him. Perhaps the baby would, in some small way, make up for the loss of his title and lands. It would mark a new beginning for them. They could form a Fortune dynasty right here in Virginia. Hugging herself, she twirled about, unaware that she was being observed by a pair of smiling eyes.

"I can see that you've finally figured out that your pregnant."

Alexandra spun about, her hand going protectively to her abdomen. Betsy was framed in the doorway, grinning from ear to ear.

"Quick, come in and shut the door," Alexandra ordered.

Betsy laughed. "What's all the mystery, Miss Alex? If I was having a baby, I would be shouting it from the rooftops, not trying to hide it."

Putting on her wrapper, Alexandra tied the silk sash tightly around her waist. "I want it to be a surprise. I haven't quite decided how I'm going to break the news to Nicholas yet."

"Have you told your mother? She's going to be beside herself with joy."

Alexandra shook her head. "I haven't told a soul. Which brings me to ask, how did you find out?"

Smiling, Betsy crossed to the bed, stripping off the covers. "You forget who washes your monthly linens, Miss Alex."

Alexandra's face reddened. "I should have known better than to try and keep a secret from you."

"When will you tell his lordship?" Betsy inquired, bundling up the soiled bed linens to take downstairs.

"Nicholas has gone with my father to call on several prospective clients. Father has offered Nicholas a partnership. He says he is getting too old to handle the business by himself. Since Ben isn't interested in becoming a merchant, Nicholas was the logical choice.

"I don't want to burden Nicholas with too many changes at once. After he gets used to the idea of having to work for a living, then I'll spring the baby on him."

"That's probably for the best," Betsy concurred. "It hasn't been easy for his lordship, adjusting to his loss and all."

Biting her lip, Alexandra nodded. She still carried a large measure of guilt around with her concerning Nicholas's loss. "I know this sounds selfish, Betsy, but I'm glad we won't be moving to England. I didn't want things to happen the way that they did, and I would take them all back if I could, but I can't say I'm sorry to be staying in Virginia. Do you think I'm terrible?"

"No, Miss Alex," Betsy said, her blonde curls bouncing as she shook her head from side to side. "I feel the same as you. I know Will pines for the land of his birth, but I have no desire to leave this land I call home."

"I guess things have worked out just as you said they would," Alexandra said.

Betsy's look was knowing. "They always do, miss. They always do."

348

* * *

The following morning, just as Nicholas and Alexandra sat down to their morning meal, a loud pounding on the door ensued.

"I wonder who that could be," Alexandra said, motioning to rise.

Throwing down his napkin, a disgruntled expression on his face, Nicholas pushed back his chair. "I'll answer it. Habersham is on an errand, and Betsy is outside in the wash house."

Her curiosity piqued as to who could be calling at such an unfashionable hour. Alexandra followed Nicholas to the door. As he threw it open, the sight that greeted her sent a shiver of fear down her spine. Standing on the porch were two British soldiers. Her stomach lurched, her hands instinctively going to her abdomen.

Nicholas's eyes narrowed at the sight of the King's men littering his porch. "What is it you want?" he demanded.

The taller of the two men stepped forward. "Sergeant Millford at your service, sir." His complexion turned as red as the freckles on his face when he caught sight of Alexandra hovering behind her husband dressed only in her wrapper. "I beg your pardon, but we are here on official business of Governor Dunmore."

"What kind of business?" Nicholas asked, his tone harsh.

The young soldier swallowed. "Lord Dunmore has asked me to convey the following message: your presence and that of your wife are requested at your earliest possible convenience. The governor would like you to attend him in his private chambers at the palace."

Nicholas and Alexandra exchanged startled glances before Nicholas turned his attention back to the caller.

"Is that all?" At the soldier's nod, Nicholas slammed the door in his face.

"Nicholas, shame on you!" Alexandra scolded. "That poor boy looked as if he was about to have a fit of apoplexy."

Nicholas sneered. "Good. I hope he does. If the governor thinks I'm going to jump when he calls, he's very much mistaken."

Threading her arm through his, Alexandra led Nicholas back into the dining room. "Sit down and eat your breakfast. We need to discuss the governor's request a bit more calmly."

Stabbing at the plate of sausages as if they were his worst enemy, Nicholas replied, "Since when do you heed the summons of the governor? You've never hid the fact that you despise the man."

"That's true, but I've matured a bit in the last year, in case you hadn't noticed. I think it would be prudent to find out what the governor is up to. Perhaps it can aid our cause in some way."

Nicholas's eyebrow rose. "Our cause! Am I to infer by that remark that you consider me a patriot?"

Alexandra smiled a small, secretive smile but did not reply. Instead, she buttered a hot, flaky biscuit, popping it into her mouth.

Eyeing her carefully, Nicholas remarked, "It seems your appetite has increased tenfold lately. At the rate you've been eating, you'll be as plump as Betsy in no time."

Two spots of color the exact shade of strawberry jam appeared on her cheeks. "Will doesn't seem to mind," she replied, licking her fingers.

"Will! It's Will now, is it? By God, to think how you and that opinionated housekeeper of yours have taken a perfectly respectable valet and turned him into a henpecked housewife!"

Alexandra's laughter tinkled through the air. "You

are purposely changing the subject. Are you going to meet with the governor?''

Nicholas sighed. ''Yes, I'll go.''

# Chapter Twenty-Nine

A light rain began to fall as the Fortune carriage moved slowly down Nicholson Street toward the Governor's Palace. The occupants were silent, each lost in his own disquieting reverie.

Nicholas's anger was tempered by uncertainty. He had pondered the reasons for Lord Dunmore's summons but could not come up with a logical explanation. The only possible reason he could think of was that perhaps Basil's ship had sunk at sea. That thought buoyed his spirits enough to make him want to find out if it might not be true.

Alexandra fidgeted nervously with the folds of her blue dimity gown. What could have happened to spark the governor's request? she wondered. Lord Dunmore's summons, coming on the heels of the recent battles at Lexington and Concord, had her worried. Perhaps in some sort of twisted way, they thought Nicholas was somehow responsible. She knew the idea was preposterous—but so was his initial charge of treason.

"Alexandra."

Alexandra jumped at the sound of her name, and her hand flew up to cover her heart, which beat wildly in her chest. She swallowed.

"We're here," Nicholas said. "Are you all right? You look a bit pale." His brows drew together.

Smiling, Alexandra patted his hand to reassure him. "I'm fine, just a bit nervous." She could see by the concerned expression on Nicholas's face, he wasn't entirely convinced.

Entering the palace again, under quite different circumstances, caused bitter bile to rise in Nicholas's throat. Throwing his shoulders back, he lifted his head high. He had no reason to be ashamed. It was the governor and his blue-blooded council who had cause for reproach.

Holding Alexandra's arm in the crook of his own, he guided her up the stairs to the second floor. As they approached the northeast bedroom, they paused, staring into each other's eyes. The room held many memories for both of them, some happy, some sad. Without speaking, they followed the servant to the governor's quarters.

Lord Dunmore was waiting for them when they entered. Nicholas had never seen him so relaxed; the smile he wore on his face was welcoming, bringing instant suspicion to Nicholas's mind.

"Come in, come in. Thank you both for answering my summons so promptly."

"What is it you wish to speak to us about, Governor? I assume if it were not important, you would not have requested our immediate attendance." Nicholas's voice was cold, the words he stated matter-of-fact. There was no hint of the previous friendship that had existed between the Duke of Blackstone and the Earl of Dunmore.

Lord Dunmore's smile was full of regret. "Please sit down. I believe the news I have to impart this spring day will brighten your afternoon despite the nasty weather outside."

Nicholas and Alexandra exchanged questioning

glances and took their seats on the gingham-covered occasional chairs.

With hands clenched behind his back, Lord Dunmore paced nervously, back and forth, in front of the young couple. For the first time in his life, he felt at a loss for words. At the sound of Nicholas's impatient cough, he stopped, turning to stare intently into the concerned faces of the Fortunes.

"Yesterday I was paid a visit by a mutual acquaintance—Miss Sabrina Montgomery."

Nicholas's sharp intake of breath was clearly audible. Looking over, Alexandra found his face reddening in anger. She took hold of his hand, trying to forestall the interruption she knew was coming.

"Miss Montgomery has given testimony to the fact that your brother Basil perpetrated the entire charge of treason against you." Alexandra gasped, squeezing Nicholas's hand.

The governor paused, letting the full import of his words sink in before he continued. "She also confessed to Basil's murdering of Davey Johnson. With her confession, I was able to go before the council yesterday and have all the charges against you dropped."

Nicholas was too stunned to speak. He sat there, mouth agape, trying to absorb the bitter truth he had suspected that was now confirmed by Lord Dunmore's words. Taking a deep breath, he forced himself to quell the rising anger welling up inside his breast.

Noting her husband's shocked expression, Alexandra quickly recovered her own surprise and asked, "Does this mean Nicholas will have his title, fortune, and lands reinstated?" Her voice shook as she asked the question, fearful of what the answer might be.

Smiling, Lord Dunmore nodded. "Indeed, madam, that is exactly what it means. The title of Duke of Blackstone, and all that it entails, has been fully restored to your husband. You, my dear, are once again a duchess."

Alexandra paled, leaning heavily against her seat.

Nicholas finally stood, facing Lord Dunmore. His face was hard; his tone as acerbic as the fruit of the lemon tree when he spoke. "What will happen to my brother and his accomplice?"

Lighting his clay pipe, Lord Dunmore inhaled deeply. "I have already dispatched orders to the naval department to have the ship your brother is sailing on, boarded. He will be placed in custody and brought to England to stand trial. With Miss Montgomery's testimony, and the murder of Davey Johnson to his credit, the only realm your brother will be lording over will be Newgate Prison."

"And Sabrina?" Nicholas questioned, his eyes narrowing.

"Miss Montgomery was given full immunity for her testimony."

"That's not fair!" Alexandra shouted, jumping up. "She assisted Basil in his plan to have Nicholas hanged. She is as guilty as he is."

"Please calm down, Lady Blackstone. I really had no choice in the matter. Although what you say is true, without Miss Montgomery's testimony, we had no case against your husband's brother."

"The governor is right, Alexandra," Nicholas said, although he was loath to admit it. "Sabrina's testimony was vital. But do not think she will escape unscathed. There are other ways to make her suffer." Sabrina would not get away with any of her fraudulent activities, Nicholas vowed bitterly. She had made a big mistake when she chose to harm Alexandra. His eyes glittered dangerously.

"Really, Lord Blackstone! I cannot countenance cold blooded murder."

Nicholas almost laughed aloud at the look of outrage plastered on John Murray's face. "I was thinking more of social ostracism rather than murder, my lord. To a woman in Sabrina's position, who you know and who

356

knows you is everything. When she returns to England, she will find the doors to society slammed shut in her face.''

Alexandra couldn't contain the smile crossing her lips. Nicholas was right: for a social butterfly to have her wings clipped would be tantamount to a death sentence. Resuming her seat, she focused her attention on the governor.

"I'm sorry all this came to pass, Nicholas. I know these past few months haven't been easy for you.''

Nicholas's mouth spread into a thin-lipped smile. ''I doubt that you know anything of the kind, my lord, but I accept your apology. Now if you will excuse us, Alexandra and I have a great deal to discuss.''

Alexandra's stomach tightened. A feeling of panic welled up inside her. What would happen now? she wondered. With England and her colonies on the brink of war, and her husband a member of the British aristocracy once again, where would his sentiments lie? Where would hers?


A newspaper tucked securely under her arm, Alexandra picked her away around the mud puddles that dotted Duke of Gloucester Street after the previous night's rain. The hem of her pink muslin gown was becoming hopelessly soiled as it dragged through the mire. Grimacing at the sight of it, she dared not think what Betsy was going to say when she saw it. Why hadn't she taken the time to wear her pattens this morning? she chastised herself. Now, not only her slippers were ruined, but her dress as well.

She had been in such a hurry to escape the house this morning, she really hadn't been thinking straight. She had been inventing excuses all week to get herself out of the house, and today was no exception. Sighting a lack of reading material, she had given Nicholas a kiss on the cheek and fled to the printer's.

She had been full of nervous energy of late caused by the current political events and her own uncertainty about the future. Running errands and doing chores was the best method she had found to keep her mind occupied.

Nicholas had made no mention of leaving. She had not had the courage to broach the subject, and so she waited on tenterhooks for some sort of decision to be reached. The waiting was unbearable. She knew it was coming. The only questions was, when?

The political events that had taken place recently were sufficient cause in themselves for her nervous state. With Benjamin Franklin's return to the colonies, and Patrick Henry's recent demands on the governor, things were going from bad to worse.

Patrick Henry had marched on Williamsburg with one hundred and fifty men to collect reparation for the powder that was stolen from the magazine last month. Fortunately, before anything disastrous occurred, he was intercepted about fifteen miles outside of town by a representative of the governor's staff. A truce had been declared, and Mister Henry had been given a bill of exchange for three hundred and thirty pounds, which he took with him to the Continental Congress in Philadelphia.

Her brother Benjamin had been one of the volunteers to escort Mister Henry to the Maryland border after Governor Dunmore had declared him an outlaw.

Shaking her head, Alexandra sighed. She feared for her brother's safety during these turbulent times. Ben had not yet returned from his mission, and she prayed that he remained safe.

Deciding that Tom would probably know something about Benjamin's whereabouts, she turned around, heading in the direction of the cooper's shop.

Approaching the shop, she stopped to pause by the white picket fence that surrounded it. Bending over, she picked a handful of lovely white peonies. The peony root was said to have medicinal powers. She wished they could cure what ailed her at the moment, but she knew there was no remedy for uncertainty and self-doubt. Hiding her bouquet behind her back, she entered the shop.

The pungent odor of freshly hewn pine brought a lump of bile to her throat. Taking a deep breath, she leaned heavily against the doorframe. Lately, many familiar odors caused nausea to overtake her. She closed her eyes, waiting for the feeling to pass.

"Alex!" Tom shouted in greeting, his smile quickly turning to alarm when he noticed her pale complexion. Escorting her to a wooden bench, he pressed a cup of water into her hands.

"Thank you," Alexandra finally managed to reply, taking a sip of the cool liquid. "I don't know what came over me."

Tom studied her intently. "Don't you?"

The blush on her cheeks had little to do with her near fainting spell. Handing Tom the bouquet she had picked for him, she smiled sheepishly. "I never was a very good liar."

Tom smiled. "Does Nicholas know?"

The mane of black curls came loose beneath her mobcap as she shook her head emphatically. "No one does, except Betsy and now you. I would appreciate it if you would keep my confidence."

"Of course," he replied, his expression puzzled. "What brings you by here today? There is nothing the matter with Alicia, is there?"

Tom's look of concern touched her. How happy she was that Tom and Alicia would soon be married! They had set the first Saturday of October as their wedding day.

"Alicia's fine. It's Ben I'm concerned about. He hasn't returned from escorting Mister Henry to Maryland."

"You are not to worry about Ben, especially in your

359

condition," Tom scolded. "Ben is perfectly capable of looking after himself. 'Tis a good thing the British don't monitor his movements as stringently as you and Prudence."

"Has Prudence been by?"

"Yesterday."

Alexandra felt guilty that she hadn't spent more time with her future sister-in-law. She vowed to rectify that situation immediately.

"I heard about Nicholas having his title reinstated. Congratulations."

Forcing a smile between her lips, Alexandra replied in a small voice, "Thank you."

"You don't seem very happy about it."

She felt the heat rise up her neck. "I am happy for Nicholas. I think that it's wonderful, but. . . ." She paused to consider her words.

"But?"

"I do not want to live in England—to raise my child among strangers." Her voice caught; she broke down, covering her face with her hands.

"Alex," Tom said, kneeling beside the distraught woman, "surely if Nicholas knew how you felt, he would not ask you to leave."

"You don't understand. I can't tell him how I feel. I can't ask him to choose between his ancestral home and me. He was devastated when he thought he had lost everything. I can't ask him to leave it all behind."

"We are always faced with difficult decisions to make, Alex. It's never easy. You've been confronted with worse situations than this. I know you will find the answer to your problem."

Standing up, Alexandra shook her head. "I'm not sure there is an answer to this problem."


Nicholas sat with his knees propped up under his chin, staring out at the blue waters of the James River.

If only his life could run as smoothly as the current that passed in front of him, he thought wistfully.

He had come to the spot where he and Alexandra had picnicked so long ago—the spot where Alexandra had first asked him to make love to her. God, that day seemed like a lifetime ago, he thought, tossing another pebble aside.

He could hardly remember what his life was like before Alexandra had become a part of it. It was lonely—he remembered that much. And devoid of anything that could remotely be considered joy. He hadn't laughed or been as happy in all the years before he had met Alexandra. He smiled, thinking of her sprightly ways and impish smile. She always found a way to bring a smile to his lips.

He didn't want to mar Alexandra's happiness by making the wrong decision. Since the reinstatement of his title, he had pondered the question of what he was going to do a thousand times. He still had not found the answer. He wasn't immune to the worried looks and nervous glances she cast his way. He knew Alexandra would no more want to travel to England to live than she would embrace King George to her bosom.

He heaved a sigh. He had obligations to his title—to his estates. As competent as his estate manager, Mr. Weberly, was, he did not feel comfortable relegating the entire control of the Blackstone lands into his hands. He couldn't abandon his duty for the love of a woman, even if that woman was his life. In time, Alexandra would learn to adjust to her new life—her new role as duchess. He laughed. Who was he kidding? She would never adjust. It just wasn't in her to fawn and scrape to her betters. Wasn't that what this whole damn conflict between England and her colonies was all about?

Gazing at the raw beauty of the land, its openness and freedom, he thought about the confining role he must return to in England. Could he do it? Could he go back to his old life as if nothing had happened—as if nothing had changed within him?

He had changed. He'd had his eyes opened by the likes of the Joseph Walkers and Patrick Henrys of the world. How then could he go back and pretend everything was the same? He shook his head. There didn't seem to be an answer to the questions nagging at him.

Alexandra's anguished screams split the stillness of the night. Nicholas came instantly awake, reaching for the terrified woman by his side. She was shaking uncontrollably, staring straight ahead, her eyes glazed with fright. Her screams continued with such ferocity, Nicholas leaned over to light the chamber stick next to the bed.

The dark shadows hovering in the corners were immediately dispelled by the golden glow of the candle. "Alexandra," Nicholas said, shaking her shoulders to try and arouse her from her nightmare. "Alexandra, wake up. It's me . . . Nicholas."

Suddenly, she quieted; her eyes flew open; she stared at him in horror until the dawn of recognition reached her consciousness. "Nicholas?" she whispered.

"Yes, my sweet. I'm here; I will never leave you."

Tears streamed down her cheeks. Oh, God! It was only a dream. Nicholas was still here by her side. They were still in Virginia, not the cold-damp country of her nightmare.

"You were having a nightmare, my sweet. Do you remember what it was about?"

She shook her head in denial. She couldn't reveal what had frightened her so. Her dream had seemed so real. She had been surrounded by a sea of angry, unfriendly faces. When she reached out to Nicholas, they pulled him away, shouting, "Go home, Yankee . . . go home, Yankee." The harder she tried to reach him, the farther away he got, until at last he had disappeared into the mist, leaving her all alone in a foreign land. She trembled at the memory.

"It was only a dream. Go back to sleep," Nicholas said, leaning over to blow out the candle.

"No! Wait," she pleaded, pulling on his arm. "Don't blow it out just yet."

Kissing the top of her head, he gathered her into his arms. He could feel the dampness of her nightdress pressed against his skin. "You'll catch your death in this," he said. "I'll get you another."

"Why not remove this one instead?" she suggested, relieved when she saw Nicholas's smile. She needed the closeness only Nicholas could provide—the security of being held against his chest—to listen to the steady beating of his heart. She needed his love to chase away the shadows in her mind.

"Why not, indeed!" he replied, lifting the garment over her head and tossing it onto the floor.

Nicholas's eyes ignited into glowing embers as they traveled over every inch of her body, darkening into two black pools as he studied her naked form.

"You are very beautiful," he whispered. "I never tire of feasting my eyes on such perfection."

Alexandra smiled shyly, a warm blush suffusing her body. Slowly and seductively, his gaze slid downward, coming to rest on the soft patch of curls nestled at the apex of her thighs. With gentle fingers, he explored, stoking a gentle, growing fire. The tiny bud swelled, growing hard with her need of him.

"Nicholas, I love you so," Alexandra whispered, writhing beneath the intimacy of his touch. Closing her hand around his shaft, she felt the pulsating life within. Nicholas's need for her was as great as hers for him. She smiled in contentment, grateful that she was able to satisfy his needs.

Nicholas had given so much of himself during their lovemaking. He had unlocked her heart and soul. Now it was her turn to give a small measure of pleasure back to him.

With gentle but firm hands, she pushed him down onto his back. Noting the question in his eyes, she smiled. Covering his body with her own, she slid sensuously down the length of him, trailing her long dark mantle of hair over his hard muscled form.

Nicholas writhed beneath her ministrations. A sheen of perspiration covered his entire body; she licked at the glistening droplets of sweat that clung to the hairs on his chest. "Alexandra," he choked out, ecstasy softening his tone as she took the hardened member into her mouth.

She gave of herself freely, with an abandon that surprised her. When his breathing came shallow and she knew the point of his climax was near, she lowered herself onto him, sheathing his shaft within the velvet softness of her soul. Riding him with unbridled passion, she was flooded with uncontrollable joy as they reached their fulfillment together.

Contentment and peace flowed between them as they lay nestled in each other's arms. Every day her love deepened and intensified. Whatever tomorrow might bring, tonight they still had each other.

# Chapter Thirty

"I can't believe you are actually going to resume your position as Governor Dunmore's aide," Alexandra ranted. "Not after everything that has happened."

Nicholas stared at the angry woman before him, unable to believe that this termagant was the same woman he cradled so tenderly in his arms last night. To think that a mouth such as hers, capable of inflicting so much pleasure, could also inflict such pain.

He felt guilty enough about what he must do; he was torn by his loyalties to King and country and the new life he had carved for himself in Virginia.

Shrugging into his frock coat, Nicholas picked up his tricorn and made ready to leave. "I would have expected someone so loyal to your cause as you to understand my attitude in this matter. I have a certain position to maintain—a certain responsibility to my King. My orders were to serve Lord Dunmore, and that is exactly what I intend to do."

"Your country turned its back on you—cast you aside. How can you go back as if nothing has happened? Where is your pride?" As soon as the words were out of her mouth, she wished she could call them back. The look of hurt in Nicholas's eyes tore into her soul. She shrank from the anger now directed at her.

Rancor sharpened his voice. "As my wife, you are

not in a position to question my motives. As you were born a commoner, I can't expect you to understand the intricacies of noble birth. With my title go hundreds of years of tradition and custom. Try to understand," he said before slamming out the door.

Plopping down on the bed, Alexandra tried to hold back the tears of anger and frustration threatening to spill forth at Nicholas's words. "Damn his arrogant hide!" she shouted, punching the pillow on the bed. If being of noble birth meant you had to bow down to some egotistical jackanapes, then she was glad that she was as common as good old Virginia peanuts, she thought.

Thinking of peanuts made her realize how hungry she was; her stomach rumbled. Walking over to the wardrobe, she flung open the doors, searching for a dress that wouldn't make her feel like a stuffed turkey. Her stomach growled again. Damn! She had better stop thinking in terms of food and get over to Chloe's kitchen. Chloe could always be counted on to supply her with a hearty meal and a soft shoulder to cry on.

Nicholas strode into the governor's office, taking a seat at the desk. The window was open; it was a very warm first day of June. The fragrant odor of lilac drifted in, accompanied by the melodic tones of a blue jay perched on a branch nearby.

Eyeing a stack of documents waiting for his attention, Nicholas frowned. The work had certainly piled up in his absence. There were dozens of letters of correspondence that needed to be answered as well as a heap of bills needing to be paid. He shook his head. 'Twas a wonder the creditors weren't beating on the door of the palace demanding payment.

Picking up a quill, Nicholas proceeded to record the information in the appropriate ledgers. Absorbed in his chore, he did not hear the door open.

"Good morning, Nicholas. Good to see you back at work," Governor Dunmore stated, approaching the desk. "I don't mind telling you, I've sorely missed your competent assistance."

Nicholas looked up. The governor's jovial manner and ingratiating words set his nerves on edge. He couldn't help but recall Alexandra's stinging criticisms as he stared at the pompous fool dressed in his frippery. "Good day to you, my lord. How may I be of service?"

Taking a seat, the governor reached into his pocket, securing a gold engraved snuffbox. Inhaling, he flipped the case shut, stuffing it back in his pocket. It was a ritual Nicholas had observed countless times. He sometimes wondered if the man wasn't addicted to the odious stuff.

"I intend to summon a session of the General Assembly. Lord North has proposed a compromise, which I intend to present as soon as possible."

Nicholas's eyebrow rose. Finally the Prime Minister had heeded his appeals, he thought. "What is the extent of the proposal, if you don't mind my asking?"

The governor smiled, seemingly pleased by Lord North's directive. "The Prime Minister has promised not to tax the colonists if they will agree to taxing themselves in accordance with quotas to be sent from London."

Nicholas almost laughed. The Prime Minister had the right idea, but it came about a year too late. He shook his head. Fools . . . don't they know that their time has run out? he thought.

"You don't seem pleased by the proposal, Nicholas. Is something the matter?" Lord Dunmore asked, his brow furrowing in consternation.

Everything was the matter, Nicholas thought, but he wouldn't waste his breath trying to explain it. "I wish you good luck with your plan, governor," Nicholas said. You're going to need it, he added silently.

* * *

Taking the last bite of her waffle and washing it down with a large glass of milk, Alexandra pushed herself away from the old wooden table, hugging her stomach as if she were in agony. "I vow, Chloe, you have stuffed me fatter than a Christmas goose. I'm not sure I'll be able to rise from the bench."

The black face, beaded with sweat, broke into a smile. "Looks to me like you been puttin' on a few pounds, chile. That dress you is wearin' is none too big."

Alexandra felt the heat rise to her cheeks. "Do you want me to take a turn churning the butter?" she asked, hoping to divert Chloe's attention away from her increasing girth.

Leaning on the long wooden handle, which rested inside the large earthenware crock, Chloe shook her head. "I done started churning dis heah butter early dis mornin'. The butter is stickin' to the sides of the crock already. It won't be much longer now." Chloe continued pulling the paddle up and down through the sweet cream, over and over again.

Alexandra smiled wistfully as Chloe's strong arms moved in rhythm to the spiritual she was humming softly. It seemed like only yesterday that she and Alicia had begged to churn the cream. Of course, at the ages of eight and eleven, the chore seemed more like play than work. She knew better now. Making the butter was a daylong process. Once the cream had been separated from the milk, it had to sit and ripen. Then it was poured into the churn, and mixed for up to six hours, depending on how fresh it was. It wasn't fun anymore, but the end result was definitely worth it. She licked her lips in anticipation.

"How come you ain't eatin' with your husband this mornin', chile?" Chloe asked, staring at the young woman suspiciously. "You should be home takin' care of him, instead of spending your time with an old woman.''

''Nicholas left early this morning. He had work to do for the governor,'' she said, her tone contemptuous.

''I see . . . ,'' she said, pausing, those two words carrying a wealth of comprehension, ''. . . and that didn't set well with you?''

''Something like that,'' Alexandra replied, running her nails across the roughened wood of the table's surface.

''Has you told your husband about that baby you is carryin'?''

Alexandra's head shot up to find Chlòe's knowing smile upon her. She sighed. ''How long have you known?''

Chloe's smile was enigmatic. ''I had me a notion you was wid child. You knows better than to try and put one over on old Chloe.''

''I haven't told Nicholas. I can't.'' Tears formed in her eyes, but she blinked them away.

Wiping her hands on her apron, Chloe took a seat on the bench next to Alexandra, wrapping her comforting arms around her. ''You gots to tell your man, honey. It's his baby too.''

''I know, Chloe, but Nicholas is going to leave soon for England. . . .'' She paused, not sure if she could actually voice the decision that had been forming in her heart. Lifting her head, she stared into the kind dark eyes. ''I'm not going to go, Chloe. I can't.''

Once the words were uttered, she knew she had made the right decision. If Nicholas decided to go back to England, she would not go with him. He must never learn about the child she carried beneath her breast. If he ever found out, he would force her to go and no one, including her parents, would fault him for it.

''Are you sure you knows what you is doing? You love dat man. If you let him go, a part of you will die.''

Pressing her hands against her abdomen, Alexandra nodded; the tears she had tried to hold back, slid slowly down her cheeks. "You're right, Chloe, part of me will die. I love Nicholas with all my heart, but part of him will always remain." She patted the growing mound beneath her hands. "I will not raise my child in a land of oppression where a man is only as good as the title he bears. Nicholas's problems with the Crown convinced me of that." She shook her head. "I want my child to be free."

Pushing herself off the bench, Chloe resumed her place at the churn. "Life's a lot like makin' butter, chile. It's full of ups and downs. When you separate the milk from the butter, you still have something of value." She poured out a tall glass of buttermilk, setting it on the table. "But life isn't always that easy. When you separate two people who love each other—who belong together—what you got left?" She held out her empty hands. "Nothin', that's what."

"You don't understand!" Alexandra protested, rising from her seat.

"I understand this: you and the duke belong together. You're two parts of a whole. One without the other is no good."

"But. . . ."

Chloe held up her hands to forestall Alexandra's argument. "I know more about freedom than most. But I tell you somethin', I'd give up my freedom right here and now if I could hold my man and my two babies against my breast. Freedom ain't nothin' when the one you love is gone."

The two women embraced, each lost in her own private battle. The older woman thought of the man she had lost—the love that had been taken from her; the younger woman thought of the man she still had—the love she was throwing away.

* * *

Like a spring ready to uncoil, the residents of Williamsburg were ready to strike out at the least provocation from the Crown.

The limits of their patience were sorely tested on the first Saturday of June, when two local youths were injured slightly by the blast of a spring-triggered shotgun, when they had tried to break into the powder magazine.

The church service the following morning was filled with bitter accusation and condemnation for the man who was touted as a would-be assassin. Governor Dunmore and his family were conspicuously absent from the service that day.

When the final hymn was sung and the benediction had been given, the angry parishioners filed out of church, gathering outside in the courtyard to continue their heated debates.

Standing beneath the shade of a flowering magnolia, its great white flowers and dusty green leaves providing a sweet fragrance to the bitter atmosphere, Nicholas and Alexandra exchanged pleasantries with the elder Courtlands.

"What did you think of the service today, Nicholas?" Samuel questioned. "The Reverend Price was particularly hard on the governor today."

"With just cause!" Alexandra interrupted, twirling her parasol in agitation. "Imagine setting a vicious trap like that! Those poor boys were lucky to have escaped with their lives."

Nicholas's eyebrow shot up. "Those 'poor boys,' as you put it, had not the right to be breaking into the magazine," he reminded her. His tone reflected the underlying hostility that had plagued their relationship since he had resumed his position as the governor's aide.

"I might have known you'd defend the governor's action. Once a Tory, always a Tory," she chanted childishly.

371

"Alexandra!" Samuel's tone was full of censure. "I believe we are all on the same side here. The side of truth and justice."

Blinking back the tears that surfaced so quickly these days, Alexandra nodded. Turning on her heel, she walked away.

"Alexandra," Nicholas shouted, taking a step forward.

Grabbing onto his arm, Catherine pulled him back. "Let her go, Nicholas. She needs some time alone. This is a difficult time for Alex. The tensions between our two countries is pulling her apart. She is torn between her loyalty to you and loyalty to her country."

"Catherine is right, I'm afraid," Samuel added. "Alex just hasn't been herself these past few months. I think she carries a bigger burden than any of us realizes."

Nodding, Catherine smiled to herself. Alexandra carried more than just a burden if the thickening of her waist and the fullness of her breasts were any indication. Why had she kept the fact of her pregnancy a secret? she wondered. It was obvious Nicholas didn't know. She shook her head. Men . . . they were perfectly capable to head governments and lead armies into battle, but when it came to understanding a woman's needs, they were as useless as a flea on a dog.

"You're both right, of course," Nicholas agreed. "These have been trying times for all of us."

"What are your plans, Nicholas? When do you leave for England?" Samuel asked, adding, "I must admit, I'll be sorry to see you go. I still think you would make an excellent merchant." He slapped Nicholas on the back.

Observing the worried look on Catherine's face, Nicholas smiled to reassure her. "In truth, I haven't finalized my plans. I need to make a decision soon. The waters will be unsafe for travel if war breaks out."

"Well, whatever your decision, you'll always have

our love," Catherine said, placing a kiss on his cheek. "Take care of Alex. She needs you more than ever right now."

Catherine's enigmatic words flowed through Nicholas's mind as he watched the Courtlands walk away. *She needs you more than ever right now.* He needed Alex, too. But it seemed of late, they were drifting farther and farther apart. Like two poles of a magnet, they fought to come together but never seemed to click.

# Chapter Thirty-One

The banging on the bedroom door brought Nicholas instantly awake. The eerie stillness of the predawn hours made the pounding seem that much louder. Jumping out of bed, he reached for the red satin robe hanging on the bedpost. "I'm coming," he yelled, shrugging into the sleeves of the garment.

Alexandra bolted upright, clutching the sheet to her pounding chest. "What is it? What's happened?"

Ignoring her questions, Nicholas opened the door to find his usually staid and immaculate valet standing in the hall, bare-chested and with his pants half unbuttoned. His eyebrow shot up in question. "What is it, Habersham?"

The servant colored, shifting his feet to hide the fact that they were bare. "I'm sorry to disturb you, my lord, but there is a group of men waiting downstairs to see you. One is a gentleman by the name of Cyrus Willoughby. He says it's most urgent that he speak with you."

Nicholas's mouth dipped into a frown. "Show the men into the parlor. I'll be down directly," he ordered, closing the door. What the devil could the governor's secretary have to talk with him about at this hour of the morning? he wondered.

Stepping back to the bed, he stared down at Alexandra, who had lit the candle and was staring up at him with a look of trepidation on her face. "I'm sorry to disturb you, my sweet. It appears the governor's secretary needs my assistance on some urgent matter. Go back to sleep. I shouldn't be too long."

"What do you think has happened?" she whispered.

Fastening his breeches, Nicholas shook his head. "I have absolutely no idea." He saw the look of concern on her face and sought to reassure her. "You're not to worry. I'll be back as quickly as I can."

An hour later, Nicholas reentered the bedroom to find Alexandra dozing fitfully with her head propped up against the headboard. The candle still burned on the nightstand, illuminating the frown she wore in her slumber. Tiptoeing over to the bed, he sat heavily upon it.

The mattress sagged and creaked under Nicholas's weight, jarring Alexandra awake. Her blue eyes widened in surprise at the sight of her husband. "Nicholas, you're back. Is everything all right?" she asked, frightened by the mask of worry he wore.

Heaving a sigh, Nicholas replied, "It seems the governor and his family slipped out of town in the wee hours of the morning."

Alexandra sat up, staring at him in astonishment. "But where did they go? Why would they do such a thing?"

Nicholas didn't bother to hide the look of disgust that crossed his face. "Apparently, they have taken refuge on a ship—the H.M.S. *Fowey,* at Yorktown. Why he left is anybody's guess. Mine would be that the incident with the spring-gun proved to be more than he could handle. Lord Dunmore was never one to manage criticism or conflict with any type of diplomacy."

Grabbing onto his arm, Alexandra replied, "There is another possibility, Nicholas." Her heart beat loudly in her chest.

"What's that, my sweet?" he asked, unfastening his shirt.

"What if the British are getting ready to launch an invasion of Virginia?" she asked, her fear turning quickly to anger at the sound of Nicholas's laughter.

"That's preposterous. Don't you think, if that were the case, I would have gotten wind of it?"

"Perhaps you did and you've kept it from us," she accused, studying him carefully.

Rubbing the back of his neck, Nicholas shook his head. "Let's drop it, Alexandra. I'm tired, and I want to go back to sleep." Removing his boots, he dropped them one by one onto the floor.

The thud of each boot echoed in Alexandra's heart. Her brows drew together in a frown; the seed of suspicion that was planted in her mind began to take root and grow. What was Nicholas hiding? Did he know something he wasn't telling her? After all, they were hardly on the same side of this conflict. Laying her head back down, she pulled the covers up to chin, chilled despite the warmth of the evening.

The next morning, Alexandra awoke to find Nicholas gone. Staring at the empty space next to her, she couldn't stop the feelings of mistrust and foreboding that continued to assail her. Nicholas's vague attitude about the governor's flight bothered her. He was too flippant—too self-assured. She was certain he was holding something back from her.

Now that she had finally reached a decision about their future, she wanted to make certain it was the right one. Since her conversation with Chloe, she had agonized over what she should do. And now she had decided. Life without Nicholas wasn't worth living. Despite everything—their political differences—his noble birth, she loved him. She would put aside her prejudices—her reservations—and follow her heart. She would go to England with her husband.

Jumping out of bed, she stuck her head out the door

and called for Betsy. A moment later, Betsy, carrying a silver tray laden with chocolate and warm rolls bustled into the room.

"You called, Miss Alex?" She walked straight to the window, pulling the drapes apart and throwing the sash. The breeze ruffled the fabric, the fresh morning air replacing the stale odors of the night before. It was the same ritual she had performed over and over again the past fifteen years.

"I need you to send Habersham up to the attic for the trunks," Alexandra said, scarcely believing her own directive.

"But why?"

Taking hold of Betsy's hand, Alexandra's smile was bittersweet. "I've decided to go with Nicholas, Betsy. I can't leave him; I love him too much."

Betsy's eyes filled with tears. "But, Miss Alex, I thought you said you wouldn't go . . . that you didn't want to raise your baby among strangers."

"I don't want to raise my baby without a father. Nicholas deserves to see his child grow up—share in his life. I can't deprive him of it."

"Who will help you with the baby? You'll be among strangers there?"

Tears misted Alexandra's eyes. These were the same arguments she had used to try to convince herself to stay, but in the end, she knew they weren't strong enough. "I'm sure Nicholas will have many competent people on his staff."

Drawing herself up to her full height, Betsy stuck out her chin. "I'll not have you traipsing off to some godforsaken place by yourself. If you're bound and determined to go, Will and I will go with you."

Rushing forward, Alexandra hugged the little woman to her heart. "Oh, Betsy, you don't know what this means to me. Are you certain you want to go? It won't be easy, you know."

Smiling, Betsy patted the young woman's cheek.

"I'll not have strangers caring for our baby. Now don't you worry about a thing. I'll have Will bring down the trunks and we'll be packed up in no time." Pausing in the doorway, Betsy turned, "When will we be leaving, miss? I have a few friends; I need to bid farewell."

As do I, Betsy, Alexandra thought sadly. "I'm not sure. I haven't told Nicholas of my decision. When he returns home this evening, I'll take care of the details."

But Nicholas didn't return home. Not that evening, nor the evening that followed. Alexandra had received a brief note, stating that it was imperative that he travel to Yorktown to visit with Governor Dunmore. That was all it said. Not when he would return, not how long he would be gone, not even that he loved her.

Seated in the rear yard, beneath the shade of the crepe myrtle tree, Alexandra hugged her knees, staring listlessly into space. Even the antics of the two gray squirrels frolicking on the picket fence couldn't bring a smile to her lips.

Nicholas was gone. Ben had told her yesterday that Lord Dunmore's ship was no longer anchored at Yorktown. The governor had gone, and she was certain, Nicholas had gone with him.

It had been days since his initial departure. She had waited anxiously that first day, eager to tell him of her plans. When he didn't return, she had packed the trunks with all of their belongings, supervised the closing of the little house on Nicholson Street, and waited. Too much time had passed. He would have sent word by now; he wouldn't have wanted her to worry.

Alexandra's tears slid slowly down her cheek, one for every day of her life she would spend without Nicholas. They fell unchecked into a puddle of sadness, staining the blue gingham of her gown. Laying her head down on her knees, she sobbed piteously for her unborn child—for the love she had tossed away, for the

379

man she would never see again. "Oh, Nicholas, why did you have to leave me? I love you so."

"I love you too, my sweet."

Looking up, the vision before her was blurred by her tears. Wiping them away, she focused on Nicholas's face. He was smiling at her, extending his hand out to her. She grabbed hold of it, certain she would never let it go.

"Nicholas," she cried, jumping up. "Nicholas, you've come back!" She ran her fingers over his face, making certain her eyes hadn't deceived her. "My God, it's really you."

Nicholas laughed, drawing her into his embrace. "Of course, it's me. Who did you think it was?"

She shook her head, laughter bubbling up inside her throat. "I never thought I'd see you again."

Frowning, he tipped up her chin. "Not see me. What nonsense is this? I'm your husband. Did you forget?"

"Yes . . . no . . . I mean, you didn't come back. You left without a word."

"But I sent you a note."

"Nicholas, that was over six days ago. Ben told me Governor Dunmore's ship had left Yorktown. I thought you had gone home."

Drawing Alexandra into his embrace, he hugged her to him tightly, placing kisses on her eyes, her nose, her chin, until finally he captured her mouth in a heart-melting kiss. Lifting his head, he stared into her eyes. "My sweet, I am home."

Alexandra smiled, her joy lighting the blue of her eyes so they shone like brilliant sapphires. "Does this mean you don't wish to go home to England?" She waited breathlessly for his answer.

"This is my home now. Wherever you are is home. We shall make a new beginning here—a new life for our son." He patted the growing mound with reverent hands.

Alexandra's eyes widened. "You know?"

Nicholas nodded. "I have for a long time, my sweet. Did you think you could hide it from me? I know your body better than my own."

Alexandra blushed, realizing the truth of his words. "I love you, Nicholas. I always will. Whatever happens from this day forward, that fact will never change."

"There are troubled times ahead, my sweet, but I can face anything as long as we are together."

"Even living with a sharp-tongued seditionist?" she teased.

Nicholas smiled, kissing her nose. "Even that."

## Contemporary Fiction From Robin St. Thomas

**Fortune's Sisters**                                    (2616, $3.95)

It was Pia's destiny to be a Hollywood star. She had complete self-confidence, breathtaking beauty, and the help of her domineering mother. But her younger sister Jeanne began to steal the spotlight meant for Pia, diverting attention away from the ruthlessly ambitious star. When her mother Mathilde started to return the advances of dashing director Wes Guest, Pia's jealousy surfaced. Her passion for Guest and desire to be the brightest star in Hollywood pitted Pia against her own family—sister against sister, mother against daughter. Pia was determined to be the only survivor in the arenas of love and fame. But neither Mathilde nor Jeanne would surrender without a fight. . . .

**Lover's Masquerade**                                    (2886, $4.50)

New Orleans. A city of secrets, shrouded in mystery and magic. A city where dreams become obsessions and memories once again become reality. A city where even one trip, like a stop on Claudia Gage's book promotion tour, can lead to a perilous fall. For New Orleans is also the home of Armand Dantine, who knows the secrets that Claudia would conceal and the past she cannot remember. And he will stop at nothing to make her love him, and will not let her go again . . .

# HISTORICAL ROMANCES BY VICTORIA THOMPSON

## HEART SOARING ROMANCE BY LA REE BRYANT

**FORBIDDEN PARADISE** (2744-3, $3.75/$4.95)

Jordan St. Clair had come to South America to find her fiance and break her engagement, but the handsome and arrogant guide refused to a woman through the steamy and dangerous jungles. Finally, he relented, on one condition: She would do exactly as he said. Beautiful Jordan had never been ruled in her life, yet there was something about Patrick Castle that set her heart on fire. Patrick ached to possess the body and soul of the tempting vixen, to lead her from the lush, tropical jungle into a FORBIDDEN PARADISE of their very own.

**ARIZONA VIXEN** (2642-0, $3.75/$4.95)

As soon as their eyes met, Sabra Powers knew she had to have the handsome stranger she saw in the park. But Sterling Hawkins was a tormented man caught between two worlds: As a halfbreed, he was a successful businessman with a seething Indian's soul which could not rest until he had revenge for his parents' death. Sabra was willing to risk anything to experience this loner's fiery embrace and seering kiss. Sterling vowed to capture this ARIZONA VIXEN and make her his own . . . if only for one night!

**TEXAS GLORY** (2222-1, $3.75/$4.95)

When enchanting Glory Westbrook was banished to a two-year finishing school for dallying with Yankee Slade Hunter, she thought she'd die of a broken heart; when father announced she would marry his business associate who smothered her with insolent stares, she thought she'd die of horror and shock.

For two years devastatingly handsome Slade Hunter had been denied the embrace of the only woman he had ever loved. He thought this was the best thing for Glory, yet when he saw her again after two years, all resolve melted away with one passionate kiss. She *had* to be his, surrendering her heart and mind to his powerful arms and strong embrace.

*Available wherever paperbacks are sold, or order direct from the Publisher. Send cover price plus 50¢ per copy for mailing and handling to Zebra Books, Dept. 3251, 475 Park Avenue South, New York, N.Y. 10016. Residents of New York, New Jersey and Pennsylvania must include sales tax. DO NOT SEND CASH.*